"This is where we made love the last time."

Feeling her body heat rise, she looked at the bed again. It was a king-size, big enough to get lost in, but for one brief time they had found each other instead.

"When . . . ?" she whispered.

"When we closed on the house. You were ecstatic. I didn't see you that way very often, and I wanted to share it. I wanted to feel . . ."

"Feel what?"

He gave a shake of his head. "Just feel."

She wanted to know so much more. Was it day or night? Did he turn to her in bed, slide in behind her, awaken her with gentle caresses and erotic kisses? Did he catch her in the middle of something else, distract her with one steamy look and boldly seduce her? Or was he blunt, the way he sometimes preferred, the way *she* had sometimes preferred?

Had their lovemaking been tender or greedy? Hard, demanding, raw? Had they made love, as he'd called it, or engaged in slick, hot, potent sex for its own sake?

Deliberately tormenting herself, she asked in a throaty voice, "Were we good?"

"We were always good, Maggie. You can't have forgotten that."

Always. Yes. From their very first time together.

What if she locked the door, closed the drapes, stripped off her clothing and his, and demanded the use of his body . . . She knew how to cut through his resistance, how to heat his blood and fog his mind, how to arouse him beyond bearing and satisfy him beyond belief.

"Maggie?"

He touched her hand, and she swore she heard a soft sizzle.

SOME
ENCHANTED
SEASON

Marilyn Pappano

BANTAM 🐓 BOOKS

New York Toronto London Sydney Auckland

SOME ENCHANTED SEASON

A Bantam Book

PUBLISHING HISTORY
A Bantam Book / December 1998

ISBN 0-553-57982-7

Published simultaneously in the United States and Canada

Bantam Books are published by Bantam Books, a division of Bantam
Doubleday Dell Publishing Group, Inc. Its trademark, consisting of the
words "Bantam Books" and the portrayal of a rooster, is Registered in U.S.
Patent and Trademark Office and in other countries. Marca Registrada.
Bantam Books, 1540 Broadway, New York, New York 10036.

PRINTED IN THE UNITED STATES OF AMERICA

WCD   10 9 8 7 6 5 4 3 2 1

SOME
ENCHANTED
SEASON

Prologue

THE TEARS WERE OVERWHELMING.

Maggie McKinney had thought she could escape without them. They hadn't threatened when she'd told Ross she was leaving him. She'd been calm and cool when she'd said she would be seeing a lawyer about a divorce first thing Monday morning. She'd been dry-eyed and composed when she'd packed a few items and carried them down the stairs while he watched from the living room, and she had remained that way as she'd walked out the door, even though part of her had been sobbing in silent entreaty.

Please don't let me go.

Please say you don't want this.

Please tell me you're sorry.

Please don't let it end this way.

But he hadn't stopped her, hadn't asked her to stay,

hadn't said a damn word to her, and so she'd had no choice but to keep walking out of the house. Out of his life. Out of their marriage.

Before she'd driven ten feet down the snowy street, the tears had burst free, hot and bitter. Like a dam suffering from years of neglect and damage, her marriage had crumbled, and now her spirit was crumbling too. There'd been too many arguments, too many different dreams, too much disappointment and disillusionment.

Tonight was the final, killing betrayal. Tonight she knew beyond a doubt that there was nothing left of their marriage to save. Affection had turned to hate, respect to derision, love to ashes. They were finished, and her heart ached with it.

It was a Christmas Eve to remember.

Gripping the steering wheel with one hand, she groped in the passenger seat for her purse and the tissues inside. She dried her eyes, blew her nose, then tried to concentrate on the road. It was a sorry night for traveling. Thick, fat snowflakes fell in a flurry of white, covering the highway and reducing visibility to practically nothing. A smart person would be at home, celebrating the holiday with her family, warm and snug and contemplating the big day tomorrow.

But she didn't have a family. Ross had seen to that.

And she didn't have a home. He'd seen to that too.

Fresh tears spilled over. She wiped them away as the windshield wipers cleared the glass of snow. Ice was gathering on the road that climbed out of the valley into the surrounding mountains, causing the tires to slip, then grab.

As the truck fishtailed over a slick patch, she tightened her grip and considered for an instant returning to the house and waiting out the snow. But how could she go back? How could she give him another chance to hurt her? How could she stay in the same house with him, knowing how he felt? Heavens, he'd stood there, utterly disinterested, and watched her go, knowing what the weather was like, what the roads were like, and he hadn't said a word. How like him to provide further proof of how little he cared.

Why *she* cared was a mystery. She should be angry. Anger was strength. Angry was the best way to be when dealing with Ross. Angry was how she would survive this.

But first she had to go through the pain. Things between them had gotten so miserable that she'd thought the end, when it came, would bring relief. She hadn't known it would feel as if her whole world had shattered. She hadn't known she would feel so betrayed. Disappointed. Lost.

She hadn't known it would *hurt*.

Praying for the ache to ease, she didn't feel the gentle slide of the car right away. When she became aware of it, she jerked the steering wheel, worsening the skid. In a panic, she tapped the brakes, but the truck continued to slide, picking up speed.

It reached the edge of the road, bumping across the narrow shoulder, then falling, rolling bottom over top, breaking trees, crashing over rocks. The air bag deployed with startling force, pushing her back, but it couldn't stop her head from slamming sideways against the door frame, couldn't protect her, as it deflated, from the truck as it crumpled around her.

When finally the truck came to a sudden and violent stop against a tree too strong to plow over, she lay motionless, trapped between the seat and twisted metal. She tried to move but couldn't, tried to lift her head to check herself for damage, but couldn't manage that either.

Blood pooled on the leather seat beneath her cheek. She thought she should be feeling a great deal of pain—sharp, agonizing, life-threatening—but she felt nothing. Her breathing sounded loud and labored, but the air she was taking in was sweet, cold. Snowflakes drifted through the broken window beside her, landed on the seat, and brought with them the cool, clear realization that Ross didn't have to worry about a nasty divorce.

She was going to die. Right there. Alone in her truck on a quiet, snowy Christmas Eve.

He probably couldn't think of a better gift.

Chapter One

ROSS MCKINNEY STOOD AT THE MAS-
sive window that made up the outer wall of
his office and gazed out across the city. It was
a cold, gray morning, not the sort that put
Buffalo in its best light. The city looked dreary, unwelcoming. He felt that way.

In the past eleven months, he'd spent an inordinate
amount of time staring out windows. Last Christmas
Eve the windows had been in a newly refurbished
house in Bethlehem, and he'd watched the snow come
down, obscuring all but the nearest houses, and worried about Maggie. For the first two months of the
year, the window had been in an intensive care cubicle
dominated by a hospital bed and its frail patient. Ma-
chines had supported and monitored her, their
whooshes and beeps the only signs of life in the small
room for nine weeks.

There had been more windows—in another hospital room, the rehab center, the quiet, still place he called home, this room. Most of his time had been spent here, where, on good days, he could lose himself in the demands of his business, where, when he was lucky, he could put aside his anger, his regret, his guilt, and concentrate for a time on something else. Something productive. Something not Maggie-related.

In a few hours he would have traveled full circle. He would be back in Bethlehem, back in Maggie's house, where this most recent tragedy that their marriage had become had gotten its start. Where he had started it. Where together they would end it.

Ironically, due to the head injuries she'd suffered in the accident, she didn't remember the town of Bethlehem, or the house, or the events that had set in motion the accident. He was taking her to recuperate in a place she might never remember—a place he would never forget.

"This isn't necessary."

Ross didn't look over his shoulder at the lawyer shuffling papers on the other side of the desk. Tom Flynn had made clear his opinion of Ross's plans. It was what Ross paid him to do, and usually he followed Tom's advice. But not this time.

"You have an office at the house in Bethlehem with a computer, a modem, a fax. It would mean some reorganizing, but—"

"No." Finally Ross did turn from the window. "If I didn't know you better, Tom, I'd say you were afraid of the responsibility."

As he'd expected, Tom took the words as a challenge. "I can handle it."

"I know." Next to him, Tom was one of the better deal makers—or breakers, as suited his purpose—around. He was smart, tenacious, quick to understand the intricacies of business, and, like Ross, he was driven. He'd created himself out of nothing, had chosen a slot and shaped himself to fit it. There was nothing Tom couldn't achieve—except, perhaps, a satisfying personal life.

Again, like Ross.

"I just don't see the point in these changes. Do you really think you're going to spend twenty-four hours a day playing nursemaid to Maggie?"

"She doesn't need a nursemaid."

"She doesn't need *you*. But the company does."

Ross opened his briefcase and began removing folders. Tom was right. Maggie didn't need him. There was a time when she had, when no one or nothing was more important to her than he was, but that time was long past. She'd grown used to being alone, to rarely having his complete attention. She'd learned to entertain herself, to fulfill her emotional needs elsewhere, to live without him, and he'd done the same.

But she needed *someone*. After eight months of intensive therapy, Dr. Allen was releasing her from the rehab center today. He'd recommended that she complete her recuperation someplace familiar, someplace where she'd been happy. Ross hadn't been able to think of one place that met both requirements. His house here in the city was familiar, but she hadn't been happy there, and so he'd chosen Bethlehem, where she had been.

Dr. Allen had suggested that she go with some*one* familiar as well. She'd had her fill of strangers poking, prodding, examining, and treating her. Now she wanted someone she knew with her, and he was the only candidate.

The doctor had made it clear before asking Ross that they'd explored other options and come up empty-handed. There was Maggie's mother, who'd disowned her for marrying Ross sixteen years ago. Janet Gilbert had wanted more for her only child than marriage to a poor bastard with big dreams that, she was convinced, would never amount to anything but heartache. He'd proved her wrong a few million times over, but it hadn't mattered. Janet had never forgiven Maggie.

As parents went, Frank Gilbert was an even bigger disappointment than Janet. He'd run out on his family when Maggie was barely six and, at the urging of his new young wife, broken off all contact with his first family. Maggie hadn't seen him since she was ten, although a child support check had arrived every month like clockwork until her eighteenth birthday. That month Frank had prorated the check and removed himself completely from her life.

There had also been the possibility of asking a friend to help out, but it was a hell of a favor to ask. After all, Maggie's friends had families and responsibilities of their own.

So that was how Ross had gotten selected to spend

the last few months of Maggie's recuperation in Bethlehem with her.

He could have refused, could have said he was too busy, too vital to the company to take up residence five hours away, and it would have been mostly true. But was two or three months of his time so much to ask considering their sixteen years together? Considering that the responsibility for the sorry state of their marriage rested on his shoulders?

Considering that the bulk of the responsibility for her near death also rested on his shoulders?

"No one would blame you if you refused to go," Tom said.

He would blame himself, though, and he carried too much guilt already. "I want to go. I want to do this for Maggie." It wasn't much of a good-bye gift, but it was the best he could manage. "The decision to turn the business over to you was mine, not Maggie's. I know myself, Tom. It's all or nothing. If I try to work while I'm there, I'll end up leaving Maggie alone all the time. That's not what she needs, not what the doctor had in mind."

"But you're going to leave her alone in a few months anyway."

The words were quiet, empty of emotion, harmless little sounds that carried no accusation, but he felt the indictment anyway. No condemnation, but he still felt damned.

After a few moments, he returned to his work. He offered no response, neither confirmed nor denied Tom's assertion. He hadn't discussed his plans with anyone, hadn't even fully thought them out.

He'd made the decision a year ago. After the holidays, he'd planned to file for a divorce that would have been far more civil than the marriage had become. Years before, he'd given Maggie a fair share of the business, back when the deal hadn't been worth the paper it was written on, but now it was worth millions. She would have gotten more money on top of that, would have taken with her a fortune in jewels, another in art.

She would have lived the rest of her life in luxury, and he would have been free to pursue what was important to him—business. A friendship or two. Maybe a relationship with a woman who hadn't learned to hate him, who didn't resent the hell out of the attention he gave his work.

But he'd put the decision out of his mind soon after making it. How could he think about divorce when the doctors hadn't expected Maggie to live? Make plans to be free when she hovered in a coma between life and death? Be so callous and selfish while she struggled to relearn all the skills robbed of her—little ones like feeding and dressing herself and major ones like walking and talking?

If only they'd spent last Christmas Eve the way they'd spent most evenings—apart. If only he hadn't angered her, if only she hadn't left the house, been on that road . . .

Regrets, he'd learned in the last eleven months, were pointless. He couldn't change the past. Because of him, Maggie *had* left, she *had* been on the road, and because of it, she was still his wife. His responsibility.

And for that reason, he was accompanying her to Bethlehem.

Deliberately he changed the subject. "You'll have to make an effort to get along with Lynda while I'm gone. I would hate to replace her, so don't harass her into quitting."

"I think I could replace her quite easily," Tom said with a scowl. "Any idiot walking down the street would probably do just fine."

If Tom was Ross's right hand in running the business, Lynda Barone was his left, and if there was one thing she certainly was *not,* it was an idiot. And one thing she definitely was was a major annoyance in Tom's life. The two barely managed civility most of the time. Often they regressed into outright hostility. Maggie had once commented that sometimes such hostility between a man and a woman was a screen for something personal, intense, sexual.

But, as they'd learned in their own relationship, sometimes hostility was simply hostility.

"Maybe I'll send Lynda to Japan to work on the deal from their end," Tom muttered. "That should keep her busy for a few months."

"If you did, she'd come back speaking fluent Japanese and have the consortium insisting on doing business solely with her." Ross glanced at his watch. He had an eleven-thirty appointment with Dr. Allen. It was time. "If you have any problems that truly require my attention, call me. Otherwise . . . I'll see you in two to three months." He closed his nearly empty briefcase, smiled a smile he didn't feel, and offered a hand to his lawyer.

Muttering something about damned principles, Tom shook hands, then Ross left the office. He took the elevator from the twenty-first floor to the open top tier of the three-level parking garage. The city was even colder and grayer than it had looked from his office. It had been a mild winter so far, but they would get snow soon. Probably while he was in Bethlehem, where he could get snowed in for days, with nowhere to go and nothing to do.

With no one for company but Maggie.

He shook off the apprehension that settled over him, put his briefcase in the trunk with his luggage, and got into the car.

He knew the way to the rehab center in his sleep. When the hospital had done all they could for Maggie, Tom had researched the options and selected the Allen-Ridley Institute as the next best step. Located on a twenty-acre tract in a Buffalo suburb, it looked more like a gracious old hotel than a rehabilitation hospital. The main building sprawled across a lawn that was emerald green in summer and neatly groomed even in winter. The broad veranda, lined with rockers and wicker planters, was a welcoming place to spend a sunny afternoon.

All the chairs and planters were empty today.

He followed the veranda to the front, where double doors in the center led into a lobby that was an elegant parlor. The patients' rooms could pass for any well-appointed bedrooms, and the dining room was truly a dining room, with cherry tables, chandeliers, paintings on the walls, china cabinets in the corners. Only the therapy rooms indicated that the center was a high-tech facility.

A young secretary showed him to Dr. Allen's office.

He'd been there many times before—had sat in this leather chair and listened to the doctor's assessment of Maggie's condition, had heard reports of improvements and regressions, had been cautioned, warned, and encouraged.

A week ago, when the doctor had called him in to arrange Maggie's release, his future had changed—once again—in this room.

"Today's the day," Dr. Allen said after a perfunctory greeting. "Do you have any questions before we meet Maggie?"

Ross shook his head. They had talked at length the previous week about the minimal care she required. His role in the next few months wasn't loving husband welcoming home his fragile wife but, rather, a companion on hand in case something went wrong. She was able to do much for herself, but some questions about her abilities could be answered only away from the controlled environment of the center. Answering those questions was the goal of the next few months.

At the same meeting, the doctor had gone over her remaining impairments in detail—a mild expressive speech disorder. The various symptoms of posttraumatic syndrome—headaches, sleep disorders, personality changes. Residual problems with the hip she'd broken, particularly with extended weight bearing. Difficulty climbing stairs, trouble concentrating, dizzy spells.

And the amnesia. Much of her memory of the year preceding the accident was spotty. The months immediately prior were missing altogether. When or if those memories would return, according to the doctor, was anyone's guess. If she hadn't been in the accident, if the amnesia were the only problem, he would presume that she would make a complete, or nearly complete, recovery.

But the accident changed things. There had been bleeding in and swelling of her brain, causing some damage, and she'd been in a coma for weeks. Still, the doctor had thought that being in Bethlehem would be good for her, that it might jog loose forgotten memories.

Ross wasn't proud of it, but he wouldn't mind if those memories stayed unjogged awhile longer. At least for the next few months they were together.

The doctor had told him everything he possibly could, except how he and Maggie were going to get along. They were two people who had once been in love, had once been intimate, who had watched their love die. And now there was only awkwardness. Distance. One stranger with another.

"This will be a period of adjustment for Maggie," Dr. Allen said. "She's going to find out just how independent she can be—what she's capable of and what she's lost. There will be the temptation to do things for her, but don't give in until she's proven that she can't complete a task."

. . . *how independent she can be* . . . That was the big question. Would she be able to manage alone, or would she require a live-in companion? At the end of these few months, they would know.

"I would recommend that she continue to meet with a psychiatrist for a time," the doctor continued. "At least until we see how well she adjusts to being away from the center. Dr. Olivetti, her psychiatrist here, has recommended a doctor in Bethlehem by the name of Grayson. Maggie's first appointment should be within the next week or so. Have I raised any new questions?"

When Ross shook his head, the doctor slid a stack of forms across the desk for him to sign, then rose from his chair and smiled out of habit. "Let's go get Maggie, Mr. McKinney."

MAGGIE MCKINNEY WATCHED FROM HER seat on the bed while an aide did a final sweep of the room. "Looks like that's it, Mrs. McK," the young woman said with a bright smile. "Everything's packed, and your husband's on his way up with Dr. Allen to pick you up. You must be so excited."

Excited? Yes, that was part of what she was feeling. When they'd wheeled her in there eight months earlier, she'd been afraid she would be stuck there forever. She'd been unable to perform the simplest tasks— couldn't pick up a fork, couldn't talk worth a damn, couldn't walk two steps. She'd lost her dignity and her independence and had been unable to imagine winning them back.

But she was almost there. The next two months would prove how much she had regained. They would prove that she could live alone, that she could make a life for herself.

That she had no further need of Ross.

The words still had the ability to stir an ache deep inside. There'd been a time when not needing Ross in her life had been utterly inconceivable—a time when he'd *been* her life. That time was long past now, but the regret wasn't. The sorrow wasn't.

And even if their marriage was over, she owed him so much. It was his money, his forceful personality, and his steadiness—along with her own damn hard work— that had gotten her through the past eleven months. From the first day, she'd gotten the best care his money could buy, the special treatment he had imperiously demanded.

And he had stood by her. Her parents had let her down, and so had her friends, but Ross had been there week after week, when she couldn't walk, couldn't talk, couldn't even get her thoughts in logical order. He, and the endless hard work, had been the one constant in her life, and she was grateful to him.

Of course, she knew why he'd spent all that money and made all those visits to her both at the hospital and the rehab center. While he was a decent man, he was also an image-conscious man. He'd worked hard to present the perfect image, both professionally and privately. He'd had to stand by her, like it or not, until she could stand on her own.

But he wanted to be free too. She was sure of it. So, after the next few months, she intended to say goodbye—if he didn't say it first. Another person may think that was cold and manipulative, but it wasn't. Goodbye was simply all that was left for them to say.

While the aide loaded her suitcases onto a wheeled cart, Maggie made her way into the bathroom. After closing the door, she stared at herself in the mirror, taking stock. Her auburn hair, shaved completely in the operating room for the surgery to remove blood clots from her brain, had grown back months before and looked much the same as ever. It completely covered the scar that arced across her scalp from front to back.

Makeup camouflaged the thinner scars on her forehead, her cheek, her jaw. Those were where her face had come into contact with various parts of the truck. The thicker, elliptical scar at the base of her throat, visible when she tugged down the neck of her sweater, marked the incision where the ER doctor had inserted the tracheotomy tube that allowed her to breathe in those first few hours.

Other than the scars, she looked like the same old Maggie. But she wasn't. She was more afraid than the old Maggie, less confident. She felt less intelligent, less capable, less competent.

But she was more determined. She'd already proven wrong the doctors who'd said she wouldn't survive the wreck, the others who'd said she wouldn't recover. Now she was going to prove just how much she had recovered. She was going to declare her independence, to live her life for herself and no one else.

For the first time in far too long, she was going to be happy.

The knock at the door made her gaze shift in that direction. "Mrs. McK? They're here," the aide called out.

They. The two most important men in her life. The doctor who had treated her so well these last eight months, and Ross, who had once loved her with all his heart. Whom she had once loved with all her soul.

Taking a deep breath to ease the tightness in her chest, she looked at herself again. Her face was pale, and her eyes were wide and dark. She looked afraid. Though she'd waited for this day to come, now that it was here, she wanted desperately to stay at the center, where everyone was familiar, where everyone understood her shortcomings and the reasons for them, where there were other people like her. She wanted to stay where she felt safe and protected.

There was another tap on the door. "Maggie?" That was Dr. Allen. He was being polite. There was no lock on the door—no unbreachable privacy for any of his patients, not even in the bathroom. If she didn't answer, he could, if he wanted, simply turn the knob and let himself in.

She turned it instead.

Her large, comfortable room seemed smaller with so many people in it. She pressed her palms together and avoided eye contact. "I—I guess it's time." Her voice sounded breathy because she'd forgotten to breathe. She filled her lungs before gesturing toward the wheelchair. "I'm not riding in that."

"Now, Maggie," Dr. Allen began, but she interrupted.

"You people spent a lot of time teaching me to walk again. You're not putting me in a wheelchair now."

"It's our last treat for you. Just policy, Maggie. You know that."

She appreciated that he gave her credit for knowing simple things—some people didn't—but it didn't sway her. "I don't want to feel like some—some—" She knew the word, could see it in her mind, could hear it but only in its second meaning. Invalid. Not valid. Null. Useless. No good.

Ross broke in in his rich, powerful CEO voice that no one—not even Tom Flynn, certainly not Maggie—argued with. "Take the wheelchair away. She worked hard to learn to walk. Let her walk."

The aide looked at Dr. Allen. He shrugged, then smiled at Maggie. "All right, Maggie. Dazzle us all. Walk out of here."

She circled the bed and left the room for the elevator. The doctor walked alongside her, with Ross a few feet behind, the aide behind him with the luggage cart.

After recovering from the fractures that had required surgery on her left leg and right hip, she'd been walking one way or another for several months—with a walker, followed by crutches and, most recently, a cane. In the last few weeks she'd gotten around on nothing but her own two feet. But today whatever grace she had recovered was temporarily gone. Her movements felt jerky and awkward because fate or luck or whatever the hell it was couldn't let the moment pass without reminding her how much she had changed.

But she would get stronger. However strong she needed to be to live alone, she would achieve it.

The elevator doors opened, and she moved inside with the others. The car was mirrored. By turning her head just a bit, she could see Ross's reflection. The first time she'd ever seen him, she had been in her second year of college, and she'd thought he was the most handsome man who ever existed—black-haired, blue-eyed, with a wicked grin and more ambition, intelligence, and sex appeal than one person should ever possess. She'd been half in love with him from that moment on, had fallen all the way in a few short weeks.

All these years later she still found him startlingly handsome. His hair was longer than he normally wore it, shorter than she normally liked it, and the expression in his eyes was guarded in a way it had never been before. He was still ambitious, intelligent, and sexy as hell, but she never saw that wicked grin anymore. She never saw him smile at all unless she happened to be looking when he smiled at someone else.

The day she'd realized that was the day she'd decided to return to college to finish the education she'd interrupted to put him through school. It was the day she'd known their marriage was past saving.

It was the saddest day of her life.

The bell rang for the first floor, and the aide stepped off first, pushing the luggage cart toward the side entrance with its automatic door. Dr. Allen accompanied Maggie and Ross through the front door and onto the veranda. When they stopped at the top of the steps, he was saying something about questions and needs and calls, but she wasn't listening. Instead, she stared across the grounds.

It was nearing the end of November, eleven months less one day since she'd taken up residence in hospitals. The sky was overcast, and the air was chilly with a reminder that winter had arrived. It was her favorite time of year. Autumn, changing leaves, Thanksgiving, Christmas, nesting in for winter. She was a great nester.

She loved warm clothes, cold weather, hearty stews, and roaring fires.

Ross loved business meetings, eighteen-hour workdays, and takeovers. He wouldn't adapt well to nesting, to twenty-four hours a day with her, to living in a tiny town hours away from everything important to him. He would make the effort because she, through Dr. Allen, had asked it of him, because his image of himself demanded it, but she was sure he would be glad when it was over.

So would she, she reminded herself.

"Well, Maggie." Dr. Allen claimed her attention as well as her hand. "We'll miss you."

"I'll miss you too."

"Take care of yourself. You can do it now."

Smiling at his reassurance, she stepped forward and hugged him. "Thank you for everything."

"We just helped. You did all the hard work yourself." When she released him, he extended his hand to Ross. "Mr. McKinney."

"Doctor." They shook hands, then Ross looked her way. She felt it. "I'll bring the car around—"

"No." She tilted her face to the gray sky and smiled. "I can walk."

She held the rail, smooth wood painted black, and took the first careful step, placing her left foot on the step, gingerly shifting her weight, bringing the right foot alongside. Ross descended easily to the bottom, then waited. He didn't know what it was like to have to think about the mechanics of walking, to give commands and coax muscles and work and struggle so hard for every step. He didn't realize how incredibly lucky he was. *She* did. She was lucky to be alive.

When she reached the bottom, she slowly turned and smiled triumphantly at Dr. Allen. "Thank you."

He smiled back. "You're welcome."

Buoyed with the confidence of success, she found the walk to the end of the sidewalk easier. Ross's attention was on the parking lot, not on her, and she looked that way too. His last car, to the best her battered brain could recall, was a Jag—expensive, impressive, part of the image. There were only a dozen cars in the lot, but she didn't see it. "Which one is yours?"

She felt him glance her way, as if startled that she'd spoken. "The Mercedes." Then, noticing that about half of the dozen cars were Mercedes, he gestured to a midnight-dark car. "The gray one."

The aide met them at the car. After settling in, Maggie took a quick look around. Luxury and beauty. Ross had a fine appreciation for both qualities and had worked hard to earn the fortune that enabled him to surround himself with both. Unfortunately, whatever fortune he had was never enough. The ambition she had so admired back in college had become a relentless drive to have more, always more. If he could live comfortably on a six-figure income, then he would be more comfortable with an eight-figure income. If he owned six companies, he wanted twelve. If he was a powerful, wealthy man, he wanted to be the most powerful, the wealthiest.

All she'd wanted was enough. Enough money to pay their bills, provide a comfortable house, put food on the table, and a little extra for fun now and then.

Enough to support a houseful of babies and let her be a stay-at-home mom. Just enough.

There had been a time when that was all he'd wanted too. How had they grown so far apart?

They'd left the center grounds and were several miles away before he spoke. "Do you want to stop somewhere for lunch?"

"I ate early." She'd had her reasons. She hadn't sat down to eat a meal with him in at least eleven months. She hadn't eaten a meal in a restaurant in that long, hadn't tried out her relearned skills—feeding herself, walking, talking, socializing—in public in that long. She wanted to delay the experience.

"Is there anything you need to do before we leave the city?"

"Like what?"

"Visit your friends. Pick up clothes from the house. Go shopping." He finished with an uncharacteristic shrug, the only outward sign of the awkwardness he was feeling. It was funny, the things she knew about him when she really didn't know him at all anymore.

"I've said all my good-byes."

"So you want to go straight to Bethlehem."

"Yes." Though she sounded certain, she was just guessing. When Dr. Allen had asked her where she'd been happiest, she hadn't had a ready answer. Certainly not in the mansion Ross had built. She'd hated the place from the moment he'd showed her the plans, but he'd built it anyway, and she had lived in it, but she'd never been happy there.

She'd been happy in the little two-room apartment where they'd lived when they were first married. Everything about the place had been shabby, but they'd been wildly in love, and that had been enough. She'd been happy everyplace they'd ever lived—the drafty old house subdivided into dreary rental units, the starter house of red brick where the roof leaked above their bed, the middle-class ranch in a neighborhood crawling with kids, the stately Georgian with enough trees to screen out neighbors and kids. She'd been happy everyplace . . . except Ross's place.

It was Ross who had suggested Bethlehem. He said she'd picked out the house herself, had overseen the remodeling, had made every decision. He said she'd been happy there.

Happy. In a house she couldn't remember in a town she couldn't remember filled with strangers she couldn't remember. *Happy.*

It was a concept she sometimes had difficulty grasping.

After another few silent miles she asked, "Where is the Jag?"

"Home."

"Why did you buy this car?" For years he'd had a short list of requirements when purchasing an automobile: It must have a touch of flash and a whole lot of class. He'd never bought anything even remotely resembling a family car.

"I thought it would be more comfortable for you. Once you start driving again, you can have it or pick out whatever you want."

"I don't have much desire to drive again," she remarked as she gazed out the side window.

"It'll come."

"That's what Dr. Olivetti said. I told her she was wrong. She said at the rates you were paying for her services, she couldn't afford to be wrong." She drew a steady breath, then forced out two awkward words she'd waited eleven months to say. "Thank you."

"For what?"

"All the money you paid for Dr. Olivetti and Dr. Allen, for the center and the hospital. For not letting the accident kill me. For not leaving me to recuperate alone and for not divorcing me when you had plenty of reasons."

When he remained silent, she finally looked at him. Both hands were on the steering wheel, his fingers tightened. His knuckles were pale, his face flushed. Embarrassment over her gratitude? She didn't think so. More likely guilt, because he'd stayed with her not out of obligation to her but to himself. But it didn't matter. All that mattered was that he'd been there when no one else had.

"Give me a couple more months," she went on, hearing the casual, carefree tone of her voice and admiring it even as she hated it. "Then you'll be free. It was almost my Christmas gift to you last year. We'll consider it a late Christmas gift this year." Glimpsing the startled look that crossed his face, she turned away and saw her reflection in the window smile, just barely, with bittersweet anticipation and the slightest bit of fear as she finished.

"After the holidays, we'll file for divorce."

Chapter Two

AS DUSK BEGAN TO SETTLE, THE HIGH-
way began its slow, gentle descent into the
valley.

Ross glanced at Maggie, asleep for the last
few hours, and wondered if he should wake her for a
look at her new hometown, then decided against it.
She had plenty of time to refamiliarize herself with it.

He followed a well-maintained street past neat
houses and prospering shops right into the heart of
Bethlehem, to its town square, with businesses on three
sides of it, the courthouse on the fourth side, and a
bandstand in the middle. There was one small hospital
and two grocery stores, one elementary school, one
middle school, one high school, and a dozen or more
churches. It was a well-preserved piece of history, visu-
ally appealing and quaint as hell.

And Maggie—at least, the Maggie before the accident—had loved it. He hoped the post-accident Maggie was just as taken with the place.

Her house was located at the intersection of Fourth Street and Hawthorne Avenue, just a few blocks north and east of downtown. Two weeks earlier he had contacted an attorney in town to prepare the house, remove the Christmas tree, pack up the gifts, and store them in the basement. Alex Thomas had volunteered his wife to stock the refrigerator and cabinets, and Ross had agreed. The easier settling in would be for Maggie, the better.

He pulled to the curb in front of the house. The place had been built at the turn of the century and was meant to last. It was deep red brick with broad porches both front and back and a porte cochere on the left that led to the detached garage in back. Though it wasn't a particularly large house—barely a fraction of the square footage of their Buffalo house—its square lines, thick walls, and generous use of brick and concrete gave it a solid, permanent feel. That was part of what had drawn Maggie to it—the fact that it looked as if it had been there a hundred years and fully intended to be around a hundred more.

After the last eleven months, she needed that sense of stability.

He turned into the driveway, stopping underneath the porte cochere. A few feet from the car, a French door led into a small foyer with a brick floor and steps up to the corridor. A few feet behind them, a broad set of concrete steps rose to the front porch. He had considered building a ramp in one place or the other and save Maggie the hassle of stairs. After the discussion about the wheelchair at the center, he was glad he hadn't.

"Maggie?"

Her head was turned toward him, her expression unguarded in sleep. For a moment he simply looked at her. Her features were delicate, though her jaw was stubborn. Her once-perfect nose now had a bump just below the bridge.

She was incredibly beautiful, and that was nothing less than a miracle. When he'd rushed into the emergency room at Bethlehem Memorial last Christmas Eve, he'd thought there had been a mistake. That bloodied, battered woman lying there couldn't possibly be Maggie.

Then he'd recognized the emerald stud in her ear. He'd stood less than a foot away, staring into his wife's face, and her earring was the only thing he recognized. The shock had been overwhelming.

"Maggie?"

Her lids fluttered open, and he found himself staring into clear green eyes. He'd seen every emotion in existence in those eyes, had dreamed of them when he was young, had avoided them when he was older. He had matched emeralds to their rich, deep shade and had watched them turn as cold, as hard, as the stones themselves. This late November afternoon, even newly awakened, there was nothing in her eyes for him to read. It was like looking at a stranger.

"We're here." Not *home*. Just *here*.

She straightened in the seat and turned to look at the house. It wasn't particularly impressive from this angle. By the time he got out of the car and circled to her side, she had unfastened her seat belt and opened the door. She moved slowly, turning in the seat, carefully pulling herself to her feet. For a moment she clung to the door, and he wondered if she needed the support emotionally or physically.

"So this is the house I wanted." She moved down the driveway to the sidewalk out front. There she faced the house as he'd done only minutes before and subjected it to the same long scrutiny.

He found the unfamiliar key on his key ring, unlocked the door, and set their luggage inside before joining her. "You don't remember it, do you?"

"No. But it's a great house."

"That's what you said the day you told me about it." He hesitated, then went on. "We first came to Bethlehem in August of last year. One of my business associates was visiting family in the area, and we agreed to meet here. You came along to . . ."

When he trailed off, she completed the sentence. "To play at being the perfect wife."

He didn't deny it. She'd always been one of his most valuable assets, both professionally and socially. She'd known exactly what to say, how to dress, when to interrupt, and when to blend into the background, and she'd had the art of being gracious down to a science.

In the beginning Maggie's support had been genuine. In the end it had been an act, a performance for which she had been well compensated.

"You liked the town," he went on. "You felt at home here, and you came back a few times. You found the house in September and asked me to buy it, and I did."

"Just like that."

"You wanted the house. It would make you happy."

"And you wanted me to be happy, didn't you?"

He didn't have to listen hard to hear the mockery in her voice. He shrugged and responded with a simple statement of fact. "When you were happy, you weren't making me *un*happy."

She started walking, her gaze on the broad concrete steps, edged with low stairstepping brick walls, that led to the front door. There was no rail to hold on to, so she took the first step with caution. He walked beside her, close enough to catch her if she faltered, distant enough to give her some sense of independence. Her pace was slow and made him feel edgy.

At last she crossed the threshold and stood just inside the door while he switched on lights down the hall and up the stairs, in the living room on one side and the office on the other. The air was warm and smelled faintly of spices, reminding him that he'd missed lunch. The makings for a fire were laid on the hearth, and a bouquet of fresh flowers bearing a Welcome Home greeting sat nearby.

A flight of stairs, long enough to make Maggie's eyes widen, stretched in front of them to the second floor. Down the hall were the kitchen, pantry, and utility room that occupied the back third of the house, and in between those rooms and the front rooms were a dining room and side hallway on the left, a library on the right.

"How much of this did we re—re—" She gave it a moment's thought, then settled on an easier word. "Redo?"

He removed his jacket. "I don't know. This was your project." He hadn't seen the house before they'd bought it, and he hadn't paid much attention when he was there. That was the way they'd lived—not paying much attention.

She turned in a slow circle, looking in each direction. "It's pretty. I had good taste."

Slowly she moved, going into the office first, where the simple chandelier, with not a shard of crystal in sight, banished the gloom into the farthest corners. The walls were hunter green, the furniture leather, the desk and wood filing cabinets antiques. This was where Ross had stayed from early morning until late into the night, making calls, sending faxes, waiting for responses. He'd kept the pocket doors closed and had been grateful for the Christmas preparations that kept Maggie just as busy.

She went into the living room next, and he followed, watching as she circled the room, touching something here, studying something there. The last time he'd seen this room, it had been decked out with Christmas finery—a twelve-foot tree with gifts piled high beneath it, garlands made from fresh pine boughs, mistletoe and holly and white candles in every window.

All that was gone now, and what was left was the room as Maggie had envisioned it. Overstuffed furniture comfortable for sprawling. A fireplace with a serpentine marble surround and a carved white mantel. White casings and moldings against vivid yellow walls. The faint smell of mulberry potpourri.

Bending in front of the flowers, she removed the

welcome message. "Who are Melissa and Alex Thomas?"

"He's a lawyer here in town. I hired him to get the house ready, and his wife stocked the kitchen for you. I believe you knew her."

She fingered the card while a distant look crept across her face. After a moment she shook her head, laid the card on the mantel, and turned away.

She left through the side doors, crossed the hallway leading to the porte cochere, and went into the dining room. It was fairly casual, with a set of good antiques, more white trim, and deep coral walls. He'd forgotten her love of color. The lack of it in the Buffalo house must have left her cold.

At last she came to the kitchen and stopped short. "Oh, wow."

"You wanted a place to cook, to be comfortable and to curl up and watch the snow." And the kitchen had it all. Plenty of cabinets and work counters. A marble pastry slab. Restaurant-quality appliances. Windows across the back wall with padded benches topping storage cabinets. A brick fireplace with two rockers in front of it. All on a heavily padded vinyl floor, more comfortable on the feet and legs for hours at the stove—though, according to Dr. Allen, she wouldn't be spending hours on her feet for a long time.

She circled the island, drawing her hand across the granite surface. "I haven't cooked in . . . almost a year, at least. Hardly at all for five years. I loved cooking and baking." Abruptly she looked at him. Her tone was curt, almost accusing, when she asked, "You didn't hire a staff, did you?"

"That would defeat our purpose, wouldn't it? You can't learn what you can do if I'm paying someone to do it for you."

Our purpose. The words brought Maggie a faint longing. It had been ages since there'd been an *our* in their marriage. After so many months of traveling on different paths, they finally, once more, shared a common goal. It would feel good if that goal wasn't the end of their marriage. Better, she decided, to say the beginning of their new lives. Endings were sad and unhappy. Beginnings were filled with promise, and she had such promises to fulfill.

She looked around the room while he waited near the hall. She might not remember the house, but she had no doubt Ross was right in saying she'd loved it. It was everything she'd ever wanted—a comfortable, welcoming home with a yard for flowers, room for children, and freedom to live and relax.

When she glanced at him, Ross had moved to gently rock one of the chairs in front of the fireplace. With bread baking in the oven, snow coming down outside, and a fire crackling on the hearth, the rocker would be a perfect place to while away an afternoon. She could hardly wait for the first snowfall to try it out.

"I must have loved cooking in here last Christmas."

With a shrug, he shoved his hands into his pockets. "I guess so. You cooked every day, baked a lot of cookies, pies, and breads. The house smelled of food all the time."

She bit back the impulse to comment that she was surprised he'd noticed. She had become such an unimportant part of his life that even obvious hints of her activities had escaped his attention. But the remark would sound petty and would put him on the defensive. Besides, being critical and snide was the old Maggie. The new one wasn't going to fall into those traps.

She looked inside a few more cabinets, the refrigerator, and the freezer, located coffee and filters for the coffeemaker on the counter, then crossed to the central hallway.

A door on the right opened to a small bathroom. Another revealed a closet. Double pocket doors on the left led into a library of built-in bookcases with tall windows, walls of deep crimson, and a carpet plush enough to sleep on. She imagined she would spend much of her time in there.

Ignoring the discomfort in her hip, she circled the room, drawing her fingertips over the spines of old favorites read long ago and newer books that, if she'd read them, she'd forgotten. She loved to read, though it was no longer the effortless pastime she'd taken for granted. Sometimes the blurred vision that accompanied her chronic headaches made it impossible to focus. Sometimes her ability to concentrate just wasn't there, and sometimes her mind wandered off on its own to other places and happier times—both those lost in the past and those in the future awaiting discovery.

The hallway led her back to the front door and the stairs. She looked up with some trepidation. "The bedrooms are upstairs?"

Ross nodded. "I'll help you this time, then—"

"No, thanks," she said politely. "I can manage." It was neither easy nor quick, but she made it to the top of the stairs in the same way she'd made it through these last months—slowly, doggedly, one step at a time.

There were four bedrooms on the second floor, three sharing the same large bath. The master bedroom, at the back on the right, had its own bath. The room was dark blue, the bed a queen-size four-poster. The sitting area was cozy, the bathroom as gorgeous as the rest of the place, and the closet was huge.

She walked inside, opened drawers, examined shelves. Only a small portion of the closet was in use— one clothes rod, one shelf, one drawer—and everything there, left over from last year, belonged to her. Maybe Ross had had time to remove his own things. Or maybe he hadn't used this closet—or this bedroom. Maybe their marriage had been even closer to death last Christmas Eve than *she* had.

Only one person could tell her exactly how far apart they had grown in those missing months. He hadn't followed her into the room but was standing in the doorway, hands in his pockets, watching, waiting.

She didn't phrase the question as bluntly as she would have liked, but she didn't dance around it either. "Which room did you use when you were here last Christmas?"

He looked startled, the same way he had looked in the car when she'd told him they would file for divorce after Christmas. Then his expression became still and thoughtful. "The one across the hall."

"So we weren't sharing a bedroom. Things were worse than I'd realized."

"We weren't even sharing a life, Maggie. And how

much worse could things have gotten? You were planning to file for divorce. So was I."

Deep inside she'd known that, but this was the first time he'd told her so. It had never mattered to her who did the leaving, just as long as she got out. Yet it hurt to hear that he'd been as eager to leave her as she'd been to leave him.

Glancing out the window into the night-dark sky, she noticed lights in the houses behind them. "We have neighbors. We haven't had neighbors for a long time."

Slowly Ross came into the room, coming to stand at the opposite end of the window. "Are you changing the subject, just making a comment, or is this one of those head-trauma things I'm supposed to be patient with?"

She gave him a long, steady look. "Just making a comment. Was that genuine perplexity, or have some fragile remains of your sense of humor actually survived your obsession with business?"

His only response, before changing—or returning to—the subject, was what might have been the fragile remains of that wicked grin she had so long ago fallen in love with. "We've always had neighbors. It's just been eight or ten years since they've been this close. You'd met the people in all these houses and had grown rather fond of the two elderly sisters who live in the Victoria catercorner from us. You said they were great bakers, wonderful surrogate grandmothers, and grand ladies."

"Did they like me too?"

"I suppose. They invited you to their parties, and

you went—to one, at least." He shrugged. "What's not to like?"

Maggie glanced around the bedroom—*her* bedroom, where she had slept alone while her husband slept across the hall—and felt another twinge of pain. "You tell me."

Ross grew more serious too, and withdrew just a little. "Not tonight, Maggie," he said quietly. "I'm going to bring our luggage up. After we unpack, why don't we see about dinner, then call it a night. It's been a long day."

She nodded in agreement, then went to the bed as he left the room. The mattress was so thick that sitting down required a boost. Her feet dangling above the floor, she let her shoes drop, then inspected the night-stand's single drawer. It held a novel, one of last year's blockbuster hits according to the dust jacket, plus a box of tissues, a bottle of antacids, and a bottle of lotion.

Underneath it all was a picture frame, facedown. She pulled it free, turned it over, and saw that the glass was shattered, with several jagged pieces missing. The damage was new to her, but the photo was achingly familiar. It was their wedding picture, taken by a disinterested clerk in the judge's chambers. She was wearing her best outfit—a simple green sheath and matching jacket—and Ross wore jeans and a white cotton shirt. They had been so young, so much in love.

And look at them now.

At the sound of Ross's footsteps in the hall, she quickly returned the frame to the drawer. He set her suitcases at the foot of the bed, then asked, "Do you need help unpacking?"

She shook her head.

"Then I'll get my stuff. I'll be across the hall or downstairs. If you need anything, call." He left the room, closing the door behind him.

Maggie slid to her feet, then heaved the heaviest of her suitcases onto the bed. One of the first things they'd taught her at the rehab center was how to dress herself, and she'd been happy to learn, to escape the hospital gowns and nightgowns in which she'd lived the preceding three months. She had started simply, with sweats, before graduating to jeans and T-shirts, button-front shirts and sweaters. In the summer months she had developed quite an affection for light, airy dresses that slipped easily over her head.

Her current wardrobe was a far cry from the elegant, dressy, sophisticated clothes in the closet. She liked the sight of denim and cotton sharing the same space with velvet and silk, liked overwhelming all that formality with her rediscovered taste for the casual.

She was placing the last of her shoes on the shelves in the closet, when the built-in jewelry chest caught her attention. In the fifteen years of their marriage before the accident, Ross had given her a not-so-small fortune in jewelry. It had started with the piece that mattered most—a plain gold wedding band inscribed with the date and one simple word: *love*. She'd worn the ring constantly until the anniversary—their ninth? tenth?—when he'd replaced it with a diamond monstrosity that weighted her hand and made her cringe to look at it.

The only other jewelry that mattered was a pair of emerald studs. When they were first married and living in a shabby apartment, he'd promised her that one day he would buy her emeralds to match her eyes, and, keeping that promise his first year in business—a grand extravagance for which he'd worked hard and sacrificed much—had meant the world to him. Because of that, the earrings had meant the world to her.

But it was difficult to keep treasures she no longer had. Though the monstrosity was in the chest, along with everything else she must have planned to wear over the holidays last year, there was no sign of the little gold band or the emeralds. Maybe she'd left them at the house in Buffalo. Maybe she'd had them with her at the time of the accident, and they had been given to Ross.

Maybe they were gone for good. Like their marriage.

Like their love.

R OSS WAS PULLING A COLANDER OF GRAPES FROM the refrigerator when Maggie came into the kitchen. Walking with a slight limp in Ragg socks, she crossed to the island and eased onto a tall stool there. He faced her. "I told you to yell if you needed anything."

"I know. I didn't need anything."

"You shouldn't be going up and down the stairs alone."

She picked up a handful of grapes. "If I'd fallen, I would have yelled."

"That's not funny," he said sharply—too sharply,

judging by her look and the carefully controlled tone of her voice when she answered.

"Trust me, I've fallen enough to know that it's not funny. Why do you think they had all that padding in the physical therapy rooms?" She popped a grape into her mouth, then asked around it, "What do we have for dinner?"

"Whatever you want to cook. Or we can go out."

She answered too quickly, too casually. "No, thanks. I'd rather cook."

Rather cook than what? he wondered. Go out with him? Or go out in public, where she might meet people she'd once known but had since forgotten, or strangers who might wonder about the thin scars and the slight limp? If she was self-conscious about making a public appearance, she would have to deal with it. She was too young to become a recluse.

But for one night, it couldn't hurt. "How about sandwiches? Then you can start tomorrow off cooking breakfast. Nothing fancy—just some crepes. Maybe eggs Benedict. Fruit compote. Homemade croissants."

She looked wary. "I don't think I should be quite so ambitious to start. Maybe oatmeal with sliced bananas."

He wasn't sure how serious she was—but then, that was nothing new. Too many times in the last few years, he hadn't had a clue what she thought, meant, or wanted. For most of that time he had cared. Then he hadn't.

Instead of wondering about it now, he gathered sandwich ingredients. The bread was wrapped in

Thanksgiving-themed paper and secured with a seal that read FROM THE WINCHESTER KITCHEN.

"Who are the Winchesters?" Maggie asked, reading the label upside down.

"I think they're the elderly sisters across the street."

She took a deep whiff as he unwrapped the bread. "The great bakers," she murmured. "Absolutely."

"You're a great baker too," he reminded her, and she got that wary look again.

"We'll see. I don't have the best of luck concentrating these days, and following directions isn't always an option. Sometimes I just can't do it."

"You don't sound too broken up over it."

With a shrug that didn't achieve the casual effect she was aiming for, she parroted words he knew she'd been told at the center. "I've gotten better, and Dr. Allen says I should continue to improve. But plenty of people who *haven't* had brain injuries can't follow directions. If I can't, I'll adapt. And even if I can't follow orders, I can give them. Put that knife away and get a bread knife. There should be one in the same drawer—long, thin, with a serrated blade."

He did as she instructed and started slicing the bread. "Don't get too bossy. It's not an attractive trait."

"Tell me about it," she murmured as she claimed the first two slices for her plate.

He paused, the blade poised above the loaf. "What do you mean by that?"

"Nothing. I was simply agreeing with you."

"You were implying that I'm bossy."

As if her attention stretched to only one task at a time, she made her sandwich: turkey and ham, provolone and mozzarella, topped with spicy mustard. Then she looked at him, her expression flat and steady. "You treated me like an employee. You told me how to dress, how to act, where to go, what to do, who to be friends with, and who wasn't suitable. When I did my job well, I got rewarded with another fabulous piece of jewelry. When I didn't do it well, you made your displeasure known and gave me the cold shoulder until you needed me again."

"I did not—"

"Oh, please," she interrupted. Though it had been absent a long time, he had no difficulty recognizing the subtle scorn in her voice. It had become a familiar companion, there every time she'd bothered to speak to him. "I'm not up to your version of our history tonight. I don't like fairy tales until bedtime."

"The only fairy tales you ever liked were your own anyway." Pulling a stool around the island, he sat down opposite her and put together his own sandwich. Before he took the first bite, though, he said, "So tell me this, Maggie. If I was such a bastard, why did you stay with me so long?"

Something in her face shifted, and he felt it within himself—the realization that they'd so easily slipped into old habits, old resentments. She toyed with her food, pinching bits of crust from the bread, before finally meeting his gaze and replying in a quiet, subdued voice. "I assume for the same reasons you were still with me. In the beginning, I still loved you. And in the end . . . I didn't get the chance to leave."

There was nothing he could say to that. She was absolutely correct. In the beginning—practically from the first time he'd laid eyes on her—he had loved her passionately. She'd made all the hardships worthwhile, had been part of his drive to succeed. He'd wanted to repay her for all her sacrifices, to show his gratitude, to give her things as beautiful and precious as she was.

And in the end . . . He hadn't gotten the chance to divorce her before fate, bad weather, and an icy mountain road intervened.

"I suspect we'll get along much better as exes than as husband and wife," she said thoughtfully. "If, of course, we ever see each other, which we won't, once you leave here."

"I suspect you're right."

Abruptly, unexpectedly, she grinned. It was a sight he hadn't seen in far too long. "It's been a *long* time since you've said that."

His smile was faint. "You haven't even seen the town yet, but you think you'll want to stay."

She nodded.

"Based on what?"

"This place. You were right—and I know, it's been a long time since *I* said *that*. I did love this house. I can feel it. I can tell just by looking at it. I was planning to stay here then, and I knew the town then. I knew some of the people. I'm trusting that I made a good decision."

"What will you do?"

Her shrug made her hair shift, reflecting the lights overhead, the red tones gleaming. "I don't know. I must have had plans, but they're gone now. Maybe I'll get a job. Maybe I'll do volunteer work."

"Maybe you'll get married again and have those babies you wanted." As far as Ross was concerned, that would be the best-case scenario. For years she'd wanted children, and for years he'd put her off. He wasn't making enough money, he wanted to be able to give their kids the absolute best, he was traveling too much, the business was too demanding. He'd had excuses lined up, just waiting to be given, until suddenly she stopped asking. She stopped talking about a family, stopped doting on their friends' babies. At the time, he'd been relieved. He wondered now if that had been, for her, the beginning of the end.

"Maybe I will. I'm only thirty-four. That's young enough."

"Thirty-five. Missing your birthday because you're in a coma doesn't entitle you to take a year off your age."

"It should," she said dryly. "Still, thirty-five is young enough. If I got started right away, I could have four or five babies before I turn forty."

"I wouldn't be surprised." He paused. "You didn't ask what my plans are."

She snorted, a coarse sound coming from such a delicate woman. "You'll do what you've done the fifteen—excuse me, sixteen—years we've been married. You'll work hundred-hour weeks, buy new companies, expand your old companies into every conceivable market in the world, make millions more, and impress the hell out of everyone with your business acumen."

Her prediction was on target, but its limited scope—strictly business, as if he would have no personal life—left him feeling prickly. "Maybe I'll get married again too."

"Maybe. But why bother when you can get everything you want—someone to plan your parties, to accompany you to business functions, to put in appearances on your behalf, and to satisfy your occasional need for sex—simply by contracting with the appropriate businesses on a need-by-need basis? It's much more cost effective that way, and there's never a need for a divorce."

"You have complaints about the sex?"

"What sex?" she asked with the innocence of a child. "I can't even remember the last time we had sex."

He smiled cynically. "That's right. You can't. Trust me though. You weren't complaining." Then he deliberately, coolly, added, "It was a pleasant change."

For a long time she simply looked at him, her expression calm. For the first minute, he endured, then he began getting edgy again. Suspicion that he was somehow being manipulated made him uneasy, then annoyed, then guilty for insulting her.

"I thought we might get through the next few months as polite acquaintances, if not friends," she said softly. "Let's at least make the effort. I don't want to fight with you. We've done enough of that to last a lifetime, and frankly, I'm just not up to it. I'm sorry I suggested you should buy a companion. I'm sorry I brought sex into the conversation at all. And I'm sorry that my being pleasant was a rare occurrence in our marriage."

He'd been manipulated, all right, but he wasn't sure if it had been Maggie pulling the strings, or his own conscience. "It wasn't so rare," he admitted grudgingly. "Under the circumstances, I can't blame you."

"Of course you can. There's plenty of blame to go around." She smiled sadly. "I—I think I'll go to my room now."

"I'll walk up with you."

"It's not— All right."

He accompanied her to the top of the stairs, waited there until she closed the bedroom door behind her, then returned to the kitchen. After cleaning up, he made his way to the front of the house again.

For a moment he paused in the office doorway. Less than twelve hours had passed since he'd officially turned everything over to Tom—less than twelve hours free of business responsibility. The computer tempted him, invited him in, reminded him of all the work he could accomplish in the next few hours. It offered to keep his mind occupied, to leave him not even one moment to think about Maggie, or their marriage, or their divorce.

But he had promised Maggie and himself no work for the next few months. Besides, work wouldn't make him forget the reminder he'd just gotten that no divorce, no matter how eagerly anticipated, was painless. Even though they both wanted to be free, they still had the ability to wound egos and hurt feelings.

And why shouldn't they? They had loved each other more than anyone else in their lives had ever loved them. Though the love was long gone, there was still so much left—so many intimacies, so many disappointments, so many regrets. Those things hurt, and the simple fact of saying "In two months we'll file for divorce" couldn't change that. Only time could.

Instead of giving in to the urge to use work to hide from life, he closed the pocket doors, shut off the hall lights, and headed up the stairs. Maybe if he'd set limits on work years before instead of on Maggie, they wouldn't be where they were now.

But they were there, and the best he could do was no less than she deserved. No routine work, no accusations, insults, or arguments. She needed him for friendly support, and that was what he would give her.

And then she would give him his freedom. Forever.

Chapter Three

MAGGIE AWAKENED AT HER USUAL time Tuesday morning and, for a moment, simply lay with her eyes closed. The sounds that had greeted her for the past two hundred and forty–odd days were noticeably absent—the doctors making rounds, the staff going to help those patients who needed it, the housekeeping staff getting an early start on their day. The house was quiet, with no sound from Ross across the hall, and so was the neighborhood, except for the faint passing of a car.

When she opened her eyes, she saw that the sun was shining. Throwing back the covers, she eased out of bed, rubbing the stiffness from her hip. Quickly she dressed, brushed her teeth, combed her hair, then reluctantly opened the makeup case on the counter. She'd never been one to consider makeup an essential part of her morning routine, but these days she felt she had little choice. Though she disliked the implication of vanity, she wasn't yet ready to display her scars to the world. She couldn't hide her occasional limp, her speech problems, or difficulty concentrating, but she could darn well hide her scars.

Once that task was completed, she left her room and made her way carefully downstairs. From the hall closet, she chose a heavy jacket, then went outside.

The front porch was broad, lit around the edges by the morning sun and made for kicking back, relaxing, and doing nothing. She sat down on the glider, propped her feet on the concrete shelf that capped the brick, and gave a soft, satisfied sigh.

Listening to the quiet, looking at the peaceful streets around her, she found it easy to believe that this was where she belonged. Bethlehem was a small-town–family sort of place, and she was a small-town–family sort of girl. She didn't want to be rich, had no use for power. She wanted to putter about her own kitchen, to kneel in her own dirt and plant her own flowers, to exchange recipes and baby-sitting with neighbors who were also friends. Ross said some of these people had been her friends last year. She sincerely hoped they would be again.

As if conjured by her thoughts, two women came out of the big Victorian across the way on Fourth Street—the Winchester house, according to Ross—and turned in her direction. Coming to see her? she wondered with more pleasure than a simple visit with strangers should generate.

The women were elderly, but their step was lively as

they crossed Fourth, then Hawthorne, and turned onto her sidewalk. Seeing her on the porch, both women beamed welcoming smiles and one called a greeting. "Hello, Maggie. It's so good to see you again."

Maggie lowered her feet to the floor and started to rise as the women climbed the steps.

"Oh, no, dear," the stouter one admonished. "Don't get up. Stay right where you are."

She obediently sank back as they came to a stop in front of her.

"You probably don't remember us, dear—"

"You *know* she doesn't remember us," the other chided in a loud whisper.

"But I'm Agatha Winchester—"

"And I'm her sister, Corinna Humphries, and we're your neighbors." Corinna seated herself on the glider and patted Maggie's hand. "We met you last year, dear, before that dreadful accident—"

"And we're happy to see that you're recovering so nicely." Agatha sat on the brick wall and offered a foil-covered plate. "Fresh rolls. We love to bake—"

"And cook. Of course, you do too. You're very good at it, you know."

"You baked the bread we had with dinner last night. It was wonderful." Maggie accepted the plate, lifted the foil, and breathed in the heavenly scent of cinnamon rolls fresh from the oven. "I love cinnamon rolls. I remember . . . in the hospital . . ."

Both women beamed their million-watt smiles again, and Agatha bobbed her gray head. "We sent some with the sheriff when you awakened and he was able to interview you about the accident."

Maggie remembered. She hadn't been allowed food yet—she had still received her nourishment via IV—but the aromas, after nine weeks in a coma, had been almost as good as actually eating. Though he'd no doubt thought it best, it had nearly broken her heart when Ross had them taken away.

"So . . . we understand you and your husband are going to live here for a while," Corinna said. "Once you're settled in and feel up to it, we'll have a welcome-home party to reintroduce you to all your neighbors."

"Let's not wait for a party." Agatha leaned close to pat her knee. "Thanksgiving is the day after tomorrow. We always cook a big dinner and have a lot of people in—family and friends and neighbors. Why don't you and your husband join us?"

"Oh, please do," her sister chimed in. "Thanksgiving is meant to be shared by a crowd. It's much too big a holiday for just two people. Please come. You met everyone last year, and they'll be so glad to see you again."

Maggie felt a flutter of panic at the thought, no matter how well intentioned, of being on display for a crowd of strangers who knew her but had no place in her memories. At the same time, part of her relished the notion of spending a holiday with people who were genuinely happy to see her. That same part liked the idea of being welcomed into the community. After all, she was going to be a part of it.

"It sounds nice," she said, meaning it in spite of the panic. She was going to have to face her fears at some point, and being a part of the holiday they were describing seemed a perfect opportunity. "I'll have to check with Ross, but it shouldn't be a problem."

"Everyone starts gathering around eleven, and we eat at one or thereabout. We'd be happy to have you—and you don't need to bring a thing. We always have plenty. Now, go ahead, eat," Agatha encouraged. "There's a napkin underneath the plate, though I prefer to just lick my fingers. Corinna, we should have made some hot cocoa. What good are cinnamon rolls on a nippy fall morning without hot cocoa?"

"They're wonderful all on their own," Maggie said as she broke off a piece. She savored the first bite and the next, until half of one roll was gone.

That was when Corinna took a look around. "Is your husband here, my dear?"

"He's inside—still asleep, I think."

"We never met him last year. On the rare trips he made here, he was always working." Corinna clucked her tongue. "Young people need to learn to take it easy, to make time for what counts. Life doesn't last forever, you know." Abruptly, her cheeks turned pink. "I'm sorry, dear. That was insensitive of me."

Maggie smiled to put her at ease. "Not at all. It's all too true, as I found out for myself."

"You're a very lucky girl. We saw your truck when the sheriff had it towed out of the ravine. It's a miracle that you survived." Agatha's expression shifted from grave to joyous. "You got your very own Christmas miracle. We love miracles here in Bethlehem."

"Then it's a good place to be." And as long as she was there, Maggie could use a few more small miracles—if she hadn't already used up her share.

"Well, dear, we must get back," Agatha said, getting to her feet. "We've got planting to do."

"Planting?"

"We're dividing our bulbs," Corinna replied. "It should have been done weeks ago, but . . ." She waved one hand dismissively. "Things happened. But as long as we can work the ground, it's not too late. Why don't you bring your husband over sometime? We'd love to meet him, and we're usually home, unless we've gone to the library with the children—"

"Or to help out at the church," Agatha added, "or with something at the school."

"I will," Maggie agreed, though the chances of getting Ross to drop in unexpectedly on two old ladies whom he'd never met were slim, to say the least. "Thanks for the rolls. They're really wonderful."

"Take care," one sister called as they made their way down the sidewalk. The other added, "Don't be a stranger."

Maggie watched until they disappeared inside their house. As she started on the second roll, a car left from the stone house directly across the street. Another stopped in front of the Winchester house, and a small boy barreled out and across the yard to the porch at full speed. Ross had called them surrogate grandmothers, and the boy's eagerness to reach them seemed to support that.

Around the corner, shouts and laughter from unseen children were followed by the rumble of a school bus. Children in their Buffalo neighborhood were chauffeured to private schools in luxury cars by employees whose sole job was catering to their juvenile charges.

Maggie took such delight in the big yellow bus belching black smoke as it lumbered around the corner that the click of the front door hardly registered.

"We're going to have to reach an agreement about you and the stairs."

She glanced up as Ross crossed the porch and sat down at the opposite end of the glider. He wore jeans and a steel-gray sweater and looked too handsome for his own good. There'd been a time when every sight of him had made her heart beat faster and her hands tremble. Now she could simply look and appreciate him the same way she would appreciate anything of beauty. She didn't have to feel a thing.

"A welcome gift from the Winchester sisters," she said, offering him the final roll. Once he'd taken it, she responded to his comment. "Every morning for two hundred and forty days, I've gotten up at exactly the same time, gotten dressed, wheeled myself or hobbled or limped to the dining room for breakfast, then spent the rest of the morning and all of the afternoon in one sort of therapy or another. This morning I wanted to do something different, and I didn't want to wait for you to wake up to do it."

"You could have knocked or opened the door and shouted or thrown something across the room."

She smiled faintly at the image of herself throwing anything more damaging than a tantrum. With all the exquisite breakables in his mansion, if she'd yielded to such desires, she certainly could have gotten his attention.

"Dr. Allen says you're not supposed to take the stairs alone. He says you can't afford to break your hip or

your leg or your head again. You could end up perma-
nently disabled, which is a hell of a price to pay for
being stubborn."

"So what are you going to do? Tell on me? I've been
discharged from his care. He's not my boss any longer,
and neither are you." Then she yielded with a sigh.
"Never mind. All right. I won't come downstairs by
myself again."

"Or go up."

"Or go up," she agreed.

Ross took his victory quietly and changed the subject. "So you met the sisters. Did they seem familiar?"

"They reminded me of someone's grandmother.
Does that count?" Without waiting for a response, she
shook her head. "They seemed to like me, though, and
they want to meet you. They make a big deal out of
Thanksgiving—fix a huge meal and invite a ton of
people—and they asked us to join them."

"Do you want to go?" Neither his face nor his voice
gave any hint of his own preference.

"Yes. No." She shifted uncomfortably on the glider.
"I haven't dealt with strangers in a long time—and
these people are worse than strangers. They know me,
but I don't know them. Frankly, the whole idea leaves
me feeling . . ."

"Scared?" he suggested, his voice softer and more
sympathetic than she'd thought it could be.

After a moment's hesitation, she nodded.

"You always loved the idea of that kind of holiday
celebration—in part, I guess, because you'd never had
it. It would be a shame to turn it down now just be-

cause you don't remember the people. Did you feel awkward with the sisters?"

"No. They're sweet old ladies."

"Do you think they would let you feel awkward as a guest in their home?"

She gazed across the street at the Winchester house. Sometime in the last few minutes, Agatha and Corinna had come outside again, still bundled up, and were now on their knees in the side yard, digging up, then replanting, bulbs with the help of the little boy. He crouched beside them, intent in his concentration, rarely speaking but quick to respond to their directions. She wondered who he was, which Winchester friend was lucky enough to have him in her life.

"No, probably not," she murmured before turning away from the scene.

"As far as the rest, no one's going to comment on any of it. You don't need to feel self-conscious."

He was right, of course. Nice people weren't likely to point out her shortcomings. They might wonder what scars her makeup and clothing hid, but they wouldn't ask.

"It's up to you," Ross said with a shrug. "You can see what you've missed out on all these years, or we can have another quiet Thanksgiving at home."

Just like they'd had for sixteen years. On rare occasions there'd been one or two guests at their table—Tom Flynn, when he hadn't gone off with whatever woman was temporarily in his life, or sometimes a business associate of Ross's—but for years it had been just the two of them. In the early years they'd cooked the meal together, stuffed themselves, then watched

TV or napped away the afternoon. In recent years the staff had done the cooking before going home to their own meals, and she and Ross had dined in stiff formality before separating to spend the rest of the day in solitary pursuits.

She would love to see what a *real* Thanksgiving was like.

"Okay," she agreed. If it was too much to face when the day arrived, she could always beg off, could always come up with a legitimate medical reason to excuse her cowardice or to cut the visit short.

She turned her attention back to the scene around them, and Ross took advantage of her distraction to watch her. That morning was as big a change in his routine as hers. Normally, he was in the office by seven, eating breakfast at his desk, taking care of business, planning the day with Tom and Lynda. He couldn't remember the last time he'd slept past six, or had an entire day ahead of him with nothing scheduled and no one demanding his attention. It made Maggie feel free. It made him feel free, too, but *she* liked the feeling. He was pretty sure he didn't.

"What do you want to do about breakfast?"

She pointed to the empty plate. "The cimmanon—cin-na-mon rolls were breakfast."

"One roll?"

"Actually, I had two. Sleep late around here, you miss out." She gave him a look, made an uneasy offer. "I can make toast."

Last night she'd suggested oatmeal with bananas. Now her confidence had been reduced to burning a slice of bread on both sides. He hated that the woman who'd once created gourmet delicacies out of nothing now doubted her ability to turn water and rolled oats into oatmeal.

Standing up, he offered his hand. "Come on. Let's go in. It's cold out here."

"That's why I put on a coat."

"Well, I didn't."

"And they say *I'm* the brain-damaged one," she murmured. Ignoring his hand, she picked up the plate and stood up without any problem. The instant she tried to take a step, though, she faltered and reached for the closest thing—his arm—for support.

"Sitting in the cold can make your joints stiff," he murmured mildly as her fingers curved around his forearm.

Sending a scowl his way, she took one small step, then another, then let go. By the time they reached the door, she was walking with only the slightest of limps. With her smug look as she crossed the threshold, she made sure he noticed.

At times her stubbornness and determination had driven him out of his mind. There was no such thing as a simple argument with her, and too often compromise wasn't part of her vocabulary. She'd decided that she hated his work and had never relented, had determined to despise their house before the plans were even finished, and to this day hated it intensely. She held grudges for ages, stood her ground long after a reasonable person would have surrendered, and consistently refused to admit that she might conceivably be wrong.

But there were also times he'd admired those qualities tremendously. If she hadn't been so stubborn, her mother would have manipulated Ross right out of her life. If she'd lacked determination, she never could have worked two jobs to put him through his last two years of school. She never could have pushed him the way she had, never could have loved him as long as she did. Stubbornness and determination had brought her back from death last Christmas Eve. They'd brought her through a difficult recovery, and, with a little help from him, they would see her into a new, independent life.

He wished for a little of her determination for himself, to help him into his own new life.

Inside, he refused to open the office door and glance inside, to see if the message light was flashing on the machine, if pages awaited his attention in the fax. He'd broken every promise he'd ever made Maggie. This last promise was one he would keep, no matter how difficult.

The kitchen was warm and made warmer by the sunlight that came through the east windows, falling in brilliant wedges across the vinyl floor. It was a great room if you were the sort of person who spent a lot of time in the kitchen. Over the last five years, he'd forgotten that Maggie *was* that sort.

He was ashamed to admit that he had forgotten a lot about her.

He watched as she started the coffee. He'd watched her make coffee before, a haphazard operation at best, but that morning her movements were deliberate—removing one and only one filter from the stack, fitting it inside the basket, carefully scooping the grounds from a canister marked COFFEE, measuring the water. She turned it on, frowned, then remembered to plug in the cord. When the red on light appeared, she smiled with satisfaction.

That satisfied look gave him a queasy feeling in the pit of his stomach. She was one of the smartest and most capable people he knew. She could arrange a last-minute dinner party for fifty without blinking, could coordinate a formal ball for five hundred with ease, could put together the most elaborate feast with no need for recipes or an extra set of hands.

And that morning she was inordinately pleased because she'd gotten the coffeemaker running with only one hitch. Life was so damn unfair.

Which was one way to look at it, he acknowledged. He could feel sorry for her and frustrated over all that she'd lost. Or he could be encouraged by all that she'd regained, could take pride at her resolve.

It was an easy choice.

"What should I try this morning besides toast?"

"Do we have eggs?"

"Yes."

"Bacon?"

She glanced in the refrigerator. "Yes."

"You can't get much more traditional than that."

She agreed with a nod. As he lit a fire in the fireplace, she gathered ingredients and equipment on the island. Her concentration as she worked was extraordinary, as if the fate of the free world depended on the quality of this meal. Even with all that effort, the eggs were runny, the bacon charred or undercooked. She'd put the toast in when she'd started the bacon, so it was cold long before the strips were done.

They sat in the rockers in front of the fire, their plates on their laps, coffee on a small table between them. Maggie moved the eggs on her plate with a fork, then gave a glum sigh. "I used to be a wonderful cook. Everyone said so. I even thought about opening my own restaurant."

"You did?" It was news to him. He didn't know she'd had any interest in restaurants besides eating in them regularly.

"For a while. I even went so far as to scout out locations and plan a menu."

"I never knew."

Maggie shrugged. "You don't invest in restaurants, and at the time, you weren't very invested in me."

Though he wished he could dispute the accuracy of her response, he couldn't, not truthfully. "Why didn't you give it a shot?"

"Frankly, I didn't think our marriage could survive both of us up to our necks in business matters."

"It's not too late. As I recall, Bethlehem has a couple of places downtown, a steak house, and the restaurant at the inn. They'd probably be happy with someplace new."

"Great. I find a good market, and I can't even fry bacon."

"So . . . you want to feel sorry for yourself?"

She gave him a long, wry look before shifting her gaze to the windows. "No. I want to go out."

"Out as in outside or out into town?"

"Into town."

"Where do you want to go?"

"To a—a—" She grimaced, and her cheeks turned

pink. "A place that sells flowers and bulbs and—and gardening things."

"A nursery," he supplied quietly.

"Nursery." She repeated it softly to herself, as if doing so might ensure that she wouldn't forget again. "I want to go to a nursery."

"Why don't you check the phone book for one?"

With a look around, she spotted the phone above the built-in desk near the fireplace. The phone book was on its side in a cubbyhole underneath, a slim volume only a fraction of the size of the Buffalo directory. She flipped through the Yellow Pages, passed the N's, and returned. "There's only one," she said after a moment's scrutiny. "Melissa's Garden. On Eighth Street. Do you have any idea where that is?"

"The street on the side here is Fourth."

"So Eighth is four blocks in one direction or the other."

Ross nodded. "What are you looking for?"

"Bulbs. Irises, tulips, daffodils."

"Isn't it kind of late for planting flowers?" The instant the question was out, he wished he could call it back. Before the accident, he would never have questioned her knowledge of anything. But she'd awakened from the coma knowing nothing about a lot of common, everyday things. His careless question was now making her wonder whether she knew anything about gardening.

For a moment she looked as if the insecurity might win. Then she squared her shoulders and lifted her chin, and the determined look came into her eyes. "I don't know. But the Winchesters said if the ground can be worked, then it's not too late, and they're across the street, planting, right now." A faint humor crept into her expression. "What can go wrong? Bulbs are forgiving. Even if you plant them upside down, they grow down an inch or so, then turn and come up anyway."

"Then get your coat while I take care of the fire."

He hadn't even reached the fireplace, when the phone rang. Maggie's jaw tightened as she passed it. "It's for you."

She was right. It was Lynda, looking for someone to vent her frustration on. With the phone balanced between his shoulder and ear, Ross half listened while he banked the fire and moved the metal screen into place.

"You have to do something, Ross," Lynda finished in a hot-tempered rush, "or he's going to blow this whole deal. You have to talk to him."

He wavered. It would be so easy to agree, to tell her to call Tom to the phone, to mediate this dispute just as he'd mediated countless others. But if he did, then Lynda would have just one more question. Tom would want his input on one other issue, and before he knew it, it would be as if he'd never left the city.

"I'm not going to talk to him for at least a few more months," he said, hoping he sounded more determined than he felt. "You two are in charge, remember? Work it out. And don't call me again unless it's an emergency."

Lynda was stunned into silence, and he took advantage of it to hang up, then joined Maggie at the porte cochere door. She looked surprised. "Let me mark this day on the calendar. For the first time in history, Ross

McKinney finished a business call in under two minutes."

"I'm on an extended vacation. Don't you know what that means?"

"Yes. It means you spend a lot of money to travel someplace new and exotic so you can do exactly the same work you would be doing at home if you were there."

He paused before opening the door. "That's not fair. We took some real vacations."

"Name one."

"When we went to St. Thomas."

"Work."

"London."

"All work." She began ticking off destinations on her fingertips, speaking in a tone he couldn't quite read—not friendly, but not really antagonistic either. "Paris—work. Rome—work. Tokyo—work. Tahiti—work. Birthdays, holidays, anniversaries, even Christmases—work."

"What about . . ."

When his voice trailed off, she shook her head. "Work. Always. Do you remember our twelfth anniversary?" She paused for the briefest of moments, obviously not expecting him to. "I told you I wanted to go someplace really isolated, where we could be alone, where we wouldn't be disturbed."

Sparked by her words, the memory came slowly into focus. "And I picked a very small resort on a very private Caribbean island."

"There were no phones, no televisions, no cars, no planes. We had to take a boat to the island and a horse-drawn carriage from the dock to our cottage, where you immediately plugged in your notebook computer, hooked it up to your cellular phone, and proceeded to take care of business the entire time we were there. You were in this beautiful, romantic place with your wife, and you never walked on the beach, never went for a swim, never had drinks in the lounge with the rest of the guests. You were obsessed with work, Ross. It dominated your life."

And, in her opinion, it ruined their marriage. He knew that from previous arguments. Because he appreciated her restraint in not mentioning it again, he kept his response to her indictment mild. "Okay, I'm on vacation—a real vacation," he said once they were settled in the car. "So before we find Melissa's Garden, let's do something vacationy, like taking a tour. Let's reacquaint ourselves with Bethlehem. Are you interested?"

"Sure."

"There's another Bethlehem in New York—south of Albany," he said as he backed out of the driveway. "Did you know that?"

"I didn't know *this* one was here until you told Dr. Allen about it." She gazed out the window at the neat houses that grew smaller with each passing block. "How many times did you come here last year?"

"Four. For my business meeting, to sign the papers on the house, to see it just before the work was finished, and to spend Christmas."

"How many times did I come?"

"Practically every weekend between August and

Christmas. Sometimes, while the renovations were going on, you were here during the week too."

He turned past the courthouse, drove by the square, then turned right on Main. All the shops and businesses were decorated in fall colors with a Thanksgiving theme. Before long, though, turkeys and pilgrims would give way to the most extensive Christmas decorations he'd ever seen. With a name like Bethlehem, he supposed it was required.

Maggie was wide-eyed, looking from side to side, trying to absorb everything. Though he had little interest in quaint shops, Ross slowed, then pulled into a parking space. "Want to make this a walking tour?"

"Can we?" Her smile was bright with anticipation, and its very presence reminded him of all the long months it had been absent from their lives. Over the years he'd tried to buy such delight with diamonds, emeralds, and sapphires, when all she really needed was a simple little indulgence like this.

Why hadn't he known that? She was his wife, damn it—the one person who knew him best, the one person he should have known best. Why hadn't he known?

Maybe because he *was* the selfish bastard she'd described last night.

They were on the west edge of downtown. With coats zipped against the chill, they started at a leisurely pace toward the other end. Hardly aware of the cold, Maggie gazed in each display window, making mental notes of places she would return to regularly—the gift shop and bookstore, the pharmacy, the clothing store, and the post office. She wondered if she'd bought supplies for the house at the hardware store across the street, if she'd stocked Ross's office from the office supply shop, if she'd taken her dry cleaning to the little corner establishment.

She wondered how lucky she'd been to find this place at exactly the time she'd needed it most. It must have been fate. Destiny.

Destiny. Her last brush with destiny had come seventeen years earlier on the university campus. Some guy rushing by in the rain had knocked her books into a puddle, and the handsomest man she'd ever seen had helped her fish them out. They'd cut their next classes and gone to the student union for coffee, and when they'd parted eight hours later, she'd known she had met the man of her dreams.

Now she'd found the town—the home—of her dreams.

How sad that they were separate dreams.

She stopped to admire a display of Christmas china and wondered if she'd bought anything similar last year. If not, it could be her welcome-home gift to herself, because she intended to have an active social life. Of course, she'd had that in Buffalo and hated it, but in Bethlehem it would be different. She would entertain people because she liked them, not because Ross did business with them, and it would be small, intimate groups in her wonderful kitchen, not formal events with a guest list longer than Santa's. There would be cocoa and egg nog rather than champagne, finger foods instead of catered hors d'oeuvres, poinsettias and not hothouse orchids, and children. Definitely children, and they would be heard and not just seen.

"They have an interesting mix of stores here," Ross said. "When you're sick, you can pick up your prescription, rent a video, and grab a bowl of homemade chicken noodle soup all in one stop. Here we have china and sporting goods, obviously owned by a Chicago Bulls fan."

She shifted her gaze to the sign above the door—THE BULLS IN A CHINA SHOP—and smiled. "If you want to survive in today's business climate, you have to diversify."

"So you did listen to me from time to time."

"I listened a lot. I've probably learned from you the equivalent of an MBA, which would be great if I were interested in business."

He grew serious. "You always pretended to be—for the first ten or twelve years, at least."

"I never cared about the business. I was interested in *you*." Her answer caught him off guard and held him still while she moved on, passing an office building shared by one lawyer, two doctors, and three dentists. That brought her to the square in the middle of town. She looked at the wrought-iron benches, thought about how cold they would be for sitting, then settled her gaze on a diner across the street. "Want some coffee?"

That caught Ross off guard too. He looked at the diner, moderately busy, then back at her. "You mean, go in, sit down, and have something to drink?"

"You could have something to eat too," she said dryly. "Judging by the number of customers there, they have better luck in the kitchen than I do."

"You don't mind?"

"If you eat someone else's cooking?"

He brushed away her intended humor with an impatient gesture. "Going in. With strangers."

She watched the traffic, saw drivers waving at people, heard a man on one side of the street call a hearty greeting to a woman on the other. A year from then, she wanted to be like those people, running into friends and neighbors while she took care of all her errands in a few square blocks. One sure way *not* to accomplish that was to remain self-conscious. "I'll admit it doesn't thrill me, but I've got to face strangers sometime."

He took her arm—so she couldn't change her mind, she suspected. As they approached Harry's Diner, a group of men in suits came out, one of them holding the door open.

Inside, she chose the lone empty booth, and the waitress brought them menus and coffee. "I'll be right back to take your order, folks—Maggie? Why, Maggie McKinney, it *is* you. How are you?"

Maggie hoped that her smile looked more genuine than it felt. "I'm—I'm fine."

"Oh, and you look fine! I heard you were coming back to town. You couldn't have picked a better time for it, with Thanksgiving only two days away and then Christmas— You *are* staying for Christmas, aren't you?"

"I'm staying." Maggie tried to read the name tag pinned to the waitress's left shoulder, but the lace hanky it secured fell over all but the first letter. Taking a deep breath, she gathered her courage and blurted out, "I'm fine, but there's a lot I don't remember about

last year, and names, I'm afraid, are part of it. You
are . . . ?"

"Maeve. I'm sorry, honey. Sheriff Ingles told us
about the memory problem, but I was so surprised to
see you that it slipped my mind." Hearing her own
words, she smiled broadly. "If you're forgetful, honey,
you'll fit in just fine with us. Why, half the people in
here have forgotten that they're supposed to be at
work."

"Yeah," a diner at a nearby table chimed in. "And
Maeve's forgotten that she was supposed to be getting
me some decaf."

"You just hold your horses, Charlie. If you're in
such a hurry, you know where the coffeepot is." She
turned her attention back to them. "I'm Maeve Carter,
and I run this joint."

"So there's no Harry?"

"Oh, sure. Harry Winslow. He's the cantankerous
old goat behind the counter. He owns the place,
but"— she smugly patted her carefully styled hair —"it
would be nothing without me."

"I heard that, Maeve," Harry called. "Don't believe
a thing she says, Maggie girl. She's full of talk. And
welcome back. That big house has missed you."

"So have we, sugar," Maeve added before shifting
her attention across the booth. "So . . . who's this
handsome fellow?"

"This is my husband, Ross."

"Welcome to Bethlehem, Ross." Maeve offered her
hand. "You're going to like it here. It's a wonderful
change from big-city life."

Murmuring something appropriate, Ross shook her hand, then Maeve excused herself.

"That wasn't so bad."

"No, it wasn't," Maggie agreed without looking at Ross. And it hadn't been, except for the embarrassment she'd felt at admitting her memory lapses and the bit of guilt that nagged her. She feared that she had given the impression, however innocently, that she and Ross were there to stay—as a couple. What would people think after the holidays were over, when she no longer needed him and he returned to the city?

They would think it was a shame the marriage had ended, she assured herself, and they would continue to welcome her. Bethlehem was a small town, but it wasn't removed from modern social ills. She wouldn't be the first divorced woman in town. They wouldn't make her an outcast because of it.

"You want a late breakfast or an early lunch?"

Maggie refocused her attention on Ross. He was, as Maeve had so bluntly stated, a handsome man, and sometimes—like then—when she looked at him, she felt such regret. Sometimes she thought about a future without him in it and panic fluttered through her. Sometimes she wanted to stamp her feet and wail that this wasn't how her life was supposed to go. She hadn't worked so hard and made so many sacrifices only to end up all alone. It wasn't *fair*.

But life *wasn't* fair. If nothing else, the last year had taught her that. And it was too important to mope over lost dreams. She could have all the regrets she wanted about Ross and their marriage, but she couldn't lose sight of her future. She intended to make it a good one—the best.

"Maggie?"

She smiled as she opened the menu. "A late breakfast is fine."

And *she* was too. Absolutely fine.

Chapter Four

IN THE BACK ROOM OF THE NURSERY, ME-lissa Thomas was knee-deep in poinsettias and humming a Christmas carol to herself. Even if the holidays weren't the busiest time of year for the shop, she would love them anyway. She was eager for Thursday to bring Thanksgiving, which she and Alex would spend with the Winchester sisters. She couldn't wait to drive down Main Street Friday morning and see the decorations that would go up the afternoon before, was looking forward to Saturday evening, when they would put up their tree, following Thomas family tradition. She loved the shopping, the parade, the Tour of Lights, Santa Claus, and even the cold and snow that were scheduled to arrive that weekend.

The only way she could love the holidays more was if she and Alex had a real family to spend them with. Oh, they had Alex's uncle Herb, the Winchesters,

Holly McBride, the Bishops, the Walkers—all good friends. But she wanted a *family*. Children, toys underfoot, puppies and kittens, trikes in the driveway, diapers on the shopping list.

More than anything else in the world, she wanted a baby—a bunch of babies, but one would be a wonderful start. One would make her life complete.

Shaking off the melancholy that always accompanied such wishful thinking, she turned in a slow circle. The delivery truck had dropped off its load a half hour before, and she'd made little headway. Perhaps she should save her wishes for something more within her grasp, like a prospective employee answering the help wanted ad she'd placed in the paper. Then she could be up front putting together the autumn-hued centerpiece she was taking to the Winchesters Thursday, or the delicately shaded peach roses Nathan Bishop had ordered to mark the first anniversary of meeting his wife, Emilie, or any of the other dozen orders that waited on the counter.

The bell over the front door rang, and she scooped up an armload of artificial poinsettias to deliver to the shop. She deposited them on a shelf, then approached the customers. "Hi. Welcome to Melissa's Garden. Can I help you?"

The man turned first—a stranger with dark hair and less than friendly blue eyes. His movement revealed the woman behind him, whom Melissa recognized by her sleekly styled auburn hair. A quick glance at her face confirmed the identification. "Maggie, how nice to see you. I'm Melissa Thomas. We met last year."

For an instant, Maggie's expression was utterly

blank. Even when she smiled, there was no hint of recognition. When her husband had asked Alex to ready the house for them, he'd mentioned that Maggie had no memory of Bethlehem. It hadn't quite registered with Melissa that that meant no memory of the people either. As far as Maggie was concerned, they were complete strangers. She didn't know that they'd had lunch together from time to time, didn't remember coming to the shop and choosing the flowers that had decorated her house last Christmas, didn't remember the long evening of conversation during one of the Winchesters' holiday parties.

It was an odd feeling for Melissa, knowing things about Maggie while Maggie didn't know *her* from the man in the moon. How much odder it must be for Maggie.

Melissa turned her attention back to the man. She'd heard a great deal about Ross McKinney—that he was arrogant, aggressive, ruthless. That he put business first and people last. That he was a hard, cold man who cared little about his wife or her obvious unhappiness. Standing there, he merely looked like any man who'd followed his wife someplace he didn't care to be—a little uncomfortable, more than a little out of his element. For that reason, she offered her hand and injected extra warmth into her voice when she spoke. "Mr. McKinney, we've spoken on the phone a few times. It's nice to meet you."

It was clear as he shook her hand that her words puzzled him; then abruptly he nodded. "You're Alex Thomas's wife. You stocked the kitchen for us."

"I hope you don't mind that I opted for conve-

nience foods. They're the mainstay of my kitchen."
Truthfully, restaurants were the mainstay. While eating
at a table for two in a restaurant was bearable, at home
it wasn't. The empty chairs were a harsh reminder of
the family that wasn't.

She wondered if Maggie minded not having children. They'd never gotten close enough for a question
like that. She suspected, though, that the answer was
yes. Call it instinct or women's intuition, but she
would bet Maggie McKinney could understand the
emptiness in her life.

She would also bet that Ross McKinney couldn't.

"You sent the flowers," Maggie said. "They're
beautiful. Thank you."

"Just a little welcome back. What can I help you
with today?"

Maggie looked around, her gaze skimming over the
flower shop that filled half the space and the gardening
supplies that occupied the rest. "I want to plant some
bulbs."

"They're down here." Melissa led the way, stopping
near the end of the first aisle. "I'm afraid I don't have a
very big selection. It's near the end of the planting
season, so I haven't reordered." Truth was, she hadn't
sold a bulb in weeks. She just hadn't gotten around to
taking the leftovers off the shelves.

"Is it too late?" Maggie asked as she picked up a fat,
rounded bulb.

"It's not the optimal time for planting," Melissa
said. "But we've had a fairly mild fall, and the ground's
not frozen. They may not do as well as the bulbs
planted a few months ago, but you should get some

lovely blooms out of them. I'll leave you to make your choices and get back to work. If you need anything, yell." On impulse, she gave Maggie's shoulder a gentle squeeze. "It really is good to see you again."

Ross watched her walk away, then he looked back at Maggie. "I wonder how many people you met while you were here."

"So do I," she said ruefully.

She didn't waste time picking through the boxes with color photos stapled to the front. She simply picked up one box, emptied all the others into it, then wandered along the aisles, adding a box of fertilizer, a pair of gloves, a few hand tools. She paused for a moment, then looked at him. "I want to decorate the house for Christmas."

"Of course you do."

"I mean me. Not some designer you hire."

Her scowl brought him more than a little discomfort. Christmas decorating at their house in Buffalo had been, at his insistence, a carefully planned process. They'd had a top-quality silk tree, with no bare spots, crooked limbs, or other natural imperfections allowed. The decorations Maggie had collected over the years had been relegated to the attic, replaced by perfectly matched sets of white ornaments and silver ribbons. There'd been no creche, no candles, no colored lights twinkling. No garlands, bows, or fragrances. The minimalist effect had been cool, elegant.

And awful.

Their old decorations had been the first boxes Maggie shipped to Bethlehem when the house was nearing completion, and she'd used them all. Ornaments had covered every inch of the twelve-foot-tall fir. Her collection of angels had spread their wings across the mantel. A dozen Father Christmases had taken up residence on the antique library table against the wall. Music boxes, each playing a different carol, were scattered through the house. There were creches in every room. A wreath as wide as the front door. White lights outlining the house, woven through the shrubbery and over the bare branches of the trees in the yard, and colored ones by the hundreds inside. The entire house had been an explosion of color, scent, and sound, and Maggie had loved it.

"You're perfectly welcome to decorate however you want," he said as they started toward the cash register near the door. "You'll have to see if you can top last year."

"But I don't remember last year."

He smiled faintly. "Then it'll be a challenge, won't it?"

He was about to call Melissa Thomas from the back, when he realized there was a clerk on her knees behind the counter, unpacking a box filled with baskets and red velvet bows. In the fluorescent light her brown hair seemed to gleam with silver, but as soon as she looked up, he saw that it had merely been an illusion. "I'll be right with you, Maggie, Mr. McKinney."

The name tag on her sweatshirt identified her as Noelle. He watched Maggie read it, watched the frustration—or was it becoming resignation?—of not remembering edge into her expression.

"Doing some planting, are we?" Noelle flashed a

brilliant smile as she got to her feet. "I like a person who plants late in the season."

"Why is that?" Maggie asked.

"It tells me two important things—that you're optimistic, looking ahead to spring's reward for today's hard work, and that you have faith."

"Faith?"

"Anyone can plant daffodils in September and expect to see blossoms in the spring. But only a gardener with faith would plant in winter with the same expectation." The woman's look moved to Ross. "Faith is a rare gift these days. One should nurture it when one finds it."

He shifted uncomfortably under the directness of her gaze even as he silently agreed with her. His mother had had faith in God and in him. For a good many years, Maggie had had faith in him too, but not many others had. His father had insisted he would never amount to anything. So had Maggie's mother. His high school teachers had believed college was out of his reach. He'd been told he should quit dreaming and accept what life held for him—a job in the same factory where his father had worked and his grandfather before him, a plain little house in a shabby neighborhood, with no bigger goals than drinking his way through the weekend games on TV.

Now he owned the factory. He funded scholarships at the high school. He lived in a mansion, and if he ever had any desire to see a game, he wouldn't settle for TV. He would take the corporate jet, have the best seats in the house, and celebrate with the winning team owner afterward.

He was a success. He had measured up to his mother's faith in him.

But not Maggie's.

When Noelle rang up the last item and announced the total, Maggie looked at him. "I don't have . . ." She turned her empty hands palms up.

He pulled his wallet from his pocket and paid the woman.

"Any tips on planting these?" Maggie asked.

"Good soil, water, sunlight, and food. Nothing can live without proper care and nourishment. You can't ignore them and leave them to starve in the winter cold, then expect them to do their best for you next spring." Noelle nodded for emphasis. "Care and nourishment. Those are the keys to everything."

They were halfway to the car when Ross spoke. "I bet she talks to her plants."

Maggie smiled. "Probably. It must work for her though. She works in a nursery." She gave the last word a subtle emphasis. Pleased that she'd remembered it this time, or mocking that she'd forgotten it the first time?

He took the back way home, making one short detour at the McBride Inn. He stopped alongside the gravel road that led to the main entrance, giving her the full effect of the gracious old farmhouse-turned-inn. "This is where we stayed when we were in Bethlehem."

Her gaze took in the rambling structure, the porches, the porte cochere, the trees, the pond, the dormant fields. "I don't remember . . ."

"Do you want to go inside? I'm sure the owner would let you look around."

She looked a moment longer, then shook her head. "No. I don't remember. I'd rather go home and plant."

With a nod, he pulled onto the road again. A few minutes later they were home. But Maggie had no interest in going in. She headed for the backyard instead, and, with bags in hand, Ross followed her.

The yard was a nice size, fenced on three sides with board planks atop a low brick wall. The grass had been mowed short sometime before dying, and the flower beds had been cleaned out and covered with mulch. The space had a lot of potential, and Maggie probably knew just what to do to fulfill it.

Even if she was looking a little lost right now. "I must have had plans for this yard, but I don't remember."

"Then it doesn't matter. Come up with new plans."

"If I can't remember something, it doesn't matter? Is that how it works?"

He shrugged. "It works for me."

"That's because you never forget anything. You still remember every detail of every deal you ever made."

Not every one, he acknowledged grimly. He could think of one deal in particular where he'd forgotten too much, where he'd paid too little attention, where he'd made promises and offered guarantees and failed miserably. *Forever and ever, till death do us part.* Death had almost succeeded last Christmas Eve. Now they were giving in to something that sounded so much less ominous but was every bit as destructive—indifference.

How had they made this journey from passionate lovers to polite acquaintances? What had gone wrong? What could they have done differently? Who was to blame?

He didn't have any answers, didn't know any truths save one. If he and Maggie could stop loving each other, then anything could happen. Nothing—no one—was safe.

He shook off the melancholy that accompanied his thoughts. "Where are you going to plant your flowers?"

She looked up at the sun, then around the yard before gesturing toward a distant corner. Taking the bags from him, she started in that direction and gave him a dry look when he followed. "I can do this by myself."

"I hope so. I'm under orders from Dr. Allen to not do anything until you've proven that you can't."

"I meant you could go inside."

He shoved his hands into his pockets. "I don't think so."

"I'm perfectly capable—"

"I'm sure you are. Humor me, Maggie. Before long you'll be able to do whatever you want. But we're not there yet."

With a haughty sniff she turned her back on him and faced the corner of the yard instead. Reaching into one bag, she pulled out a handful of bulbs and threw them across the grass with more force, he thought, than was necessary. One bounced off the brick wall and landed upright a few inches away. The rest scattered around.

"Is this some gardening ritual I'm not familiar with?"

"You're not familiar with any gardening rituals besides the one where you take out your checkbook to pay the grounds staff." She tossed the rest of the bulbs three or four at a time until the entire corner of the yard was littered with them.

"So what are you doing?"

After handing the bags to him, she pulled on the cotton gloves, then took a trowel from another bag. "Naturalizing. In the wild, daffodils don't grow in neat beds. They're scattered all over."

"I didn't know daffodils grew in the wild. Don't they interfere with mowing the grass?"

"By the time you have to mow, the bulbs are through for the year." She fell silent as she carefully knelt and began digging. Underneath the dead grass was rich, dark soil.

Back in the early years of their marriage, they'd shared the yardwork. He had mowed and she'd tended the flowers. Mowing their tiny yards had always been quick and easy, and afterward he'd stretched out in a lawn chair with a cold beer, sometimes talking to her, sometimes simply watching her.

The more successful he'd become, the more expensive their houses, the bigger their lawns, and the more willing he'd been to pay someone else to do the work. Maybe that was where things had started going wrong—when he'd stopped indulging in the simple pleasure of watching her garden.

She planted in the same methodic manner she'd made coffee—digging the hole exactly the right depth, sprinkling in just the right amount of fertilizer, positioning the bulb just so, tamping the dirt back in around it. When she finished, the yard looked as if it had been attacked by a crazed mole. Dark patches of dirt dotted the grass, showing exactly where to imagine sunny flowers next spring. She would be there to see them.

He wouldn't.

When Maggie started to rise, he moved forward, taking both her hands, pulling her to her feet. She was unsteady for a moment, then she tugged free and took a few careful steps. "I forget sometimes that I'm not good as new."

"That'll come."

"When? In two months? Nope, I'll be going back for more surgery sometime around then. Two months after that? Four? Eight?"

"What surgery? When?"

"To remove the plates in my left leg. Probably in February."

"I didn't realize they would be removed." Some emotion must have shown in his face—dismay?—because she shrugged.

"Don't worry. I won't ask you to stick around through it. I'll pay some sweet, motherly nurse a fortune to come in here and pamper me." She readied a garden hose as she spoke. "I'd move if I were you."

He did as she suggested, and she directed the water over the newly planted bulbs. He wondered why the news of her impending surgery had caught him off guard. Maybe because he'd seen too much of her in a hospital bed. Because she looked so small and vulnerable there. Because she already bore enough scars from that damnable accident.

"The surgery is something of an accomplishment."

He looked at her, but her attention was on the ground. "In what way?"

"It means that the bones have healed completely. That they're strong enough to support me without the plates and screws. It's the last procedure I have to undergo, and then this whole thing will really, truly be behind me."

He had to admire her outlook. If he'd been through half of what she'd undergone in the past eleven months, he would be desperate to avoid any future contact with the medical establishment. But then, he might not have been strong enough to endure her ordeal.

"I don't mind staying until after the surgery."

"Oh? Then what caused that look of revulsion?"

"I think the idea of having pieces of metal screwed directly into your bones would cause any reasonable person a moment of revulsion—to say nothing of going back a year or so later and unscrewing them."

She shrugged carelessly. "I was unconscious when they put them in, and I'll be unconscious when they take them out. It's no big deal."

No big deal. He shook his head in disbelief. "You're a remarkable woman, Maggie."

That stopped her short, and then she quietly said, "Thank you. It means a lot to hear you say that."

The moment was broken by the squeal of brakes out front. Ross watched as a deliveryman carrying an express package and a clipboard climbed out and started up the driveway.

"Too bad your staff isn't a little more remarkable," Maggie murmured. "It's a good thing you're not on a *real* vacation. They would never leave you any time to relax. I'll be inside." She released the trigger and cut off the flow of water, then recoiled the hose a little less neatly than before.

The uniformed man greeted her with a nod, then double-checked his package. "I've got a delivery here for Ross McKinney. That wouldn't happen to be you, would it?" he said to Ross.

He watched Maggie disappear inside, then forced his attention back to the deliveryman. "Yes. Yes, it is. Where do I sign?"

"A FTERNOON, MISS AGATHA. AFTERNOON, son."

Stopping where the sidewalk crossed the McKinney driveway, Agatha Winchester nodded regally and replied to the deliveryman, "Good afternoon, Fred."

Beside her, four-year-old Brendan Dalton mimicked both the nod and the greeting, bringing a grin from Fred as he climbed into his truck. The boy watched the truck rumble away, while Agatha turned her attention in the opposite direction.

Standing at the end of the driveway, scanning the contents of the package just delivered, was their new neighbor, the mysterious Ross McKinney. She knew little about him—that he was a businessman, successful and very wealthy. Holly McBride, over at the inn, had already told her that he was handsome as sin—not a description that a God-fearing woman like Agatha particularly cared for, though she could certainly understand where it came from, with his black hair, sharp eyes, and forbidding scowl.

She knew that on his few visits to Bethlehem last year, he'd stayed shut up in their suite and kept at least one phone line and usually two tied up practically the entire stay. He'd left his lovely wife to her own entertainment and had usually taken work even to the dinner table. He'd also left Maggie all the responsibilities of remodeling this big old house and had neglected to accompany her to even one Christmas party.

In Agatha and Corinna's opinion, Maggie might as well have been single, for all the attention her husband paid her. She'd tried to make the best of it, but it had been obvious that she was a lonely, unhappy woman.

And then she'd had that dreadful accident. Her husband had told the sheriff that she'd been on her way home to Buffalo, with no explanations, no excuses. While Sheriff Ingles had accepted that—after all, it *was* an accident—Agatha knew there must be more to the story. Home to Buffalo? On Christmas Eve? Impossible! Maggie had been looking forward to the Christmas Eve service in the square. She had been excited about celebrating the holiday in her new home and had planned an elaborate Christmas Day feast. She wouldn't have decided to return to Buffalo that night unless something dreadful had happened.

And it involved her husband. Agatha was sure of it.

"Miss Agatha." Brendan tugged her sleeve. "The truck's gone."

With a sense of purpose, she gave the boy a bright smile. "Come along, Brendan. Let's say hello to our new neighbor."

He wrinkled his nose. "Uncle Nathan says doan talk to strangers."

"*Don't* talk to strangers. Uncle Nathan's exactly right. But it's all right when you're with me. I know everyone. Come along." Pulling on the hand of the ragged bear they held between them, she started up the driveway. "Good afternoon, Mr. McKinney. It's a beautiful day, isn't it? I'm Agatha Winchester. My sister, Corinna, and I live in the Victorian on the corner over there."

He blinked as if startled, then accepted the hand she offered. "Ross McKinney."

"And this is Brendan Dalton. He lives in the blue Victorian right over there." She pointed directly across the street, where just a corner of the second floor of the Bishop house showed behind its neighbor. "Say hello to Mr. McKinney, Brendan."

The boy shifted the bear's paw to his other hand, then extended his right hand. "Hello, Mr. Mc-Kinney."

The man bent to shake his hand and greeted him with the same polite reserve he'd shown Agatha. The action moved him up one notch in her estimation, but the man who'd played a part in dear Maggie's unhappiness a year before still had quite a long way to go.

"Corinna and I brought Maggie a little welcome-home gift of cinnamon rolls this morning. We were so sorry to hear about her accident and are so glad to see her back in her house. She did a wonderful job on the old place."

"Yes, she did." He sounded stiff. Guilt over the accident? Resentment that she'd referred to the house he'd paid for as Maggie's house? Or perhaps just plain old wariness about discussing his wife with a total stranger?

"We issued an invitation to Maggie to join us for Thanksgiving dinner. It's such a big meal to prepare for only two, and with her just getting discharged from the rehabilitation center yesterday . . . Well, we'd love to have you both. What do you say?"

He looked uncomfortable. "I—I don't know. Maggie's a little self-conscious about meeting a lot of . . ."

"Strangers," Agatha said with a gentle smile. "We know she's forgotten everything about the town, but we haven't forgotten her. We were her friends a year ago, and we'd like to be her friends now. There will be plenty of people there to make her feel at home— Corinna's children and grandchildren, Brendan's family, the Thomases, the Walkers, Holly McBride. We'd love to have you both."

His smile was polite but insincere. "I'll tell her, Mrs. Winchester."

"Oh, it's Miss. Miss Agatha will do fine." She gave him her brightest smile. "We'll let you get back to whatever you were doing. Come along, Brendan. Nice meeting you, Mr. McKinney."

Agatha rather liked doing things for people, helping them solve their problems, making life a little easier, a little better. Last Christmas it had been Nathan Bishop and Emilie Dalton who'd needed her and Corinna's help.

Emilie had been up in Boston, doing the best she could for the three little angels placed in her custody, when catastrophe struck. She'd been cheated out of an entire month's paycheck by an unscrupulous employer and evicted from her apartment because she couldn't pay the rent. Desperate to keep her family together, she'd taken them from the homeless shelter and would have fled to Atlanta, her hometown, if a snowstorm and car trouble hadn't stranded her in Bethlehem.

At the time, Agatha remembered with a smile, Emilie had thought getting stuck there was one more disaster in the string of disasters that had become her life, but now she saw it for what it had really been: the beginning of a miracle. For if the snow hadn't stranded her there, she never would have met Nathan. They wouldn't have married last New Year's Day, and they wouldn't be so incredibly happy and so blessedly in love.

Agatha liked to think that she and Corinna had played a part, just a small one, in getting those two together. Maybe they could play another small part in fixing whatever was wrong between Maggie and Ross McKinney. At the very least, they could be Maggie's friends. She needed friends, needed to be surrounded by people and happiness and life—needed it for her heart, needed it for her healing.

And, she rather suspected, Ross needed it too.

• • •

GRIPPING THE ENVELOPE ALONG WITH the contracts, Ross went into the office and seated himself behind the desk. It wouldn't take more than a few minutes, twenty at most, to go over them, and then he could let Tom know that he was sending them back. As long as he had him on the phone, he could also make sure that whatever had set Lynda off had been resolved and—

Or he could remember that he was on vacation and set them aside for now, the way someone *really* on vacation would do. Later he could come up with a plan for dealing with the inevitable intrusions from Buffalo—a once-a-week schedule, something he could stick to, something that would leave the rest of his time free—and he could make sure that Tom and Lynda understood and respected it.

Reluctantly he slid the contracts back into the envelope, left it on the center of his desk, and returned to the hall. For a moment he simply stood there, listening for some hint of Maggie's whereabouts. The old house was too solid for creaks and squeaks. The only sounds that broke the quiet were the ticking of the mantel clock in the dining room and faint music from the back of the house—a lone voice, singing softly.

He hadn't heard Maggie sing in months, probably years, even though she'd always loved music. She'd cleaned house to it, cooked to it, seduced him to it. More times than he could remember, what had started as innocent fun—singing along with the radio during after-dinner cleanup, followed by a dance or two around the kitchen table—had ended in erotic pleasure in their bed.

They hadn't shared *that* in months either, and they never would again.

The thought unsettled him.

She was sitting on the bench in front of the kitchen windows, cookbooks scattered around her. Her shoes were kicked off, and one socked foot tapped the air, keeping time with her out-of-tune tune.

She wouldn't stay single long, he thought suddenly. Some smart guy would grab her up, and before long she would be well on her way to having those four or five babies she'd talked about. Before long she would have everything she'd ever wanted—a home, a town, a place to belong. A husband and kids to belong to. He hoped the guy came from a large family, all settled around there, and that they would welcome her as if she were their own daughter.

He hoped she got it all. Every hope. Every wish. Every dream.

Everything *he* hadn't given her.

She looked up. "There you are. Have you been talking to the deliveryguy all this time?"

"No. Miss Agatha came by."

" 'Miss' Agatha? How sweet. What did she want?"

"To be neighborly, I suppose. Maybe to see for herself that I really do exist."

"You do tend to be a bit invisible when you get away from Buffalo," she said matter-of-factly. "Usually, the hotel housekeeping staff are the only people who see you."

The comment was too true to disagree with, so he ignored it. "She also wanted to repeat the invitation to Thanksgiving dinner. I told her you'd be there."

Maggie stared at him. "You what?"

"You said just this morning that you wanted to go."

"Yes, but—"

When she didn't finish, he did. "But you thought you wouldn't give them an answer either way so that if you wanted to back out at the last minute, you could." Her wide-eyed and wary nod made him relent. "Well, you still can. I told Miss Agatha that I would talk to you about it. But I think you should go. These people are your friends, and they're going to be your neighbors. Thanksgiving will be a perfect time to start getting to know them again. And who knows? Thanksgiving dinner with a crowd might be fun." Like being away from the office with nothing to do was fun. Like living even temporarily in a small town that offered none of the attractions of the city was fun.

"It might be." Finally her startled look dissolved into a yawn. "Sorry. It's warm and I'm tired—a perfect recipe for an afternoon nap."

"Why don't you take one?"

"Actually, I was hoping you would bring the Christmas stuff out from wherever it is. I want to start decorating after Thanksgiving, and I'd like to go through it first."

The request made him stiffen. If his instructions had been followed, the stuff, as she called it, was in the basement. The ornaments, lights, angels, Santas, and all the presents that had been left unopened last Christmas.

Plus one that *had* been opened. One that he needed to get rid of before Maggie saw it. Before she wondered about it.

"I can do that," he agreed, his voice remarkably empty of the tension inside him. "If you take a nap."

She yawned again. "All right. I'll lie down for a while, but you have to bring up *everything*. Okay?"

"Okay." He escorted her to the top of the stairs, then made his way to the basement door at the rear of the house.

A switch just inside the door turned on lights above a flight of stairs and every eight feet through the cavernous space. The boxes he'd had delivered from Buffalo were stored there, just a few feet from the bottom of the stairs. All the Christmas things were there too, in cardboard cartons clearly marked GIFTS, ORNAMENTS, or DECORATIONS. Underneath those labels, some incredibly organized person had been even more specific: ANGELS. SANTAS. MUSIC BOXES. If a person knew exactly what he was looking for, he could find it in one of the three dozen boxes in minutes.

What *he* was looking for was in the stack of boxes that held last year's presents. As his business prospered and grew each year, his gifts to Maggie had become showier, costlier. Five years ago he'd gotten so busy that Lynda had taken over the shopping for him, buying outfits Maggie refused to wear, handbags she refused to carry, trips she refused to take. The only gift he had continued to choose himself was the jewelry, always something to take away the breath of the most avaricious woman around—and always something that failed to impress Maggie.

Last year he'd bought two pieces of jewelry—an emerald pendant in the deep, rich shade she favored, and a bracelet of two-carat round diamonds alternating with matching sapphires. They were both dazzling pieces, but only the bracelet had made an impression on Maggie—one hell of an impression.

Soon after he'd made arrangements with Alex Thomas to oversee the reopening of the house, the lawyer had called him about the bracelet. The cleaning service had found it on the living room floor and turned it over to him. What did Ross want him to do with it?

Give it to your wife had been Ross's first response. He didn't want to see the bracelet again as long as he lived, and he sure as hell didn't want Maggie to see it.

But Alex had refused, and finally Ross had told him to pack it with the rest of the gifts. He would dispose of it later, before the time came to pull out the decorations for this Christmas.

This was probably his best chance at "later."

He opened the top carton and found the bracelet exactly where Alex had said it would be, in its velvet-lined box in the corner. Even under the less than adequate lighting, the stones glowed. From the first gems he'd bought—emerald studs to the last, this was the most stunning, the most exquisite—and the one piece Maggie had hated most. He and this bracelet had almost killed her.

After sliding it into his pocket, he headed upstairs to the office. He sealed the bracelet in an envelope and addressed it to Tom, with a terse note instructing him to get rid of the piece. Keep it himself, give it to a girlfriend, sell it, flush it down the sewer—Ross didn't care, just as long as he never had to acknowledge its existence again.

Leaving the envelope on the hall table, he returned to the basement for the boxes. By the time he made his final trip up the steep steps, Maggie had enough boxes to keep her busy for days. He was tired but he still had one more thing to do before he could relax.

He flipped through the phone book until he found the address for the delivery service, only a half dozen blocks away. He could be there and back before Maggie realized he was gone.

Ten minutes later, as he watched a clerk toss the padded envelope into a bin of overnight packages, relief settled over him. Tom would get rid of it as requested, no questions asked, and Maggie would never know of its existence.

Unless she remembered.

He wouldn't wish her memory lapses on anyone. He'd seen too clearly how it frustrated and haunted her. But the old saying was true. Some things really were better off forgotten.

Chapter Five

THANKSGIVING DAY DAWNED BRIGHT and sunny, with a chilly reminder that Christmas was less than a month away. While Ross was still in bed, Maggie slipped downstairs, started the coffee, and pulled out her favorite cookbook. Originally intended for use as a photo album, the book held recipes instead of snapshots—some handwritten, some cut from magazines, others collected from friends. These were all her old favorites, her reliable standbys that everyone loved most. Some were fairly simple, others complicated. The one she wanted that morning was on the simple side.

Grandma's pumpkin pie. She didn't remember where the recipe had come from and didn't have a clue who Grandma was—certainly not *her* grandmother. Though her father's parents had lived little more than an hour away, she'd seen them only three times after the divorce. As for her maternal grandmother, Maggie remembered her from the annual summer trips she and her mother had taken to Ohio. To a little girl, her grandmother had seemed far older than her years. She'd been crotchety, cantankerous, and critical of everything Maggie or her mother did, and the week-long visits had ended with relief all around.

The last visit had come when Maggie was ten, when they'd gone back for the old woman's funeral. It was winter, with six inches of snow on the ground and not a hint of genuine sorrow to be found. She'd worn a navy blue dress, white socks, and black shoes, and kept her hands in her coat pockets because her gloves were too gaily red for such a somber event. She'd thought she would freeze to death before the graveside service ended.

That the memory was so clear was ironic. She could remember all the details of a—sorry to say—relatively minor event more than twenty-five years ago, and yet major things from only a year before were wiped clean from her mind. Dr. Allen and her psychiatrist, Dr. Olivetti, had warned her that might be the case. People who suffered generalized psychogenic amnesia often had fantastic recall of distant events and yet knew nothing of their lives in the weeks or months preceding the amnesia.

She slid the pumpkin pie recipe from its plastic sleeve and laid it on the counter. She and Ross had gone to the grocery store the day before, and she'd purchased all the necessary ingredients. She hated to show up at the Winchesters' empty-handed and had thought her super-easy, never-fail pumpkin pie was her best bet.

After pouring herself a cup of coffee, she sat down on the nearest bar stool and read over the instructions. She could do this. She'd bought a refrigerated crust— she knew not to push her luck too far—and the rest was a simple matter of measuring, mixing, pouring, and baking. All she had to do was concentrate for a while.

All she had to do . . .

Some days she'd have more luck turning back the hands of time than concentrating. Some days thinking was so hard that it gave her a headache, and on the really lousy days, she got dizzy too. So far, she'd been spared that since leaving the rehab center. She'd had a few sleep disturbances—restlessness, wakefulness, a vague recurring dream—but for the most part she was doing all right. Better than expected. Maybe better enough that when Ross returned to the city, she would be able to live completely on her own.

If she needed live-in help, she could accept it. But she wanted the choice. She needed to know that she *could* be totally independent if she wanted to be.

Her gaze fell on the recipe card. Was her mind wandering because of the post-traumatic syndrome? Or was she delaying the moment of truth by delaying the pie baking?

In this instance she preferred the former to the latter.

Sliding to the floor, she circled the island and gathered the ingredients she'd left on the counter yesterday. She spread everything out in the order the recipe called for, gathered measuring cups and spoons, bowls and utensils, and her favorite pie plate. She read the instructions on the pie crust box just to make certain there was nothing more vital to do than fit the crust into the dish, and she carefully measured the ingredients—spices into one bowl, cream and eggs into another, pumpkin into the third.

"Good morning."

She looked up as Ross came through the doorway. He wore jeans and a ragged sweatshirt proclaiming his long-forgotten college loyalty. His feet were bare, his jaw dark with stubble, and his hair looked as if it'd been combed with his fingers—and he was still too damn appealing for any woman's good.

"The coffee's hot," she said in greeting. "It's . . . you know, the almond stuff."

"Amaretto."

"Yeah, amaretto. For breakfast, there's banana nut bread. Butter and cream cheese are in the refrigerator." Miss Corinna had delivered the bread the day before, along with a copy of the recipe. The lengthy directions for the low-fat, whole wheat, yogurt-enriched bread were now tucked into Maggie's photo-album cookbook, awaiting the day she felt capable of doing it justice.

"What are you making?" Ross asked, taking a seat across from her with coffee and a pinched-off piece of cold bread.

"Pie."

"To take to the sisters'?"

"If it turns out."

"It'll be fine. Why wouldn't it be?"

She gave him a dry look. "Because nothing else I've cooked has been."

"The stuffed potatoes last night were good."

"They were frozen. All I had to do was put them in the oven and remember to take them out when the timer buzzed." And that was a good thing, because the rest of the meal had been barely edible. The chicken cutlets were overcooked, the broccoli was mushy, and the simple cheese sauce had been thick and rubbery.

"So? The first meal you cooked was all bad. Last night you got one dish right." He grinned. "You're making progress."

She simply stared at him, at that dear, familiar grin, before abruptly turning away. Her hands shook, and she spilled cream on the counter. After cleaning it, she went back to mixing with less force.

"Why don't you teach me to cook?" Ross suggested.

"Why would you want to learn that? You have one of the best cooks in Buffalo as your personal chef."

He shrugged. "I happen to have some time on my hands."

"And you think you have a better chance of getting good food if you're doing and I'm merely reading from the directions."

He had the grace to sound guilty, if not contrite. "You said yourself that sometimes you can't follow directions because your concentration's out of whack."

"And I've got to learn to deal with those times." She used a spatula to scrape the mixture into the crust, and was about to place the pie in the oven, when Ross apologetically spoke.

"Seeing that you're making an attempt at independence, I don't suppose this would be a good time to mention that you left out the spices, would it?"

Heat flooded her face. Very carefully she straightened, turned, and carried the pie back to the island. Sure enough, half hidden under the dish towel was the small ceramic bowl of the spices.

Her first impulse, born of frustration, was to dump the pie, plate and all, into the garbage and walk out, but that would be admitting defeat, and she hadn't gotten where she was today by accepting defeat. Without saying a word, she emptied the filling into the bowl, stirred in the spices, then refilled the crust. And as soon as the pie was in the oven, she walked out through the back door and onto the porch.

How could she have forgotten? She had stood there just moments earlier and measured the spices so precisely, and then they'd slipped from her mind. She felt as if she had a sieve for a brain.

On the other hand, it would have been so much more embarrassing to take the pie to dinner and find out her mistake from strangers.

"Our first Thanksgiving."

She didn't turn to look at Ross but listened to his footsteps on the concrete as he crossed to her, laying a jacket over her shoulders—one of his, she realized immediately as the scent of his cologne perfumed the chilly air. Pulling it close, she breathed deeply of the fragrance as he leaned against the wall in front of her.

"Do you remember it?"

"Our first Thanksgiving? Of course. We were living in that awful little apartment, and we had no money."

That was no exaggeration. They'd subsisted those first years on macaroni and cheese, peanut butter sandwiches, and mostly vegetarian meals.

Ross took over. "We couldn't afford a turkey, and there was no reason for dressing without turkey, so we had roasted chicken, mashed potatoes and gravy, and green beans. And for dessert we had our only traditional Thanksgiving dish."

"Pumpkin pie." She raised one hand to massage the ache in her forehead. "Only instead of pie filling I'd bought plain pureed pumpkin, and I forgot to add sugar, and it was awful."

He pulled her hand away. "It was an honest mistake. You were distracted. That was all."

Then or now? she wanted to ask, but it didn't matter, because the answer was both. This time she'd been talking with him—had been defensive with him—about her cooking. That time they'd slept late, celebrating a rare day off from both school and work. She'd just started making the pie when Ross had come in to entice her back to bed. Reading directions had been impossible when he was whispering wicked words in her ears, when his hands were doing wicked things to her body. Dazed and barely able to stand, much less think, she'd finished the pie in a hurry, and they'd made it only as far as the sofa in the next room before they made love.

Funny. She hadn't thought about that day in years, and yet even then she remembered the heat, the longing, the need. Even then she felt the intense hunger, absent for so long, beginning to stir.

Hot, embarrassed, flustered, she pulled her hand

back and tucked it inside the jacket, curling her fingers into tight fists. "Thank you," she murmured.

He didn't ask for what, but merely shrugged. After a moment he did ask, "Is that really how you remember our first apartment? As an awful place?"

"Three tiny rooms, no hot water half the time, no air-conditioning in summer and enough heat only to keep from freezing in winter?" She sat down a few feet away. "No, it wasn't awful."

"It gave us a good reason to generate our own heat."

And they had, every chance they got.

He looked up at the house, in a different universe from that shabby apartment, and gave an awed shake of his head. "God, we've come a long way."

"You have," she corrected him. "After you finished college, I was just along for the ride."

"That's not true, Maggie. I couldn't have done half what I've done without you."

Her smile was faint. "Better be careful. Under the circumstances, your pet shark would warn you not to say such things. I might repeat them to the judge in an attempt to get more than I deserve."

"Tom's not a shark. And you deserve damn near all of it. You can have as much as you want."

Her smile broadened and made her feel a few years younger. "You feel safe saying that because you know I don't want it all, because money can't buy the things I want. But thank you for offering."

He looked at her for a long time, his blue eyes solemn, a little sad. "I'm going to miss you."

She opened her mouth to respond, then clamped it shut and pointedly looked away.

His gaze searched her profile, then finally, quietly, he asked, "What were you going to say?"

"Nothing."

"Obviously it was something. What?"

Her exhalation sounded loud and formed a puff of vapor before disappearing. She gave him a sharp look. "Why didn't you miss me before? When I would have done anything to get your attention? When I missed you so much I thought I would die? When it would have done some good? Why didn't you miss me then, Ross?"

His gaze shifted away from her to some point on the floor, and his jaw set tightly.

"Do you know how much time I've spent alone—how many nights I've slept alone?" She heard the anguish in her voice but couldn't make it go away. "Do you know how many times I've tried to talk to you only to discover you weren't listening? How many times you've shut me out? How many times you looked right through me as if I had no place in your life?"

"I imagine about the same number of times you've ignored me, shut me out, and turned your back on me," he said stiffly. "I had to work long and hard in the beginning, Maggie, you *know* that. If I wanted to succeed, I had no choice."

"You worked long and hard because you *wanted* to. Because the business was important to you. *I* wasn't." She stood up, walked to the door, then came back to plant herself in front of him. "We were supposed to love and honor and cherish each other forever. When did it end? *Why* did it end?"

"Because we wanted different things. I wanted success. Power. And you wanted . . ." His shrug appeared as casual as his gaze was intense. "Someone who wasn't me."

For a long while she stared at him. She wanted to deny his last words, but there was too much truth in them. With another heavy sigh the tension left her. "Is it that simple?" she asked wistfully. "Wanting different things destroyed all that love, all that commitment, all that passion? Were we that fragile? That weak?" Her throat grew tight with anger and emotion. "Damn it, Ross, how did this happen to us? How did we get here?"

"I don't know." His voice was weary, flat. It made her feel the same way. "I just don't know."

Moments passed without notice as they stared at each other, sorrowful and regretful and each of them alone. After a time she sighed one final sigh. "I'd better check on the pie." When he made no move to stop her, no move to speak, she went inside and closed the door. She left him in the cold and thought it was only fair.

After all, he'd left her there a long time ago.

M ORE THAN ANY OTHER HOLIDAY—EVEN Christmas—Thanksgiving seemed to Ross a family holiday. Growing up an only child with no relatives nearby left him with limited experience with family. His mother had come from Alabama, where Ted

McKinney was stationed during a short army stint. She'd been only seventeen when he'd sweet-talked her into bed with promises of marriage, kids, and a better life as an army wife, traveling to bases in places that sounded foreign and exotic to a south Alabama girl.

Against her family's wishes, she'd married him, and right away he'd begun breaking his promises. There was no army career, no exotic new homes. Instead, he'd finished his enlistment and headed back to Buffalo for a factory job that provided a paycheck-to-paycheck existence and a life no better—and in many ways worse—than the one she'd dreamed of leaving behind.

There hadn't been much of a family either—just Ross, and the old man had decided that was plenty. The older Ross got, the more his father had regretted that decision. He'd thought any son of his would be the spittin' image of him, just as he was of his own father. He'd believed there could be nothing more important to Ted McKinney's boy than sports, drinking, and scoring with the girls. He'd mocked Ross's desire to go to college, had scorned Maura's support of that desire, and had declared a hundred times too many that there was no way in hell such a worthless kid could possibly have come from him.

Nothing would have made Ross happier than to find out that the old man was right, but there was no chance. Maura had been the sort of woman who never looked at another man while turning a blind eye to her husband's endless affairs. Besides, the proof had stared them in the face every damn day—the same black hair, the same blue eyes, the same angular jaw. He hadn't seen his father in nearly twenty years, not since his mother's death and his own graduation from high school, but he imagined the resemblance was still there.

So was the scorn, the bitterness, the animosity.

So, knowing so little about families and all that meant, what was he doing spending a family holiday with a bunch of total strangers?

Giving Maggie the support she needed to rebuild her friendships with her new neighbors, he reminded himself. That he felt uncomfortably out of his element, that he would rather be home alone, was irrelevant. This was for Maggie.

A blond woman answered the door and greeted Maggie like an old friend. She sent the pie to the kitchen in the care of a coltish young girl, sent their coats off to the guest room with a younger girl, then made introductions as they passed through the living room. Ross shook hands with the men, endured pats on the arm from women old enough to be his mother and too young to be his wife. He wasn't accustomed to such casual touches. Beyond brief, impersonal handshakes, he rarely made physical contact with anyone. It wasn't, he discovered quickly, an entirely comfortable experience.

"Welcome to our home, Maggie, Ross." Miss Agatha rested her hand on his shoulder. "Did you meet everyone? Don't worry—you'll get the names straight eventually. Ross, help yourself to something to drink, then find a place to sit and talk while I steal Maggie away for a minute."

He wanted to protest, wanted to stay close to Maggie's side on the pretext that she might need him.

Truth was, she might protect him—might act as a buffer between him and these too-friendly people.

But she had come to meet her neighbors and forgotten friends, not to deflect attention from him. So when Miss Agatha led her away, he let her go, then turned to survey the crowd that filled the living room and spilled over into the other rooms. He was the only stranger in the house. Everyone knew everyone else. The snatches of conversation he overheard were about mutual acquaintances, common experiences, shared memories. Even if he wanted to take part, he couldn't.

He made his way to the sideboard in the dining room, doing duty today as a bar. There was a large crystal bowl filled with punch, bottles of soda in a half dozen varieties, a sterling coffee urn, and boxes of juice for the kids. He poured himself a soda—one minute gone, a hundred or more left—and found a quiet place against one wall, where he waited for Maggie to return.

He wished he were home in Buffalo. That was his city, his place, even more than Bethlehem was Maggie's. He knew the city like the back of his hand and was known in all the places worth going to. That was where he belonged on this family holiday—in some elegant restaurant, the subdued luxury of his office, or the quiet of his house. Failing that, he should have stayed at Maggie's house. Obviously, she didn't need the support he'd smugly thought he was providing, and he didn't need to feel like a leper plunked down in the middle of—

"Hey, Ross, you like football?"

The question startled him out of his thoughts. He

turned a blank look on Alex Thomas, who'd spoken from the hallway. Most of the younger men were gathered around him.

"Football?" he echoed, then lied. For Maggie's sake? Or his own? "Yes. Sure."

"Come on. The TV's this way."

He followed them to a sunny sitting room, where the television, a big old console model, was tuned to an all-sports channel. Taking the last empty chair, he considered the men as they talked amiably around him. Though he hadn't paid them particular attention, these people were easy to recall, maybe because instinct had told him they would most likely be important to Maggie. Or, maybe, he thought with a hint of cynicism, just because he was good with details. It was part of business.

There was Nathan Bishop, one of Bethlehem's finest who'd come there from the New York City police department. He lived across the street in the blue house, was married to Emilie, the blonde who'd answered the door, and was uncle to the little boy who'd visited Tuesday with Miss Agatha.

Mitch Walker was the chief of Bethlehem's finest and seemed well suited to the position. He gave the impression of possessing just the right mix of reliability, trustworthiness, respect for what was good and right, and compassion for the people he served. His wife, Shelley, was the very pregnant woman Maggie had looked longingly at when they'd met.

Dean Elliott was a few years older than Ross and another refugee from elsewhere. He was single and an artist of some sort. According to Melissa Thomas,

Maggie had purchased several of his pieces last year for the house.

Ross wondered idly if Elliott was interested in getting married, then backed away from the idea. He wasn't playing matchmaker. He wanted Maggie to be happy, but how she accomplished that was entirely up to her. He wouldn't trust his choice for her anyway. After all, until the last couple of years, he'd thought *he* was her perfect mate.

The last two men in the room were Alex and J. D. Grayson. *Dr.* Grayson, the psychiatrist Maggie's Buffalo doctor had recommended. Based on his knowledge of Dr. Olivetti—in her sixties, no-nonsense, blunt spoken, caring but never coddling—Ross had expected the doctor she endorsed to be similar. But J. D. Grayson wasn't even half the doctor's age and looked more like a lumberjack than a respected psychiatrist. He'd roughhoused with the kids, quoted football statistics with authority, and talked about the house he was building for himself halfway up the mountain.

But his manner was all professional when he struck up a conversation with Ross. "Are you aware that Harriet Olivetti asked me to schedule a few sessions with your wife while you're here in Bethlehem?"

Ross nodded. "I thought I'd call for an appointment Monday."

"Let Maggie do it. I'm in the phone book." A groan from the others shifted his gaze to the TV screen for an instant before he looked back. "How is she?"

"She's fine."

"Any adjustment problems?"

Ross shook his head even as he wondered why he

didn't want to talk about Maggie to this man. It wasn't as if he hadn't discussed her in great detail with any number of physicians and therapists over the last eleven months. They were all professionals, all charged with her care. Being young and single didn't make Dr. Grayson any different.

Did it?

"What about the post-traumatic syndrome? Has she been having any problems with that?"

"She wakes up during the night." He deliberately didn't mention that he'd heard her from his room across the hall. The first night he hadn't realized what had awakened him until finally he'd recognized the sound—the slow, rhythmic creak of the rocker in front of her bedroom window. He had lain there in the dark, listening, wondering what she was thinking as she looked out into the dark night. Was she peaceful? Regretful? Sorrowful?

He didn't have any idea, a fact that shamed him.

"Does she go back to sleep fairly soon?"

"Sometimes." Tuesday night, after twenty minutes or so, silence had settled over the house again. Last night he'd fallen asleep listening.

Whatever the doctor had intended to ask next was lost in the commotion in the hall. A half dozen kids literally fell into the room, calling out amid grunts and squeals, "Dinner's ready! Miss Agatha says turn off the TV and come eat!"

Alex and the doctor untangled the kids, then ushered them from the room. As he stood up, Mitch Walker commented, "You and Maggie don't have kids, do you?"

Ross shook his head.

"You're missing out on a lot of fun. Kids are wonderful. Incredible. Never a moment's trouble." Then he grinned. "By the way, those were my two who tripped everyone else."

"And two of our three who landed on top of everyone else," Nathan Bishop added dryly. "But Mitch is right. You're missing out on a lot."

"A lot of what?" Elliott asked. "Noise? Chaos? Dirty diapers?"

A lot of responsibility. A lot of changes.

And, Maggie was convinced, a lot of love.

A line had formed through the dining room and into the kitchen, with mothers and children at the head. With more relief than he wanted to admit to, Ross located Maggie near the refrigerator, talking with Melissa while both women watched the children with the same sort of yearning in their eyes. He knew too well why Maggie had no babies, but he wondered about Melissa. A medical problem, he would bet, because Alex seemed the likeliest candidate for fatherhood around.

When he joined the women, Maggie offered him a vague smile. "Where have you been?"

"Watching the football game in the other room."

"You don't like football."

He shrugged and changed the subject. "Are you glad you came?"

"Yes."

He liked her quick, decisive answer. "How do you feel?"

"Fine. I've been sitting down with my feet propped

up, at Miss Corinna's insistence. You know, I'm *not* an invalid."

"No, you're not," he agreed before mildly going on. "But you're also not back up to a hundred percent. You don't want to take it too easy, but you also don't want to push too hard."

Before she could respond, the sharp tinkle of a knife against glass hushed the crowd and drew all gazes to Miss Corinna. "Let us have your attention for just a moment, please. Reverend Howard, would you bless the meal for us?"

The reverend stepped in beside her, and everyone automatically bowed their heads. "Our heavenly father, we are gathered here today . . ."

Ross stared down at the vinyl floor, neat squares of ivory ingrained with a pale blue pattern. When he was growing up and they'd had the good fortune to eat dinner without his father, his mother had always insisted on saying grace—simple little prayers giving thanks, asking for blessings. She had believed in the power of prayer, had kept her faith through long years of miserable living and even through the hellish year it had taken the cancer to kill her.

He had prayed, too, that last year—first for her to live, and later for her to go quickly. God hadn't been listening though. She'd died one agonizing, heartbreaking day at a time, and he had never prayed again until he'd stood beside another hospital bed with another woman he'd loved. But was Maggie's survival a testament to the power of prayer, or merely to the medical miracles money could buy?

He neither knew nor cared. He was simply thankful she had survived.

"Go with us today, Lord," the pastor intoned, "and keep us safe in Your love. Amen."

A chorus of amens echoed through the rooms, then the chatter returned to its earlier volume and the line slowly began to move. Ross leaned forward, his mouth close to Maggie's ear. "See the guy in the plaid flannel shirt?"

She looked and nodded.

"That's Dr. Grayson, the psychiatrist Dr. Olivetti referred you to."

She looked again, with more interest this time. "He's cute," she said with surprise. "The rehab center may have had the best doctors in the country, but none of them was good-looking. I bet his female patients fall all for"—impatiently she tried again—"all fall for him."

Ross looked at him again, making brief notes—big, tall, blond, blue-eyed. "I didn't know the rugged, outdoorsy type appealed to you."

Her smile softened as Grayson swung someone's two-year-old into his arms and carried her through the crowd to her mother. "Not particularly, but the sweet, compassionate, soft-spot-in-his-heart-for-children type will get me every time."

And he missed on all three counts, Ross thought moodily.

"Are you talking about J.D.?" Melissa asked, turning to include Ross in the question. "We've been trying to get him married ever since he came here last year, but we're not having much luck. I don't suppose you have an unmarried friend who's looking to leave Buffalo for the slower and much sweeter life we have here in Bethlehem."

"I'll see if I can think of anyone," Maggie said with a secretive smile. She would soon be single, she intended to stay in town, and she very much wanted a family. He wanted her to have one too—but not with J. D. Grayson. She didn't need a full-time shrink.

"He's good catch," Melissa went on. "He did his undergraduate work at Boston College, went to medical school at Harvard, then set up practice in Chicago. He was highly respected there."

"So why did he come here?" Ross asked.

"Because he discovered that there's more to life than twelve-hour workdays, big-city living, high crime rates, pavement, crowds, and traffic everywhere you turn."

"If Bethlehem can support a highly respected, Harvard-educated psychiatrist, then it must not be as wonderful a place to live as everyone thinks."

Melissa gave him a gentle smile. "Life is simpler here. The cost of living is more manageable. In addition to his private patients, J. D. does counseling at the schools, works with social services, and sees patients at both the hospital and the nursing home. It's enough to meet his expenses, but not enough to interfere with having a life. What more could a person want?"

He could want a hell of a lot more, Ross acknowledged, and did. If Grayson didn't want his work to interfere with his life, great. But all Ross wanted was for his life to not interfere with his work.

It was an incredibly selfish attitude. He understood

that. But it was the way he was and he couldn't change. He also understood that.

He hoped Maggie did too.

THE FEASTING WAS OVER AND EVERY woman in the place was gathered in the kitchen, all trying to help the sisters with the cleanup.

"Out," Miss Corinna commanded. "Everyone under the age of fifty, go away and leave us old ladies to catch up on our visiting while we clean."

Her mother's strict upbringing forced Holly McBride to resist, even though doing dishes was her least favorite chore in the world. "Now, Miss Corinna, that doesn't make any sense. Why don't all you 'old ladies' pat yourselves on the back for a meal well done, then go make yourselves comfortable and catch up on your gossiping—I mean visiting," she amended with a grin. "We'll take care of this mess in here."

"This is my kitchen, child, and if something's being done in it, I'll be here to help. Go on now. Scoot, all of you."

Years of dealing with guests and the inn's everchanging staff had taught Holly when to argue and when to retreat. She'd never known anyone who'd won an argument with either Winchester sister, and so she retreated. "Come on, guys. Let's find our own quiet place and visit for a while."

Followed by Maggie, Emilie, Melissa, and Shelley, she led the way through crowded rooms, down the hall, and into a dimly lit parlor. Matching wing chairs curved in front of an overstuffed sofa, with a petitpoint hassock in the middle. They settled in, kicked off their shoes, and propped their feet on the hassock.

"Has this mob scene thoroughly confused and bewildered you, Maggie?" Holly asked.

"I still have a few short circuits in my brain, but I think I've kept most things straight. You own the inn where I used to stay when I came here." When Holly nodded, Maggie turned to Emilie on her left. "You live across the street, you're married to Nathan, who's a police officer, and your nieces and nephew live with you."

"Alanna, Josie, and Brendan," Emilie answered, the sounds softened by her Georgia accent. "Lannie's ten going on twenty, which is a great improvement, because last year she was nine going on ninety. She's learning to be a child again. And Josie and Brendan are the sweetest, quietest, most demure angels you've ever seen."

Amid a round of snickers and snorts, Holly chided her friend. "You shouldn't fib this close to Christmas, Em. Santa won't bring you anything."

Emilie wasn't concerned. "That's okay. Last Christmas I got a home, a husband, all new friends, and permanent custody of the kids. Those gifts are enough to last a lifetime."

"And in the spring you and Nathan will have a baby of your own," Melissa added. Her smile was gentle, but it couldn't hide her envy. It was no secret that she and Alex had been trying for years to start a family. Her first three pregnancies had ended in miscarriages, and a fourth had simply never happened.

Holly wasn't the mothering type at all, but she felt

sorry for Melissa. If she ruled the world, all women who wanted babies would have them and women who lacked the nurturing instincts—like her, like her own mother—wouldn't. But she didn't rule the world, just her own very small part of it, and that gave her no power beyond wishes and prayers to help the Thomases.

Maggie returned to her recitation of the facts she considered important. "Melissa owns the nursery, does beautiful flower arrangements, sings in the church choir, and organizes the Christmas pageant every year because she was going to be an actress before she got married and came here."

"No, no, she *was* an actress," Shelley clarified, "and a very good one too." When Melissa protested, Shelley overrode her. "It doesn't matter if they were just local productions. You were good. The reviewers said so."

And she was still good, Holly thought privately. After the last miscarriage, she'd been able to convince practically everyone in town that her heart wasn't breaking a little more each childless day. Holly wasn't sure how much more of the disappointment Melissa could take.

"And Shelley . . ." A flush tinged Maggie's cheeks. "I tried to pay attention when we talked, but I think the whole time I was envying you your baby. When is it due?"

"Two weeks. An early Christmas blessing."

And the women, Holly thought, were a blessing in themselves. She'd gone through a long period when she'd had little use for women, when running the inn had consumed her days and looking for love—while settling for affection or lust—had filled her nights. The experience—and the failure to find anything more meaningful than a short-term affair—had left her skeptical of the whole concept of love.

Oh, she knew it existed. Miss Corinna had had forty wonderful years with her husband, and it was clear to anyone with eyes in their head that Nathan, Alex, and Mitch absolutely adored their wives. But she'd never experienced it firsthand—not romantic love and not much in the way of familial love.

And so she'd given up looking—well, had significantly cut back. In doing so, she had given up the idea that all other women were potential competitors in the search for Mr. Right and had discovered some wonderful friends. They were her support, her family, sometimes her sanity.

She tuned back into the conversation—still about babies—and noticed the faraway look that had claimed Melissa. Heaving a great dramatic sigh, she pleaded, "No more talk about pregnancies, please. My feet are starting to swell, and I'm beginning to experience cravings. Maggie, how would you feel about giving us a tour of your house? I've been dying to see what you did with it, and you did plan a party last year to show it all off before . . ."

The look Maggie gave her was steady and friendly. "Before I slid off the mountain. What kind of party?"

"A post–Christmas, pre–New Year's, pre–Emilie's wedding party," Shelley said. "It was scheduled for the Saturday after Christmas."

"You had invited everyone from the inn, the neighbors, everyone you'd met—even the work crew,"

Holly went on. "But then you had the accident and the party was canceled. So how about showing us around now?"

Maggie got the keys from Ross, then they left, walking the short distance to the brick house.

The house was beautiful—Holly had expected that—and cozy. She *hadn't* expected that. She'd seen a photo spread in some magazine of their home in Buffalo—the most sterile, unwelcoming, unlived-in-looking place she'd ever seen. She couldn't imagine Maggie living in that house—or Ross living in this one. They had just settled in the living room to discuss Bethlehem's holiday affairs, when the doorbell rang. Being closest to the door, Holly volunteered to answer it.

The man waiting impatiently on the porch wasn't exactly handsome. His brown hair was a little too unruly, his face a little too rugged, his manner a little too arrogant. He looked like someone too used to giving orders—like someone too much like Ross McKinney.

"Can I help you?"

"I'm here to see Ross."

Irked by his imperious pronouncement, Holly lounged against the doorjamb. "He's not here."

"Where is he?"

"At a neighbor's house."

"When will he be back?"

Holly shrugged.

"What about Maggie?"

She stepped back and pulled the door open wide with a sweeping gesture. "She's in the living room."

Giving her a look of pure annoyance, he walked

past. The faint scent of aftershave lingered in the air. He stopped in the wide doorway, and his dark gaze settled on Maggie.

"Hello, Tom," she greeted him. The coolness of her voice told Holly she'd been right to start off disliking him.

"Maggie. I sent Ross some papers a few days ago to sign and return. Do you know where they are?"

"Probably in his office across the hall. Feel free to look."

He nodded curtly and went into the opposite room. With a devilish smile Holly followed him again. When he opened the brightly colored envelope from the corner of the desk, he swore. "He didn't sign them." He combed his fingers through his hair, then seemed to notice her for the first time. "Do you know the number where he is?"

She nodded.

"Would you give it to me so I can call him?" He sounded impatient now.

"I'll call." As she made her way to the phone on the desk, she said politely, "It's Thanksgiving, you know. A holiday. When most people don't work."

"I'm not most people."

Oh, she could see that. Absolutely. She could also see, on second examination, that while he wasn't exactly handsome, he was arresting. Interesting. And so absorbed in his work that he had no time for anything else. Not her type. But definitely interesting.

Mitch Walker answered the Winchester phone, and she asked him to tell Ross that Tom somebody was waiting at the house to see him. She half hoped as she hung up the phone that Ross would keep the man waiting. It was no more than he deserved for interrupting their Thanksgiving with business.

"Couldn't you have just called instead of coming here all the way from Buffalo?"

He gave her another of those irritated looks. "Not that it's any of your business, but I did call. I called a half dozen times." He glanced at the answering machine with its blinking message light, swore again, then scowled at her. "You don't need to stand guard until Ross gets here. He put me in charge of his company. He won't object to my being alone in his office."

She went as far as the door before turning back. "Holidays. There are about a dozen of them every year. Great time for resting and relaxing and being with friends. It's a wonderful concept. You ought to try it sometime."

His only response was another grumbled curse that she barely caught. Even though he was definitely not her type, it was a good thing he lived so far away.

Because when it came to men and her type, she was nothing if not flexible.

Chapter Six

I N T H E M I D D L E O F T H E C O N V E R S A T I O N
about Bethlehem's annual Tour of Lights, Ross returned from the Winchesters'. Maggie watched as
he went into his office, wondered as she gazed at
the closed doors what was important enough to bring
Tom Flynn so far on a holiday. Of course, like Ross,
Tom recognized holidays only as days when it was difficult to catch people in their offices or answering their
calls. Also like Ross—and like her—he had no family,
or at least none who claimed him, and he shied away
from any woman who might try to take him home to
share the day with her own family.

She would feel a little sorry for him—as sorry as she
could feel for a cold-blooded snake—but she doubted
he had any clue what he was missing.

Realizing that the room had gone quiet, she
refocused her attention to find all four women watch-

ing her. With a faint flush staining her cheeks, she asked, "So when is the Tour of Lights?"

"It starts in a couple of weeks." Emilie Bishop's tone was perfectly normal, but there was something about it that told Maggie it was a repeat.

"You just told me that, didn't you?"

"A few minutes ago."

"Sorry. Sometimes I get easily distracted."

"Then let me distract you some more." Holly glanced over her shoulder at the office doors, then lowered her voice. "Who's this Tom person?"

"He's Ross's lawyer. He's running the company for him while Ross is here."

"Attractive and capable. Nice combination. Is he married?"

Maggie stared at her for a moment, then burst out laughing. "No, no, no. You are *not* interested in Tom, believe me."

"Why not?"

"He's not married because no woman with half a brain would have him—and that's the kind of woman he prefers. They're all cool, beautiful, elegant, with an IQ smaller than their bust size. They're all blond, with legs up to their necks, and they're all greedy enough for his money to put up with his perpetual bad humor—for a while. None of them sticks around, and none of them ever comes back to give him a second chance."

"But he's attractive in a ruthless way."

Maggie glanced across the hall again, though the solid doors hid the topic of discussion. Attractive? Tom? *She'd* never thought so—but then, she had never liked the man. From the day he'd gone to work for Ross, it seemed to her that things had begun to change. Each man's ambition had fed off the other's, until they'd no longer been merely doing their best, striving to make a place for themselves, working hard for success. They had become driven, with all the negative connotations. Business had become more and more important, and gradually she had become less important.

For years she'd blamed Tom, but it wasn't his fault. Without Tom's help Ross would have still reached that point where nothing else mattered. The lawyer was just a convenient scapegoat.

But that didn't make him suitable for a relationship with a woman she liked, and she liked Holly McBride.

"Maybe he is attractive, but he's an exercise in futility. He's never remained on a friendly basis with a woman he's dated. They all go away hating him. The most important thing in his life is business. He came all the way out here on Thanksgiving Day for some papers, for heaven's sake."

"That's an awfully long drive," Melissa remarked.

"Oh, he didn't drive. I promise you, he called one of Ross's pilots and made him give up his holiday to fly him to the nearest airport where he could rent a car."

" 'One of Ross's pilots,' " Emilie repeated with a sigh. "It must be *nice*. Last year, when things had gotten about as bad as they could get, I'd get the kids to sleep, then I would fall asleep there in the homeless shelter and dream about having money. Not just having enough, as I'd had before, but being *rich*. Rich enough to never worry again, to protect the kids, to always keep them safe." Smiling, she shook her head at the memory.

"And then she went and married a cop," Shelley said with a laugh. "A profession not known for its fabulous salaries."

"No," Emilie agreed, "but it's enough."

And she meant it. Maggie knew, because that was all *she'd* ever wanted. Just enough—and Ross. He would see to it that they both always had enough, but the price had been too high. They'd lost each other.

The money wasn't worth it. If she could go back ten years and change everything, if she could trade the money and the success for a happily-ever-after for the two of them together, she would do it. But, of course, she couldn't. All she could do was make certain that her future was better than her past.

Across the hall the pocket doors slid open, and Ross and Tom stepped into the hallway, then left through the front door. Would this visit and whatever business they'd discussed whet Ross's desire to get back to work? Would she go looking for him later today or tomorrow or the next day and find him on the computer or the phone, right back in the thick of things? Probably. And would she be disappointed? Maybe. A little.

She expected Ross to squeeze in a few last instructions on the walk to the car, then return to the house. But it was long after the sedan drove past the front windows that he came back, and he was carrying a plastic grocery bag filled with foil-wrapped packages.

"The sisters are divvying up the leftovers," Holly said as she slid to her feet. "That means it's about time to head home. Maggie, thanks for the tour. Come by the inn sometime. We'll have lunch. Shelley, Melissa, you come too. My assistant manager, Emilie, and I, of course, will be there."

"I'd like that." Maggie accompanied them to the door, exchanged good-byes, then watched as they returned to the Winchester house. She was smiling when she turned and found Ross waiting a few yards away.

"I went to thank the Winchesters for their hospitality, and they sent me home with enough food to last through next week."

"So you're saved from eating my cooking for a while."

"Would you have preferred that I turn down their offer?"

The edge to his voice surprised her. "Of course not. Leftovers are the best part of Thanksgiving dinner." Then she remembered their discussion that morning about cooking. "It wasn't a criticism, Ross. It was just a comment."

She went back into the living room and sat down on the sofa. As she tucked her feet between the cushions, he settled in the armchair she'd just vacated. "I had a really good time. I'm glad we went."

"So am I," he agreed.

She wondered if his words were sincere and decided to believe they were. So what if loud, homey family gatherings suited him even less than large formal affairs without a single genuine friend in the place suited her? Maybe he'd truly enjoyed himself, or maybe he was just saying so for her benefit. Either way, she would take his words at face value.

"You look worn out."

She tried to resist a yawn. "I am. I haven't talked to so many people in . . . well, longer than I can remember."

"Since last December. The Fairingtons' Christmas party."

"Gala," she said sleepily. "Candace Fairington always calls it a gala."

"You wore a red dress that made Candace turn green with envy, and you danced with the governor and charmed the mayor, and all the time you were wishing you were here."

And now she was, she thought, her eyes slowly closing. And she was here to stay.

Home to stay.

TOM FLYNN DROVE SLOWLY DOWN THE streets of one of Buffalo's poorer neighborhoods. His Porsche was out of place on the empty streets where the only cars were burned-out hulks stolen from someplace more prosperous, stripped, then set afire. *He* was out of place in his five-thousand-dollar suit, his custom-made shoes, his fifteen-thousand-dollar wristwatch.

Of course, appearances could be deceiving. No one belonged there more than he did. He'd grown up in that building over there, had stolen food from the market across the street, had been kicked out of the school down the block, and said confession at the church up ahead. Empty, abandoned, haunted buildings—all except the church.

The place was shabby, run-down. The diocese had never been a wealthy one, and Holy Cross had been the poorest of its churches, serving the neediest of its people. The building should have been condemned fifteen years earlier, and would have been if there'd been a building inspector brave enough to come into the war zone.

Nobody cared but Father Pat. Patrick Shanahan had come in a young, idealistic priest. He'd done his best, helped a few souls, lost hundreds more. Thirty years down there had made him old, but he kept trying.

The church doors were unlocked despite the punks who ran the streets. Few lights were on—trying to keep the electric bills down—and few candles were lit, giving the place a spooky air. Even in better days, though, it had always scared the hell out of Tom.

He stopped a few feet from the confessional, remembering the sweaty palms, the cramped space, the fear of retribution. He hadn't been to confession since he was sixteen, hadn't set foot in church since then either.

"Have you come to say confession?" The quiet old voice came from behind him, startling him more than could be explained by dim lights and deep shadows.

Bless me, Father, for I have sinned.

His list of sins was long and detailed, spanning more than twenty years and destined to spin out across the next twenty. There wasn't a priest in the world with the power to absolve him of all he'd done and all he would do.

"I've come to make a donation." He turned to face the old man, reached into his coat pocket, and pulled out the bracelet. He turned the priest's hand over, then let seven inches of gold and twelve carats of flawless diamonds and sapphires puddle in his palm. When the clasp slipped through his fingers, Tom folded Father Pat's hand over the treasure. "Happy Thanksgiving, Father. Put that to good use."

And then he walked out, back into the cold, back into the night, and he drove out of the old neighborhood for the last time.

T HE SNOW STARTED SOMETIME DURING the night. When Maggie settled in the rocker in the kitchen with a cup of fresh coffee, the backyard was completely covered with white. Clumps of snow topped the fence, and drifts piled wherever the wind blew it. It looked incredibly cold and beautiful outside but it was warm and cozy in the house. All she needed to make the scene perfect was the smell of something baking and a fire popping in the fireplace. She wasn't adventurous enough to try her hand at baking again, not yet, and Ross would build a fire when he came down. . . .

The thought gave her pause. It was so easy, after so many years, to still think in terms of his responsibility or hers. She could build a fire. She had logs, matches, kindling—even better, a supply of compressed sawdust fire starters. Soon the chore would be hers every cold morning she spent in this house. Why not get some experience now?

Within minutes the well-seasoned wood was burning brightly. She reclaimed her coffee, then stayed on the floor, leaning against the hearth, staring into the flames.

At the Winchesters' yesterday, she'd learned that last year the house had been done up with hundreds of white lights and dozens of farolitos. It had looked beautiful, everyone agreed, and so she'd decided to do it like that again.

Her first Christmas tradition.

Next weekend she would put up her tree—her second tradition—and sometime before Christmas she would have that party she'd missed out on last year. This time she would have to cater it, but next year, and every year to follow, she would do all the cooking herself. The house would be filled with people, and there would be music and laughter, and she would—

Long fingers appeared before her face and snapped, jarring her out of her reverie. She blinked, then turned to find Ross seated on the hearth, a cup of coffee beside him.

"Where were you?"

She smiled dreamily. "Christmas future." She moved to sit on the brick and felt an immediate blast of heat on her back.

"And what did you see there?"

"People. Kids. Bethlehem." She wondered what he saw in his own future Christmases. *Not her,* came the immediate answer with a quick stab of pain, a sharp, tight breath. Probably work, work, and more work. He would fulfill all his holiday social obligations, but other than that December would be just another month, the twenty-fifth just another day. She felt sorry for him, but if he was happy having no life outside his office—

and she knew from experience he was—then that was all that mattered.

"And what do you see in the near future?" he asked. "Like for breakfast?"

"We have turkey, ham, dressing, pumpkin bread, pumpkin pie, banana cream pie, the Winchesters' home-baked rolls, candied yams—"

"How about a turkey sandwich?"

"Sounds fine."

He headed for the refrigerator, and she watched him. When building the mansion, he'd insisted that the kitchen be perfect—large, state-of-the-art, with enough room and equipment to prepare dinner for fifty—but once it was completed, he'd never set foot in it. He'd hired the staff before they'd moved in and had trusted them to know what was where.

He seemed at home in *this* kitchen—as at home as he could be in a place as foreign to him as Bethlehem was.

"What are your plans for today?" he asked as he worked.

"I want to unpack the ornaments."

"When are we getting the tree?"

"Next weekend. Melissa's getting in a shipment of live trees. After Christmas we can plant it in the backyard."

"If you're not getting the tree for more than a week, maybe you should wait—"

"I know. But I want to do it today." She wanted to look at every ornament, wanted to remember when she got it and why, wanted to feel the warmth of nostalgia wash over her the way it did every year.

"If that's what you want," Ross agreed with a shrug. "Mayonnaise or mustard?"

"Mayonnaise." After sixteen Thanksgivings together, he should know that she always put mayonnaise on her turkey sandwiches. Maybe the fact that he didn't had something to do with why there wouldn't be a seventeenth.

As he brought the sandwiches to the fireplace, she commented, "If you were home, you would have been in the office at least two hours ago. Do you miss it?"

He shrugged.

"Come on. You're starting your fifth day away from work. You haven't had five con—consec—" She grimaced. "Five days off in a row since you got your first job twenty-one years ago. Be honest. When Tom was here yesterday, didn't you have the urge to lock the door and talk business for a few hours? When he left, didn't you envy him, just for a moment, because he was working and you weren't?"

"Honestly?" He was silent for a moment before answering. "Yes, I might have been a little envious." Then he shrugged. "All right. *Damn* envious."

"There's no reason you shouldn't work here. I don't need your attention all the time. As long as you're available in case something happens . . ."

He was obviously tempted even as he shook his head. "I don't know how to work just a few hours at a time. It's a talent I never developed."

"When we first met, I really admired your dedication—to your work, your studies, to me."

"But over time, dedication became obsession, and it wasn't very admirable."

Maggie shook her head. "Oh, I still admired it. But I resented it too, because it consumed you, including the part of you that was supposed to be mine." She gazed out the window at the snow and moved an inch closer to the warmth of the fire. "Could you ever imagine yourself living the same kind of life as the men you met yesterday? Alex Thomas, Nathan Bishop, Mitch Walker—they're all good at what they do, but their jobs aren't their lives. They go to work, they dedicate those eight or ten hours to their job, and then they go home. They have families, friends, hobbies. They go to church. They take vacations. They have *lives*. Could you ever be satisfied with that?"

Again, Ross remained silent a time before answering. "Do you remember when you were finally able to quit your job?"

Maggie nodded. It had been the start of his fourth year in business, and for the first time he'd made enough money that not every spare penny had to be pumped back in. To celebrate, he'd wanted her to quit her secretarial job and be a woman of leisure, like the wives of the successful businessmen he knew.

"You'd worked long enough and hard enough, putting me through school and supporting us while I got established. Finally you were able to sleep in. You had the time and the money to fix up the house, to indulge in some shopping, to relax and take it easy. I thought you would be happy." His smile was self-deprecating. "You weren't."

That was putting it mildly. For the first week, she *had* slept late—a true luxury that she'd rarely been allowed. But sleeping late was no fun when she woke up alone. And yes, she'd had time for long, leisurely lunches—but no one to share them with. All her friends worked full-time. The shopping had been fun for the first new wardrobe and the first houseful of new furniture, but she'd soon lost interest.

"You were bored. You didn't know how to live like that. And I don't know how to live the life these people live."

"All we're talking about is a little moderation."

"I don't know moderation. For me, it's all or nothing."

How true, she thought. In the beginning, even when they'd been chronically broke, they'd had it all—all the love, the romance, the passion, the commitment. And in the end they'd been left with nothing.

"If that disappoints you, I'm sorry."

He was giving her an earnestly regretful look. She patted his arm as she got to her feet. "I got over being disappointed a long, long time ago. I was just curious. Nothing more." She stretched, then headed for the boxes stacked neatly against the wall. "I'm going to start on this. Why don't you go to the office and see if you can do a little work?"

"Maggie—"

"Just a little. I've done this alone for ten years. It's kind of become a tradition." And traditions were worth observing, even if they weren't happy ones.

He looked as if he wanted to argue, but how could he when she'd made it clear that his presence wasn't needed—and when he really wanted to do what she suggested? As she arranged a half dozen boxes in a single layer on the floor, he carried their dishes to the sink, then stopped in the hall doorway. "I'll be in the office," he said grudgingly.

"Thank you," she said with a smile. "If I need you, I'll call."

And who knew? Though she'd needed him hundreds of times, had called for him in hundreds of ways, and he'd never answered, this time he just might.

A FTER A TREMENDOUSLY SATISFYING DAY'S work, Ross returned to the kitchen late in the afternoon and found the room looking as if a hurricane had swept through—Hurricane Maggie, to be precise. Cartons stuffed with boxes, wrapping paper, and bubble wrap were pushed against one wall, and their contents covered every flat surface in the room, including much of the floor. There was no sign of the source of the chaos, though, and no sound of her either.

"Maggie?"

The dining room was empty, though she'd left signs of her passage—nutcracker soldiers in every size marching across the table. The living room was empty too. At the bottom of the stairs he called again and thought he heard a soft sound in response. It came from the library, though, not upstairs. He went to the room he'd passed by only moments before and found her curled up in the chair-and-a-half there, her feet resting on the matching ottoman, her eyes closed in sleep.

She had come in, he suspected, to deposit an armload of haphazardly coiled strings of lights and opted for a moment's rest. With the drapes drawn, the room was dimly lit and welcoming, and the chair was obviously comfortable. It was a good place to snooze.

He backed out of the room without disturbing her and went back to the kitchen. It took only a few minutes to return the unpacked boxes to the basement, quite a few minutes more to bring some order to the things she'd scattered about. The larger items he lined up on the floor in front of the window seat. The smaller pieces went into a dozen baking pans and baskets.

He didn't recognize many of the ornaments—proof of how little attention he'd paid to such things in recent years—but more than a few brought back memories. There was the glass ball, painted in delicate colors, that had been his only present to Maggie the first Christmas they were married. A tree had been an extravagance they couldn't afford, and so the ball had hung from a ribbon in the middle of the living room. They had treated it like mistletoe, kissing every time they passed underneath it.

They had passed under it a lot.

The miniature Mardi Gras mask hung with curling ribbons in purple, green, and gold marked their first vacation. To justify the expense when they were still living on a tight budget, they'd made it their birthday, anniversary, and Christmas presents rolled into one with a belated honeymoon, and they'd made the most of it.

Not once in those four days had he thought about work.

The crystal icicles—two of them, heavy, faceted— had come from Paris, the Father Christmas from Amsterdam, the tiny bean pot from Boston. There were dated ornaments, a full set of fifteen, one for every year of their marriage. He imagined there would soon be a sixteenth—after all, they were still together—but no more. He wondered if she would hang them next year or if they would be relegated to some dark corner of the basement, too meaningful to throw away, too full of sad memories to use.

Maggie came into the room. He watched her reflection in the window glass as she took a soda from the refrigerator, then came to lean against the nearest end of the island. "See anything you remember?"

"A lot." He picked up a handmade piece, a gnome's face with a pointed hat and a long beard that also flowed to a point. "The art student who lived across the hall from us in the last apartment made this."

"Venita. She also did the cornhusk angels."

"And the next-door neighbor at our second house made these." He picked up a pair of beanbag snowmen with stick arms and red plaid stocking caps that matched the scarves around their necks.

"Maureen."

"And you made these." She'd stacked the decorations crocheted from cotton string in no particular order. He knew if he laid them out on the counter, he could pick out the first one, and the second and the third. The later ones were perfectly shaped and proportioned, but the early efforts held more charm—the lopsided stars, the wobbly hearts, the bumpy stockings.

She'd made others too, from store-bought clay and homemade salt dough. There were cinnamon-scented creations, bright-colored felt pieces and tiny hand-pieced quilts. Satin balls elaborately decorated with beads and braid. Shiny gold bows with long, curling streamers. Fat wooden Santas meticulously painted. A punched tin heart with a red satin bow. If he turned it over, he could read the inscription, but he didn't need to. He remembered.

Maggie loves Ross.

Forever.

There was a time when he'd thought forever meant forever—a lifetime—and he'd felt cheated finding out differently. What was his next lesson? That *always* was actually a finite number of years? That *never* was only a matter of months?

"Do you remember these?" Maggie opened a small box and held it for him to see.

Inside was a set of nineteen ornaments—glass, fragile, faded. They started with Baby's First Christmas and progressed up to Friends. The latter was inscribed with a sappy verse about how "you'll always be my daughter, but now you're also my friend."

So *always* must be nineteen years, since that was when Janet Gilbert disowned her only daughter and friend.

"I remember them," he said shortly. Janet had collected the ornaments for Maggie so that when she eventually married, she would have a starter set for her first Christmas away from home. When that time came, though, she'd refused to hand them over. Instead, she'd thrown them away, and a neighbor had rescued them and passed them on to Maggie. Maggie had kept them, but she'd never hung them on a tree.

Too meaningful to throw away, too full of sad memories to use.

"Did she know about the accident?"

Ross took the box from her unsteady hands, secured the lid, and laid it aside. "I don't know. Two years ago she moved away from Buffalo. No one knew where she went. Some of her coworkers thought she was getting married, but they couldn't come up with a name. Tom spent weeks trying to locate her, but he couldn't."

"And my father?"

He would really rather not talk about her parents, though he supposed, it being the holidays with its intense emphasis on family, her questions were only natural. "He knew."

"You told him?"

"Tom did."

He waited, but she didn't ask what her father's response was, whether he'd come to see her, whether he'd given a damn if she lived or died. She knew where she ranked in her father's life—had known since she was a little girl. Most of the time she was past caring. Sometimes, though, the bastard still held the power to hurt her.

He was glad she didn't ask for details, because the story Tom had repeated to him wasn't a pleasant one. The old man hadn't even recognized his daughter's name—had put her so completely out of his life and his mind that he'd needed reminding that he had a daughter from his first marriage. Tom had come back from the meeting thoroughly disgusted—and, since he was a ruthless bastard himself, it took a lot to accomplish that.

"I can find a good private detective for you if you'd

like to locate your mother. Tell her that I'm gone, and she's likely to forgive everything and welcome you back."

The look Maggie gave him was sharp with derision. "I'm not the one in need of forgiveness. I did nothing wrong. I'm sorry she felt the need to remove herself from my life, but it was her decision—her mistake."

"It *was* her mistake, but you've had to live with the consequences. You've missed her."

"I miss the ideal of a mother, but my reality was far from ideal. Even before I met you, things weren't easy. My mother was controlling. She had my entire life mapped out, and if I did anything that deviated from her plan, she punished me by withholding her affection. I wish I had a mother like Miss Agatha or Miss Corinna—a mother like I hope to be once I'm blessed with children. But I've long since accepted that my mother isn't what I need."

She didn't need so much, Ross thought regretfully as she picked up the box of ornaments. Just a husband whose commitment to her couldn't be overshadowed by anything else and children to love. Instead, she had everything but that.

Finding no storage carton for the box, Maggie stuck them in a cabinet under the window seat. Straightening, she busied herself with bringing order to a tangled string of gold beads. "How did it go in the office?"

"Okay." He'd spent all but a half hour lunch break at the computer or on the phone. It had felt good to get back to work, though he'd caught himself more than once paying little attention to the task he was doing and listening intently for sounds from the kitchen. He could have closed the door, as he'd always done at home, but then how would he hear her if she called?

Not that she had, except to tell him that lunch was being served in the living room. The rest of the day she'd spent happily alone, doing a job that a husband and wife should share. That she hadn't wanted him to share.

"So . . . what about dinner?"

"What about it?" he asked.

"Let's go out."

"You mean you don't want leftovers again?"

"Sorry, but turkey and/or ham four meals in a row is my limit. I want a thick, juicy, rare steak. You said there was a place in town."

"McCauley's. Do you want to go now?"

"After I clean up. Care to escort me upstairs?"

He gestured toward the front of the house, then followed her. She went into her room and he turned into his own.

The room was large, high-ceilinged, comfortable. The walls were colonial red, the linens deep green and muted red paisley, the floor gleaming oak planks scattered with rugs. With her taste and his money, Maggie could have worked wonders on their house in Buffalo, if only he'd let her.

He couldn't remember exactly why he hadn't. It had been important to him that the house be perfect, as defined by him, his neighbors, his associates—everyone but his wife. What he'd gotten was the perfect showplace.

But it wasn't much of a home.

Though it seemed an insult to Maggie, he would probably sell the house, he realized. After forcing her to live in it for five years, knowing how much she hated it, he had little use for it by himself. He had impressed all the people he wanted to impress. There wouldn't be many huge parties without Maggie there to plan them, wouldn't be much socializing at all. For all the time he spent at home, a condo near the office would be a wiser choice. In fact, there was a high-rise condominium about a mile from his office with all the luxuries he required and only a fraction of the space he didn't need. It would be perfectly suitable for him.

Too bad he couldn't ask Maggie to decorate it for him. Then he might have a real home, too, instead of merely a place to hang his clothes.

He pulled on a sweater. The garment was bulky, the color creamy ivory, the knitting intricate and expertly done. Maggie had bought it for him on a trip to Ireland, and then she'd done most of its wearing. She'd dressed from his closet as much as from her own, claiming shirts, borrowing sweaters, even taking his socks for around-the-house wear. For years she'd slept in his T-shirts—or in nothing at all.

When had she stopped raiding his closet? When had she given up wanting that intimacy?

He was staring out the window, contemplating those questions, when she rapped on the open door. "I'm ready."

She wore brown slacks and a sweater the color of a well-used penny. The collar points of a brown, white, and rust plaid shirt extended over the sweater's ribbed neck. Her hair, gleaming in the light, fell sleekly into place, and her makeup had been redone to hide the scars. She looked fresh, wholesome, innocent. She looked incredibly lovely.

He stared at her so long that she shifted awkwardly. "Ross?"

He shook his head to break the moment, but it lingered with him—the surprise at how beautiful she was. He knew it, of course, and was reminded every time he looked at her, but occasionally it startled him anew. She was a truly lovely woman, and over the years many people had envied him for having her. Soon, within a year, surely no more than two, it would be his turn to envy some other man, but his envy would be tinged with regret. He had little doubt of that.

"You look nice," he said as he crossed the room. She smelled of vanilla and jasmine when he grew close and something subtler—honeysuckle, perhaps. Altogether, it was a pleasing fragrance. "Let's go. Probably everyone in town who's tired of turkey leftovers will be standing in line for steak."

It was cold enough outside to make the breath catch in his chest. The snow had stopped sometime while he worked, leaving a few inches on the ground, but the street was more or less clear. "Why don't you wait in the house while I get the car warm?"

Maggie struck a pose. "I should be warm enough, don't you think?"

Her brown cashmere overcoat reached almost to her toes, which were warm in a pair of fleece-lined boots. A vivid gold scarf was wrapped around her throat, and gloves the same shade as her coat covered her hands. He compared her winter gear to his own—a leather jacket—and rephrased his question. "Why don't *I* wait inside while *you* get the car warm?"

She smiled smugly as she slid into the passenger seat, and he joined her inside.

At the first intersection, when he would have gone straight, she touched his arm. "Turn left here, will you? I want to go down Main Street. Shelley said they would have the Christmas decorations up."

He obeyed her. On Main, the Thanksgiving decorations were gone, and Christmas had appeared everywhere. Wreaths and bows decorated the streetlights. Mistletoe hung in shop doorways, twinkling lights outlined the windows, and canned snow provided the base for brightly painted Christmas scenes on the glass. Evergreens planted two to the block were hung with ribbons, bells, and bows, and wooden soldiers stood at stiff attention on every block, wearing coats of red, yellow, or blue and gripping holiday flags firmly in one hand.

He slowly drove the length of the downtown district. He heard Maggie whisper, "This is nice" with such satisfaction, such this-is-where-I-belong certainty.

He was glad she felt that way. Really. But he also felt a little envy. The only place he belonged was in his office, and while he was certain that was where he wanted to be, he couldn't help but wonder if, as choices went, it might not be the best he could make. Maybe Maggie was right. Maybe it really was just a question of moderation. Maybe he could learn to separate business from pleasure, to set limits on work and actually have a life that had nothing to do with business.

For a moment he considered the possibility, then, with a bit of relief, brushed it away. Business *was* his pleasure. Small-town living, a family, hobbies—those things were fine for Maggie, because they were what she wanted. But all he wanted was his work. It was his life.

And he wouldn't have it any other way.

Chapter Seven

B ETHLEHEM MEMORIAL HOSPITAL WAS a redbrick building, two stories, oddly shaped as if new wings had been placed on a whim. As hospitals went, it was on the small side, probably no more than thirty beds, and was situated in the middle of several acres of snow-covered lawn. A block to the west was the elementary school, a block to the east the nursing home. Convenient for Dr. Grayson, who, according to Melissa Thomas, worked in all three places.

Maggie studied the building. She'd spent enough time in hospitals not to be intimidated by them. On the other hand, she'd spent enough time in them to find the idea of voluntarily walking into one, even for just an hour, somewhat repugnant.

"Wait inside while I park the car," Ross told her.

"Just let me out, then go on home."

"But—"

"I can do this."

He studied her for a moment, then nodded. "I'll meet you here at four."

Fighting a brief moment of panic as he drove away, she walked into the lobby and forced herself to the information desk. The silver-haired volunteer there directed her to an office down the hall, where another volunteer escorted her into the doctor's office.

"I somehow missed meeting you on Thanksgiving, Maggie," he said as he came around the desk to shake hands. "I'm Dr. Grayson. You can call me J.D."

"I'd rather not," she said with a wan smile. There seemed something not quite right about being on a first-name basis with your psychiatrist. She never would have dreamed of calling Dr. Olivetti by her first name—after nine months of treatment, she didn't even *know* her first name—and she preferred to keep her association with this doctor on the same impersonal footing.

Then the ludicrousness of that thought struck her. *Impersonal?* Dr. Olivetti knew more about her than anyone else alive. But Dr. Grayson's only job was to ensure that she was adapting to life outside the rehab center, and he didn't need to probe too deeply into her psyche to establish that she was.

"Whatever you're comfortable with. Can I take your coat?"

She handed it to him, then settled in the chair in front of his desk, a leather piece that had seen better days. Everything in the office, in fact, was well worn and only a few steps away from shabby—except the frames on the wall that held his degrees.

He noticed the direction of her attention as he sprawled in his own chair. "It's an humble abode for a Harvard degree, isn't it? I went the elegant-office, astronomical-fee route in Chicago. Here I'm a bit more down to earth."

She nodded once, glanced around again, then blurted out the first thing that came to mind. "Do you actually know Dr. Olivetti, or did she recommend you because you're the only psychiatrist in town?" Hearing the implication in her last words, she flushed, but the doctor didn't take offense.

"We did our psych residencies together. She didn't start college until after her kids were grown, you know."

"I didn't know she had kids. She's not much on sharing personal information. It's a one-way street with her—all her way."

"She's good. She's one of the best." Without boasting, he added, "I'm good too. Don't let the fact that I'm a small-town doc fool you."

"Why did you come here?"

"Why did you?"

"It's a lovely town. I like the people here. There are no traffic jams, no crowds, not much in the way of crime. The pace of life is slower. People know their neighbors and care about them." She shrugged. "It's a great place."

"That's why I came too. You sound as if you're planning to stay."

"I am."

"How will your husband run that multibillion-dollar corporation of his from here?"

She stiffened for an instant, then forced her muscles to relax. "Give him a computer, a modem, and a couple of telephone lines, and he can do business from anywhere in the world," she said, her voice a little too bright, her tone a little too flippant.

Dr. Grayson said nothing, but simply continued to watch her, his blue eyes sharp, probing, giving rise to the same twinge of guilt she'd felt when Maeve, at the café, had assumed that she and Ross were a happy couple come here to live. Everyone at the Winchesters on Thanksgiving had probably thought that too, and though she'd done nothing to encourage their mistake beyond showing up with Ross, she'd done nothing to clear it up either.

After a moment of that steady gaze, she sighed and quietly said, "Ross isn't staying. He's going back to Buffalo sometime in January or February."

"I see."

"I don't mean to mislead everybody, but it would be a little awkward to say to a stranger, 'Nice to meet you—and, oh, by the way, my husband and I are splitting up in a few months.' " Though her tone remained casual, the words stung. They sounded so damned impossible. So real. So *wrong*.

"You don't owe anyone warning of what's going to happen in the future of your marriage, Maggie. Telling your friends and neighbors after the fact is perfectly acceptable." He paused. "I take it this is a mutual decision."

"Why do you assume that?"

"Neither of you seems particularly broken up over it. I would expect substantially different behavior if you both didn't think this was for the best."

Was divorce ever *for the best*? Of course, if one spouse was abusing the other, if children's futures were at stake, if all the love, commitment, and respect were gone. But *this* divorce . . . Were their differences really irreconcilable? Couldn't they compromise, find acceptable solutions to their differences, salvage the love, commitment, and respect that had carried them through sixteen years?

The answer left her with an incredible sadness that softened her voice when she responded. "We do."

Dr. Grayson changed the subject and, with his grin, the tone of the conversation. "So what's it like, having escaped the institute? *Institute*. That sounds so rigid, like it should have bars on the windows and straitjackets on the patients."

"That's why I prefer to call it the center," she said dryly, then, unable to resist, she grinned too. "It's nice. I'm really very grateful to them for everything they did, but I hope I never see the place again. Independence is vastly underrated by people who have never lost theirs."

"Any problems?"

"None."

"Headaches?"

"A few minor ones."

"Dizziness? Depression? Sleep disturbances?"

She shook her head to each symptom.

"Are you sure about that?"

She sighed again. "What did Ross tell you?"

"That you wake up during the night."

It was true. She'd been awake some portion of every night the past week. A time or two she'd laid in bed until sleep finally returned, but usually she got up, wrapped a comforter around her, and sat for a while in the rocker, looking out the window. A few of those nights it had been dreams that awakened her, vague scenes that she couldn't recall five seconds later. Those nights she'd rocked until her heartbeat slowed, until her breathing settled and the thick panic that tightened her chest receded.

It was unsettling to know that across the hall, Ross was listening.

"Sometimes I don't sleep through the night," she admitted. "Sometimes I have trouble concentrating. I sat down to watch a movie yesterday afternoon, and I couldn't even follow the story. I can't cook the way I used to either."

"Is that good or bad?"

"I loved to cook. I was a great cook. Now the directions are too complicated to follow."

"I would imagine that culinary skills get rusty just like any other unused skill. Give yourself a little time. Pick some simpler dishes. Get Ross to help."

She shook her head. "I want to do it myself. When he's gone, I'll *have* to do it myself."

"Unless he has some sort of ironclad prenuptial agreement, when he's gone, you'll be financially comfortable, at worst. You'll be able to hire someone to do whatever you can't."

"No, there's no prenup," she admitted. Ross's circle of acquaintances who came closest to achieving the status of friends had been appalled that he hadn't thought to take such a precautionary measure. They were unwilling to share any credit for their success with their wives or any financial gain with their ex-wives. But Ross wasn't like them. "I'll have the money, but I don't want to hire someone unless there's absolutely no other option."

"So, like I said, give yourself some time. You know, with most patients who suffer post-traumatic syndrome, the symptoms lessen, then disappear within the first year or shortly thereafter. In a few more months you could be perfectly fine."

"Or some of what we're attributing to post-traumatic syndrome could actually be brain damage," she said with a sardonic smile. "I could be like this the rest of my life."

"But you're alive and otherwise healthy. You can lead a normal life—and hiring someone to cook for you would be normal in your life. Don't tell me you didn't have a full household staff in Buffalo."

"We did. I hated it."

Another brief silence settled between them as he watched her. Often in her sessions with Dr. Olivetti, the doctor hadn't even looked at her—had instead made copious notes while listening intently. Maggie suspected that Dr. Grayson learned almost as much from watching his patients as he did from listening to them, and he hadn't yet made a single note.

"So . . . what are your plans after Ross is gone?"

"I don't know. When things started getting bad, I went back to school and finished my degree, so I'd like to work, I think. For years the only job I've held was being his wife. The pay and benefits were great, but the emotional satisfaction . . ." Flushing, she let her voice trail off, then murmured, "I'd like to do something with kids. My degree is in early childhood development. I'd like to use it."

"That shouldn't be too difficult. Bethlehem has kids coming out of the woodwork. When do you plan to start looking?"

"After Ross goes home."

They talked a few minutes longer, then Dr. Grayson said, "That's about it for today, Maggie. Before we call it quits, is there anything you want to ask?"

"Yes. What are they doing out there?" The scene out the window had caught her attention more than once while they talked, but she'd forced herself to ignore it, to concentrate on his questions and her answers. Now that their hour was almost up, though, she felt no such compunction.

Dr. Grayson turned in his chair to look. Across the lawn was a tall building of the sort used to house heavy equipment. In spite of the cold, the wide doors were open and a small group of adults and children were busy inside. Occasionally one child raced out into the snow, followed at top speed by another, then disappeared inside again.

"They're working on the hospital's float for the Christmas parade," Dr. Grayson replied. "It's this Thursday night. If you'd like to volunteer an extra set of hands, I'm sure they'd be happy to have you."

She was tempted—very much so. But she had little artistic talent, knew nothing about building floats, and wasn't quite up to inviting herself to join a group of strangers.

Reading at least part of her reluctance accurately, Dr. Grayson said, "You've already met some of them. The Winchester sisters are over there—they're two of our most reliable volunteers—and they always bring the Dalton kids. Shelley Walker's kids help out too, and some of the other folks who shared Thanksgiving dinner with us. All you have to do is twist paper and poke it through chicken wire." Rising from his chair, he got both her coat and his own from the hook on the back of the door. "Come on. I'll walk over with you."

Even as she protested, she stood up and slid her arms into the coat. "I'm supposed to meet Ross in the lobby at four."

"So we'll just say hello, and you can talk to them about helping out later. It won't take but a minute." He ushered her from the office, out a back door, and across a walk that had been partially cleared of snow.

As they stopped in the open doorway, Josie Dalton, Emilie Bishop's niece and Maggie's neighbor, ran forward and leaped into Dr. Grayson's arms. "Dr. J.D., look what I got at school today," she said, then closed her eyes so he could better appreciate the bruising that encircled her right eye.

"Nice shiner, kiddo," he said admiringly. "How'd it happen?"

Opening her eyes again—well, one eye, at least—she pouted, looking angelically pretty with her blond hair, blue eyes, and delicate features. "Kenny Howard did it. I'm gonna tell Uncle Nathan, and he'll go arrest him and put him in jail, and Kenny'll be sorry 'cause Santa

Claus won't bring him nothin' for bein' bad." Switching her attention to Maggie, Josie turned off the pout and grinned. "I 'member you. You live in the brick house that had candles in paper sacks that didn't burn up last Christmas. I'm gonna ask Aunt Emilie if we can't have 'em too. I'm Josie Lee Dalton."

"Hi, Josie. I'm Maggie."

Josie's elder sister, Alanna, joined them in time to hear the introduction. "That's *Miss* Maggie to you, Josie," she said. "Come on. Miss Agatha wants your help."

"She's a beautiful child," Maggie murmured as the two girls walked away.

Dr. Grayson knew immediately which child she was referring to. Josie was a doll—a bright, funny, precocious doll—but Alanna was lovely. "She is," he agreed. "Have you ever seen a ten-year-old girl who looks that incredibly serene?"

Serene. It was a perfect description—and the *incredibly* was pretty accurate too, based on what Maggie had learned on Thanksgiving about the Dalton children's background. Their mother was a severely dependent personality who had abdicated her responsibilities to her children in favor of men, alcohol, and drugs. She had spent last Christmas in a court-ordered rehabilitation program and was back there again this Christmas. As for their fathers—each child had been born of a different relationship—they had never been a part of the children's lives.

How fortunate for them that their aunt Emilie and uncle Nathan loved them as if they were their own, and how lucky the Bishops were to have them.

"Hello, Maggie girl," Harry Winslow from the diner greeted her. "Have you come to work, J.D.?"

"Afraid not. I've got an appointment in a few minutes. But I brought you someone who thinks working on a parade float would be a wonderful way to while away a few frigid hours." Ignoring her chastening look, Dr. Grayson pushed her farther into the cavernous space. "I'll tell Ross where you are, and I'll see you again soon."

As he left, Harry offered her his arm. "We're pretty proud of our handiwork here. Let me show you around, and then the sisters can put you to work. How does that sound?"

She looked at the float surrounded by its bundled-up creators, all talking and obviously having a good time, then offered the elderly man a smile. "That sounds wonderful."

And it really did.

T HE HOSPITAL LOBBY WAS NEITHER LARGE nor imaginative. It was a square room with plate-glass windows decorated with fake snow, a nativity scene on one side and equal time for the secular sector and Santa on the other. Rows of hard plastic chairs in garish orange lined two walls, and a vinyl couch faced one. The information desk was strictly that—a desk situated between the elevator and a corridor—and was manned now by a teenage candy striper who'd replaced the grandmotherly woman present when he'd arrived five minutes earlier.

Ross wondered how Maggie's appointment with

J. D. Grayson was going—wondered what they were talking about. He'd never asked her what she discussed in her sessions with her psychiatrist. If anything was sacred, surely that was.

But he wouldn't be surprised if the impulse to ask this time was stronger than the need to resist. And he couldn't deny that it had something to do with the fact that the doctor wasn't a sixty-something, gray-haired, fatherly type. That he was their age, single, and, by Maggie's own description, *cute.*

"Can I help— Why, Mr. McKinney. What are you doing here?"

He focused his gaze on the woman in front of him. He'd seen her before—at the Winchesters, perhaps, or— "You work at the nursery."

She smiled brightly. "I was there the day Maggie got her bulbs. Did she get them planted all right?"

"Yes, she did. Do you work here too?"

With one slim hand she tugged the lapel of her lavender lab coat, drawing his attention to the name tag pinned to it. NOELLE, VOLUNTEER, it read. "I help out wherever I can. Maggie's not sick, is she?"

"No. She's with Dr. Grayson."

"Wonderful doctor. Bethlehem's lucky to have him."

Just what he needed—another of the doctor's fans, Ross thought sourly before she continued.

"Just as you're lucky to have Maggie. It was a miracle that she survived such a nasty accident—a genuine Christmas miracle. I guess she hadn't yet fulfilled God's purpose for putting her here." Once more she smiled that light, lovely smile. "I see the doubt in your eyes. Is it miracles you don't believe in, Mr. McKinney? Or God's purpose?"

He didn't offer an answer. She didn't require one.

"We all have a purpose here—a place to belong, a life we should be living. Sometimes, though, we get too caught up in the world to recognize our place when we find it. I think Maggie has found her place. Have you?"

Uncomfortable with the question, he opened his mouth to tell her politely that his place was none of her business, but whistling from the hallway distracted him. "There's Dr. Grayson now," he said, moving to meet the man halfway.

"Maggie and I are finished for the day," Grayson said. "She's out back now helping the Winchesters work on the hospital float. Come on, I'll show you where they are."

"Is everything all right?" Ross fell into step with him but took one quick look back before they turned the corner. Noelle, with her pesky questions, was already gone.

"Everything's fine." Grayson stopped at a short corridor. "Go out that door and follow the sidewalk. Tell Maggie to give me a call . . . oh, in three weeks or so. I don't think we'll need to meet more than another time or two. She's remarkably well adjusted, considering."

Considering *what*? Ross wanted to ask. All she'd gone through with the accident? Or all she'd gone through with *him*? Had Maggie confided the fact that the image they were presenting to the people of Bethlehem was misleading at best? He knew it bothered her. She was too honest by nature and wanted too much to make a lifelong place for herself among these people to want to deceive them in any way.

But he couldn't ask, and even if he could, Grayson couldn't answer. So Ross simply acknowledged that he would pass the message on, then went out into the cold.

The aluminum-sided garage was only a few degrees warmer inside than out, although Harry Winslow was in the process of correcting that. He was building a fire in the woodstove against the back wall with help from Brendan Dalton and Mitchell Walker, the police chief's younger son. Once the logs caught, he called to several of the older kids to close the massive doors, and they did so a moment after Ross walked in.

At first he saw no sign of Maggie, but the float that dominated the space blocked much of his view. It was built on a flatbed, a wood-and-chicken-wire fabrication without enough substance to make sense of it.

"Doesn't look like much now, does it?" Harry stood beside him, looking warmer in his insulated coveralls than Ross was in jeans and jacket. He really had to learn to dress warmer than he was accustomed to back home, or he wouldn't survive the next few months to *get* back home.

"What is it supposed to be?"

"That shape there—it's going to be a crib like in the hospital nursery. It'll be too cold for a real baby, so we'll use a doll instead. That'll be a wheelchair for the mother, and the father will stand behind her. There'll be three doctors over there—a family doc, an anesthesiologist, and a pediatrician—and a couple of nurses over here. These sides will be like nursery walls decorated for Christmas, and on the back, in red and green, it'll say SEASON FOR HEALING."

A newborn baby, mother, and father, three wise men, and the shepherds who tended to the needs of the flock. "It's a hospital version of the Nativity."

Harry beamed. "That's right. And there'll be a star mounted above the cab. You caught right on. Apply a little imagination, and it looks better now, doesn't it?"

He went off to see to some task, and Ross wandered to the other side of the truck, where he found Maggie seated astride a wooden bench with a supply of brightly colored paper in front of her. Miss Agatha and Miss Corinna were there too, comfortable in folding lawn chairs with lap quilts tucked around them, along with several other women, dressed in nursing uniforms underneath their heavy coats.

The women were talking about some child who needed a good spanking or, at the very least, grounding for a month. "Kenny's a little heathen," one of the nurses declared. "You know that saying about how preachers' kids are always the worst of the bunch? Well, *this* preacher's kid sure proves it."

A young girl appeared in front of him. "Hey, look at my eye. Nice shiner, isn't it?"

Maggie noticed him then, looked up, and smiled. She had a dozen different smiles—cool, warm, disinterested, polite, distant. This one was gentle and soft, and for an instant it made him ache inside. I think Maggie has found her place, Noelle had said. Looking at her now—at the peace, the contentment—he would have to agree that she had.

But why, he wondered with a great sense of injustice, couldn't her place have been with *him*?

With the tone of a child not used to being ignored, the girl again demanded his attention. "Well? What do you think?"

Slowly—reluctantly—he pulled his gaze from Maggie to agree with the kid. "It's a great shiner. How does the other guy look?"

"Ugly. And mean. I didn't get to hit him at all, not even once. He's just a big bully, and I'm gonna have Uncle Nathan arrest him."

Ross wasn't at all sure how to respond to that. Fortunately, she required no response as she settled on the blanket spread across the floor near the sisters.

"Pull up a seat, Ross, and help us for a while," Miss Agatha invited.

The only seat available was a few spare inches on the bench where Maggie sat. He opted to remain standing. "What are you doing?"

"Working on the float decorations," the old lady replied. "We each have our own little job. Maggie cuts the colored paper and passes it to us, and we make the . . . what do you suppose these are called?" She held one up for inspection. It consisted of a square of red paper wrapped around a wad of crumpled newspaper, with the excess red twisted tightly and the ends poufed out.

"I'm sure they must have a name," one nurse said, "but I don't know what it is."

"The technical term is 'thingie,'" the other nurse announced.

"Whatever." Miss Agatha dropped the paper into

the box on the floor in front of her. It was about half filled with red thingies. "We're each doing a color, but you could help Corinna with the white ones, since we'll need many more of those than the colors."

"Actually, Agatha, he came to claim one of our workers, not volunteer his own help," Miss Corinna chided. "We mustn't be pushy. Maggie has already agreed to come back tomorrow and help us, haven't you, dear?"

Without meeting Ross's gaze, she nodded. "Just let me know when you're coming, and I'll be ready."

The girl with the shiner said, "You have a car. I seen it at your house. Why don't you just drive yourself?"

"I don't drive, Josie," Maggie said.

Josie stared incredulously at Maggie. "You're all growed up and you don't drive?"

"I used to, but I haven't in a long time."

"So what do you do when you want to go some-wheres?"

"Ross takes me."

"But what about when he's not around?"

Good question, Ross thought. What would she do once he'd gone back to Buffalo?

Maggie's smile was strained. "Well, I haven't had that problem yet, Josie. I'll have to think about it."

What she would have to do was start driving again. Even if she never ventured out in bad weather, even if the car never budged from the driveway between November and March, she needed the security of knowing that if she *must* go somewhere, she could.

"You look tired, dear," Miss Corinna said, leaning forward to take the supply of colored paper. "Why don't you go on home? We'll call you tomorrow after-noon."

Ross thought Maggie might refuse, but she nodded. They said good-bye to everyone and left through a small side door. They were halfway to the car, when he broke the silence. "Nice people." At the look she gave him, he scowled. "Yes, I recognize nice people."

"I should think it's fairly easy for you. They're ex-actly the opposite of the people you're normally ex-posed to."

Irritated, he sarcastically asked, "Didn't you like *any* of our neighbors and friends in Buffalo?"

"Neighbors and acquaintances. Associates. *Not* friends." She pretended to think about it. "Umm . . . no. The women were all shallow, the men were all boring, and everyone was obsessed with money, power, and success."

He fingers clenched tightly. "We were all just alike, so you must have found me boring too."

"No," she said. "Most of the time I couldn't find you *at all*. I wasn't allowed to disturb you in your office at home. I had to go through about ten levels of secu-rity guards, receptionists, secretaries, and assistants to reach you at the office—when you were even *in* the office and not in London, Munich, or Tokyo, in which case you accepted phone calls only from Tom or Lynda but not from me. I rarely saw you, Ross. How could I possibly be bored by you?"

She kept walking, but he stood still, taking a few moments to mutter every curse he could think of. Then he went after her. She didn't acknowledge him at all even when he caught up with her. Not until he caught her arm. "Why are we fighting?"

She stared past him at the darkening sky, then blew her breath out heavily. It fogged in the air between them, then vanished as her faint, weary smile appeared. "Because that's what we do, Ross. Old habits. Sometimes I can't resist being sarcastic and you can't help being defensive. I'm sorry."

"So am I." He let her go, and slowly they began walking again. "But, you know, Maggie, you paint a bleaker picture of our life in Buffalo than it really was. We had friends. You enjoyed some of the things we did. You liked some of those people. Life wasn't really so bad."

"Yes, I did have some good times and I did rather like some of those people. But life *was* bad—at least for me." She stopped beside the car. When he opened the door, she turned to get in, then turned back. "All you ever wanted was to be rich and powerful, and you had that, Ross. Of course life wasn't so bad for you. But all *I* ever wanted was you and a family, and I didn't have either one. I had plenty of money to spend, an impressive mansion to live in, servants at my beck and call, exquisite jewels to wear with fabulous clothes, but all that is pretty cold comfort when you're as alone as I was."

What could he say to that? he wondered as she got into the car and closed the door. How could he deny the emptiness he'd created in her?

He couldn't. Whether his perception matched hers was meaningless. When talking about *her* feelings, *her* opinion was the only one that mattered. The only thing of his that mattered in this instance was his apology.

Once in the car, he started the engine and turned the heat to high, then faced her. "Maggie, I'm really sor—"

"I know you're sorry. You never meant for things to turn out like this. Neither did I. It just happened, and it's unfortunate and sad, but life is like that sometimes. All we can do is accept it and move on." She smiled sweetly. "And I can watch what I say. Just because we used to fight all the time doesn't mean we have to now. I'll behave, and you'll behave, and we'll make it through the next two months without a problem. Deal?"

He glanced from her face to the hand she offered, then back to her face. It wasn't the biggest deal he'd ever made, or the most profitable, and certainly not the most complicated—though he knew from experience that the two of them behaving together wasn't as simple as it sounded.

But it just might be the most important.

He shook her hand, then wrapped his fingers tightly around hers. "Deal."

THE BIG OLD BUILDING BEHIND THE HOS-pital took on something of a party air Wednesday night when the volunteers met to put the finishing touches on the parade float. With the McBride Inn float all ready to go, Holly was donating her evening— and a big pan of her cook's best lasagna—to the hospital's cause.

"Did you make this lasagna?" J. D. Grayson asked as he came back for a second helping.

"Bite your tongue. These hands don't cook."

"Too bad. If you did, I might have to marry you."

"And what makes you think I'd have you?"

He gave a great, exaggerated grimace of pain. "Ah, Holly, you wound a man's ego."

"So I've been told," she said with a scowl that instantly changed his expression from teasing to leering, overblown interest.

"Why don't you pull up a chair and tell Dr. J.D. all about it?"

"And why don't you—" Seeing the hospital administrator's elderly wife approach, she bit off the retort and gave the old woman a stilted smile instead.

Following his own advice, J.D. pulled up a chair and joined her at the serving tables. In addition to the lasagna, there was pot roast with savory vegetables provided by the Winchesters. Harry had donated a pot of beef stew from the café, and others had provided salads, desserts, and drinks.

"So . . . did you come tonight to work, serve food, or just to see me?" J.D. asked.

"Oh, just to see you, of course. I live for these occasional glimpses. They make the rest of my dreary, drudgery-filled life worthwhile."

"You're a hard-hearted woman, Holly."

She'd been told that before too, but she knew it wasn't true. If anything, she was too soft-hearted, though she tried her best to be otherwise.

"How do you like the float?"

She shifted her gaze to their reason for being there.

The truck, on loan from Lloyd's Garage and Salvage, looked about as festive as a flatbed could. The white cab was decorated with red, green, and gold streamers. Poster-board placards identifying the float as Bethlehem Memorial's and outlined in glittery gold garlands hung on each door, and virtually every hole in the yards of chicken wire was filled with a pouf of white or colored paper. "It looks great." Then she looked at the human components testing their places in the tableau. "And sexist."

"It's a nativity scene. What could possibly be sexist about that?"

"All three of the wise doctors are male. We have a female doctor, you know. Oh, but why use her? The lowly shepherds are female. Of course."

"The Bible did say wise *men*," J.D. said mildly. "And of course the shepherds are women. It's the women who do most of the nurturing and caring and watching over in this world. Other than that, what do you think?"

"It's okay."

He rolled his eyes. "Don't overwhelm me with praise."

"Every other female in town worships you, J.D. Do you need me at your feet too?"

"As I recall, the few times I had you there were quite enjoyable. Are you coming to the parade tomorrow?"

"I haven't missed one yet." Even when she'd gone away to college, she'd always cut classes the first week of December to come home for the parade and the following week for the Tour of Lights. They were two of the highlights of Christmas in Bethlehem.

"Want to have dinner with me before it starts?"

Batting her eyes at him, she answered in the breathy, my-aren't-you-wonderful tone that too many women took with him. "Why, Dr. J.D., it almost sounds as if you're asking me for a date."

He laughed. "No way. Been there, done that. I'm asking a friend to share a meal with me."

"Sure. I'd be happy to," she replied, and with a satisfied grin he left the table, taking his throwaway dishes with him. She watched him go.

They'd done the dating routine soon after he came to town last year. They'd shared a number of pleasant evenings—and an equal number of steamy nights—and had been fortunate enough to realize that they weren't exactly meant for each other. The friendship was fine, the sex was great, but the deeper connection was missing, and so they'd become strictly friends.

Luckily, she was able to remain friends with *all* the men she'd dated. Otherwise, Bethlehem would be a mighty uncomfortable place for her.

"Mind if I join you?"

She shifted her gaze from J.D. and focused on Maggie instead. With her hair mussed, her cheeks flushed, and her eyes bright and free of shadows, she looked as if she was having a ball. "Sit down," Holly invited. "Are you about floated out?"

Maggie grinned. "This is great. I've never done this sort of thing before."

"You mean you didn't build chicken-wire floats in the big city and stuff them with paper?"

"I can't say that I did. I never took part in this kind of gathering either. It's wonderful. I'm glad we found this place."

Other people shared her sentiment, and though Holly had been born and raised in Bethlehem, she thoroughly understood it. There was something special about her town. It was a community in the best sense of the word—the ideal place to grow up and grow old, the best place to come back to after you'd been away, the best place to stay.

"Except for four years in college, I've lived all my life here. Kids I went to school with dreamed of escaping, but not me. I want to stay here forever."

"Me too."

"It's just a shame there aren't a few more single men around," Holly said with a regretful shake of her head. "I do believe I've dated all of the current crop. I'm going to have to start importing them." And the first one she would bring in was Ross McKinney's tall, dark, and handsome lawyer. Who cared that he was as ruthless in his personal life as he was in business, that he wasn't looking for a commitment? She wasn't interested in marrying the guy. She'd just like to have a little fun with him.

"If you don't mind being accused of robbing the cradle, I've seen how these boys here look at you," Maggie teased.

"Robbing the cradle, robbing the grave." Holly shrugged. "I'll take 'em where I can find 'em."

"And then do you put them back where you got them when you're done?"

"Most of the time." She glanced around the

crowded room. "Lord, I've dated every man in here over the age of twenty-five and under the age of fifty except your husband."

"Ah, so you're a popular girl."

For the right reasons—she was smart, nice, and often entertaining—as well as the wrong ones, Holly acknowledged. Too many of her dates scored the first time out, which left them no goals to strive for. Complacency set in, followed by boredom, and soon they were just friends again, leaving her one more notch in her bedpost and one step further from believing that Mr. Right existed.

"That's me," she agreed in an airy voice. "Little Miss Popularity. Of course, you're no wallflower yourself."

Maggie smiled. "I never had the chance to be popular with the boys. I didn't date until college, and even then Ross was the only one I went out with. Once I met him . . ."

"Love at first sight?" It was a rhetorical question. Holly didn't believe in love at first sight. People confused hormones with heartstrings and usually suffered for it in the long run. Now, *lust* at first sight . . . That was a concept she could embrace—and had. It was safer than the other.

"Actually," Maggie said softly, "yes. I knew at the end of our first date that I was going to marry him."

The memory saddened her, and Holly couldn't help but wonder why. To say that their relationship pre-accident had been adversarial was a major understatement, but this time around they seemed about as good together as it got. Holly had assumed that Maggie's near death had softened them both—had reminded them that life was fragile and love should be nurtured.

Maybe instead it had convinced them that life was too precious to waste on someone who brought out the worst in you. Maybe they seemed good together now because they both knew that it was only for a limited time.

Holly wished it wouldn't be totally rude and insensitive to ask, but of course it would. Until she got to know Maggie better, until the other woman gave some indication that she wanted to confide in her, Holly would just have to wait. And wonder.

Injecting just the right amount of carelessness into her voice, she responded to Maggie's last comment. "You're a braver woman than me. If I met some guy and knew right away that I was going to marry him, I'd run the other way so hard and so fast that he wouldn't even get a good look at me."

"But if he was the *right* guy, he'd track you down. He would know you anyway, even without a good look."

Holly shuddered dramatically. "If I believed that for an instant, I'd be worried. But since the only signal I send out is the one that says 'For a good time, call . . .' I'm safe." And alone. But better that than with someone and wearing that exquisitely sad look Maggie had worn a few moments ago. Better a lonely heart than a broken one.

At least, that was what she told herself. Tonight, in a busy crowd filled with the holiday spirit, with friendship and caring and love, she even believed it.

Chapter Eight

BY SIX FORTY-FIVE THURSDAY EVE-
ning, downtown Bethlehem was packed. Main
Street was blocked off, concession stands had
been erected along the street to sell hot drinks
and snacks, and at least half the town was shuffling
along the sidewalks, window-shopping, greeting
neighbors, and simply passing time until the seven
o'clock parade began.

Bundled against the cold, Maggie stood beside a six-
foot-tall wooden soldier. Against Ross's wishes, they
had walked over from their house. He had wanted to
drive—had worried that the half dozen blocks each
way was more than she could handle—but she felt fine.
In fact, she was so excited, she felt she could walk the
parade route a time or two, stand in line in the square
to see Santa, and still have the energy for the walk back
home. She was having a ball.

A chilly wind whistled down the street, and Ross stepped closer, using the soldier and his body to provide her with a windbreak. She looked up at him over her shoulder and smiled appreciatively.

"When was the last time you went to a Christmas parade?" he asked.

She glanced across the street. People were starting to claim their spots, with curbside seats for the little ones, the adults gathering in groups or taking shelter from the wind in the recessed doorways of shops closing for the evening. She and Ross had been invited to join the Winchester sisters, given a place of honor at the square, and Holly and Dr. Grayson down by the hardware store. The Thomases had offered them the warmth of Alex's second-floor office that overlooked the street, at least until the parade started, but right there, alone with Ross in the wooden soldier's shelter, seemed the best place to her.

"My last Christmas parade," she repeated thoughtfully. "We went every year when I was little. It was always a big deal. We huddled together until it started, and then my father lifted me onto his shoulders so I could see everything. Afterward we went to my parents' favorite restaurant for a celebratory meal. It was the only time all year I was allowed to go with them to such an adult place, so it was really special."

"What happened after your father left?" Ross asked softly.

She gave him an uneasy smile. "Haven't I told you this all before?"

He shook his head, and she shrugged as she continued.

"When my father left, most of the family traditions disappeared too. We didn't have much of a Christmas the first year, or the second. The third year, though, Mom made an effort to revive the traditions. We made the Christmas cookies, put up the tree, decorated the house. We went to the parade and stood in our usual spot, and when it was over, we went to the same restaurant. It was an expensive place, and she'd saved two months for the meal. Right after we ordered, my father came in with his new wife and their baby daughter. They had just come from the parade. We left without eating, and my mother grew even more bitter, because *he* hadn't given up the family traditions at all. He'd just made himself a new family to celebrate them with." Her voice had grown softer with each sentence, until she was practically whispering. Giving a shake of her head, she returned to her normal tone. "We never went to the parade after that. What about you?"

"My mother loved parades. She watched them on TV on Thanksgiving and New Year's Day, and we went to every single one held in town. Just her and me. Without my father." He smiled faintly. "That was *our* family tradition."

"I'm going to bring my kids to this one every year," she said dreamily. "We'll volunteer to work on the float, and on the big night we'll walk over and have dinner at Harry's, and we'll sit on Santa's lap, and we'll have a wonderful time. Those will be *my* family traditions."

Traditions that she'd started this year with Ross, but next year he wouldn't be a part of them. His absence would surely diminish some of her pleasure. After all, her family was supposed to be his too, and her traditions his. She would miss him and would regret that he was gone. But regret was a part of living. Without suffering, how could a person fully appreciate joy?

But hadn't she done enough suffering in the last few years? Wasn't it her turn now for the joy?

Down the street the flash of red and blue lights drew her back from the melancholy direction her thoughts had taken. A police car was making a slow crawl along the center of the street, and its approach sent a buzz through the crowd. A few kids raced across the street well ahead of the car as everyone pressed forward, eager to see. Behind her, Ross moved closer too, and rested his gloved hand on her shoulder.

It was a casual touch. Under normal circumstances she probably wouldn't have noticed it. But their circumstances were so far from normal. The further apart they'd grown, the harder they'd found it to bridge the distance for simple contact. Even when they'd lain side by side in bed, they had rarely brushed one against the other unless it was the result of sleep and a body's natural inclination to seek out another body nearby.

She was hungry for normal casual touches. She'd had a lifetime's fill of the impersonal, purposeful kind—received daily from the nurses, the therapists, the doctors—but she desperately needed the other kind. She needed to be held. She needed to be kissed.

She needed to feel alive.

She was hardly aware of her own longing sigh, but Ross heard it and bent his head close. "What's wrong?"

"Nothing."

"Are you tired?"

Tired of living alone. Of living in limbo. Of waiting for that day when she would truly start living again. For several years now she'd been preparing for it. She'd gotten her degree, admitted that her marriage was over, found the courage to accept a future without Ross. The accident had been a major setback, but the worst of that was behind her. She wanted to reclaim her life—not in two months, not when others had decided that she could live on her own, but *now*.

Whether she was ready or not.

She looked up to assure Ross that she really was fine but found herself distracted by the flakes that were dotting his dark hair. "Snow," she murmured with pleasure as she tilted her head back to watch it fall. The flakes drifting down were the perfect touch for the parade—not too heavy, not too wet, just delicate crystals that landed, shimmered, then dissolved.

With an indulgent smile Ross turned her back toward the street. "Pay attention. You can watch the snow all winter long, but right now the parade's passing you by."

After the police car, followed by jalopies carrying the mayor, the state senator, and the school superintendent, the real parade started. What the participants lacked in professionalism, they made up for with enthusiasm. The Scouts might have marched in straighter lines, but they couldn't have had more fun. The dance school's banner could have been more neatly painted, but it made no difference to the students tapping their way down the street in costumes of the season.

"Hey, Miss Maggie." Josie Dalton left her ragged

line and danced in place in front of them. Her brown paper outfit covered her from chin to ankle, and her bright yellow headpiece swayed in the breeze. "Look. I'm a far—far— A candle in a paper bag. I was s'posed to be a tree"—she rolled her blue eyes comically—"but we got lots of trees, and this is neater anyway."

"You look wonderful, Josie," Maggie said with a laugh. "You're the best dancing farolito I've ever seen."

The girl grinned, then realized she'd been left behind. Calling good-bye, she raced back to her place between two trees, then resumed her less-than-rhythmic tap dance.

The first float was a small version of the McBride Inn, complete with pond and woods and a mechanical horse-drawn carriage that clip-clopped up the lane and back again. It had been built by Holly's grandfather, Maggie knew, and had been an entry in the parade for the last forty years.

Tradition.

There were floats for every church and many of the businesses. Firefighters rode on an antique engine, and civic club members distributed candy through the crowd. The hospital float brought up the rear, followed only by the high school band and Santa, and looked *just* the tiniest bit better than the rest. Not that she was prejudiced, of course.

After Santa, who bore a strong resemblance to Mitch Walker, passed, the crowds began breaking up. Those with young children headed for the square, where Santa would hold court, and the rest began to make their slow way home.

Maggie closed her eyes and lifted her face to the

snow. She was chilled all the way through, and she'd lost contact with her toes a long time before, but she couldn't remember ever feeling warmer or happier or more perfectly at home. She would remember this night—and this feeling—forever.

When she finally opened her eyes, Ross was watching her, his expression impossible to read. He might not understand how a simple parade could make her feel so much, but he'd understood *something*. He hadn't spoken or taken her arm, hadn't urged her to head home and bring this long, cold evening to an end.

After one moment passed, then two more, he finally asked, "Are you ready?"

When she nodded, he took her arm, steadying her as she stepped off the curb. Their pace was leisurely until they reached Hawthorne and the crowd thinned. After two blocks they had the sidewalk to themselves.

"What are you thinking?" she asked, expecting some comment about work. Since she'd persuaded him to try working at least a little, he'd spent much of his time in the office—most of Monday and all of Tuesday, Wednesday, and that day. There were times when she'd regretted her encouragement, but most of the time she was fine alone. It was a good time for daydreaming.

"That you're going to have some great traditions, like the parade."

"You could come back for it if you wanted. I don't have exclusive rights."

"It wouldn't be the same. Next year you'll be with someone else."

He said the words so easily, but they struck her as so impossible. *Next year you'll be with someone else.* How could she be, when she'd spent nearly half her life with *him*? How could she ever feel for someone else all the things she'd felt for him? How could any other man ever take his place in her life, in her heart?

Right that moment she couldn't imagine being married to anyone but Ross, loving anyone but Ross, and the knowledge sent a rush of panic through her. Now, because of the parade, she was feeling incredibly sentimental, but what if it were true two months, six months, or a year from then? What if all her grand hopes were simply dreams that she couldn't make come true? After all, she'd tried with Ross and failed. What if she kept failing?

She had to believe that she wouldn't, had to believe that there was a future out there better than the past she was leaving behind. After all, this was Bethlehem, a place for miracles. Her miracle wouldn't include Ross, but it would include *someone*.

Please, God, it would.

The glow from their house caught her attention the instant she stepped onto their block. Yesterday the workers she'd hired had spent much of the afternoon putting up lights. The strong, straight lines of the house lent themselves well to the white bulbs that stretched from one end to the other and from top to bottom. The farolitos along the porte cochere roof were electric, but the real thing, currently unlit, lined the sidewalk and the porch steps.

"I'll make you a deal," she said as they turned onto their sidewalk. "You fix dinner, and I'll light the candles."

Shaking his head, he repeated her offer. "*You* fix dinner, and *I'll* light the candles."

"No fair. You got the fun part." Though she knew from last night's experience that replacing and lighting three dozen votives in the cold wasn't entirely fun. She'd gone through an entire small tree's worth of fireplace matches, and a nagging ache in her back had kicked in somewhere around the tenth candle. Maybe next year she could turn the lighting job over to Josie—supervised, of course—who thought candles in paper sacks were pretty neat.

"But all right," she continued. "I'll fix dinner. But I won't be responsible for the results."

"And I won't be responsible if I set the yard on fire," he retorted, unlocking the door.

"You don't know how to *not* be responsible," she said with a laugh. "It's one of the things I always admired about you."

"With the others being . . . ?"

"Fishing for compliments? Or just trying to delay going back out into the cold?"

"All right. I'll go out now, and we'll talk compliments later." He gathered the candles and matches started his cold task. Though traditionally farolitos were lit for only nine nights, Maggie chose to ignore that part of the tradition. She liked the lights, and Josie did too, and that was reason enough to bend tradition.

Yesterday morning he'd come down to breakfast to find her sitting on the kitchen floor surrounded by the paper lunch bags. She'd been completely absorbed by the job of opening each bag, then folding over the top edge an inch or two. When she'd lined up the finished products, he hadn't been surprised to see that the folds were virtually identical on all thirty-six. When her difficulty concentrating forced her to focus her attention so narrowly, the results could be amazing.

From each bag he removed a blob of melted wax, leveled the sand, and positioned a new candle. He burned himself only a time or two and considered it an accomplishment when he finished that he hadn't set a single bag on fire.

For a moment he stood on the sidewalk out front and simply looked at the scene while his mind wandered back downtown. He hadn't expected more than slight entertainment that evening—hell, if he wanted to see a parade, he could command plum seats at the Macy's Thanksgiving Day or the Tournament of Roses parade—but he'd enjoyed this one. Somehow, homemade floats, pint-size gymnasts, and the midwinter queen and her court freezing in formal gowns and convertibles held more charm than the professional industry big parades had become. Parents and grandparents had taken pride in watching their kids, and everyone on the sidelines had gotten a kick out of knowing everyone in the parade. It had been fun.

And it'd been a hell of a long time since he'd thought that about anything.

A stiff wind blew snow against his face, but he was so cold that he barely felt it. He didn't move to go in though. Something—some sudden emptiness, some ache—held him where he was, staring at the farolitos, the lights, the house. The *home*.

Though the bags protected the candles, the flames flickered slightly, casting their light first to one side, then to the other. For the first time, he understood Maggie's desire for the farolitos. In the quiet dark night, with snow falling and the sounds of carols fresh in his memory, the bags became more than just paper, sand, and wax. They were bright, golden beacons, welcoming, lighting the way home.

But it was Maggie's home, not his. He missed the city, missed all the things she had wanted to escape. She belonged here—should have spent the first thirty-five years of her life here, would spend the rest of it here—but *he* didn't. He didn't know how to fit into this good, decent place filled with good, honorable people. He didn't know how to be one of them—didn't know if he would if he could.

He felt lost in Bethlehem.

For a man used to being in total control, lost was not a pleasant way to feel.

Feeling colder than he ever had—and not entirely due to the temperature, he suspected—he picked up the box and went inside. Maggie was standing beside the island, warming her hands on a pottery mug while watching hamburger patties sizzle on the cooktop grill. Her cheeks were still red from the cold, her hair mussed from the cap she'd worn. She'd kicked off her shoes and stood on a thick nubby rug, her right foot resting atop her left as if one might warm the other. She looked . . .

He'd meant to finish the sentence in a meaningless, stating-the-obvious sort of way. Beautiful. Adorable. The word that came to mind, though, was anything but meaningless.

Appealing.

He didn't *want* to find her appealing. He didn't want to get that personal. *Beautiful* was impersonal. People who simply saw her on the street and didn't know the first thing about her found her beautiful. But appealing . . . That implied some emotional connection—desire, if nothing else. Wanting.

He couldn't afford to want her.

"Want some cocoa?" she asked when she became aware of him standing there. Without waiting for a reply, she slid a mug to the opposite side of the island, then flipped the burgers and added a slice of cheese to each. On the griddle, thick slices of buttered bread were browning, and a plate on the counter held onion slices and homemade pickles. "We're having burgers and soup."

He stood there, too cold but warming quickly. The heat came from the inside, pumping with his blood, raising his temperature in seconds from frigid to feverish. It made his hands unsteady and thickened his voice when he finally thought to speak. "What—what kind of soup?"

"Whatever kind you want." With a flourish, she opened a cabinet door to display a full shelf of canned soups.

He forced himself to look at them, but the names made no sense when panic had scrambled his brain. It was perfectly natural, he told himself. They'd been married for sixteen years. He knew her intimately, was as familiar with her body as with his own. He'd been alone a long time. Seeing her there, looking so damn—yes, appealing, on a night when he was already

feeling a little lost . . . Hell, he'd worry if he *didn't*
feel something.

It didn't mean a thing.

"How about chicken noodle?"

He nodded blankly, then picked up the cocoa. He
took a long drink, then grimaced and blurted out before he could stop himself, "Jeez, what did you put in
here?"

She turned, an open can of soup in hand, and gave
him a worried look. "Just the usual—cocoa, sugar,
milk, and a few drops of vanilla. I thought it tasted . . .
Oh." Color crept into her face. "We were so cold that I
thought . . . Well, I added a little rum. I found it in
the cabinet. I must have made rum cake last year—I do
every Christmas—and I thought . . . So I put a tiny
bit in mine. I haven't had any alcohol for a year, and I
never could hold it very well. But since you do drink
and you were outside longer . . . Is it too much?"

He drew a deep breath as he set the mug down.
"Not if you have another quart or so of cocoa to di-
lute it."

"No. Sorry." Her contrition turned to dismay as
they both became aware of the smoke drifting up from
the grill. She removed the burgers, only slightly
charred, to a plate, then took the toast, also charred,
from the griddle. Morosely, she scraped the toast, assembled the burgers, and slid a plate to him. "Dinner."

"Come sit down." Catching her hand, he drew her
around the island and didn't let go until she was seated
on a stool. Then he fixed their drinks while the soup
heated in the microwave. Once the noodles were
dished up and he'd located silverware and napkins, he

turned back to find her, head bent, hands over face, shoulders shaking.

No crying, he silently pleaded as the panic returned. He'd never had to deal with tears from her, not in all those long months in the hospital, not ever. God help him, he wasn't up to learning how tonight.

But whether he was up to it didn't matter. The fact was, she was distressed and he had to do something about it.

He moved a few cautious steps closer. "Maggie?"

She didn't lift her head, try to compose herself, or silence the soft, strangled sounds muffled by her hands.

"Maggie, it's okay. The meat's just a little well done. You know, even in the best burger joints now, that's required by law in most states."

Making a choking sound, she finally looked up. Her eyes were damp, all right, but not because she was sobbing over another bad meal. She was laughing.

"You find this funny." He felt thickheaded, as if he didn't have a clue.

She wiped her eyes and gave a great sigh. "Oh, Ross, if I don't laugh, I'll have to cry, and I've cried enough tears in my life."

He didn't want to know—honest, he didn't—but the question slipped out anyway. "When?"

In an instant, she became utterly serious. "Nights when you were in the office. Weeks when you were out of town. Years when you were out of reach. A woman can't watch her husband create a life for himself with no room for her without shedding a few tears."

"I—I'm sorry. I didn't know . . ."

"Maybe not about the tears, but you knew you were moving me out of your life. You just didn't care." She spoke matter-of-factly, as if she had long ago accepted that fact. Before the acceptance, though, there must have been heartache and disillusionment, because she, at least, had tried to make things work.

That was more than he could say for himself.

She tried her burger and shrugged. "It's not too bad. I've had worse. I've *cooked* worse." After another bite she said, "All those dinner parties I planned for you . . . What was wrong with them?"

"Nothing. The food was great. You were always great. They were fine."

"Then why did you take them away from me? Why did you suddenly insist on having them catered?"

Sliding onto the stool beside her, he thought back to when he'd made that decision. He tried to remember what her response was. Had she been resistant, or had she quietly, meekly, gone along? Had she been grateful to be freed of so much responsibility, or had she felt rejected?

That last was easy enough to answer. *Why did you take them away?* wasn't the question of a grateful woman.

"It was a status thing," he said at last. "A way of subtly pointing out that we could afford such extravagances." Seeking to ease his own discomfort, he said, "You never enjoyed those parties anyway—not the hours of planning or the days of shopping or even the cooking. What did it matter to you if someone else did it?"

"Because it was one less way you needed me. You're

right. I didn't particularly enjoy the parties. But I liked doing them for you. I liked feeling that I had some-place in your life besides bed." Suddenly she grinned. "But I have to admit, whatever problems were building between us, the sex was still great. I was always grace—grateful—that you never replaced me there. But you weren't that type. All those times you were gone, all that distance between us, I always knew that there would never be another woman. That counted for a lot."

The chill that hit Ross was guilt laced with shame. It made his lungs tight and filled his ears with a rushing that distorted her words as she continued to talk. She sounded so confident, so certain that she could trust him at least on that score, but she was wrong. Her gratitude was misplaced, because for one brief, un-forgivable time, he'd been exactly that type. He had betrayed her and himself for a few hours' pleasure, and in the process he had almost destroyed her.

Now he was betraying her again, because even as she hoped and prayed for her missing memories to return, he prayed that she would never remember.

God forgive him.

Because Maggie wouldn't.

FOR CHRISTMAS TREES, WHETHER YOU cut your own or chose from the display near the road, Bill Grovenor's farm was the place most of Beth-lehem went. For live trees, though, with the root ball intact and ready for post-holiday planting, Melissa's Garden was the only source. Maggie was determined to have just such a tree to mark the momentous occasion of her first Christmas in Bethlehem. Last year didn't count, after all, since she'd been whisked away only minutes after midnight on Christmas Day and didn't remember anything prior to that.

"My selection of trees is a little on the thin side," Melissa said apologetically as she led the way through the nursery to a secured area outside. "Most of my customers special-order, and I keep only a few extras on hand. Here they are."

The trees she indicated ranged in size from four feet to ten and in color from the blue-green hue of a blue spruce to rich green. Maggie admired the littlest tree even as she thought about all the years of growth it would require to be as impressive as the others. But what did a few years matter? She would be there.

Once she turned her attention to the other trees, it took only a moment to make her choice. It was the biggest tree there and was as full at the bottom as it was tall. The branches were strong enough to support the most treasured of her ornaments, the needles weren't prickly, and its scent—with a hint of orange—was heavenly.

Brushing her hand over it, she glanced at Ross. "This one?"

He nodded—not exactly the response she was looking for. She wanted him to agree, of course—she could love this tree for its fragrance even if it wasn't perfect—but would it have hurt him to at least walk around it one time to check its shape? Would it hurt him to show a passing interest?

He had promised her companionship, she reminded

herself. Not interest. She should accept what she was getting and be grateful, because he wasn't going to offer more.

And she *was* grateful. These nearly two weeks in Bethlehem would have been wonderful without his companionship, but not quite as much. She owed him a lot for this gift of his time.

But it was only natural to want more, and before long she would have it. Just not with him.

Shifting away from the thought, she flashed a smile at Melissa. "We'll take this one. Can we get it delivered?"

"No problem. The guys are going out with a delivery today. They can bring it by sometime this afternoon." Melissa pulled a tag and pen from the apron underneath her coat and handed it to Maggie. "Just write your name and address on there, and I'll add it to the delivery order."

Maggie braced the paper on her knee to write their name, then looked at Ross again. "I don't know our address."

He opened his mouth, closed it, then shrugged. "I don't either."

When they both turned to Melissa, the other woman laughed. "Don't ask me. I certainly don't know. Just put 'the brick house on the corner of Hawthorne and Fourth.' These guys have lived here all their lives. They'll find it."

Once the tagging process was finished, they returned to the nursery and the cash register near the door. "Tell me, Maggie," Melissa said as she figured the sale. "Do you sing?"

Maggie burst into laughter. "Only to myself. You must be working to start—" She gave an exasperated shake of her head. "Starting to work on the church pageant."

"Yes, and as usual, I'm in need of a little divine intervention. I've got backstage help coming out my ears. The speaking roles were taken the first day. Even singers aren't hard to find. It's just the soloists I have to beg for." She looked measuringly at Ross. "Do *you* sing?"

He looked as startled as if she'd asked him to unbind his wings and fly away. "Sing?" he repeated blankly. "Out loud? In front of people?"

"I'll take that as a definite no."

Maggie was amused by his response. Actually, his voice was as pleasant in song as it was in speech—a baritone, nice and rich. Once upon a time, neither of them had thought twice about singing along with the radio or going a cappella in the shower. Now he listened mostly to songs without words, and as for the shower . . . It'd been a long time since they'd shared a bathroom. She didn't have a clue.

Melissa told Ross the total, and he wrote her a check. "I hope you enjoy your tree," she said. Then, before they could turn from the counter, she asked, "Maggie, how about lunch at the inn Monday?"

"I'd like that."

"Do you want to meet there, or should I pick you up?"

Maggie glanced out the door at the Mercedes in the parking lot. If she wanted, she could have it for her own, Ross had told her the day he'd picked her up at the rehab center, but she hadn't given it any thought. She hadn't felt the slightest temptation to reacquaint herself with the pleasures of driving. Even Josie Dalton's incredulity hadn't prompted her to consider it.

But a simple lunch invitation might.

"I—I'll get there," she said carelessly.

"Around noon?"

"That sounds fine." With a wave she walked out the door Ross was holding for her.

"You know, you drove tens of thousands of miles without ever having even a minor fender-bender," he commented as they approached the car.

"And I drove less than five miles from home and almost killed myself."

"The weather was bad. The road was icy. It could have happened to anyone."

"But it happened to *me*."

He stopped behind the car and held out his hand. The keys dangled from their ring, swaying hypnotically. "The keys to independence," he said, then the teasing disappeared. "You've got to give it a try sometime, Maggie. Why not today?"

"There's snow on the ground."

"On the ground. Not on the streets."

She looked at the keys again and thought about taking them, about walking around to the driver's side, sliding behind the wheel, starting the engine. She thought about driving through the streets of Bethlehem as she'd done last Christmas Eve, and then about rolling violently down the mountainside. The muscles in her stomach clenched, and an ache began to throb behind her eyes.

Without saying a word she walked to the passenger side and waited for him to unlock the door.

When he joined her in the car, the look he gave her was sympathetic. "It's okay, Maggie. You've got plenty of time."

She turned away to stare out the side window. What had she thought that Christmas Eve night when the truck began its skid? Had she worried about the impending damage to her vehicle? Had she realized in those first few seconds that the damage to *her* could be far more extensive? Had she suspected that she might not survive, or had unconsciousness come too quickly for such morbid thoughts?

"You don't have to drive at all. We can make arrangements—"

"Do you know where it happened?"

Her question startled him into silence. He delayed answering by starting the engine, adjusting the heat, locking the doors. Finally he said, "Yes, I do."

"Show me."

Again he delayed before responding. "I don't think that's a good idea."

"I didn't ask for your opinion, did I?" She regretted her sharp tone immediately when she saw the way his mouth tightened, but she couldn't bring herself to apologize. The other was more important. "I want to see it."

"There's nothing to see, Maggie. Just the highway and rocks and trees."

"I want to see."

For a while she thought he would refuse. After all, what could she do about it? Go without him? Of the two of them, only he knew the location. Only he had the courage to drive. Then, angrily, he relented, shifted into gear, and left the parking lot.

The anger remained between them through town and up the mountain. It guided his movements when suddenly he pulled to the side of the road where the shoulder was wider and shut off the engine. It colored his voice when he finally spoke. "This is the place. I remember the vehicles parked here and on that road."

He gestured, and she looked at the lane on her right. It extended twenty feet off the roadway, then ended in a pile of dirt.

"There's a cabin down there." Again he gestured, this time to the opposite side. "You can't see it from here, but the man who lives there heard the crash. He investigated and called it in. The first deputy on the scene called the sheriff, who came to the house to notify me. We could see all the emergency lights from down below. There were sheriffs' cars, wreckers, an ambulance, a fire truck, and the rescue truck. When we got here, they were just bringing you up. There were so many people working on you at once that I couldn't see a thing."

She tried to re-create the scene in her mind—a cold, snowy night. Red, blue, and amber lights casting colored shadows on the snow. A frantic rescue effort. A victim more dead than alive.

"I could see what was left of the truck in the ravine, and I thought there was no way on earth you could have survived."

His voice was so flat, so dark, it made Maggie shiver. "It would have been easier for you if I hadn't."

His head jerked around, and his eyes made contact with hers. He looked shocked. Stricken. "How can you say that? How can you even *think* that? My God, Maggie . . ."

She felt guilty even as she gave a careless shrug. "My medical care over the last year must have come to more than a million dollars. Your life has been in limbo, now more than ever. You're facing a divorce and giving up some of that fortune you've worked so hard for. If I had died, other than giving the public appearance of mourning, you would have been free to live exactly the way you wanted. It would have been much more convenient for you."

He stared at her a moment longer, then turned away so that she barely caught his whispered words. "Damn you."

The headache that had started back at the nursery worsened. She ignored it, and the edginess that rippled through her, and unfastened her seat belt. Her fingers didn't want to work right, but finally she managed to free herself and left the car.

It was colder up there than it was in the valley. The wind blew harder, whipping her hair around her face. If she had any sense, she would get back in the car, apologize to Ross, and ask him to take her home. But then she would just have to come back some other time—she knew that—so she might as well get it over with then.

There was no traffic in sight in either direction. Shoving her hands into her pockets, she crossed the road to stand on the narrow shoulder on the opposite side. There were a dozen places along the road where a person could drive off, fall no more than twenty feet, and walk away with a few bruises or less. But not her. No, *she'd* had the misfortune to fall into a deep, steep ravine.

Ross had been right. There was nothing to see but the road, rocks, and trees. Some of the rocks were scarred. So were some of the trees, with great gashes ripped across their trunks. Smaller trees lay uprooted, and the earth showed where one large boulder had been forcibly moved a half dozen feet from its original resting place.

So this was it. This was the place where she had almost lost her life, where instead she'd been given a second chance.

She drew a deep breath of frigid mountain air, held it a moment, blew it out again. Turning, she saw Ross standing beside the car and took a step, then went down on one knee as the world spun around her. He called her name, then his legs—three of them?—appeared in front of her an instant before he lifted her to her feet. Without thought she leaned against him, resting her head on his shoulder. Closing her eyes, she breathed deeply of clean air, pine, and masculine cologne—slow, measured breaths intended to ease the pain in her head and the unsteadiness that had claimed her body.

The breathing would work, if only he'd quit trying to push her away, to hold her back far enough that he could see, and stop talking. "Maggie, what's wrong? Are you okay? What's—"

Blindly she raised one hand to his mouth. "Shhh. Give me a minute."

He fell silent and did exactly what she needed— simply held her. His leather jacket was cold beneath her cheek, his body solid. For years simply being held by him had been one of her greatest pleasures. She'd always felt so safe in his arms, so protected, so loved.

Today two out of three wasn't bad.

It was just unbearably sad.

With one last breath she lifted her head, straightened her shoulders, and gently pulled free of his embrace. He let her step back, but he held tightly to her arms. "I'm okay. I just got a little dizzy. The atti—altitude, you know."

He looked as if he didn't believe her, and he was right not to. The difference in altitude there near the top of the mountain and down below in the valley wasn't substantial enough to cause dizziness, but it was a nice pretense to blame one of her problems on something that affected a lot of people rather than on her damaged brain.

When he continued to stare at her with such intense concern, she forced another smile. "I'm all right, Ross, honestly. I just have a headache, and sometimes that brings on a dizzy spell. But I'm fine now. I'd just like to go home."

He still didn't look convinced, but he escorted her to the car and hovered there while she settled in the seat. Once he joined her, she laid her head back and closed her eyes. She didn't open them again until they reached the house.

He took her upstairs to her room. "Where are the pain pills Dr. Allen gave you?" he asked.

"I'll get them. I'm headed to the bathroom anyway." She left him lowering the blinds and closed the bathroom door behind her. The pills were in a small bottle in the linen closet, secreted behind a pile of towels. She had no intention of taking them. Only one would put her out for the afternoon and leave her feeling groggy and disoriented for the rest of the evening. She didn't want that, not when she had a Christmas tree to decorate. Just a few aspirin and a few hours sleep, and she would be fine.

When she returned to her room, he'd turned down the covers and was waiting with a scowl. "We shouldn't have gone up there."

"Yes, we should have. I needed to see it." She kicked off her shoes, stripped off her jeans. In the dimly lit room, wearing a sweater that came to mid-thigh and suffering a headache that made her feel weak, she felt neither modest nor self-conscious.

As she settled in bed, he started to leave. She spoke before he got too far. "Ross? I never, ever believed that you wanted me to die."

His expression when he turned back was wary. "Then why did you say that?"

"I said it would have been *easier* for you. Not that it was what you wanted."

He came to stand at the end of the bed, his hands gripping the curved wood so tightly that his knuckles turned white. "We had an argument that night. You left the house because of me. You were on that road in that weather because of me. Do you understand, Maggie? You almost died *because of me*." His voice rose, sharpened, and he made an obvious effort to control it. "There would have been nothing easy about that. It would have destroyed me."

With that, he walked away, leaving her alone.

Chapter Nine

ONCE UPON A TIME, DECORATING THE Christmas tree had been a special event in the McKinney home, Ross mused as he studied the tree three teenage boys had delivered two hours before. Back then, he and Maggie had ignored the phone and any unexpected guests who might drop by. They'd shut off the television, put carols on the stereo, and spent the entire evening getting all the lights and all the ornaments just right. Dinner was simple and intimate—sandwiches, chips, something freshly baked for dessert—capped off with Irish coffee or mulled cider.

And when they'd finished, when the food was gone and the decorations were hung, they'd turned off the lights to admire their handiwork. Inevitably one of them had made a move—a touch, a kiss. One particularly memorable year Maggie had made a minute adjustment to their first-Christmas-together ornament, then simply, boldly, erotically, removed her clothes before approaching him, and he—

Scowling, he shoved the memory away. All that was past. It had no bearing on the present. Though they would work together that night—there was no way he was letting her get on a ladder after what had happened today—it wouldn't be the same. There would be little laughter if any, and little sense of sharing. No intimate dinner, no freshly baked dessert, no Irish coffee.

And certainly no making love. No laying Maggie down naked on that handloomed rug in front of the tree. No sliding inside her the way he'd done hundreds of times before. No losing himself there the way he had every one of those hundreds of times.

His jaw tightened—and so did his body. He *didn't* want her. It was just the power of old memories and the curse of having gone a very long time without sex. It didn't matter that she was beautiful, that they'd been married a long time and were still married. He didn't want her. Couldn't have her.

Couldn't.

He moved toward the tree. The boys had set it up in the same place last year's tree had stood, in front of the large windows that looked out on the street. It filled the space, stretching toward the ceiling and overwhelming the room with its fragrance. He hoped Maggie wanted it there, because there was no way the two of them alone would be able to move it.

She'd slept soundly all afternoon. Neither the doorbell nor the three boys had disturbed her. He'd checked as soon as they were gone, and she was still curled on her side, breathing deeply. For a longer time than he could justify, he'd stood beside the bed and watched her. He had deliberately blanked his mind—had refused to think, to feel—and had simply stood there while she slept, and in spite of his best intentions, he'd felt something anyway. Hurt. Lost. Afraid.

The hell of it was, he wasn't sure what he was afraid of. The marriage ending? He was prepared for that, had been for a long time. Maggie no longer being a part of his life? She had been only a very small part for several years. The truth coming out?

His smile was thin, its bitter mockery directed at himself. He'd been afraid of that from the beginning. From the first moment he'd realized that he was actually going to bed with a woman other than Maggie, he'd feared the truth, the pain, the anger. He had hoped desperately that she would never find out, but in the end, after all the lies and careful subterfuge, he had been the one to reveal his own sins. One careless act, and Maggie had known everything. That night she had paid the price.

Then he had hoped she would never know. Now he prayed that she would never remember. Maybe it was stupid—certainly it was selfish—but some small, vain part of him liked knowing that she thought him a better man than he was. It meant something that after all they'd gone through, she still believed in him. He didn't want to destroy her faith a second time, didn't want to see the scorn and revulsion once again darken her eyes, to know he'd hurt her once more.

Please, God.

With a sigh he turned away from the tree. There

was a ladder in the utility room and strings of tiny colored lights in the library. The least he could do while waiting for Maggie to wake up was get the tree ready for her.

He worked in silence, concentrating on nothing more than his task. After positioning the final light—number eight hundred by his count—he stepped back to look.

"It's beautiful."

He turned to face Maggie standing in the doorway. Looking at her, a person would never guess that there'd been anything wrong with her a few short hours earlier. She looked well rested, lovely, and her eyes were bright with anticipation. That didn't change when he spoke two chiding words. "The stairs."

"I held on to the banister very tightly." She came to stand beside him. "Thank you for doing my least favorite part of the decorating. Isn't it gorgeous?"

He murmured in agreement, but he wasn't looking at the tree. He didn't want her, he reminded himself as he felt the first stirrings of desire. So she was standing only inches away looking lovely and warm and touchable. So the fragrance she wore—had always worn— was so closely associated with their lovemaking that a mere whiff of it had long been enough to arouse him. All he really wanted was sex, preferably with any woman in the world *except* her. He wanted her happy and healthy and whole, but that was the extent of it. Under the circumstances, anything more would be disastrous.

After a moment she turned her attention from the tree to him. "You're so quiet. Are you still angry?"

"No. Just thinking. Remembering."

She didn't ask, Remembering what? No doubt she could guess. Her long-term recall was excellent. She hadn't forgotten all the times they'd done this ritual together, all the nights they'd made love in the glow of the Christmas lights. She remembered every little intimacy that had been so much a part of them—that they had lost, one by one, until they'd lost themselves.

"Shall we get started?" She moved to the stereo in the corner cabinet, checked, and, not surprisingly, found Christmas CDs already in the changer. With the press of a button the solemn notes of "Ave Maria" filled the room.

Ross's jaw tightened. "I'll get the ornaments from the kitchen."

"Ave Maria" had been playing when the doorbell rang nearly a year ago. He'd stood beside the tree—had stood there more than an hour, looking out the window, watching the snow fill in the tire tracks that had marked her leaving. He still held the glass he'd been holding when she walked out, and the music she'd started had played on, though he heard none of it.

Not until the doorbell chimed. He hadn't had even an instant's false hope that it was Maggie, over her anger enough to return until the weather cleared, because he'd watched the unfamiliar truck pull into the driveway and the stranger climb the steps. The man introduced himself as Sheriff Ingles, and Ross had known. That was when the soaring organ and the Latin verse of the hymn had registered.

It had seemed fitting that he'd learned his wife was dying with such a reverent score in the background.

He made a dozen trips between the kitchen and living room. By the time he'd reached the last box of decorations, the song had ended, and another had begun, this one lighthearted and silly. Inwardly he sighed with relief.

"What do you want to do about Christmas?" Maggie asked as she slid thin wire hooks into the loops of brightly colored glass balls.

"Do?"

"Well, we'll spend it here, obviously. Would you like to invite anyone? Maybe Tom or Lynda?"

He accepted the balls she handed him and hung them one at a time on the tree. "You're actually volunteering to have Tom Flynn and Lynda Barone in your house on Christmas Day?"

She smiled. "Goodwill to man and all that. My biggest problem with Tom was always that he came between us and you let him. Now that there's no 'us' to come between, I can be gracious and overlook the fact that he's a cold-blooded reptile."

Some part of that little speech settled uncomfortably on Ross. Was it the implied criticism of him for not keeping their marriage safe from Tom? The unfair insult of the man who was the closest he'd ever come to a best friend? Or the *no "us"* part?

He didn't want to know.

"And what was your problem with Lynda?" he asked instead.

She answered as pleasantly as if she were discussing the weather with one of the Winchester sisters. "Beyond the fact that she's a bitch? Nothing."

"She's not—" He broke off when she sent a sharp warning look his way.

"It wasn't that she saw more of you than I did. Or that she knew more about you than I did. It wasn't even that you used her to keep me away. I disliked her because she *enjoyed* all that. She took pleasure in the fact that she was more a part of your life than I was. She liked telling me that you didn't have time for me."

He took another handful of ornaments from her. "You never told me."

"And what would you have done? Fired her?" She gave a skeptical shake of her head. "I never would have forced you to choose between her and me, because I was afraid of what your decision would be. After all, a good wife is a lot easier to find than a good assistant."

He stared at her. "You're kidding, right?"

She picked up a handmade Santa, its white clay beard ending in a point of curlicues, and looped its red ribbon over a sturdy branch. When she turned, the look she gave him was full of challenge. "What *would* you have done? If I'd told you what I just did, would you have fired her? Would you have said you'd take care of it, then forget it? Or would you tell me that she was too valuable to lose and I should learn to deal with it?"

"I would like to say that I would have fired her, but it's not true. She *is* too valuable to lose. Probably the best I would have done was talk to her—warn her to treat you appropriately."

"She treated me the way she saw you treat me. She probably thought that *was* appropriate."

"Well, hell, Maggie, this is fun," he said. "Which of my other failings would you like to discuss tonight?"

She didn't apologize, didn't try to defend her comments. Instead, she moved around the tree, where he couldn't see her. "I was only answering the question *you* asked," she pointed out mildly.

"Pardon me for not suspecting that your answer to 'Why did you dislike Lynda?' had nothing to do with Lynda and everything to do with me."

"Of course it had everything to do with you. If not for you, I wouldn't know she existed. She's nothing to me except in the context of you." The branches between them shifted, and her face became visible in the small space. "We can discuss *my* failings if you'd prefer."

"What failings?" he asked with a scowl.

She smiled sunnily. "Thanks. I couldn't think of any either."

As the branch snapped back into place, he gritted his teeth, then finally gave in to the faint smile that she'd meant to coax from him.

"I know you're smiling," she said from the back side of the tree. "You can't resist, because I'm being charming."

"*This* is charming?" he asked dryly.

"I know. It's been so long that you've forgotten what it's like—and I'm a little rusty at it, to say the least. There was no need for charm at the rehab center. That was the staff's job. The patients were expected to be irritable, frustrated, and depressed."

"I never saw you irritable or depressed."

"I was. Especially in the beginning, when the therapists would say 'Just try one more time' after I had already tried—and failed—a hundred times. Or when they forced me to work when the only thing I wanted to do was curl up in a corner and die. There were times when I was irritable enough to do someone physical harm. I just didn't have the bodily control to do it. I couldn't even tell them to go to hell."

She spoke of her helplessness so matter-of-factly that it somehow seemed even worse. He couldn't begin to understand what she'd gone through. He'd never had a broken bone, never even a sprain, and finding the right words to say exactly what he wanted had never been a problem.

Except in those weeks after she awakened from the coma. Back then he hadn't known what to say to her except *I'm sorry* a million times over, and *sorry* lost some of its cathartic value when she didn't have any idea what he was apologizing for.

"Before I wiggle out of here, why don't you hand me a tray or two of ornaments?"

"You ever planning to use those baking sheets for baking?" he asked as he did so. "You can start with white chocolate macadamia cookies. Those were always my favorite."

She remained silent for a long time, then returned to their earlier subject. "I don't think I ever told you," she said quietly, "but your visits to the center meant the world to me. They broke up the monotony of the therapy and gave me something to look forward to. They made me work harder because I wanted to show some progress every time I saw you."

Shame warmed his face, tightened his throat. Four

to five hours a week—that was all he'd given her. He'd made it part of his routine—had written it in on his calendar, had treated those four visits as inviolable appointments. He'd left his pager in the car, turned off his cell phone, and given his staff strict instructions not to disturb him for any reason.

Why hadn't he set such limits years ago? Why hadn't he declared evenings with his wife as private times to be interrupted by nothing less than the end of the world? If he had made it clear to everyone that nothing took priority over her, if he had shown her that kind of commitment and respect, none of the last year would have happened.

So many ifs. So many regrets.

Satisfied with the distribution of ornaments on the back of the tree, Maggie eased out from behind it in time to catch the remorseful look on Ross's face. She'd known practically from the beginning why he'd made the effort, but she hadn't cared, not then, not now. All that mattered was that he had.

He put aside the remorse quickly, and she pretended not to have noticed it. Instead, she walked back to the doorway to check their progress, then claimed a pie plate filled with small clay figures from the coffee table. "What do you want for Christmas?" she asked as she hung the first of nine reindeer on the tree.

"Do you know how long it's been since you've asked me that?"

"Ooh, so I do have one failing after all." She cocked her head to one side to study Rudolph's position on the branch, then answered his question. "Six years."

"What?" he asked absently.

"The last time I asked you what you wanted. By then, you were making so much money that you just automatically bought everything that caught your fancy. Anything I could possibly think of that you might want, you'd already bought. So I began buying you duty gifts. Maybe you would use them and maybe you wouldn't, but at least there was something under the tree. So what do you want this year? And, no, I won't buy that little company down in Georgia that you've had your eye on."

"Alabama. I bought the one in Georgia two years ago." He was silent for a time, wearing the look that said he was seriously concentrating. When he finally found his answer, he met her gaze. "I want you to be happy."

"Ross," she gently chided, but he raised his hand to stop her.

"It's a gift—trust me—and it's one that only you can give me. I want you to be happy, and I want you to not hate me."

"I've never hated you."

"Yes, you have. Last year. You just don't remember."

"I don't believe that." She had gotten angry with him dozens of times. She had resented the hell out of him, had stopped loving him, but she couldn't have hated him. She wasn't capable of it. He wasn't deserving of it.

Impulsively she claimed his hand, wrapping her fingers around his. "All right. I'll be happy, and I'll never hate you. Now, how about something I can wrap up with a bow?"

"I'll think about it. What about you? What do you want?"

She forced back her first thought—*Nothing you can give me*. It was a harsh answer, but true. She wanted love, marriage, babies, and he wanted none of that. Instead, she suggested something she really did want, that, hopefully, he could provide. "My emerald earrings. I must have been wearing them the night of the accident, because I can't imagine leaving them in Buffalo." She fingered one earlobe. "I'll have to get my ears pierced again, but I'd like to have them. If you still have them. If you'll let me have them."

"They gave them to me at the hospital here in town." His voice was low, troubled. "They're at the office."

He didn't say she could have them, and she didn't ask. She was sure he would return them to her. After all, they were *hers*. That fact wouldn't be lost on him. Satisfied of that, she changed the subject. "Did you eat lunch while I was asleep?"

He shook his head.

"Why don't you keep working here and I'll see what I can do about dinner?" Without waiting for a response, she hung the last reindeer, then went down the hall to the kitchen.

Instead of doing as she suggested, he wandered into the kitchen a few minutes later. "Can I help?"

She scanned the recipe in front of her, then separated a half dozen ingredients from the rest and pushed them toward him. "You can make the vinaigrette."

She gave him other assignments while she peeled the cooked shrimp and found herself wondering why things between them couldn't have always been this easy. If he had come home from work, changed from suits to jeans, then joined her in the kitchen to prepare together the meal they would then share, things would have been so much better. Instead, he'd come home from work only to disappear into his office for more work, leaving her to spend evening after evening alone. In some small place deep inside, she almost resented his availability now, when it was too late.

Wasn't it?

She stared out the window. *Was* it too late? They'd gotten along better in the past twelve days than in the past three years. They had talked, apologized—even laughed. They certainly had the foundation to build on. They were bright people who learned from their mistakes. Maybe they *could* resolve their problems without resorting to divorce. Maybe, if they both tried, they could . . .

She gave herself a mental shake. They could remember that these last twelve days were part of an attempt to end the marriage amicably. That it was easy to get along when the end was in sight. That they each had plans for the future that didn't include the other.

With a sigh that wasn't forlorn—it *wasn't*—Maggie finished peeling the shrimp and tossed them with the salad Ross had assembled. They took their plates and drinks into the living room, where he'd built a fire before joining her in the kitchen.

After the first bite, he declared the shrimp salad very good, and it was—better than anything she'd put together by herself. What a difference a clear-thinking assistant made. Maybe Dr. Grayson had been right to suggest that she seek out Ross's help. Now, if the give-yourself-a-little-time-and-things-will-get-back-to-normal part of his advice was also right, she'd be a happy woman.

"Do you know, by any chance, where my Christmas card list is?" she asked.

"Probably on the desk in the kitchen—you know, the thick book that has the phone company's name on it instead of yours."

She smiled. Their first few Christmases, they hadn't had money to spare for luxuries like cards. Once they could afford it, though, she'd started sending out a few. Before long, the list of friends had been joined by Ross's business associates and had become enormous, taking days to complete. But being the good corporate wife was no longer on her list of responsibilities. "Since you pay her so well, Lynda can handle your business cards this year. I thought I'd send just a few to people here and a few to Buffalo." To her new friends and to the medical staff who'd been a daily part of her life.

Maybe even one or two to old friends, she thought as she caught sight of a three-dimensional clay tree ornament resting nearby. It was gaily painted in reds and greens, with a glimmering gold star at the top, and in the center was a small photograph of herself with her friend Jessica. They'd been Christmas shopping and, on a lark, had visited Santa's Workshop in the middle of the mall. It'd been a slow morning for Santa, and he'd invited them to pose on his lap for a picture.

It was the sort of silly thing that Maggie never indulged in once Ross became successful, but Jessica and the kindly old man had persuaded her. Borrowing floppy stocking caps from Santa's college-student elves, they'd posed for two snapshots, then chosen the themed frames.

Ross hadn't been amused by either the photo or the story behind it. After work, power, and wealth, image had taken the next slot on his list of priorities—his wife's as well as his own. The fact that she'd been seen by no one he knew didn't negate the fact that, in his opinion, she'd done something childish and foolish. He'd blamed it on Jessica and demanded for the hundredth time that Maggie end their friendship.

Though she hadn't obeyed, the friendship had eventually ended anyway. Like the rest of her friends, Jessica had paid her a few visits at the center and made a few phone calls, and then she had disappeared from Maggie's life.

He followed the direction of her gaze, and she saw him stiffen when he recognized the photograph. All these years later, it still annoyed him that she'd done something so unbefitting her status as his wife—and in public, no less. He didn't ignore it, though, and there was no censure in his voice when he spoke. "Did you tell him you'd been a good girl?"

"Yes," she replied, the faint smile of remembrance curving her mouth.

"What did you ask for?"

"An 'A' in sociology. A job. A baby." The smile turned rueful. "He said he couldn't help me with the last one—said Mrs. Claus would wring his neck if he even considered it. But I got the 'A'. One out of three—that was about my average." She sighed heavily. "I can go weeks without even thinking about my old friends, but then, for some reason, I do, and I feel so . . ." Lonely. Lost. "I miss them."

He stood up, took the ornament, and in a none-too-subtle move he hung it on the back side of the tree, where she would have to go to great effort to see it. She appreciated his choice.

When he was done, he returned to his seat. "I know it wasn't easy for them to see you the way you were, because it wasn't easy for me. It was frightening how quickly you went from being a bright, capable, independent woman to being trapped in a body that didn't work with a mind that worked enough for you to be aware of your condition. In those first months you were utterly helpless—and, to make it worse, it wasn't because of something unique to you. The same thing could happen to anyone. It made us more aware of our own vulnerability—our mortality. Some people can face that. Some can't."

Dr. Olivetti had told her the same thing. But all the logical explanations in the world couldn't ease the hurt of losing her friends. She'd needed their love and support and they hadn't given it. Reasons didn't matter. Results did.

"You've made new friends here," Ross said quietly. "They're the important ones now. They're the ones who are going to be part of the rest of your life. Even if the accident hadn't happened, you would have grown away from the others anyway when you moved here."

"I know you're right. It's just . . ."

"It's nearly Christmas, and you're feeling nostalgic."

She nodded.

"So get over it. There's no point living in the past.

You've got a bright future ahead of you, and there's no place in it for old friends who let you down."

His brusque tone made her blink, then slowly a smile started. Again he was right. She had a great future to look forward to, in a home she loved in a wonderful town filled with people she adored. There was no room for old disappointments like lost friends.

Like Ross.

That last thought dimmed her smile just a little.

She didn't want to know why.

I T WAS LATE AND ROSS WAS FEELING IT when finally he climbed to the top of the ladder and positioned the angel with her flowing satin robes over the uppermost branch. While he moved the ladder to the hall, Maggie shut off the lights, then stood in the broad doorway to look. Appreciate. Wonder.

He joined her there, a safe two feet between them. "O Little Town of Bethlehem" was on the stereo— how appropriate—and they listened in silence until its last note ended. Then she said softly, "It's beautiful."

It was, he agreed. Almost as beautiful as she was. The merest of smiles touched her mouth, giving her a look of utter satisfaction—a look he'd given her more than a few times himself, often after the tree-trimming.

As the next song began to play—"What Child Is This?"—Maggie pushed away from the door. "I think I'm ready for bed."

In spite of his silent self-warnings, his body responded instantly to the image of Maggie in bed. It had been so damn long—last September, when she'd brought him to Bethlehem to finalize the deal on the house. For the first time in too long, he'd made overtures and, also for the first time in months, she had welcomed them. He had been so aroused and she'd been so satisfying that the suspicion she was acting out of gratitude hadn't diminished his pleasure one bit.

Then it had been back to life as usual. Sleeping in separate bedrooms. Living separate lives. She'd become as obsessed with remodeling and decorating this house as he was with business. She'd started spending more time in Bethlehem than in Buffalo, and he . . .

At what point had he decided that it was all right to have an affair? When had he lost that last shred of dignity and self-respect? He'd known it was wrong—some part of him *hadn't* wanted it as much as the rest of him *had*—but he'd done it anyway, and it had been an unqualified disaster. The sex hadn't even been particularly good—though the best sex in the world wouldn't have been worth the price he and Maggie had paid.

The music stopped, and a moment later Maggie passed him on her way to the stairs. "Are you coming?"

Wishing the question referred to more than accompanying her up the stairs and knowing that even if it did, he would have to refuse, he followed. Maggie safely reached the top of the stairs and her room. He stopped outside his own room and watched her turn on the lights and reach to close the door.

She hesitated. "It was a really nice evening. Thank you."

The simple words touched him. What had he done besides show up?

But wasn't showing up all she'd ever asked of him?

"You're welcome," he murmured, the words huskier than he would have liked.

With an acknowledging nod she said good night, closed the door between them, and left him alone under the bright hall lights.

"I'M REALLY NOT SURE THIS IS A GOOD idea."

Agatha Winchester gave her sister an amazingly innocent look, the kind that, in Corinna's experience, devious—meant with great affection, of course—young children like Josie Dalton managed best. "Not a good idea? We're stopping by a neighbor's house to drop off a coffee cake fresh from the oven and extend an invitation to church. Whatever could not be good about that?"

"It's Sunday morning," Corinna reminded her. "Some people don't like to be disturbed on Sunday mornings."

"Well, I don't believe Maggie's one of those people. Besides, if we can't extend an invitation to church on the Lord's day, when can we?" Agatha pulled to the curb in front of the McKinney house and shut off the engine. "Five minutes. That's all it'll take. Are you coming with me?"

"I would prefer to not give the impression that I think I can drop in whenever I please," Corinna said testily. "However, since you're determined, yes, I'll go with you, or your five minutes will stretch into thirty and make us late for Sunday school."

"Why, I've never been late for Sunday school in my life—and that's an awful lot of Sundays, I'll have you know." Agatha closed the door with enough force to rock the car from side to side, though it wasn't fueled by anger, Corinna knew. Just energy. Her sister was blessed with twice the energy of a woman half her age. In that way, Agatha reminded her, again, of Josie. The two of them could run nonstop from sunup to sundown, sleep a few hours, and be ready to do it again the next day. Of course, young Josie was partly responsible for Agatha's vigor. Being needed and loved gave an old woman a reason to thrive.

It gave *both* old women reason, she admitted as she climbed out of the car and started after Agatha. Seconds after she reached the porch, the door was opened by Ross McKinney. His hair stood on end, and he appeared distracted, needing a moment or two to focus on them. "Miss Agatha. Miss Corinna. Come in."

They crowded into the hallway, then he closed the door. He looked more than a little awkward. He wheeled and dealed with some of the most powerful people in the country, and yet he seemed at a loss as to how to treat two nosy old women who'd interrupted his morning. Corinna found the notion somehow endearing.

"I hope we haven't disturbed you, Ross," Agatha said. "We just wanted to drop this off"—she held up the foil-covered cake—"and invite you and Maggie to join us in church this morning."

"Maggie's still asleep, but—"

"No, I'm not. Hello, Miss Corinna, Miss Agatha." They all turned as one to watch Maggie approach from the kitchen. For someone supposedly still asleep, she looked remarkably alert. Her navy trousers were neatly pressed, her turtleneck sweater without a speck of lint, her hair sleekly combed, and her face perfectly made up. Trade her slacks for a skirt and add a pair of shoes, and she would be all set for church, Corinna mused—*if* she were so inclined.

"I didn't hear you come downstairs," Ross remarked.

"Because you were in the office with the door closed. Even God rested on the Sabbath, you know." Maggie greeted each woman with a hug. "Mmm, coffee cake. I smell cinnamon . . . cloves . . . and dark molasses."

"Exactly," Agatha said, beaming. "Why don't you come in the kitchen and let me serve you a piece?"

The two of them walked away, chatting about the recipe, leaving Corinna alone with Ross. "She's right, you know. Sunday *is* supposed to be a day of rest."

The gaze he turned on her was troubled. "I wasn't working. I was just . . . thinking."

About what? she wondered. Based on what she knew of him, there were only two things in his life— business and Maggie. She sincerely hoped Maggie wasn't responsible for the disquiet in his expression. After all the crises they'd survived in the past year, she would hate to think that there was trouble between them now, when their lives were practically back to normal again.

She wisely chose to change the subject. "We really would like to see you and Maggie in church."

He took a step back emotionally even if his feet

remained firmly in place. "I don't go to church. I haven't been in—" Breaking off, he counted up the years, then, for reasons only he knew, kept the tally to himself. "A long time."

"Then the good Lord would surely like to reacquaint Himself with your handsome face," she gently teased. That earned the beginnings of a smile from him even as he shook his head in rejection.

"I don't think so. I'm not sure . . ."

"That church has anything to offer you?"

"Maybe I don't have anything to offer it."

A curious answer. Though she would like to pursue it, she didn't. As Agatha and Maggie returned from the kitchen, Corinna laid her hand lightly on Ross's arm. "Going to church isn't necessary, of course. You can thank the Lord for your blessings as well right here as you can in a pew. He'll hear you from either place."

At the mention of blessings, his gaze shifted down the hall to Maggie. Whatever his troubles that morning, at least he recognized that his wife was, indeed, a blessing. Surely, she thought—hoped, even prayed, as they said their good-byes—that counted for something.

Chapter Ten

THOUGH THE ROOMS AT THE MCBRIDE Inn were lovely, the lobby was Melissa's favorite space. Once the living room in the original farmhouse, it was large and square, with a ceiling high enough to accommodate the giant Christmas tree Holly purchased every year. Several groupings of furniture provided quiet places to talk, and for solitary diversion there was a massive stone fireplace to cozy up to and big windows looking out on woods and wildlife.

She waited there for Maggie, seated in an oversized wing chair of the sort that you sank comfortably into and hated to give up. There was a cup of the cook's best mulled cider on the table beside her, and she'd already taken the edge off her hunger with a gingerbread cookie from the tray on the registration counter.

"How are you, Melissa?" Emilie Bishop asked as she

came out of the office. She eased onto the arm of a nearby chair, then adjusted her cardigan over her stomach. She was in the fifth month of her pregnancy—farther along than Melissa had ever made it—and looked radiant. Of course, she'd looked radiant ever since the courts had awarded her custody of the kids nearly a year ago and Nathan had proposed marriage. Pregnancy simply enhanced it.

Deliberately redirecting her gaze, Melissa forced a smile. "I'm fine. How are you and Junior?"

"We're growing every day. Is Alex meeting you here for lunch?"

"No, I invited Maggie McKinney. Can you and Holly join us?"

"I'm afraid not. Holly's out this afternoon, and I'm awaiting a call from one of our more troublesome suppliers." She affected a heavier version of her soft Georgia accent. "He's from South Carolina, and he usually responds much more favorably to my requests than to Holly's."

"Do you suppose that has anything to do with the fact that you display true southern gentility and say please and thank you, while Holly opens with 'What kind of idiot are you?' "

Both women laughed, then Emilie gestured toward the portico. "There's Maggie now, chauffeured by that incredibly wealthy—to say nothing of handsome—husband of hers."

Melissa turned to look as Ross opened the car door, then helped Maggie out. "He *is* handsome," she agreed. "Of course, both Nathan and Alex are pretty darn handsome themselves—though they do leave a little to be desired in the 'wealthy' aspect."

"True. But money can't buy love—or happiness. It can't protect you from bad things happening. Maggie's proof of that." Emilie rose as Maggie came in the door. Outside, Ross was driving away. "On the other hand," she said softly, "financial security can count for a lot."

Melissa silently agreed. But she knew Maggie would trade wealth in a heartbeat for a baby.

So would she.

After exchanging hellos, Emilie seated them at a table in a cozy corner of the dining room, presented leather-bound menus with a flourish, and recommended dessert before leaving them alone. Knowing what she wanted, Melissa left the menu unopened and gazed around the room.

No matter how often she went there, she fell in love with the room all over again. The long, broad hall was filled with linen-covered tables and plants that thrived year-round, thanks to the southern exposure provided by a half dozen pairs of French doors. Outside the doors was a warm-weather dining patio. Inside, fireplaces at each end helped warm the room in winter and provided a backdrop for floral arrangements from Melissa's Garden all summer. It was a lovely setting for any meal, particularly so for the wedding receptions held there throughout the year.

At last Maggie laid the menu aside, spread her napkin over her lap, and folded her hands on the tabletop. "I'm glad you suggested this. Ross has been working all morning, and I was getting restless for someone to talk to."

"If you ever get really restless, come by the shop. I'd be happy to talk your ears off while putting you to work."

Maggie smiled, then looked around. "This is a beautiful place."

"Yes, it is. You used to stay here while the workmen were getting your house ready."

"That's what Ross said. I don't remember it."

"That must be terribly difficult for you."

"It is and it isn't," Maggie said with a shrug. "It was hardest when I met everyone again. You were all strangers to me, and yet some of you knew me quite well. It still bothers me sometimes, but the rest of the time I forget that I've forgotten. It's not as if last year was a tremendously different year for me. Other than coming to Bethlehem and buying the house, the only big thing that happened was the accident, and I think I may be better off not remembering that."

"I saw your truck when they towed it out of the ravine. I think you are too." Melissa hesitated, then went on. "We were all gathered in the square for the Christmas service. They call it a midnight service, but that's usually when it ends. The first to leave was one of the deputies on duty that night, then another. Then the paramedics got paged, and a couple of doctors, and someone came to get the sheriff. Most people didn't even notice, but Alex and I did. We knew something terrible had happened to someone, but we didn't know it was you until the next day. You were in everyone's Christmas prayers."

Maggie sat silently for a long time, leading Melissa

to ask, "Would you prefer that we make the months you can't remember off limits for discussion?"

This time she was quick to respond. "I've spent the last eleven months getting up close and personal with complete strangers. I've been forced to be so open that these days, *nothing's* off limits. Do you, by chance, know what my plans were last year?"

"Beyond fixing the house?" Melissa thought about it, recalling each of their meetings. There weren't many—eight, maybe ten—and several had centered around choosing flowers for the house. The rest of the time they had talked about city versus small-town life. Melissa had shared the trials and tribulations of a Christmas pageant director, and they'd talked with the same degree of wistfulness about Christmas, family, traditions, and children. "One day, when we passed an empty storefront downtown, you said that it would be a perfect location for the restaurant you'd wanted to open. Several times you mentioned that you would like to work with children. And you talked about the house as if it were your new home—as if you intended to stay."

Maggie looked as if she wanted to say something but thought better of it and substituted another question instead. "Did I talk about Ross?"

"No," Melissa said gently. She'd heard at the time that the McKinneys had fought their way through every visit to Bethlehem. Still, it had struck her as odd that not once did Maggie ever voluntarily speak of her husband. If someone asked about him, she answered, but that was the extent of his involvement in her Bethlehem life. Heavens, Alex was so much a part of Melissa's life that she couldn't keep him out of her conversation if she tried. It just wasn't natural.

"I did intend to stay," Maggie said quietly. "We bought this house so I could live here."

"And Ross?"

"He would have remained in the city. Once Christmas was over, he probably never would have set foot in Bethlehem again. And I never would have returned to Buffalo."

So the talk about how miserable they were had been true. They had come here on the verge of a divorce. "Out of tragedy comes triumph," Melissa murmured.

"What do you mean?"

"Last Christmas was going to be your last Christmas together, but out of the tragedy of the accident, here you are—still together, better than before, about to spend another Christmas together."

A flush crept into Maggie's cheeks as she shifted her gaze to the fragrant cinnamon and evergreen centerpiece. Was she wrong? Melissa wondered. Had the accident brought them closer together? Or had it merely delayed the end of a marriage gone sour?

Fearing that the latter was true and hoping it wasn't, Melissa felt her own warm flush as she changed the subject. "So what are your plans now?"

"I'd still like to work with kids, but I don't know in what capacity. With a degree in early childhood development, I could teach or work with social services. I thought about getting my master's and doing family counseling—not that I know so much about being part of a family. What I'd really like—" She broke off.

"Go ahead," Melissa urged.

"I'd really like to have a family of my own. I'd like to be a stay-at-home mother who takes care of the house, volunteers with the PTA, cheers at soccer games, and has cookies waiting when the kids come home from school."

Though she'd wondered about it before, Melissa had never thought it appropriate to ask. That afternoon she just plunged ahead. "Why don't you have children?"

Maggie's smile was regretful. "Ross wanted to wait until we got out of debt. Until he was established in his career. Until we could afford for me to stay home. Until he made his first million, then his first hundred million. Until he could make time to be a father. He never ran out of excuses. What about you?"

"After three miscarriages, we ran out of hope." But that wasn't entirely true. Though the doctor had made clear that her chances of getting pregnant and carrying the baby to term—or even close to term—were minuscule, she still hoped. She still dreamed about babies, envied her friends, and got wistful at the smell of baby powder.

She still believed in miracles, and she still believed that someday she would get one of her own.

"I'm sorry." It was such an inadequate phrase to convey all that she felt, but Maggie knew of nothing else to offer. She pitied herself for having no children, but at least she still had the chance. All she needed was a willing partner and a little time, and she could fill her house with babies. How awful it must be for Melissa to know that all the time in the world wouldn't make her house—or her heart—any less empty.

After a moment, Melissa changed the subject to the

Christmas pageant, relating past disasters and mishaps that kept them both laughing through the rest of the meal. They followed Emilie's recommendation for dessert—Kahlua ice cream pie—then, with a sigh, Melissa neatly folded her napkin and left it on the tabletop. "Much as I've enjoyed this, I've got to get back to the shop. Can I give you a ride?"

"No, thanks. Ross is picking me up."

"You don't drive, do you?"

"You've noticed that," Maggie said dryly.

"I can't say that I blame you. After what you went through, if you never want to get behind the wheel again, then don't do it. Bethlehem's not so big that a healthy person can't get wherever they want to go on foot—or find a friend willing to give them a lift."

They paid their tab, then returned to the lobby. Melissa claimed her coat from the tree there, but Maggie left hers hanging. "Thanks for the invitation. I really enjoyed it."

"So did I. Let's do it again soon." Unexpectedly, Melissa hugged her, murmuring, "Welcome back, Maggie. I'm glad you're here."

With a lump in her throat Maggie watched her go before turning in a slow circle. She came to a stop facing the registration desk. The desk was empty, but behind it an open door looked in on the office, where Emilie was at work.

Unsure whether it was a good idea and not caring, Maggie knocked on the door. "Hi, Emilie. I was wondering . . . Could I see the room where I stayed when I visited?"

"Sure. The guests who were there checked out this

morning, and I believe the housekeeper has already finished with it." Emilie came out from behind the desk and led the way up the broad, graceful staircase. The door she opened was in the middle of the corridor and led into a two-room suite. "We haven't changed a thing in the last year. Everything's exactly as it was when you stayed here," she said from the doorway. "I'll leave you alone to look around. Stay as long as you like."

She closed the door, and Maggie slowly walked farther into the sitting room. It was beautifully decorated with plush carpet, good antique furniture, and better reproductions, warm colors and spicy, welcoming scents. She brushed her fingers over the marble fireplace surround, bent to sniff a bowl of potpourri, tried out a comfortable chaise beside a bookcase filled with well-read volumes. She had probably eaten breakfast at the delicate table positioned by the windows and watched the television hidden inside a walnut armoire.

She had definitely slept in the bedroom with its four-poster bed, had prepared for the day in the large bath and dressing room next door, had left Ross at the massive rolltop desk with his computer and telephone while she explored. She had lived for days at a time in these spacious rooms, sometimes with Ross, usually alone, but they were as unfamiliar to her as the rest of the town.

Walking to the foot of the bed, she rested her hand on the tapering carved post that reached toward the ceiling and closed her eyes. She focused all her attention inward, back one year in time, and searched intently for something familiar, something that suggested she'd ever set foot in this room before. For one breath-stealing moment she thought she'd found it. A presence surrounded her—strong, commanding—and a sense of security, of well-being, swept through her.

Ross.

Of course, she thought, vaguely amused. All the time she'd spent there alone, and it was his brief presence that registered, his presence that she felt as surely as if . . .

She opened her eyes, and the fleeting, giddy hope disappeared. Ross didn't.

He stood beside the bed with a few yards of blue paisley comforter between them. His hands were in his pockets, and his expression was all somber, filled with intense concern. "Are you all right?"

"Yes."

"Conjure up any memories?"

"No."

His expression shifted only slightly. Hiding his disappointment so she wouldn't feel her own too strongly? "This is where we stayed. Where we fought. Where we slept." With one hand he gestured to the space around them, then let his hand fall, his fingertips resting lightly on the comforter. "And this is where we made love the last time."

Feeling her body heat rise, she looked at the bed again. It was a king-size, big enough to get lost in, but for one brief time they had found each other instead. She tried to imagine the scene, tried to find it wherever it was hiding in her brain—the two of them trading kisses instead of insults, touching instead of turning away, coming together instead of drifting apart. But no matter how hard she tried, she couldn't locate the images, neither real nor imagined. Her failure was enough to make her eyes mist over and her throat grow tight, but she refused to give in to the tears.

"When . . . ?" she whispered.

"When we closed on the house."

"Who . . . ?"

"Me. You were ecstatic about the house. I didn't see you that way very often, and I wanted to share it. I wanted to feel . . ."

"Feel what?"

He gave a shake of his head. "Just feel."

She wanted to know so much more. Was it day or night? Did he turn to her in bed, slide in behind her, awaken her with gentle caresses and erotic kisses? Did he catch her in the middle of something else, distract her with one steamy look and boldly seduce her? Or was he blunt, the way he sometimes preferred, the way *she* had sometimes preferred? A simple, breath-stealing *I want you now* had gotten her into bed more times than she could recall.

Once there, had their lovemaking been tender or greedy? Hard, demanding, raw? Had they made love, as he'd called it, or engaged in slick, hot, potent sex for its own sake?

There was a lot to be said for good sex, even more for making love. Either way, she regretted like hell that she couldn't remember. Maybe it would cool the heat in her body and ease the ache in her breasts, her belly, at her very core. Maybe remembering would bring her some measure of relief . . . or arouse her beyond bearing.

Ross could do both.

She stared hard at the paisley pattern in front of her in an effort to not put him and the bed into the same scene. Right now she could deal with one or the other, but not both. Then, deliberately tormenting herself, she asked in a throaty voice, "Were we good?"

"We were always good, Maggie. You can't have forgotten that."

Always. Yes. From their very first time together, when she'd been a virgin and he'd had very little experience, they had always been good together. Whether it was passion, play, habit, or anger that brought them together, the result had always been spectacular.

She was focused so narrowly on the bed that she wasn't aware he'd moved until he was standing beside her. "Let's go home."

What if she said no? If she locked the door, closed the drapes, stripped off her clothing and his, and demanded the use of his body . . . He wouldn't say no. He might want to, but she knew him too well—all the places to touch him, all the ways to kiss him. She knew how to cut through his resistance, how to heat his blood and fog his mind, how to arouse him beyond bearing and satisfy him beyond belief.

"Maggie?"

He touched her hand, and she swore she heard a soft sizzle. Hot and edgy and all too aware that there wasn't going to be any relief, she took a step back, then headed for the door.

He stopped her halfway across the sitting room. "What's wrong?"

Her smile was brittle. "Nothing. I thought you wanted to go home."

"Do you want to stay here awhile longer?"

Her suddenly all-too-clear imagination called up an image of the bed with its paisley linens turned down, of Ross naked—she'd always liked him naked—of herself, slowly removing her own clothes in preparation of taking him deep inside. She closed her eyes, rubbed them, forced the image away. "No. I'm ready."

They didn't run into anyone as they made their way silently down the stairs and out to the car.

"Sorry I was late," Ross said stiffly as he unlocked the door.

"Got tied up in the office, didn't you?"

The tightening of his jaw was her first clue that her words were sharp, her tone snide. How easy it was to fall into old habits, to get frustrated and take it out on him, even though he hadn't a hint that she even *was* frustrated or by what. What would he think if she told him? *I was thinking about us in bed, about my hands on your body, your mouth on my body, about heat and need and that terrible, pleasurable pain, and I want it again. I want you now, and that's why I sound edgy and frustrated and about to explode.*

She had no idea what he would say.

She had a damn good idea what he wouldn't *do*.

"I was on my way out the door, when the phone rang," he said, his voice so calm and tightly controlled that she wanted to scream. "It was Dr. Allen. He wanted to know how you're doing. I told him you were fine."

She couldn't make the same sort of obnoxious comment she would have if the caller had been Tom or someone else associated with business—which was fine, because she shouldn't be making obnoxious comments at all. She was the one who'd insisted that he return to work. She couldn't blame him now for following her advice.

She certainly couldn't blame him because he hadn't magically picked up on the fact that her hormones were coming back to life—and doing so with a vengeance.

Though once, he would have known. Once he would have looked at her and known, and he would have been more than happy to accommodate her.

She missed those days when they were young, in love, and foolishly believed that it would last forever. She would go back to them in a heartbeat if only she could.

At home, before they parted in the hallway to go their separate ways, she cleared her throat. "I didn't even notice that you were late. That wasn't a problem. I—I just wish I remembered."

"I know."

With a grim nod she started down the hall. At the door to the library she turned back in time to see the pocket doors slide shut. The action left her feeling . . .

She wasn't sure what she was feeling. Frustrated. Lonely. Melancholy. Weary. Sorry—oh, yes. She was sorry that their marriage had ended, sorry she'd lost Ross, sorry she had to live through the present to get to the future. She wished she could take a nap and wake up in two hours and it would be spring, with the grass turning green, flowers starting to bloom, and both her body and her heart healed of their various aches. Life would be good then.

That afternoon it was merely sad.

I T WAS LATE FRIDAY AFTERNOON, THE END of a long, stressful week. The computer was printing the files that had come attached to Tom's most recent e-mail, and the fax was receiving endless pages of a new contract, but Ross paid neither any attention. Slumped in his chair, he'd propped his feet on the credenza and was staring out the window, watching Maggie and the Dalton girls light new candles in the farolitos. They looked as if they were having fun.

He was certainly enjoying it.

Heavy clouds darkened the sky, making it seem later than five-thirty, and snow was falling in fat wet flakes. It was perfect weather, the girls had declared in the hallway earlier, for tonight's horse-drawn wagon tour of Bethlehem. Though the prospect of spending a few hours in the cold didn't exactly thrill Ross, he and Maggie were going. There was no way she could miss one of the town's premiere Christmas events—preceded by a party at the Winchesters, another premiere event—and he wasn't about to send her alone.

Outside, the girls had finished with the last farolitos, and now the three of them stood in the grass, heads tilted back, tongues stuck out. Catching snowflakes. He hadn't seen Maggie do anything so young since . . .

The smile that had started to form faded. Since he'd

begun demanding a certain standard of behavior from her. When he'd decided that his position required the perfect wife, he'd set out to mold her into that image, and she'd let him. By the time he'd realized that the old Maggie—the one who made him laugh, who made him happy, who loved him with all the passion she possessed—*was* perfect, it was too late.

Sometimes he wished for a second chance. She had given him so much, and he'd cost her so much. He wished for the opportunity to be the husband she wanted, to give her the children and the life she needed.

Other times he knew such chances were impossible. He could never be the husband she wanted. They had both changed too much. He couldn't stop being who and what he was, and that man could never be happy with the life that would make her happy.

Could he?

The fax beeped, signaling that it'd printed the last page, but he didn't reach for the stack of papers. Instead, he slid his feet to the floor, left his chair, and, after a stop by the closet, left the house.

"You need this," he said, draping her coat over her shoulders. The sweater she wore was heavy and warm—and his, he realized after a closer look—but it didn't provide enough protection against the snow.

Though it provided *him* with a hell of a jolt of lust. The sweater had been a birthday gift years ago. They'd had a quiet, intimate dinner at home, followed by his favorite cake. After urging him to make a wish and blow out the candles, she'd left the room to get his gift. She'd come back wearing this sweater and nothing else, and he'd gotten instantly hard. As he slid inside her, he'd asked, "How did you know what I wished for?" and she had merely laughed.

It hadn't been a difficult guess. Back then they'd *always* wanted each other—anytime, anyplace. Hell, though he might have stopped loving her, he'd never stopped wanting her. He'd just lost the right to have her.

She looked at him with a smile that cut him off at the knees. "Isn't it a gorgeous night?"

He couldn't pull his gaze away. "Yes," he agreed, but he wasn't sure what he was agreeing to. All he could see, all he could focus on, was her. She looked so damn touchable that his fingers curled into tight fists in an effort to resist the temptation. He failed though. Of its own accord his hand lifted. His fingers tucked a stray strand of hair behind her ear. Her cheek was cold, but it sent a blast of heat through him.

"Hey, Mr. Ross."

He was aware of an impatient tug on his jacket, but he didn't respond. He couldn't. He could only look at Maggie—and want.

"Mr. Ross, guess what?" Josie was insistent in her demand for his attention. It required greater strength than he would have expected to give it to her. "Aunt Emilie let us have our own fire-olitos, and me and Lannie take care of them all by ourself. And we get to stay up late tonight, 'cause we're having an all-night party at Miss Agatha's so Aunt Emilie and Uncle Nathan can have a night alone." Pretending to hold someone in her arms, she scrunched up her face and made kissing noises, then laughed. "That's how Aunt Emilie got our baby. Kasey at school said so, and she knows."

Alanna tugged her sister's jacket hood. "Babies don't come from kissing, silly."

"Uh-huh, they do. That's why I'm not never gonna kiss any boy, not till I'm way growed up, like Miss Maggie." Struck by a thought, she looked from Maggie to Ross, then back. "You guys don't have a baby. Don't you never kiss?"

Alanna's tug was harder this time. "Remember what Aunt Emilie said about asking personal questions?"

"Not to. So . . . don't you guys kiss?"

Maggie crouched in front of her. "Of course we kiss," she said as naturally as if it were true.

"Then why don't you have babies?"

"Your friend Kasey is a little misinformed. Babies don't come from kissing. There's a lot more to it than that."

Thank God, Ross thought, or he and Maggie would have been in a world of trouble years ago.

Or maybe they might have been saved.

"Like what?"

"I think you need to ask your aunt Emilie that."

Josie twined her arms around Maggie's neck and swayed from side to side. "Oh, please tell me. Kasey thinks she knows everything because her dad's a *doctor,* and if you tell me, then I can go to school and tell everyone else and they'll know that she was *wrong* and she'll be all mad. Please? *Puh-leeeze?*"

She put too much wheedling into her last plea and, caught off guard, Maggie tumbled back onto the snowy grass with the girl falling on top.

"Josie!" Alanna said sharply at the same time Ross spoke Maggie's name. As he moved to help them, Alanna grabbed hold of her sister's coat and jerked her back, giving her a little shake. "You've got to be careful! You know she's been in the hospital since last Christmas!"

"It's okay," Maggie said hastily as she accepted Ross's help to her feet. She brushed the snow from her coat, then smiled at the girls. Josie's cheeks were pale with dismay, and her plump lower lip trembled.

"I'm sorry, Miss Maggie. I didn't mean to make you fall. Are you hurt? Do you need a doctor? Dr. J.D. is over at Miss Agatha's, and I can go get him. I can run fast."

"I'm not hurt. It's okay, really. I'm not going to break." Maggie's bright, reassuring smile made the rounds. "Why don't you give us a minute to lock up, then we'll all walk over to Miss Agatha's together?"

As soon as they were inside, Ross asked, "Are you all right?"

"It was only a couple of inches—and it made her forget about where babies come from. Heavens, I'd hate to suffer a *real* fall." Sarcasm entered her voice now. "The concern would be unbearable."

"A real one? You mean like down the stairs?"

She glanced to the top of the stairs, a long way from here. "Yeah, like that. Speaking of the stairs, would you mind running up and getting some blankets?"

"Which ones do you want?"

"How about the comforters from the guest room beds?"

He left the comforters in the hall near the side door

to pick up later, then shut down the office and locked up. With Josie's hand clasped firmly in Maggie's, they crossed the street to the Winchester house. A dozen cars were parked out front and along the side, and, like them, another dozen or two neighbors had walked from their own homes.

All the faces inside were familiar, though he couldn't put a name to every one, and they all greeted him and Maggie as if they were old friends. It was a curious sensation—this business of having friends. Ross was accustomed to acquaintances and associates. He socialized with people about whom he knew little and cared less, people who wanted something from him or could give him something. The only person he considered a friend was Tom, and even that was based on business. Hell, he'd never even thought he wanted friends, had certainly never needed them.

Maybe he'd been wrong.

Maggie wanted friends. She thrived with friendship—grew more serene, more content, more absolutely beautiful. With these people she was like an exotic flower unfolding under the sun's life-giving light. Having friends made her a different person—No, that wasn't true. Having friends enhanced the woman she'd always been.

He wondered if they could improve the man he'd become.

As soon as they finished their hellos, J. D. Grayson approached them with a tray of delicate Christmas china cups. "How about a cup of the sisters' special egg nog?"

Ross accepted a cup and sipped from it, expecting

something to rival Maggie's flavored egg nogs. What he got was . . . "This is just egg nog."

"The sisters don't believe in the use of spirits," Grayson said, "except for the rare medicinal dosing. How are you, Maggie?"

"I'm fine."

"Are you ready to be dazzled by the fifty-first annual Tour of Lights?"

"I've been looking forward to it all day."

All the lights in the world couldn't be as dazzling as the smile she gave the doctor, Ross thought stiffly. Grayson reacted to it the same way *he* had earlier, staring, murmuring a response with absolutely no idea what he was saying.

Feeling perverse, Ross took Maggie's arm and pulled. "Come on. We need to find Miss Corinna and Miss Agatha and say hello."

As they made their way through the living and dining rooms on the way to the kitchen, he examined the emotion that had led him to put as much distance as possible between them and Grayson—between *her* and Grayson. Surely it wasn't jealousy. He'd never experienced it before—she'd never given him reason—and there was no reason for it now. For a very long time he and Maggie had been married in name only. There was little emotion and certainly nothing physical between them. In a few more months there would be no legal bond either. For all practical purposes she was a free woman now—free to start living her own life. Free to start looking for a man to take his place in it. She wanted it. *He* wanted it.

He had no logical reason to be jealous because she'd

smiled at some other guy the way she'd just smiled at *him*. No reason at all, just because that guy looked at her in the same stunned, turned-on way that *he* looked at her.

No reason. He wanted out of her life, remember?

Didn't he?

He should be pushing the two of them together, not pulling them apart. Grayson was everything Maggie wanted—solid, dependable, a family sort of guy. He preferred small-town life over the city, wasn't interested in being rich or powerful, kept regular hours in his medical practice so he could have a personal life, and loved all these people in the same way she soon would. On top of all that, she thought he was handsome and admired his obvious affection for kids. Grayson was perfect for her.

Perfectly *wrong*.

"What are you scowling at?" Maggie asked as they squeezed between guests and a table loaded with mouth-watering food.

"I'm not—" He *was*. Consciously he forced his face to relax. "I'm not scowling."

"You don't like him much, do you?"

"Why should I?"

"I don't know. You're both intelligent, successful, respected. You're both mature adults. With that in common, I'd think you would get along fine."

And in a few more months would they also have her in common?

Just last weekend, when she'd asked what he wanted for Christmas, he'd given her a simple answer: *I want you to be happy*. He'd given that answer knowing that for her being happy meant being in love, married, and having babies—being in love with and married to another man, having babies with another man. He knew that. He'd accepted it.

But not Grayson. He was her shrink, for God's sake—though, granted, so far they'd had only one short session and would probably end the doctor-patient relationship after their next visit. He was—was— Hell, Ross didn't know *what* he was, besides unsuitable for Maggie.

He was saved from continuing the conversation by Miss Corinna's appearance. "Oh, you're here," she said, hugging Maggie, squeezing Ross's hand. "You're in for a treat tonight. We're very proud of our town, and the snow will make it perfect."

"That's what the kids said. Can I help with anything?" Maggie asked.

"No, no, we're all set. We'll eat just as soon as I make an announcement. Come along." She drew them both back the way they'd just come, then left them near the table while she took up a position in the broad arched doorway. "Can I have your attention please?"

A chorus of hushes spread through the rooms, followed by silence.

"Agatha and I are pleased to have you all join us for our fifty-first Tour of Lights opening night party," Miss Corinna said. "Some of you may have noticed that the Walkers aren't here. There's a good reason for their absence this evening. I just got off the phone with Mitch, and he told me that Shelley has given birth to a healthy, beautiful, eight-pound-eight-ounce baby girl whom they have named Rebecca Louise. Mother and daughter are doing fine." She waited a moment for the whispers and exclamations to die down, then said, "Time to celebrate. Let's eat, friends."

Ross moved closer to Maggie, who'd gone still at the announcement as the guests crowded around the table. "Are you okay?"

"Of course," she replied, and she managed a pretty good impression of being just fine. But he recognized the wistfulness in her eyes and the envy that underlaid it. "Why wouldn't I be okay? I'm not the one who just went through the rigors of childbirth."

"Precisely."

In the crush she reached for his hand, squeezed his fingers tightly. "My turn will come. Maybe by this time next year . . ."

At that moment Grayson came into sight across the room. Brendan Dalton was sitting on his shoulders, and Josie and another young girl were plastered to his sides.

Ross deliberately moved to block him from Maggie's view.

They joined the buffet line, then found a corner to share with Alex and Melissa Thomas. Soon after the meal was finished, the party began breaking up—or, rather, relocating to the park on the west side of town. They returned home to pick up the comforters and the car, then met most of the same people around the bonfire in the park.

It was a still night. The snow continued to fall, heavily blanketing anything that stood still. The logs in the fire sizzled and filled the air with their woodsy scent, and the teams of horses hitched to six hay-filled wagons waited patiently, occasionally pawing the ground or whuffling in the cold air.

It was like nothing Ross had ever experienced. Although he was cold and annoyingly aware of every move Grayson made, he was also enjoying the whole thing—and that was a new experience too.

The tickets they'd bought when they'd arrived at the park assigned them to a numbered wagon. When their number was called, they climbed into the old farm wagon with the sisters, the Thomases, the Bishops, and the Dalton kids. They settled in the hay, the sideboards at their backs, and Maggie spread the covers, tucking the first one tightly, leaving the other so the excess fabric was shared with their neighbors.

Sitting hip to hip, thigh to thigh, sharing space and body heat with people surrounding them . . . it was unbearably intimate. They hadn't been this close in well over a year, and that time they'd both been naked and hot and . . .

Swallowing hard, he looked away in time to see the last two passengers board—Holly and Grayson. Ross found an inordinate satisfaction in seeing the two of them snuggle in together. If the shrink was involved with Holly, then he was off limits to Maggie. She would never dream of coming between a friend and her boyfriend.

"This is so neat," Maggie murmured.

He glanced down at her—at the sparkle in her eyes and the flush in her cheeks. "You look more like Josie than a 'way growed-up' adult."

"I don't feel 'way growed-up.' " She pressed a little

closer, pulled the cover a little tighter, and he swallowed hard again.

"Then you're not feeling what I am," he murmured, the words barely audible.

She looked all around—at the wagon ahead of them, pulling out now, the one behind them, the crowd of people awaiting their turn—before looking at him again. "What did you say?"

"Nothing."

"Sounded like something to me."

"Well, you didn't hear it, so how would you know?"

"If it was nothing, how could I hear it?" She waited a moment, her expression challenging, before breaking into a big, smug smile. He responded deep inside with a surge of pure, deep affection. Early in their marriage he had been appreciative of the fact that he liked his wife as much as he loved her. More recently, though, the distance, hostility, and resentment had overwhelmed everything else. Everything had become so difficult—most especially him—that he'd lost track of that affection.

He felt incredibly relieved to have found it again.

Up at the front, the driver called a command to his team and, with a jingle of bells, the wagon moved out. A slight breeze flipped the end of the blanket off Maggie's shoulder, and, pretending that he did it all the time, that he had the right to do it, Ross slid his arm around her shoulders, retucked the blanket, then casually left his arm there. Every other man on the wagon had his arm around the woman with him. Why shouldn't he?

He could name a dozen reasons, if only he would. He didn't.

The tour route took them past houses, businesses, and churches, past simple, elegant displays and some tacky ones. Several times they stopped to be serenaded by carolers, and at one church they viewed a living Nativity complete with livestock. It was new, different, interesting, and he saw it all through a fog, because the more Maggie pressed against him, the closer she snuggled for warmth, the hotter he got. When she rested her gloved hand on his thigh, he was surprised that steam didn't rise through the covers.

He couldn't stand this. If there was even the slightest possibility that something would come of it, he could not only endure but enjoy the discomfort and anticipate the relief. But he was going home tonight to sleep alone, as he'd slept for a year.

All because a few nights last year he *hadn't* slept alone when he should have.

Panic and hopelessness swept over him—the same emotions he'd felt last Christmas Eve in sickening proportions. If he could change one thing in his life, he wouldn't have had that affair—and that would change all the other things that were wrong. He wouldn't have hurt Maggie like that, wouldn't have caused her to leave the house in weather custom-made for an accident, wouldn't have watched her suffer and struggle for nearly a year, and he wouldn't find himself now wanting her back with no hope of ever having her.

Wanting her back . . . The words repeated in his mind, sly, taunting echoes. Not *wanting her,* as in sex, as in, in his bed, but *wanting her back*. As in . . . In his life?

The panic increased. No. Not only no, but hell, no. He wanted to have sex with her, but only because he'd been celibate for so long—because whatever else had gone wrong, the sex had always been great. But he didn't want to be married to her, didn't want to live in this tiny little town with her, argue with her, insult and be insulted by her. He wanted just sex . . . and maybe a few quiet meals. Evenings like this one. A holiday or two. A little teasing and laughing. A few hours to simply watch her and appreciate her. To come home to her and wake up with her and . . .

God help him, he was in trouble.

Chapter Eleven

FTER THE WAGON RIDE AND A FEW
minutes warming themselves around the bonfire, Maggie and Ross had said their good-
byes and headed home. She would have liked
to stay a little longer—would have liked for the evening
to never end—but it was cold and Ross had been patient enough.

Now it was late, the middle of the night, and she
was alone in her bed. The snow still fell, but she was
warm and cozy. She knew these facts, even though she
was mostly asleep, just as she knew that the uneasiness
creeping through her wasn't real but merely the prod-
uct of a dream. Knowing didn't ease its effect though—
didn't stop her from shifting restlessly, from curling
into a tight ball to protect herself from the dark, the
fear, the hurt. She tried to wake herself, to deny the
dream its power, but it trapped her now.

Such pain, such sorrow. Tears slid down her cheeks, wetting her pillow, as heartrending sobs escaped her throat. She'd never known such anguish and couldn't bear it, couldn't stand one second more. She had to leave, to escape, but it was inside her, part of her, destroying her. How could this happen? How could she survive it? She sobbed while the semi-aware part of her wondered dispassionately what *this* was.

The pain, already unbearable, grew, turning her sobs to helpless, hopeless whimpers, making her body tremble, her chest grow tight. Please, God, she moaned, please make it go away, and in answer to her prayers, strong hands burrowed under the covers to grasp her shoulders, to shake her awake, to drag her shuddering and heartbroken out of the dark. "It's all right, Maggie," he whispered. "Honey, it's all right. Wake up. It's just a dream."

She forced one eye open, then the other, to see Ross bent over her. It was a dream, just as he'd said. She'd had them for months—vague scenes, vague emotions, unsettling but never memorable. Though there'd been nothing vague about the emotions this time, like all the others, it was just a dream.

She acknowledged that, drew a deep breath, then burst into tears.

He carried her to the rocker, slid his arms around her, and began a slow, rhythmic rocking. "It's okay, Maggie," he said quietly. "Go ahead and cry."

Pressing her face against his shoulder, she cried until there were no tears left, until hiccups ricocheted through her, until she was exhausted and relieved and feeling halfway normal again. And the entire time he held her, rocked her, stroked her hair. His touch was reassuring, incredibly comforting, and arousing. That last wasn't his intention, she knew, but rather, her need. Her emptiness.

When she was still and quiet, when even the hiccups had disappeared, he spoke softly. "Do you want to talk about it?"

"It was just a dream."

"About the accident?"

She dried his shoulder where her tears had fallen and realized for the first time that his attire was on the skimpy side—a pair of sweatpants and nothing else. His skin underneath was warm and smooth, with a scent uniquely his that she remembered from their past. She was tempted to trail her fingers along his chest as she'd done hundreds of times before, but she settled for simply resting her cheek there again.

"Maggie? Did you dream about the accident?"

"I think so. Dr. Olivetti says patients with post-traumatic syndrome often dream about whatever caused their injury." She gave the answer as casually, as matter-of-factly, as she could, but it wasn't true. The pain in her dream had had nothing to do with broken bones or head trauma, and the fear hadn't been of injury or death. No, this dream had been filled with hopelessness, despair, loss, heartbreak. Even now, safe in Ross's arms, with the impact of the dream lessened by wakefulness, she could still feel the grief, so pure and raw and overwhelming. It frightened her that she'd once felt so lost, and equal parts of her wanted to know and wanted to never know why.

"Do you remember any of it?"

She closed her eyes for a moment, felt her throat swell and her lungs tighten, then quickly opened her eyes again and forced the feeling away. "No," she said flatly. "I didn't see anything. There were just feelings, and they're gone."

"I'm sorry. I know how much you want to remember."

Not that. She hoped whatever had caused such torment remained lost forever. To know would mean living it again to some degree, and she couldn't bear it.

They fell silent again. He continued to rock and to hold her, and she snuggled a little closer. On the wagon ride, she had enjoyed the closeness to him as much as the lights and the carols. To anyone who didn't know better, they must have appeared no different from the other couples there—the happy ones, the ones in love, who'd gone home together, to bed together, and might even have made love together. In her head she'd known the appearance was deceiving, but in her heart she'd enjoyed the deception of intimacy just as she was starting to enjoy *this* intimacy.

She brushed her hair back—another deception—then, instead of returning it to her lap, she let her hand brush his chest, let them curl loosely as they came to rest at the waistband of his sweats. His muscles tightened, but he didn't push her hand away. He didn't dump her on her feet, say, Well, you're all right now, and head for the safety of his own room. For that she was grateful.

"I meant to tell you thank-you last night," she murmured.

"For what?" His voice was wary, tautly controlled.

So were his muscles. She could feel them tightening everyplace their bodies were in contact.

"Everything. Coming here. Doing these things with me—Thanksgiving, the parade, the tour. I would have a wonderful time regardless, but it's better with you to share it."

It took him a long time to respond—partly, she suspected, because he wasn't comfortable with his response. "I've enjoyed it all. It's been fun."

"Never thought you'd say that, did you?" she teased.

"No. But it's a nice break from real life."

"I bet the people here would be indignant at the implication that their lives aren't real."

"I meant—"

She rubbed her cheek from side to side across his shoulder, stopping him mid-explanation. "I know what you meant." That this wasn't *his* real life. That, although he'd enjoyed it, it would never *be* his real life. That she should never for one moment think that he might ever find himself happy, contented, and willing to stay in Bethlehem.

She had always understood that. She regretted it, but she understood. If things were different, though, if he could stay . . . She allowed herself a moment for the fantasy of the two of them passing year after satisfying year in this house, surrounded by friends, raising a family, belonging to each other and to this place in a way they never had before. It would be every wish, every dream and hope she'd ever had, all wrapped up in one.

But things weren't different. They would stick to their original plan. He would return to Buffalo and his life there, and she would remain in Bethlehem and make a new life for herself. She would meet a man, fall in love, get married, and have his babies. Those were her goals. But instead of becoming easier to visualize as the time came nearer, they'd become more difficult. The only man she'd ever loved was Ross. The only babies she'd dreamed of having were his.

She couldn't even imagine getting intimate with anyone else. Whenever she thought of making love, it was Ross's hands, his kisses, his whispers, his body. She tried to picture herself with someone else, and the picture wouldn't develop. She told herself that was natural. Once he was gone, things would change.

At that moment, in his arms, she didn't believe herself.

A soft, regretful sigh shuddered through her, and he responded—shifted underneath her, sucked in his belly away from her fingers, started to swell against her hip. The instant she recognized his arousal for what it was, she was stunned. She'd known he could still arouse her with no more than a look or a simple touch, but it had never occurred to her that she might still possess the same power with him.

Then reality overruled feminine vanity. It was the middle of the night, a time when people were at their most vulnerable; she was sitting on his lap with practically nothing between them; and he'd gone as long as she had without physical satisfaction—since last year's stay at the McBride Inn. Of course she could arouse him. Any living, breathing woman could.

She moved slightly, and he caught his breath. "I think—" he began.

"Don't think. If you do, you'll do the sensible thing

and go back to your room and whatever sleep we each get won't be worth having."

His right hand slid marginally across her arm in the tiniest of caresses. "This is foolish, Maggie." His words sounded certain. His voice, strained like his body, didn't.

"I know." She moved, and her knuckles grazed his stomach, then she flattened her palm against him. In an instant the temperature of his skin switched from warm to feverish.

"It will only complicate things."

"Or maybe simplify them. Do you want me?"

His laughter was short, coarse, as he slid one hand to her hip, held her close, and rubbed against her. "Hell, what do you think?"

"I want you too. And I can't think of anything more natural than you and me having sex together."

"Maggie—"

She slid off his lap and went to stand by the window. "I could convince you if I wanted. I know that. But it's your decision, Ross. You can go back to your room, or you can stay here with me. You choose."

He was motionless for a moment. Then he stood, and the thin light coming through the window showed just how aroused he was. The sight made her throat go dry, made swallowing impossible. Again, for a moment, he stood still, and she thought with regret that common sense was going to win out. He was going to shut himself in his room—to shut her out. Part of her hoped he did, for their own good. The rest of her would regret it.

Moving with slow, taut grace, he closed the distance

between them, maneuvered her with his body until the wall was at her back. He rested his palms against the wall on either side of her head, and he kissed her. It wasn't the kiss she expected after so many long months—neither sweet nor gentle nor tentative nor shy. He didn't coax or tease, didn't play or manipulate, but claimed her mouth in a heated, hungry kiss, thrusting his tongue inside, demanding her own heat and hunger, accepting her pleasure.

Sliding his hands down, he cupped her bottom and lifted her, rubbing, rocking his hips against her in a rough caress that made her weak. She raised her hands to his body, touching his face, his throat where his pulse beat hard and fast, his muscled chest, his narrow hips. She'd been hungry for this, she realized in a haze of sensation—for touching, for touching *him*. More than her husband and only lover, he was the other part of her self, and she'd missed her hands on his body as much as she'd missed his on her own body.

They were halfway across the room before she realized the wall was no longer at her back. Beside the bed, he broke the kiss, panting for air, and pulled her nightshirt over her head, kicked his sweats away. She had only an instant's concern for the scars before he lifted her onto the bed, followed her down, and slid inside her without delay. This first time would be fast, she knew, with just enough wicked pleasure to take the edge off their desire. But the next time . . . Ah, the next time would be slow, torturous, a test of endurance and power—how much could she bear, and once she'd borne all she could, how many times he could make her plead for more. She *would* plead, and so would he, and the result would be soul-stealing.

He kissed her, teased her breasts, thrust into her fast, hard. He made her skin burn, her muscles quiver and twitch, drew from her body every need, every fantasy, and satisfied every one. He brought her to an orgasm so intense that it made her ache, then emptied himself into her with his own completion.

Then the *real* event started.

It had been so long, and she'd been so lonely. She'd missed this, had needed it—needed *him*. His kisses, lazy and hot and designed to make her weak. His caresses, all the right ways in all the right places. His mouth relentless on her breast, his hands tormenting between her thighs. It was all too sweet, too cruel, too much but never enough. She begged for relief, and he promised it but held back, pushing her harder, making her need fiercer, until neither could wait one second more.

Some time passed before he summoned the energy to pull the blankets over them. This was what she wanted, she thought as he pulled her close, fitted his body like a glove against hers. This was what she'd *always* wanted—passion, intimacy, two-halves-of-a-whole satisfaction. So far she'd found it only with Ross.

Would she ever find it with somebody else?

HOW WAS A MAN SUPPOSED TO ACT THE morning after the second biggest mistake in his life?

Ross awakened early Saturday morning with that

thought in his mind—and Maggie's long, lean, naked body in his arms. He knew how he *wanted* to act, he thought with a scowl as his body hardened. He wanted to shift her leg, slide inside her, and wake her up with the gentlest lovemaking she could imagine. He wanted to roll her onto her back and fill her again, wanted to roll onto his own back and lift her above him. He wanted to give her again that hazy, supremely satisfied look that only he had ever given her, to take her again and again until she gave up forever the idea of another man. He wanted to brand her as his own, to make it impossible for her to ever forget it.

But she *wasn't* his. He'd given up his right to her the day he'd decided to sleep with another woman.

The memory had the effect of an icy shower. It uncurled his arm from around her waist, lifted the covers, and slid him away from her soft, silky heat. After retucking the blankets around her, he pulled on the sweats he'd discarded on the floor, nudged up the thermostat, then went to the bathroom down the hall. He would shower and get dressed, make coffee and check his mail and messages. By the time Maggie woke up, he would know what to say, what to do, how to handle this potentially fatal mistake.

But when he finished dressing after his shower, he'd found no answers and had no interest in coffee or mail or messages. Though he knew it would be best to walk away—to treat last night like the aberrancy it was—when he left his room, he didn't go away. He returned to her room, turned the rocker to face the bed, sat down, and watched her sleep.

He never should have come in last night when her

tears awakened him, but he'd been frightened, panicked. He could no more have lain in his bed and left
her to sob alone than he could go back and change
their past. And so he'd come in and left his good sense
and willpower at the door, and when things had turned
sexual . . .

Hell, he couldn't even completely regret it. Sex with
Maggie had always been the best times of his life, and
last night had been no different.

Except that they were supposed to divorce in another month or two.

The reminder forced his features into a deep scowl
that eased only after several minutes spent studying her.
She lay on her side, her hands folded beneath her chin.
There were shadows under her eyes—restless sleep and
heartbroken sobs could do that—but she was still the
most beautiful woman he'd ever known. He already
knew he would measure every woman he ever met
against her and find them lacking, which didn't bode
well for his future. She was everything he'd ever
wanted—everything he'd once turned his back on.
Now he found himself wanting her again—this morning. Next week. Next month.

Next year.

She shifted, sighed, stretched her arms above her
head. Some mornings she was slow to awaken. Others,
her eyes popped open and she was instantly alert. She
opened her eyes, yawned, saw him sitting there and
automatically smiled, then remembered last night and
just as quickly did a mental retreat. "Good morning,"
she said, not at all sure that it was. Her earlier stretch
had pulled the covers to a point above the tips of her

breasts. Even as he felt a stab of desire, she pulled them up tight around her chin. "What—what are you doing . . . ?"

"I slept here." His voice took on an edge. "Was I supposed to return to my own room when we were done? Was that a part of the agreement we didn't get around to discussing?"

Her cheeks flushed the same becoming rosy shade they took on when she was in the throes of orgasm. "I—I didn't . . . I just . . . of course not."

He should have gone downstairs—should have left her to wake up alone, to deal with what had happened before she had to deal with him. He should have given her a chance to face the dismay and the regret—because he would bet this year's profits that that was what she was feeling—but now it was too late. Now they had to face it together.

"Do you expect me to apologize?" he asked when it became clear that she wasn't going to speak.

"Of course not," she said indignantly. "Do you expect me to?"

"For what?"

"It was my idea."

"An idea I've been fighting for more than a week."

"Why?"

He gestured impatiently at the distance between them. "Isn't it obvious?"

She gave no response, but after a time she asked a cautious question of her own. "Is this what it was like after the last time?"

His smile was thin and humorless as he shook his head. "I wanted to make love to you again the next morning, but when I woke up, you were gone. When you finally came back, you pretended as if nothing had happened, and"—the male sexual ego being the fragile thing it was—"I let you. Things went back to exactly the way they were before. You lived your life, and I lived mine, and we never deliberately touched again."

After another moment's silence, she asked in a hesitant, fearful whisper, "Would you be interested in making love to me again this morning?"

For a long time he simply looked at her. When finally he offered an answer, it was simple, quiet, all too aware of the rejection she had risked, that he was risking. "Yes. I would."

She swallowed hard, then pushed back the covers in silent invitation. Slowly his gaze slid from her face to her throat, over her breasts to her belly, one smooth hip, one shapely thigh. He knew she watched him—to see if he lingered, looking for scars he'd never seen?—but he didn't.

His clothes came off easily, landing in an untidy pile on the floor, then he joined her in bed. His first simple touch sent a delicate shiver through her. The second made her breath catch. The third made his own breath catch. By the time he took her, her skin was slick with sweat, her breathing ragged, her responses raw and shocky. She welcomed him into her with a gasp, then a long, low moan that vibrated through him. She felt so incredibly good. So incredibly *right*.

They took it slowly, as if years hadn't passed since they'd shared a lazy Saturday-morning seduction, and yet always there, always present, was the need—sharp, demanding, building. Turning onto his back, he lifted her over him, then relinquished control to her, lay still, and simply looked at her. With her face flushed, her hair mussed, her body all soft and quivery, she looked like a woman on the verge of pure, sweet delight. She was the only woman he'd ever seen like this.

The only woman he'd ever loved like this.

He knew the exact instant she relinquished control too—knew when the need for satisfaction became desperate and drove her faster, harder, deeper—and then for one incredible moment he knew nothing. Nothing but pleasure so intense that he groaned with it. Nothing but heat, sensation, throbbing, filling, dying.

Nothing but Maggie.

Quiet settled around them. Her breathing eased. The rushing in his ears quieted. The shudders that racked them both calmed. She lay against him, still astride him, still gloving him. Her hair fell forward to hide her face, but he didn't need to see. He knew the sweet look she wore, the one he took such pleasure in, the one that was a twin to his own expression.

Finally, after time, she lifted her head, pushed her hair back, and somber green eyes met his. "This changes things, doesn't it?"

He nodded.

"How?"

"I'm not sure."

"It doesn't have to." Her voice took on a casual tone that he didn't like. He didn't want casual from her. He wanted passion. Need. Greed. "We can behave like two intelligent, mature adults and accept that sex between two healthy people who have been a couple as long as we have is a perfectly normal occurrence. We can ensure that it doesn't happen again, or we can fulfill each other's needs, indulge that aspect of our marriage for the time that remains, and then go ahead with our plans as intended."

He scowled at her. "We amend the terms of our agreement to include sex, then in another four or six or eight weeks we both just walk away as planned. You think it's that easy?"

She ducked her head and answered so softly that he barely heard. "No."

"And how would we ensure that it doesn't happen again? As you said, we're two healthy adults. We both enjoy sex, particularly with each other, and we've had damn little of it in the last three years. How—"

"Four years," she interrupted. "And whose fault was that? Who was always working? Who was always gone?"

He arched one brow. "So now you want to lay blame. Of course. You always get around to that sooner or later. Well, let me save you the trouble, Maggie. It was *my* fault. I was obsessed with work. I spent more time at the office than I did at home. I forced you to go to boring parties. I dressed you up in gowns and jewels to show you off and then I put you away and forgot about you until I needed you again. I made you live in a house you hated and gave you money you didn't want. I neglected you, ignored you, used you, manipulated you, abandoned you. It was all my fault. Everything that ever went wrong between us was all my fault. Are you satisfied?"

She scrambled out of bed, snatched up a robe from

the floor, and fumbled it on, in the process giving him his first look at the scars. Guilt overwhelmed him as he stared. He couldn't breathe, couldn't think, couldn't do anything but reach out a trembling hand, utter a stricken whisper. "Oh, God, Maggie . . ."

Shame flooded her face. She pulled the robe tight and tied the belt with a savage yank. "Get out."

Her voice was deadly calm, deadly angry, and too late he realized that the horror he felt must have shown on his face. He slid to the edge of the bed, but she stepped away. By the time he was on his feet, she was in the bathroom, slamming the door in his face, locking it before he thought to push his way in.

He rested his palm against the wood. "Maggie, I'm sorry." Sorry and sickened by the evidence of what he'd done to her. *He* was responsible for the obscene scars and all the pain behind them. If not for him . . .

"Maggie, please open the door."

There was complete silence in the bathroom.

"Please, Maggie, just let me explain. . . ."

The sound of rushing water broke the quiet as she turned on the shower. A moment later, from the change in tenor, he knew she'd stepped underneath the spray and, frustrated, he banged his fist on the door. "Damn it, Maggie! I didn't mean . . ." The frustration dissolved, and he turned slowly away from the door.

She'd been right about one thing. It *was* all his fault. Everything. And he had to live with that.

• • •

WHEN HER SKIN HAD SHRIVELED AND the water had turned cold, Maggie shut off the shower, but she didn't get to her feet. She remained where she'd spent the last twenty minutes, huddled on the tiles. The water had sprayed over her bowed head, cocooning her in a loud, wet world, but she'd still been able to hear Ross.

She'd still been able to see his revulsion, to feel his disgust.

Tears welled, and she angrily dashed them away. She wouldn't cry over this. So she was damaged goods. So he probably wouldn't have wanted her if he'd seen her first. It didn't matter. She didn't want any man who could look at her that way simply because she was flawed. There were worse things than having a few scars—like dying.

Like seeing that the very sight of your body sickened the man who had just made love with you.

Lifting her head, she listened to the room outside the door but heard nothing. He was gone, thank God. She didn't want to see him again, not yet.

Slowly she got to her feet, stiff, a little sore. She dried her body, combed her hair. Opening the door just a crack, she peered out and saw that his clothes were gone from the floor. Quickly, she dressed, applied makeup, fixed her hair, then ventured into the hallway, half expecting to find him waiting.

His voice came faintly from downstairs. Even at a distance she recognized anger. Once he'd satisfactorily ruined her day, he must have decided to do the same for Tom or some other poor sucker who worked for him.

Downstairs she tiptoed to the hall closet. She took out her coat and purse, added a scarf and gloves, then slipped out the side door. She needed time alone, and a walk to Harry's for breakfast seemed just the ticket.

The snow was heavy on the sidewalk but not impassable. Out there in the cold, the quiet, the solitude, she could be numb to the hurt, the shame. She could be alone and pretend that it was what she wanted. She could recapture her dreams for the future—for getting Ross out of her life and falling in love with someone new.

By the time she reached Harry's, though, she was cold but far from numb, and she hadn't come close to finding her way past the fear that a future without Ross was no future at all.

With her arms full of dishes, Maeve greeted her cheerfully. "You just find a seat wherever you can, Maggie, and I'll be right with you."

She was scanning the café for a seat when a wave from the last booth caught her attention. It was J. D. Grayson, inviting her to join him. Because any company was better than her own this morning—except Ross's—she accepted the invitation.

"Are you out alone this morning?" he asked.

"I'm a grown woman. I'm allowed to go out by myself."

"Hey, you'll get no argument from me. This is just the first time I've seen you out without Ross." When her only response was to look down at her hands, in a more serious tone he asked, "Is something wrong?"

"Nothing you'd want to know about."

"I'm a psychiatrist. I want to know about everything."

She shook her head as Maeve arrived with coffee. After Maggie placed her order, the waitress asked, "Is that handsome husband of yours joining you?"

Smiling tautly, Maggie shook her head.

After Maeve left, Dr. Grayson fixed his gaze on her. "You'll feel better if you talk about it."

She knew he was right, but she remained stubborn. "I'd rather not discuss it," she said firmly, then, for good measure, changed the subject. "I saw you were with Holly last night. Are you two involved?"

"We're friends. Does that count?"

"I think that's the best kind of 'involved' a man and a woman can have."

"Like you and Ross." At her sharp look, he shrugged. "You two certainly seemed friendly last night."

"It was thirty degrees and snowing. *Everyone* was friendly. We were trying to stay warm."

"Where is he this morning?"

"Home. Working."

"Does that bother you?"

"No." But that was a lie. It wasn't that she'd wanted to find him waiting after her shower. She just wanted what had happened to mean enough to him that he couldn't think of anything like work.

"It can't be easy, living together but not . . . well, *living* together."

"It's been fine." Unlike her previous answer, this one was true. It *had* been fine, right up until the middle of last night. *Why* hadn't she let him go back to his room when he'd started to? Why hadn't she locked the door *then* instead of in the morning, when it was already too late? So she'd had a bad dream. At least it had been one she could wake from. *This* one she had to live.

"You know, Dr. Grayson," she said, forcing calm into her voice. "I could call for an appointment Monday, and you could get paid for this."

"For having breakfast with a friend?" he asked innocently as Maeve brought their meal.

With the arrival of the food, the conversation eased into more comfortable, less significant subjects. Maggie relaxed enough to laugh a few times—to forget for odd moments that morning's scene in her bedroom. The pain always came back, though, sometimes sharper than ever.

After they paid their checks, Dr. Grayson walked outside with her. "I'm parked right over here. Can I give you a ride?"

"No, thanks. I'd rather walk. But thanks for the offer—and for the company."

"It was my pleasure. And if whatever you don't want to talk about is still bothering you Monday, make that call, will you?"

With a noncommittal nod she watched him walk away. He was about to climb into a mud-spattered sport utility truck a few yards away, when abruptly, surprising even herself, she blurted out, "He saw the scars for the first time."

His gaze flickered across her face, but those scars were well covered with makeup. He came back a few feet, and she moved closer. "I take it his reaction was less than diplomatic."

"He was appalled."

"Of course he was." Her own expression must have been appalled too, because he hastened to explain. "It's one thing for him to *know* that you had surgery. It's another to see the scars where they cut you open, and it's still another entirely when they cut you open to repair damage from injuries suffered in an accident for which he bears some responsibility."

"It wasn't his fault," she said defensively. "He had nothing to do with it."

"Why were you on the highway that night?"

She shoved her hands into her pockets so he couldn't see the fists that formed. "I—I'm not sure. We—we'd had an argument."

"And you couldn't stay there any longer. Ross took part in the argument. He was your biggest reason for leaving. By his own admission to the sheriff, he didn't try to stop you from leaving. He *does* bear some responsibility, Maggie, at least in his mind."

Stubbornly she shook her head. She might not remember what happened that night, but she knew herself well enough to realize that if she'd been angry enough to leave Bethlehem on Christmas Eve, no one ould have stopped her short of physically restraining her.

"My point, Maggie, is that Ross believes he's to blame for your injuries—for your scars. Seeing them was a vivid reminder of his guilt. He can look at you like this"—with one gloved hand, he made a sweeping, head-to-toe gesture—"and forget that anything ever happened. But it's hard to forget when you're looking at the scars."

She wanted to believe he was right, wanted it more than she would have guessed, but it wasn't easy. Appearance had always been important to Ross. He'd wanted her to look perfect, and now she hadn't a chance in hell of even coming close.

Dr. Grayson's voice softened. "Don't blame him for having an honest reaction, Maggie. Just because he found the scars—what was your word? Appalling?—doesn't mean he finds you that way too." He shrugged, offered a crooked smile. "The fact that he even saw certain of these scars tends to suggest otherwise." After a brief pause, he asked, "Are you sure I can't give you a ride?"

Her face warm with a flush, she changed her earlier answer. She was cold, sore, and had no place to go *but* home. "I would appreciate it."

They relied again on small talk to cover the short distance to the house. He pulled to the curb, and she climbed out before facing him again. "Thanks."

"Call me anytime. I keep regular hours at the hospital and at Harry's on weekends."

With a faint smile, she closed the door. As she turned to the house, though, the smile disappeared and despair stabbed through her. If only she could slip in unnoticed and hide away in her room . . .

There was just one problem: keys. She didn't have any. With all the grimness of a prisoner going to the firing squad, she climbed the steps and rang the bell. Too quickly to have come from the office, Ross opened the door. He looked cold and angry.

"I—I don't have any keys," she said as greeting and explanation rolled into one.

He walked away into the office, then came straight back to drop a key ring—house keys and car keys— into her hand. Before she could say thanks, he returned to the office and closed the doors.

Chapter Twelve

H E WAS A FIRST-CLASS BASTARD.
Ross had spent most of the day reminding himself of that and worrying about Maggie. Wondering what the hell she'd been doing with Grayson. Wanting to apologize to her. Wanting to run like hell away from her.

Just plain wanting her.

Now it was six o'clock and nothing had been resolved. Once she'd returned from wherever she'd met the damn shrink, she'd avoided him the rest of the day. They hadn't spoken one word. He hadn't made one apology.

It was time.

He left the office, where he'd accomplished nothing all day, and met her in the hall. She was dressed in leggings and a heavy sweater, and she carried a jacket—one of his—over one arm. In her free hand a pair of skates dangled by the laces. When she saw him, she stopped abruptly. Guiltily.

"Where do you think you're going?"

"Ice skating."

"Ice skating," he repeated blankly.

"At City Park. The Thomases invited us."

"And you just happened to forget to tell me."

His sarcasm made her flush. "You don't skate, and I . . . I don't want you to go."

The defiant words sent a sharp pain through him. He deserved that—and so much more—but it still hurt. Pushing it aside to deal with later, he said, "I don't think you should go either. You haven't skated in years. What if you fall?"

"One year," she corrected him. "I went with Melissa and Alex last year. And of course I'll probably fall. People do. But don't worry. J.D. will be there."

J.D. When had she started calling the shrink by his first name? he wondered as jealousy clawed through him. Exactly what had gone on between them that morning? "I don't give a damn if Grayson will be there. He won't be *here* to deal with it if you get hurt."

"You seem to think I need your permission, but you're wrong. I'm going skating whether you like it or not. My friends will all be there, and we're going to have fun. Remember having fun?" She slapped her forehead. "Oh, I forgot. Your idea of fun is making more money and accumulating more power. Well, you have your fun tonight, and I'll have mine."

When she started to move, he stepped aside to block her way. "You're not going."

"I am."

"Not unless I go too."

Behind him, the doorbell rang. He stopped her from answering it.

"That's Melissa," she said stiffly. "She said they would pick me since you couldn't make it."

"You can go with me or not at all."

Her eyes brightened like fire. "It's none of your business."

"It's always been my business. Last night made it even more so."

"Last night didn't—" She bit off the words and her jaw worked to keep them inside. Last night didn't give him any rights? Didn't change what was between them? Didn't mean a damn thing?

He didn't try to choose the most likely possibility. It would hurt too much. Instead, he coolly, obstinately, repeated, "With me, Maggie, or not at all."

The doorbell pealed a second time, and she swore. "All right. But I hope you have a miserable time."

He had no doubt he would. But miserable and watching her—especially around friends like Grayson—beat miserable and home alone anytime. "Tell Melissa that my plans have changed and we'll meet them there."

Scowling darkly, she pushed past him and walked to the door, where she told Melissa just that. The other woman responded with a cheerful "See you there," then Maggie closed the door and turned a chilly glare on Ross. Ignoring her, he went upstairs to trade his T-shirt for warmer clothes. Back downstairs, once he'd claimed his coat and gloves, they left for a silent, short trip across town.

The ice rink was situated at the opposite end of the park from the Tour of Lights setup. Bright lights illuminated the benches surrounding the rink and the skaters already on the ice. As they approached, he saw Alex and Melissa, Nathan and Emilie, Dean Elliott with a pretty blonde, Holly with a man. Everyone seemed to be having a good time, even Brendan Dalton, who glided along unsteadily, his hands securely clasped by Alanna and another young girl.

Not only was he going to have a miserable evening, he would be the only one so suffering. No doubt that would make Maggie even happier than the mere sight of her friends already had.

At one end of the oval rink, a small stone building served as skate rental, concession stand, and the only heat around. Ross looked at it longingly but followed Maggie to a bench. She was putting on her skates, when Holly slid to a stop at the rail in front of them.

"Hey, glad you guys could make it. Did Melissa tell you that we're all going back to the inn afterward for hot cocoa and dessert?"

"Yes, she did," Maggie replied.

Another invitation she had failed to mention. So she didn't want him there either. Ross felt a curious sensation—hopelessness?—take root inside.

"Ross, where are your skates?" Holly asked.

Before he could answer, Maggie did. "He doesn't skate."

"Rent a pair, and we'll teach you," Holly offered. "Melissa and I are great teachers. We taught every kid out here."

Ross was tempted to take her up on the offer, if for

no other reason than to wipe that smug look off Maggie's face. Only the fact that she so obviously wanted him here on the sidelines—on the outside, literally, looking in—made him politely decline.

She stood up, balancing carefully on the blades, and took a few wobbly steps. As she stepped onto the ice, he tried once more. "Maggie, I don't think—"

She cut him off with a sharp look. "No, you don't, do you?" Without waiting to hear his response, she pushed off with Holly at her side. Her movements were awkward and jerky at first, but soon she found the natural, graceful rhythm.

He watched for a few minutes, then sat down on the concrete bench. Though it had been swept clean of snow, it was like sitting on a slab of ice.

"Try this. It's a lot more comfortable."

He looked up, then accepted the vinyl cushion J. D. Grayson offered.

Grayson sat down on his own cushion and cradled both hands around a foam cup of coffee. "You don't skate?"

"I never had a chance to learn. In my neighborhood, skating was for sissies."

"In my neighborhood, it was for hockey players— and we weren't sissies. Why don't you let Holly teach you? I heard her offer."

Rather than admit the truth and sacrifice his pride, Ross merely shrugged.

"Not an activity of choice for the rich and powerful, huh? Why didn't you just stay home, where you could at least be warm?"

"I don't think Maggie should be here."

"Why not?"

"Because she's got steel plates in her leg holding the bones together. Because she just learned to walk again a few months ago. Because she could do a hell of a lot of damage." His tone was sharper than the question deserved. In contrast, Grayson's was milder.

"Actually, the plates and screws are titanium, and she's walking fine. As long as she doesn't try something fancy like a triple Salchow, she's not in danger of hurting anything."

"If she falls—"

"She'll most likely land on her butt, which is generally the most padded portion of the human anatomy. I know your intentions are good, but don't be overprotective, Ross. She needs to try things, to see for herself what she can do. We want her to be careful, not afraid."

He wanted her to be safe, not careful. He wanted her to never be hurt again. And he wanted to be the one to make sure of that.

Morosely, he watched as Dean Elliott skated between her and Holly, linking his arms with theirs. His gaze followed them around the rink twice, then, as Holly's date claimed Maggie's other arm, he looked away, catching a glimpse of the Bishops. As long as he was deciding who should and shouldn't be allowed on the ice, he would insist that Emilie leave too. What was Bishop thinking? If *his* wife were pregnant, the last place she'd be was sliding around an ice rink on a pair of narrow blades and only one hard fall away from disaster. If *his* wife were pregnant—

She very well might be.

The thought whispered through him, leaving cold panic in its wake. They'd gone through maybe one box of condoms years ago, before the wedding, before she'd started taking the Pill, and that was the last time he'd been given responsibility for birth control. Once, when she'd tired of taking the Pill, he had suggested a vasectomy instead, and she had quickly decided a once-a-day tablet wasn't so bad. She'd taken them right up until the accident, but as far as he knew, she hadn't started them again since her discharge. Why would she, when her dearest wish was to get pregnant as soon as possible after the divorce?

She could be pregnant right then. She would be thrilled. He would be . . . what?

His first response to even the possibility was dismay. He didn't want kids. They were a complication his life didn't need and couldn't accommodate. He'd been a failure as a husband and would probably fail as a father too, considering the example his own father had set for him.

If that response was selfish, the second was even more so. A baby would be a link from him to Maggie that she could never break. It would give him a reason to stay in her life. It would fulfill her dearest wish—and how many men got a chance to fulfill the dearest desire of a woman like Maggie?

There was just one problem: Her dearest wish was to have *another* man's baby, not his. To fall in love, marry, and live happily ever after with any other man but him. Though she would love and treasure his child, she wouldn't want *him* around. She would choose someone else—like Grayson—to take his place, to raise his child, to share their lives.

He was in a sorry state when the certain knowledge that Maggie wouldn't want him playing father to a child he'd never wanted could hurt the way it did.

Beside him, Grayson hunkered forward, elbows on his knees. "You ever consider staying in Bethlehem?"

Ross scowled. "My business is in Buffalo."

"But your wife is in Bethlehem. Your business can be moved. I don't think your wife can. Is there anything about the business that requires you to be there?"

"No." His base of operations was Buffalo only because that was where he'd always lived. Relocating would be a relatively simple process. He wouldn't have to move his entire staff, just some of his top people. Tom would have to be in Bethlehem at least part of the time, but Lynda could stay in Buffalo to oversee things there.

The last thought made him blink. A few weeks earlier he would have said Lynda's presence near his office was vital. He never would have considered moving across the street without taking her with him. Why was he now contemplating doing business with her five hours away?

Because now he knew how she'd treated Maggie. Worse, he knew how it'd made her feel.

But he wasn't seriously contemplating anything. The last thing Maggie wanted was him in Bethlehem. This was *her* town, *her* friends, and she didn't want to share them with him.

"What would it take to make such a move?" Grayson asked. When Ross simply shrugged, the doctor said, "Humor me. I'm curious, and we don't have much else to talk about. What would it take?"

To start, some assurance that Maggie wanted him there with her. That he wouldn't make such a major change, then have to watch her fall in love and make a life with someone else. "First, I would have to buy some property and build an office. I haven't seen any space around here that would be suitable."

"That could be done easily enough. Then?"

Irritation flickered through Ross. He didn't care to expend energy on games of what-if that didn't stand a chance in hell of actually coming to fruition. Still, it gave him something to do and eased the ache of watching Maggie smiling up at Holly's date the way she used to smile at *him*. "I'd choose which of my staff to bring along and persuade them to relocate."

"That couldn't be too hard. Money will persuade a lot of people. The ones who are immune to greed could probably be won over by the promise of the good life in Bethlehem. And then?"

"Then . . . move. Get everything up and running." That was simplifying things a bit, but all in all, it wouldn't be too difficult. He wouldn't allow it to be. The difficulty would be living here without Maggie.

Living *anywhere* without her.

Uncomfortable with the implication, he abruptly got to his feet. "Tell Maggie I've gone home. I'm sure someone will give her a ride to the inn, then home."

"Don't you want to meet us there?"

He did, he realized even as he shook his head. He wanted to be a part of their group, wanted to have a little of the fun Maggie considered him incapable of. He wanted to belong.

But he didn't.

"No," he said flatly, bitterly. "My lawyer was supposed to fax some records to me this evening. I need to go over them."

"You know, even God rested."

The only responses Ross could think of were flippant or pathetic, so he said nothing but good-bye and headed for his car. While the engine warmed, he watched Maggie, happy and laughing, and wished—

He had so many wishes that he didn't know where to start.

When he got home, the house was still and quiet. He paused in the office door, saw the red message light blinking on the answering machine, and the pages of Tom's records on the fax machine, but he didn't go inside. He'd already proven that he couldn't concentrate on business, not in this mood.

Instead, he turned into the living room. He took a seat in an overstuffed chair, propped his feet on the ottoman, slid down, and stared at the tree. He stared until tiny halos appeared around each light, until all the lights melded into one giant, twinkling form, and he listened. The clocks ticked. The refrigerator motor clicked on, then off. The phone rang and, a moment later, the fax printed out more work. The heat cycled on and off. Finally he heard the sound he was waiting for, that he'd waited for earlier today. A car engine out front, the solid thunk of a door closing, keys in the lock.

Maggie came inside, bringing with her a breath of

fresh air. Her skates landed on the hall floor with a gentle thud, then she came to stand in the doorway. Though he stared harder at the tree, he saw her peripherally, a shadow that remained motionless for one moment, then turned away disinterestedly. After a trip to the kitchen, she went upstairs. A moment later he heard the closing of her door. An instant after that he imagined he heard the click of the lock.

She was never going to forgive him.

Worse, he didn't deserve to be forgiven.

T HE CLOCK ON THE NIGHTSTAND READ one-fifteen when Maggie gave up on sleep. She pulled on a pair of thin cotton pants and slid her arms into her robe before slowly opening the door. Ross had gone to bed an hour ago, and his room had been silent ever since. She'd thought about waiting in the hall for him to come up, about knocking on his door after he did come up—even about inviting herself inside. Of course, she hadn't done anything.

For two mature, intelligent adults, they certainly didn't learn from their mistakes. The hurt feelings and anger never should have reached this point. If she hadn't gotten defensive that morning, blaming him for their poor sex life before he had the opportunity to blame her, he wouldn't have gotten angry and thrown back every complaint she'd made to him. And if she hadn't overreacted to his response to her scars . . .

If, if, if. She *hated* that word.

She made her way to the kitchen. She should have apologized to Ross as soon as she came back from breakfast. She shouldn't have let the silence grow. God help her, she never should have told him she didn't want him skating with her tonight. That had been cruel, and he had every right to hold it against her.

It was too corny to even think without a groan, but there were other things she wanted him to hold against her—like himself. That was why she was down there, gathering baking pans, ingredients, and her heavy-duty mixer. She was going to bake a goodwill gesture and hope they could take it from there.

She worked slowly, taking the instructions one step at a time, humming softly to herself. For the first time in months she was truly enjoying the process. She trusted the recipe, one of her old favorites. If she followed it halfway properly, the cookies were guaranteed to be good.

The first tray was in the oven and she'd just finished spooning the last mound of dough on the second tray, when she heard footsteps in the hall. She gave a moment's thought to hiding the dough and the tray, but it was too late. Ross was coming through the doorway.

He looked uneasy, as if seeing her were the last thing he wanted in the middle of the night, and bewildered. He took in the mess she'd made on the island, the sight of her in T-shirt, pants, and robe—with her hair standing on end, she realized—then sniffed the air. "You're making white chocolate macadamia cookies."

His tone sounded accusatory, but maybe she was being overly sensitive. Maybe it was just the surprise of waking up in the middle of the night to find her baking. "You said they were your favorite," she said cautiously. "When I use food to bribe someone, I try to use their favorite."

"Why do you need a bribe?"

"Because I owe you an apology, and it'll go down better with cookies." She breathed deeply, appreciatively. The cookies smelled exactly the way they were supposed to, giving her high hopes for their taste.

He came closer. He wore a T-shirt and sweatpants—a lot of clothes for a man who slept naked. He'd learned a lesson, it seemed, about running around half-dressed—and about coming close to her, she added regretfully as he stopped with the island between them.

"This couldn't wait until morning?"

"It *is* morning."

"Sure, in England or Europe or somewhere. Not in New York."

Feeling foolish now, she shrugged. "I didn't expect you to eat them tonight. I just couldn't sleep."

"Neither could I." He slid onto the nearest stool and folded his hands. He had great hands—strong, capable, with long, thin fingers. For a long time he'd worn a simple gold band on one of them. Later he'd traded it for a simple diamond band, and then one day he'd abandoned it too. She would give a lot to see that plain gold ring there again.

She would give even more if this time it would stay.

Or if she just didn't care.

"Did you have fun tonight?" he asked, yanking her from her thoughts.

Her face flushing, she used the cookies as an excuse to delay answering. When the finished cookies were on a wire cooling rack, she finally looked at him. "No, I didn't."

"Come on, Maggie, I was there. I saw you."

"You saw what I wanted you to see." Her voice had been too bright, her smile too happy, her mood too phony. She'd put on an act, and then she'd seen that he was gone and she'd wanted nothing more than to sink down right there on the ice and cry. Only pride had held her together. She would have gone home as soon as the skating was over, but she'd been afraid, and so she'd gone to the inn and continued her farce. She'd continued it right up until the instant her bedroom door closed behind her. By then she'd been too drained to cry.

"I saw you having a wonderful time and pretending that I wasn't there."

"No. You saw me pretending to have a wonderful time and wishing that you *were* there." When he started to disagree, she stopped him. "Wishing that you were with me—that you wanted to be with me."

"You're the one who said you didn't want me to go."

She clasped her hands tightly. "I lied."

"Why?"

Her shrug was small and ashamed. "After what happened in my room, you just put on your clothes and went to the office and worked all day, as if none of it had meant a thing to you. You didn't even speak to me when I came back after breakfast. You didn't eat lunch with me. You ignored me, and you worked."

"You told me to get out," he murmured stiffly.

She had, and at the time she'd meant it. She'd felt

ugly and ashamed and had wanted only to be alone with her humiliation. But later . . . Would it have hurt him to pretend that nothing had happened? To look at her instead of through her? To speak to her just once during the day?

"You regret it, don't you?" she asked. If they hadn't made love, they wouldn't have argued, he wouldn't have seen her naked, and they wouldn't be up at two in the morning, having this painful conversation.

"Of course I regret it. I never meant to . . ."

His voice trailed off, and something inside her died. An empty throb settled in her chest, and her throat grew tight. She turned away and faced the window, hugging both arms tightly to her middle.

"Damn, Maggie, how could I *not* regret it?"

"Oh, I don't know." Her voice sounded funny, teary. "Maybe because you were so willing every time that regret seemed the furthest thing from your mind."

For a long time there was silence, then . . . "What the hell are you talking about?"

"Making love. Having sex. Whatever you prefer to call it." His confusion caused her to turn around, to risk a look at him. "What are *you* talking about?"

He left the stool and walked around to lean against the island a half dozen feet from her. "I'm talking about giving you the very wrong impression that those scars make a damn bit of difference in how beautiful you are." The words were quiet, sincere, unarguable. For one moment they hovered in the air between them, then slowly they started to ease the emptiness in her chest, to make it possible for her to breathe again. "I was stunned, Maggie. The scars . . . They're obscene, and they're my fault. I did that to you, and I'll never have the words to tell you how much I regret it."

Staring at him, she focused on the one important part of his speech. "You think I'm beautiful?"

"Incredibly so."

"Scars and all?"

His faint smile was sad that she felt the need to clarify. "You're the most beautiful woman I've ever known. Scars and all."

"Then sometime you might want to—" She broke off, suddenly too shy to continue, and his smile gained strength.

"Make love with you again? I've wanted to all day. All evening. All night. I want to right now. But . . ."

She waited, edgy and uneasy, to hear his objection.

"You're not taking birth control pills. You could get pregnant."

And for him that was a major objection. He'd wanted no part of creating a baby with her when they were happily married, and he wanted it even less now. Though the knowledge broke her heart, she kept her expression smooth, her voice level. "Yes, I understand the connection between the two. What do you want? A sworn statement that I wouldn't expect anything from you?"

He looked offended, then irritated. Before he could speak, though, she did.

"It doesn't matter. This is the wrong time of the month. You have nothing to worry about." She tried to not notice the relief that eased across his face. "So . . . what do we do now?"

"First you finish with the cookies. I'll help you.

Then we go upstairs and you work off some of this tension. I'll help with that too."

She knew exactly how, knew that when he was finished "helping," she would be limp, too spent to make the slightest demand on her muscles. She would have only enough energy to curl up beside him for the rest of the night.

Seconds slid into minutes while she watched him and he watched her, until finally he gestured toward the oven. "The timer's beeping."

She glanced at the oven, then back. "I don't care about the cookies."

"Hey, white chocolate macadamia's my favorite."

"I know plenty of your other favorites." But at last she moved to the oven. She set the finished tray aside, then began spooning dough onto the next. She'd managed only one neat mound, when Ross came to stand behind her. He reached around her with both arms, pulled the spoon from her, then slid her robe down, leaving it to puddle on the floor around her feet. When he put the spoon back in her hand, for a few seconds she couldn't remember what it was for.

"Cookies, Maggie." His reminder was murmured right into her ear, tickling, followed by the touch of his tongue. She dropped the scoop of dough back into the bowl, tried again, and got it on the tray this time.

"I don't think this is what Dr. Grayson had in mind when he suggested that you help me cook," she said in a voice as unsteady as her legs, as fluttery as her heart.

"Screw Dr. Grayson."

Her laughter dissolved as his hands slid over her breasts, and her breath caught in her throat. Her

T-shirt was old and soft and heightened the impact of his caresses. She tilted her head back, closed her eyes, and lost track of everything but his mouth, his hands, and the gentle, lazy pleasure they were creating. "I—I thought . . ." It was a lie. She couldn't think just then, not without a struggle. "I thought . . . you liked . . . Dr. Grayson."

"My dislike for him is directly proportional to your liking. The cookies, Maggie."

She felt blindly for the bowl, filled the spoon, emptied it on what she hoped was the tray. "You sound almost . . ." The word disappeared as he slid one hand underneath her shirt to rub her breast, to torment her nipple with caresses gentle and teasing and wicked and hard.

"Jealous? Damn straight. He's not your type."

"Then who is?"

"Me. *I'm* your type." As if to emphasize his words, he pressed against her, thrusting, rubbing. She dropped the spoon with a clatter, braced her hands on the cold counter, and wished desperately that they were naked, that he was inside her, that they could stay that way forever. When he slid his hand underneath the waist of her pants, over her hip, between her thighs, she groaned. "If you don't stop, I'm going to . . ."

He moved his fingers gently. "To what?"

"Oh, please . . ."

"Please do that?" He stroked her, and her nerves tightened another notch.

"Please, Ross, not without . . ." Another caress, another gasp, more steamy, tingling heat. "Not without you," she whispered, and, like that, he stopped. No more erotic kisses, no more wicked caresses, no more heat and hunger and need except her own, and it was untamed, clawing through her like something wild and primitive.

He moved to the end of the island, put distance between them, then touched his cool fingers to her burning face. "I like that look on you—aroused. Womanly. Purely sexual."

She took a breath. Another. And another. When she could focus, she fixed her gaze on him. When she could speak, she softly, without rancor, murmured, "Bastard."

"You asked me to stop. What kind of man would I be if I didn't?" He tried for a smile, but it wouldn't form. He dragged in his own deep breath, and his eyes turned dark, his voice thick. "Forget the cookies. I want you now."

Her smile came as easily as his refused. She could play the same game with him, could tease him and make him ache, make him beg, then make him wait. She could toy with him until his body was tingling, straining, threatening to find its own relief without her.

She turned away from the island and took a roll of plastic wrap from the cabinet. Gathering the remaining dough, she rolled it into a ball, wrapped it in the plastic, and put it in the refrigerator. She transferred the last batch of cookies to the cooling rack, set the dishes in the sink to soak, turned off the oven, leisurely washed and dried her hands as if she had nothing better in the world to do. Then, trailing her robe behind her, she left the kitchen.

It took him a moment to follow her, and when he

did, he found her robe at the foot of the stairs. Her pants were draped over the railing at the top. Her T-shirt lay on the floor outside her bedroom door.

He stepped inside the room, turned on the overhead light, and dropped the clothes. She wanted to protest the light, but didn't. She wanted to see him. He had the right to see her. He came to the bed, stripped off his clothes, pulled away the covers. For a long, long while he studied her body and she studied his face. She looked hard but found no revulsion, no distaste, nothing but need, hunger, and pure, sweet lust.

As he joined her, joined with her, she felt a moment's regret that in the kitchen she'd eased his fears about pregnancy with the truth. She wished this were exactly the right time, wished she could know that this act—this loving—would result in the greatest gift he could ever offer. She wished she could be assured that whatever happened, she would always have a part of him in his child.

Then sensation overtook conscious thought. Her brain turned fuzzy as the promise of satisfaction began building in her belly. He gave her all she could bear and greedily demanded of her more, ruthlessly, relentlessly, taking her harder, pushing her further, until she couldn't bear any more, until her hands clenched and her body shuddered, torn into a million pieces as he filled her, as she found her own release.

Minutes passed. The night air cooled their skin. The faint aroma of cookies drifted through the house. Her fingers slowly uncurled their grip on his arms, and the tension seeped from her muscles. There was nothing more vital than that glorious moment of completion, nothing more wonderful than the lazy, well-loved languor that followed. One was best, the other better. She wasn't sure which was which.

Well-loved. The innocent words pricked her indolence and stirred a quiver of sorrow. If only the words were true, if only Ross loved her—not the habit of a long-married man for his wife, but *real* love, of a man for a woman—she would be the happiest woman in the world.

But, at least in one sense, the words *were* true. She had just been well and truly loved. No other man could have done it better. While it wasn't everything she wanted, it was more than she'd had any right to expect.

They lay facing each other, her head on his arm, his leg bent over her hip. She touched her fingers to his jaw, rough with beard, then brushed them, just the tips, across his mouth. He automatically kissed them before giving a rich, deeply satisfied sigh.

"Ross?"

His eyelashes flickered.

"What do you call it?"

He opened his eyes, and she saw that he knew exactly what she was asking. Making love, having sex, whatever you prefer to call it, she'd said downstairs. There'd been no opportunity for him to tell her what he preferred, though with his next words he'd called her beautiful. At the time she'd needed to hear that more than she'd needed to know how he would describe what they had just done.

Now she needed to know.

He touched her hair, her cheek, her throat—

touched her tenderly, as if she were fragile. Precious. Silently coaxing her forward, he kissed her—nothing passionate, no tongues, no erotic dances, just a basic, simple kiss—and then he answered.

"I call it the best part of my life."

Chapter Thirteen

A S THE HIGHWAY LED INTO THE VAL-ley below, Tom Flynn eased one hand from the steering wheel, flexed his fingers, then re-peated the process with the other. The drive from Buffalo had been uneventful but long, reminding him why he'd used the company jet last time. This time he was in no hurry, so he'd thought he would waste a sunny Monday and see what the fascination with road trips was.

He still didn't know. Driving? He'd rather take flight anytime. Seeing the countryside? He preferred his trees in parks and better neighborhoods, the only places he'd ever seen them growing up. Witnessing these slices of small-town America? God save him.

He wouldn't have come to Bethlehem at all if he hadn't found a file near the bottom of the stack Ross had given him his last day in the office. The records had been put in order according to the date by which they required Tom's attention. He'd been looking ahead to end-of-the-month assignments when he'd opened the thin manila folder. First thing that morning he'd left Buffalo.

The highway became Main Street, and the speed lowered accordingly. He noticed all the Christmas decorations just as he noticed the people crossing the street, the cars, the buildings, but they made no impression. Like Thanksgiving, Christmas was just one more day to work. It required a little planning, since so many people weren't accessible, but for the same reason it was usually a very productive day.

He turned off Main, came to the intersection with Hawthorne, and found no big brick house on the corner. A double check of the street sign showed that he'd turned one street too soon. Maggie's house was a block to the right, so he continued on. He parked out front, crossed the street, and went straight to the door. The bell sounded faintly through the solid wood, and after a brief wait, the door swung open.

"Did you forget your keys—" Ross broke off. "Tom. I wasn't expecting you."

Obviously he was expecting Maggie. Tom was glad she wasn't home. It somehow made his being there easier. "I wanted to discuss something with you, and I thought in person would be best."

"Come on in."

They settled in the office. Ross waited expectantly while Tom removed the folder from his briefcase. "I came across this last night. I think you need to reconsider your instructions."

Though Tom offered the folder, Ross made no effort to take it. His expression indicated that he knew exactly what was inside, and it suggested that Tom might have wasted ten or twelve hours that would have been better spent working.

Rather than return the file to his briefcase, he laid it on the edge of the desk. "I really don't think I should handle this. I know you think it's going to be a simple procedure, but it's not. Once Maggie's lawyer gets a look at your net worth, he's going to start making demands."

Ross remained silent.

"I can recommend a couple of attorneys who are much better qualified to handle it than I am. I know you want to wait a few more weeks, but these aren't people you call at the last minute. Even for you, it'll take some time to get a slot in their schedules."

Ross still said nothing, but his expression had grown darker, colder. Over the last eleven years, Tom had become a pretty good judge of his boss's moods, but he couldn't get a handle on this one. Ross would never lose his temper merely because Tom was looking out for his best interests. Hell, that was what he paid him the big bucks for. And there was nothing less in Ross's best interests than the instructions he'd outlined in the file. If he didn't feel so damn guilty over the wreck, he'd see that.

"You just can't go into a divorce settlement with the kind of offer you've got here. This house, the car, the jewelry, anything she wants from the house in Buffalo *and* a thirty-percent share of the company? For God's sake, that alone is a fortune." He knew almost exactly how much it was, give or take a few million, but so did Ross. "You can get out of the marriage for a fraction of that amount. It's not as if she ever had anything to do with the business. She never invested money in it. She never worked in it. All she did was live off the profits as soon as there were any. There's no reason she should continue to do so once you're divorced."

Finally Ross broke his silence. "No, she never did work in the business. But she waited tables, cleaned motel rooms, clerked in a convenience store, and emptied bedpans in a nursing home to put me through school, to get me started."

"And you paid for her to finish her degree. You're even now."

Ross's smile was thin and empty of humor. "No. We'll never be even. But you're right. I have been reconsidering. I'm not sure—"

A creak in the hallway was followed by the closing of the front door. Ross looked toward the hall, and Tom followed his gaze. A moment later Maggie appeared in the doorway. She wore only a sweater against the day's chill, and her hair was windblown, her cheeks pink. Her arms were filled with two large platters. In spite of the red and green plastic wrap that covered them, he smelled chocolate.

"Hey, Ross—" Whatever she'd been about to say was forgotten when she saw Tom. Her smile disappeared and her behavior became a shade more subdued. "Hello, Tom."

"Maggie."

She looked good. Strong. The fragile air she'd had for so many months was gone, along with the hesitance and unsureness. This was a Maggie he'd never really known—the Maggie when he'd first gone to work for Ross. The happy one. Though she wasn't his type at all, he found himself noticing that she was beautiful. Vibrantly, passionately beautiful, in ways that the women in his life could never match. For the first time, he understood why Ross had stuck around so long.

Then he looked at his boss, who was looking at his wife, and felt the first hint of concern. *I have been reconsidering,* he'd said before she interrupted them. Tom had thought he'd meant the divorce settlement. Now he knew he'd meant the divorce. He was thinking about staying with Maggie.

The idea didn't sit well with Tom. It wasn't that he had anything against her, but he recognized a bad marriage when he saw one. For years they'd done nothing but fight. Ross had nothing to give a marriage, and Maggie had had nothing to give him.

But it looked as if that had changed.

She came farther into the room, setting the plates on the desk. "I just came over to get some pans and parchment paper." To Tom, she explained, "We're making candy at the neighbors'. Would you like some?"

"No, thanks." Tom had few weaknesses. Cool, elegant blondes were one. Fine liquor was another. Chocolate didn't make the list.

She gave Ross a look that plainly said she wished they were alone, then picked up one plate. "I'll put these in the kitchen, then I'd better get back. Nice seeing you, Tom."

She wasn't even out the door, when Ross excused himself. Too wired to sit still, Tom paced to the nearest wall, examined the titles that filled the bookcases there, then was turning toward the back wall, when a sound from down the hall drew him closer to the door. Ross and Maggie were standing just the other side of the doorway into the kitchen, talking quietly, and he was combing his fingers through her hair, undoing the disorder the wind had brought.

It should have been a meaningless gesture—hell, Tom had done the same thing on occasion with one woman or another, and it'd been careless, thoughtless—but this wasn't. Maybe it was the way they were standing so close, or the way they were looking at each other. Maybe it was the way she touched his jaw, then squeezed his fingers. Whatever the explanation, there was absolutely nothing meaningless about the scene.

Feeling uncomfortable for spying, Tom returned to his chair. When Ross had told him that he was going to Bethlehem to live for two or three months, Tom had thought he was crazy. He'd thought he would never last two months away from the office. He'd been positive Ross would never survive two months alone with Maggie.

It seemed he'd been wrong.

A moment later Maggie left and Ross returned to the office with two cups of coffee.

"You mentioned you've been rethinking the settlement offer," Tom said.

Ross swiveled his chair around to stare out the window, and Tom knew without looking that he was watching Maggie, knew when he turned back that she'd disappeared inside the neighbor's house. "No," he said flatly. "I've been rethinking the divorce."

Damn. Tom hated to be wrong, but this was one time when he wouldn't have minded. "So Maggie's agreed to move back to Buffalo."

"No. I wouldn't ask that of her."

"Why not? You're the only one with a job, and that job is in Buffalo."

"The office is in Buffalo. The job is wherever I want to do it."

"So you're considering staying here." Tom gave a cynical shake of his head. "That must make Maggie happy."

"I haven't discussed it with her yet." Ross briefly toyed with a pen on his blotter. "When Dr. Allen asked me to come here, it never occurred to me that we might get along just fine. I mean, our marriage was ended. It was all over but the formalities. She was ready to be free of me, and I was ready for . . ." He faltered, lowered his voice. "For life without her."

He *was* ready—implying that he wasn't anymore, Tom thought. Cold feet? He knew from eleven years of business deals that Ross didn't suffer from last-minute doubts. More likely a reassessment of the situation. With the knowledge that the divorce they'd both wanted was just a few short weeks away, there'd been no pressure. They could both relax, put the past behind them, and just be themselves. Take away the hostility, the resentment, and the anger, and they were left with the people they really were—the people who had fallen in love all those years ago.

It was a nice trick—but it didn't satisfy the cynic within. "You think it'll last this time?"

Ross didn't answer.

"You tried this deal before, and it fell apart. You ended up miserable and hating each other."

"I never hated her. I just lost sight of what was important. I got too ambitious. Too greedy."

"You're still ambitious. You're still driven." But even as he said it, Tom knew it was no longer true—at least, not to the degree it'd been before. For eleven years he'd watched his boss put in hundred-hour weeks, year in and year out, and thrive on it. Business had been the sole purpose of Ross's existence, taking precedence over everything else, including his wife and their marriage.

Since coming to Bethlehem, he'd worked only a fraction of his usual hours. He'd forgotten deadlines and details. He returned phone calls when he thought about it, if at all, and ignored e-mails and faxes. Even when Tom or Lynda was able to get him on the phone, he sounded distracted or was impatient to get off and on to something else.

"I've worked so hard for so long that I'd forgotten what it was like to have a life," Ross said quietly, his expression distant, almost as if talking to himself. "In Buffalo it seemed normal. Everyone I knew worked hard. But here . . . People spend time with their kids. They go ice skating with friends. They build parade floats and take wagon rides and go to church and visit with their neighbors. They have families. They have fun."

And Ross had never had much of either. Tom knew, because he'd grown up the same way—maybe even a little poorer in both aspects. They'd both busted their butts to get through college. They'd dedicated a hundred and fifty percent to making something of themselves, to becoming someone no one would dare look down on or scoff at. They'd craved power and respect and the wealth that supplied them, and they'd worked damn hard to get enough, but their ambition had blinded them to exactly how much was enough. Tom had more money than he'd even dreamed existed twenty years ago, but he still didn't have enough.

Maybe, finally, Ross did.

"You said you haven't discussed staying here with Maggie. Why not?"

"She wants a divorce. She's got big plans for her future."

Maybe she'd had big plans when she came to Bethlehem. Maybe she still did. But it wasn't likely they included divorcing Ross. Tom had seen the way she'd looked at him in the kitchen, the way she'd touched him. He was no expert on relationships, but he knew those serious marriage-and-forever kind of looks. He'd faced more than a few of them himself, but he'd always escaped intact.

It didn't look as if Ross was going to.

"Did she tell you this?" he asked.

"When we first came here."

Tom made a dismissive gesture. "That was a preliminary opinion. Maybe she's changed her mind since then. You did." When Ross's expression remained bleak, unconvinced, Tom suggested, "Ask her. Tell her how you feel. Find out how she feels."

"It's not that simple."

"Why not?"

"She still doesn't remember what happened the

night of the accident. When she does—" Breaking off, he shook his head.

No one knew what happened that night except Ross. All he'd told the sheriff was that they'd argued. All he'd told Tom during the endless hours of Maggie's lifesaving surgery was that she'd left him, and all Tom had learned—guessed, really—since then was that the bracelet he'd given Father Pat was somehow involved. "Is whatever you did so unforgivable?"

"Yes." The answer was quick, decisive, impossible to argue. "When she remembers . . ."

"*If* she remembers. The doctors don't know that she ever will. You could live the rest of your lives without it happening."

"I can't take that risk. I can't lose her again."

"If you don't take the risk, you lose anyway."

Silence settled between them, heavy, oppressive. After a time, Ross broke it. "I'm sorry. This isn't the sort of counsel you're used to giving."

That was an understatement. The only advice regarding women that anyone wanted from Tom was how to seduce them, then walk away untouched. That was his specialty. But how to stay . . . That wasn't in his experience, and he doubted that it ever would be.

"It's no problem. I'd better head back to the city." Tom pulled on his overcoat, picked up his briefcase, then walked with Ross to the door. "I won't do anything yet," he said in reference to the divorce.

Ross agreed. "There's no hurry. I've still got a month or two here."

And in a month or two he could accomplish damn

near anything, Tom thought as he said good-bye, then left the house.

He might even save his marriage.

A FTER LUNCH WEDNESDAY, MAGGIE watched Ross load dishes in the dishwasher. It was such a menial task for a man like him, but he didn't mind and he did it as efficiently as she ever had.

Turning, he caught her watching and gave her an easy smile. "What are you looking at?"

"You. You used to work such long hours that I'd forget what you looked like."

"Really," he said dryly as he approached.

"No. I never forgot." She took him willingly into her embrace—brushed her fingers along his jaw, rubbed them across the fine fabric of his shirt. With his black hair and sharp blue eyes, he looked incredibly dashing in the white shirt, open at the collar, sleeves rolled back. He looked even better out of it. "I just missed you so much."

"I'm here now."

It was true. Since their cookie baking late Saturday night, he'd spent more time with her than apart. Only the most urgent business took his attention away from her, and never for long. They'd made love, gone out for dinner, shopped, taken leisurely walks, and she'd been thankful for every moment.

She wondered how long it would last.

And how would she bear it when it ended.

"Maggie?"

Blinking back the moisture in her eyes, she focused on him and smiled.

"Where did you go just now?"

"Why would I go anywhere when I'm in your arms?" Right where she wanted to be. Today, tomorrow, always. Before he could press for an answer, she patted his arm. "Are you ready to go?"

"Go where? To work? Not today. To bed? Of course. To—"

"To buy a present for Shelley Walker's baby." Mitch had brought his wife and daughter home from the hospital only two days after the big event, and tonight their friends had been invited over to meet young Rebecca. Maggie was both looking forward to it and dreading it. It was hard to be happy and so envious at the same time.

"If you insist, though I'd rather go to bed."

"Of course you would. Heavens, you act as if you'd gone without sex for a year."

"And a few months. And this has nothing to do with that."

"Then what does it have to do with?"

He touched her cheek. "You."

A lump formed in her throat to match the one in her chest. Sometimes when he looked at her like that, when he touched her like that, she thought she surely must have a forever sort of place in his life, and the idea both touched her and scared her senseless. Could she risk believing in forever with Ross again? Could she let herself be tempted by the notion of love and reconciliation and commitment, when he'd never actually spoken of those things? When the divorce they'd agreed on still loomed ahead? When he'd never even hinted that he might no longer want it?

Doing so could break her heart.

Or heal it.

Leaning forward, she pressed a kiss to his cheek. "You're a very sweet man, Ross."

He tried not very successfully to scoff. "Ask anyone I've ever done business with. I'm the toughest son of a bitch around. Powerful men tremble when I walk through the door."

"So do I." She kissed him again. "And it's so very sweet." He pressed closer and she could feel the beginnings of his arousal. With a laugh she wriggled away and headed for the closet. "Later, darlin'. Right now I need a gift for Shelley."

The boutique recommended by the Winchester sisters was unremarkable on the outside. Inside was a child's paradise, with bright colors, thickly padded carpet, play areas, and a wide assortment of everything a kid could possibly need. Maggie glanced over an array of cribs and cradles, car seats and high chairs, and felt a pang deep in her heart. She wished she were shopping for herself, for her own sweet little baby. He would have his father's black hair and blue eyes, or maybe she would look more like her mother and she would wrap her daddy around her little—

"Can I help you?"

Maggie turned to the woman who'd spoken. They'd met while skating Saturday night. The blonde had been with Dean Elliott, though they were just friends, she'd insisted. Holly and the others had teased her, but Maggie had thought she told the truth. She and Dean hadn't looked at each other the way lovers, or prospective lovers, should. No, she'd saved those looks for Holly's date, who'd never noticed.

Maggie remembered all that, but for the life of her couldn't remember the woman's name. She offered her hand. "Hi, I'm Maggie. We met Saturday."

"I remember. I'm Leanne. What can I help you with?"

"I'm looking for Shelley—for a gift for Shelley."

"Who isn't? I think my last two dozen customers have been here for her. Let me show you some of my favorites that haven't been snapped up yet."

Maggie followed her toward the more subdued side of the store, where the furnishings were pastel, the effect restful. A glance over her shoulder showed that Ross had decided to wait by the furniture.

Leanne showed her dresses, quilts, blankets knitted by a local crafter. There were leather-bound storybooks, one-of-a-kind stuffed animals, and a whimsical sculpture that she recognized as Dean Elliott's work. She chose a stuffed rabbit, easily twice the size of any newborn, of white mohair, with floppy pink ears and eyes her favorite shade of blue. On impulse, for herself, she picked up the sculpture too, and carried it to the counter at the back.

As soon as Leanne circled behind the counter, there was a soft, delighted gurgle. Leaning forward, Maggie saw the playpen set up in the small space and the bright-eyed baby it corralled. "What a doll," she said softly. "Is he yours?"

The smile Leanne gave him as she picked him up was full of love. "All mine. Being able to bring him to work with me is one of the benefits of being the boss and sole employee." One-handed, she rang up Maggie's purchases, then accepted her check without even a glance. "I don't think I have a box that'll fit Flopsy here, but I can fix a big bow around his neck. It'll take only a minute, if you don't mind watching Danny. He's good with strangers."

One part of Maggie wanted to refuse. Another part was literally aching to feel his soft, sturdy little body in her arms. That part won out as she circled the counter and took the baby from his mother.

Across the room, Ross saw the baby in Maggie's arms, and something sharp and intense swept through him. She was looking down at the baby as if she'd never seen such a creature before, and the baby gazed up at her as if she were the most fascinating thing in his world.

They looked incredibly right together—the perfect picture of beauty, love, life. Was there a place in that picture for a man who had no desire to be a father? For a man whose only desire was to get as close as possible to the mother?

Could he ever love a child? He didn't know. He'd spent so many years not wanting kids that he honestly didn't have a clue whether he could ever want a baby for the baby's sake, for his own sake, and not just for Maggie's sake. He doubted that he had the capacity to be a good father—after all, look at the role model he'd been given—but how could he ever find out? Practical experience seemed the only way, but, having grown up with a bad father of his own, he could never agree to that. If it turned out that he *didn't* have what it took, it was the child who would suffer, and that was too cruel.

And if he didn't have what it took, what would Maggie think of him then?

He tried to study the scene outside the window, but couldn't. Instead, something drew him across the shop to Maggie's side. He'd never been so close to a baby before. He'd never held one, had never noticed how sweet they could smell or how solemn they could be.

He'd never in his wildest dreams imagined that the sight of Maggie holding a baby could turn him on, but it did. That was all that ache was—lust. Longing. For Maggie.

She looked at him—he felt her gaze—but said nothing. He avoided looking back. He didn't want to see the yearning in her eyes, didn't want her to see whatever might be in his own eyes.

The clerk returned, carrying a floppy white rabbit with a giant pink bow looped around its neck. She exchanged small talk with Maggie, gave the rabbit to Ross, and reclaimed her baby.

He and Maggie left the shop and walked to the car in silence. They didn't say anything on the way home either, or as they walked into the house. She headed up the stairs, and he watched from the hall, unsure of her mood, aching to follow her but not sure she would welcome his company.

At the top of the stairs she smiled down at him. "It's later, darlin'. Come upstairs and make me tremble."

He needed no further invitation.

Their kisses were frantic, their caresses desperate, their bodies ready. As he buried himself inside her, he acknowledged the small, brief regret that their love-making would bring pleasure and satisfaction but nothing else. No hope for their future, no answer to her prayers, no baby to cherish, because the time wasn't right. The right time *would* come. She was convinced of that.

But would it include him?

"WHAT TIME ARE WE SUPPOSED TO BE AT the Walkers?"

Maggie looked up from the tray she was fixing. "Seven o'clock. Everyone's bringing a dish, so, since I got rather dis—disturbed . . . No. Dis—"

"Distracted."

She gave him an appreciative smile. "Yes. Thank you—for both the word and the distraction. Anyway, I thought I'd take the candy I made with Miss Agatha and Miss Corinna."

"*You* got distracted?" he repeated. "Who gave whom that take-me-I'm-yours look on the way upstairs?"

"I don't even know what a take-me-I'm-yours look would be," she teased.

His voice lowered, and his expression turned serious. "Of course you do. It's that look I get every time I see you."

Her hands stilled, the platter of candy forgotten. *Was* he hers? Right then, yes. But for how long? A few weeks? A few months? The rest of their lives? She wanted very much to know—too much—and for that reason she was afraid to ask.

"Well, whoever distracted whom, I'm glad. It was a lovely way to spend an afternoon." After pressing a kiss to his jaw, she turned her attention to the tray. In the center were balls of nougat glazed with honey, and piled around them were chunks of fudge, chocolate-coated peanuts, caramel-almond clusters, and white chocolate turtles. All she needed was a handful of red and green butter mints, and the tray would be ready.

"I'm going to get the rest of the candy from the office," she said. "Will you get the red plastic wrap from the cabinet beside the refrigerator?"

The office was dark, but enough light spilled in from the hallway to see. When she picked up the plate, she caught the edge of the file underneath it, dropped the papers it contained to the floor, and bent to scoop them up. Her gaze skimmed over the top page, and, with a chill, she became suddenly still, barely breathing, barely able to understand the words she was reading.

Slowly she turned on the desk lamp, sank down in a chair, and read the page again. It was addressed to Tom, detailing the action the following pages required. The rest was a neat list of property, stocks, and cash, and the lucky recipient—or *un*lucky, depending on the view-point—was Maggie.

This was Ross's proposed divorce settlement—the price he was willing to pay to get out of her life. This was why Tom had come to Bethlehem on Monday, why Ross hadn't told her that he was expecting the lawyer. Was it also why, in the two days since, he'd paid more attention to her than she'd ever hoped for?

Because he felt guilty for moving forward with the divorce without telling her?

She wasn't hurt so much as disappointed, she told herself. She'd had such hopes, such dreams.

And finding out that there was no hope *did* hurt, she admitted bleakly as the words blurred and the tears stung.

After taking a moment to compose herself, she put the file back on the edge of the desk, switched off the lamp, then returned to the kitchen. The red plastic wrap was on the island, and Ross was standing at the sink, gazing out into the night. He turned when he heard her, his smile ready.

For one painful moment she felt so betrayed. How could he tell Tom to go ahead with the divorce without discussing it with her first? And how could he smile at her like that—how could he make love to her?—knowing that Tom was going ahead without her knowledge?

Because it was what they had agreed to. Wasn't she the one who had offered the bargain—who had said, "Come stay with me, and when we're sure I can live on my own, we'll get a divorce"? Wasn't she the one who had initiated their lovemaking even knowing that the marriage was over? And wasn't she the one who had broken their bargain by falling in love with him all over again?

If she felt betrayed, she had no one to blame but herself.

After giving him the best smile she could muster, she forced her attention to the candy. Once she was finished, she cleared her throat. "I guess we should go."

"You don't sound too enthusiastic. Would you rather stay home?"

"No." She answered too quickly and covered it with a smile. Though she'd wondered if having to watch Shelley with her beautiful little girl might be more than she could bear, she knew that the alternative—staying home with Ross and her disappointment—would be worse. "Why don't you get our coats and the rabbit and I'll bring the candy."

He did as she suggested, meeting her at the side door. The floppy white bunny should have looked silly cradled against his overcoat. He was, after all, one of the most powerful, most ruthless men around. Instead, he looked charming. She didn't want him to look charming just then. She didn't want to wonder if he would ever carry a similar gift for his own child, didn't want to agonize over who that child's mother might be.

Knowing that it wouldn't be her was sorrow enough.

The Walkers lived on the southwest side of Bethlehem in a newer section of town—new being relative, Maggie thought as Ross turned onto their street. Each of the fifties-era houses sat in the center of its own neat square of lawn, with driveways on the left and porches across the front. The trees were giants and would provide leafy shade in summer and gorgeous color in autumn but now were a stark reminder that summer was a long way away.

Ross held on to her hand as they walked up the

sidewalk to the porch. Genuine affection? she wondered. A proprietary gesture? Or an act for her friends? An hour earlier she would have voted for the first. Now she had no clue.

The party was at the back of the house, in a large family room. Shelley was holding court from the sofa, with Rebecca cradled in her arms and fast asleep.

Maggie made the appropriate remarks, then, as quickly as possible, she retreated to the kitchen. It wasn't the longing for a child of her own that drove her away, though, but a need for distance from Ross.

"Coffee?" Melissa asked.

"Sure." Maggie accepted a cup and poured the last of the coffee into it, then automatically set about making a new pot. She was tucking in the filter she'd taken from a box in the cabinet above, when Melissa quietly spoke again.

"Did you know the filters were in that cabinet, or did you assume it was the logical place to keep them?"

Maggie became still. She hadn't given it any thought—had simply opened the cabinet and pulled out the box. Had she known or guessed? She honestly couldn't say. Giving a shrug, she spooned out coffee grounds from the tin pushed against the backsplash. "I guess it was logical."

"Is it also logical to keep the coffee in a tin labeled COCOA?" Melissa paused. "*I* knew it was there because I've been here before—because I've sat right there on a stool and watched Shelley make coffee after lunch. So have you. We even commented on the tin—asked her if she kept tea in the one labeled COFFEE."

Maggie looked down at the tin, then her gaze

shifted past Melissa to Ross, standing motionless a few steps behind her. He'd caught the entire exchange and looked—she wasn't sure exactly how he looked. Startled? Tense? Less than pleased? Did he think that Melissa was making too big a deal out of the incident, perhaps giving her false hope that her memory was starting to return? Or, now that he'd officially begun the legal process of ending their marriage, had he decided that it was to his benefit—his financial benefit—that she couldn't remember their last few months together?

Had he done something so terrible in that time that he feared she would use it to punish him by demanding more than the already-generous settlement he'd suggested? Impossible. He was too decent, too honest, and too consumed by business. Work had left him no time for a life or his wife and certainly no time to do anything that might be used against him.

More likely, it was that damned guilt he insisted on bearing. He blamed himself for her accident and probably thought, if she remembered, that she would blame him too. But he was wrong. Falling down the mountain was no one's fault but her own. She'd done something stupid, and they'd both paid the price.

Swallowing hard, she put on a smile and brushed off the incident. "I didn't even look at the label until you pointed it out. I keep coffee in a canister on the counter near the coffeemaker, and I just grabbed the nearest thing here." Her smile wavered, but she held it in place by sheer will as she offered the coffee she'd poured to Ross. "Here, take this. I'm going to stand here and talk to Melissa. I'll get the first cup out of the new pot."

He tried to hide the wary look in his eyes as he accepted the cup and walked away without sugar or cream. She watched him until Melissa laid her hand on her arm.

"Are you okay?"

"No." Looking at her friend, she grimaced. "No, not at all."

"I'm sorry."

"So am I. But things will work out. Sooner or later." Probably much later—a couple of years. A couple of decades. She'd fallen out of love with him once. She could do it again. For the sake of her future—her unborn babies—she had no choice.

As soon as they could graciously say good night, they did. Ross made no effort to draw her out of her silence on the way home. The phone was ringing when they walked in the door. She seized it as an excuse to find a little time to herself. "If Tom's calling this late, it must be important. Why don't you get it while I go upstairs?"

He hesitated, then, as the answering machine picked up, nodded. "I'll be up in a minute."

It took more than a minute, of course. Nearly half an hour had passed by the time she heard his footsteps in the hall. Though it was early, she was already in bed. She closed her eyes and slowed her breathing as he came in.

He undressed in the bathroom, then made his way through the dark to the bed, sliding in behind her, fitting his body to hers. "Maggie?"

She wanted to remain unresponsive, but honesty forced her to answer. "What?"

"You'll get those babies you want. I know it's hard to wait, but it'll happen."

"I know." Maybe she would get them the old-fashioned way—by falling in love—or she might find a suitable man willing to make the necessary contribution as part of a mutually satisfying business arrangement. Maybe she would have to resort to artificial means, but she *would* have her babies.

"I'm sorry I never understood how important it was to you."

"So am I."

"I was a selfish bastard."

This time she kept her agreement to herself.

Pushing back the covers, he pressed a kiss to her shoulder, then ran his hand down her bare arm to the soft cotton of her nightgown where it covered her hip. His body's response was slight but noticeable. Wanting nothing less than to share such intimacy with him when she was feeling so blue, she claimed his hand and pressed a kiss to the palm, then held it securely in hers. "Good night, Ross."

His sigh was soft with acceptance and regret. "Good night, Maggie."

I T WAS THE MIDDLE OF THE NIGHT WHEN Ross awoke, instantly aware that something was amiss. He moved his arm—the one that should have been draped over Maggie's middle—and felt nothing but cold sheets, then lifted his head. She sat in the rocker across the room, feet tucked on the wooden seat, all bundled up in a quilt.

Another bad dream? Or just sleeplessness?

He slid out of bed, wrapped the top blanket around him, then crouched in front of her. "Are you okay?"

She nodded. "I just had a little trouble sleeping. Sorry I woke you."

"You didn't. But you should have."

"That would have been rather selfish, don't you think? If I can't sleep, then you don't get to?"

He smiled at the suggestion. "You've never been selfish a day in your life." Clutching the blanket tighter, he sat on the floor. The position put him in shadow, but moonlight touched her face—her incredibly lovely, sad face. His smile faded, and his voice turned serious. "What's wrong, Maggie?"

She remained silent, staring out the window for so long that he thought she wasn't going to answer. Then, she looked at him. "I was just thinking about the dreams I had for my life back when I was in high school. I was going to go to college someplace far away, where I could be free of my mother's rules and her pressure. I would get my degree, find a job that I liked, and marry a man whom I loved. We would have a pretty little house, three kids, and a dog, and we would live this incredibly normal, incredibly satisfying life."

And instead, the only way she'd been able to afford college was to go in Buffalo and live at home. She'd sacrificed her degree so he could get his, her jobs had been drudgery, there'd been no children, and she'd wound up in a huge house that she'd hated.

"I never, ever dreamed I would be thirty-five, about to be divorced, and childless," she murmured. "My goals weren't impossible. Women achieve them every day. I just don't understand how I failed so miserably."

"You didn't fail, Maggie. You just showed poor judgment in marrying me. I'm the one who let you down on everything else."

As if she didn't hear him, she slowly shook her head from side to side. "I'm a smart woman. I'm capable. I've never been afraid to work hard. Those qualities are supposed to pay off. But here I am, almost divorced and alone. *Divorced*. God, when I was a kid, I saw what that did to my mother and I swore it would never happen to me, and now . . ."

Ross's fingers clenched tightly around the blanket. Ignoring the sharp fear in his gut, he forced his jaw open, forced the words out. "It hasn't happened yet, Maggie. Maybe . . ." He thought of the things she didn't know—his affair, the depth of his betrayal, the real reason for her accident—and the fear intensified beyond ignoring, but he ignored it anyway. He forced it back and pushed ahead. "Maybe it doesn't have to."

She stared at him. "I saw the papers in your office."

"What pape—" The file Tom had brought Monday. The file he'd had no reason to take back with him.

"You're a generous man, Ross."

"You think so?" he asked cynically.

"I saw how much you're willing to pay to get me out of your life."

"That's nothing compared to what I'll pay to keep you in it."

His mouth went dry and his hands turned clammy and he wished he could call back the words. Even more, he was glad he couldn't.

"What do you mean?" she whispered.

"You're not the only one whose life didn't turn out the way you imagined. When I was a kid, I wanted wealth and power. I wanted to *be* somebody. I knew it would take hard work and commitment and struggle, but I didn't care because it would be worth every sacrifice. I was wrong. It hasn't been worth the biggest sacrifice of all. I never wanted to be thirty-seven and living without you, Maggie. Hell, I don't even know *how* to live without you. You're my wife—the best part of my life. I love you, and I don't want to lose you."

"But—the papers you gave Tom—"

"I gave him those weeks ago, before we left Bethlehem. When he came to discuss them Monday, I told him I'd changed my mind."

"But how can we be married?"

"We've been doing a pretty good job of it."

"What about your job? It's in Buffalo. I'm here." She shook her head sadly. "I don't think I can leave here."

"I can build an office and transfer the people I need most here. I would probably have to spend a few days a month in the city or traveling, but I could be here the rest of the time."

Her gaze narrowed and an accusing note entered her voice. "You've been thinking about this."

"Since last weekend."

"Here I've been *mourning* the day you'll leave, and

you've been making plans to stay. Why didn't you *tell* me?"

"What was I supposed to do? Say, 'Hey, Maggie, lunch was good and so was your fudge, and oh, by the way, I love you and I want to live the rest of my life with you in this house'?"

The accusatory look relented, giving in to a faint, sweet smile, as she slid to the floor in front of him. "It would've worked for me."

"Would it have?" he asked wistfully. "Does that mean you're considering it?"

He waited uneasily for her answer. It shouldn't be so hard. If she didn't want a divorce, then, by default, she must want him. It should be a simple yes.

But there was nothing simple about the look on her face, nothing simple about the heavy silence or the response she finally gave. "What about babies?"

He swallowed hard. "I know you want them—"

"And you don't."

The absolute absence of hope in her voice left him cold inside. "I'm not sure what I want, Maggie—except you. I love you."

"And I love you." She squeezed his hand tightly to emphasize the words. "But I won't give up my chance to be a mother for you. I've waited sixteen years, Ross. I can't wait much longer."

The smile he intended to be reassuring felt shaky and frightened instead. "We'll work it out. If there's one thing I'm good at, it's negotiating."

She smiled too, a curious, happy-sad hybrid. "There are a lot of things you're good at—but there's not much to negotiate here. I'm going to have children,

Ross. The only questions are when . . . and who will be the father.''

He drew her into his lap, underneath the warmth of his blanket, and held her close. "We'll work it out," he said again. After all, he loved her.

That left him no other choice.

Chapter Fourteen

TWO HUNDRED YEARS EARLIER, WHEN Bethlehem was little more than a collection of ragtag buildings scattered about on a muddy road or two, Ezekiel Winchester had donated a plot of land as well as stone from his own quarry and the manpower to build its first official place of worship—hence, its simple name, the First Church of Bethlehem—and there had been Winchesters in the pews ever since. Corinna had been baptized here, had walked down that long center aisle to marry her Henry, and had made the same long walk forty-four years later behind his casket. Some of her most joyous memories were associated with this church. So were some of her most sorrowful.

This Sunday evening, though, would be counted among the joys. The Christmas pageant was one of the highlights of the season. Melissa was a talented director and coaxed the best out of those she recruited. It was always an inspiring event.

Attendance was much higher than usual for a Sunday service. Fifteen minutes before the opening prayer, the church was practically filled, but Corinna was in no hurry to go inside. No one would sit in the pew she regularly shared with her sister. If anyone tried, Reverend Howard's wife would be quick to point out that the bench was reserved.

"Evening, Miss Corinna."

"How are you, Miss Corinna?"

She smiled and returned the greetings of the sheriff and the fire chief, both students of hers years back. In one way or another, she knew every soul to walk through the door, but she was waiting for two in particular. When she'd gone across the street that afternoon to issue an invitation to the pageant, Maggie had enthusiastically accepted. She'd been baking cookies and had flour on her nose and dusted over her sweater, and she had looked happy and confident—a great improvement over the young woman who'd come to Bethlehem nearly a month ago.

The heavy doors swished open, and Maeve and Harry, accompanied by her daughter and granddaughter, came out of the cold. They made a handsome family—which they would be if Harry would only recognize the love Maeve couldn't begin to hide. The old man was stubborn, though, and believed his only reason for loving had died with his wife. Perhaps the good Lord would open his eyes before it was too late.

And perhaps Corinna would give the good Lord some assistance with the job.

The door swung open again, and Ross McKinney followed Maggie through. He helped her off with her coat, then removed his own coat. He wore a steel-gray suit and looked handsome and more relaxed, more at ease with his life and himself, than Corinna had imagined possible. Like his wife, he, too, looked as if he'd experienced Bethlehem's own special healing.

Upon seeing her, Maggie crossed the stone floor and gave her a hug. "We're not late, are we?"

"Not quite."

"I have a closet full of clothes, and nothing suitable for church that provides adequate camouflage."

Corinna's gaze swept over her—long crimson turtleneck sweater, black wool skirt, matching tights, black flats. "Well, the outfit you've chosen is perfectly suitable—though I can't help but wonder what a lovely woman like you has to hide."

"Scars," she replied candidly with a shrug.

Of course, Corinna thought, regretting her thoughtless remark. Maggie couldn't have suffered such life-threatening injuries without a few visible reminders, which might explain why she always wore pants, long sleeves, and high collars. "I'm sorry, dear. I should have realized—"

"It's all right. I'm getting over them." She gazed around the entry hall with its soaring ceiling of rough-hewn timbers, arched stained glass windows, and rugged stone walls. "What a great building—so solid and strong. It feels as if it's been here forever and always will be."

" 'The Rock of Ages,' " Corinna said, patting one

hand against the wall. "That's what they called it when we were children. After the hymn."

Maggie took another long look around. Her manner shifted, became more serious. "I've been here before, haven't I?"

"You came to the pageant with Agatha and me last year. You also brought canned and baked goods—various breads, I believe—for the baskets we distribute to the needy a few days before Christmas."

Maggie nodded slowly. "I remember . . . " As her voice trailed off, she closed her eyes, the better to concentrate. Corinna waited expectantly, Ross uneasily. "Candles . . . dozens of candles . . . an organ . . . and the 'Hallelujah Chorus.'"

When she opened her eyes again, Ross gestured impatiently. "Someone's playing the organ right now, you can smell the candles burning, and everyone sings the 'Hallelujah Chorus' at Christmas."

For just an instant, Maggie looked pleased, then acceptance swept across her face. With one blunt sentence—some might even say cruel—her husband had dashed her hopes that she might have discovered an actual memory. Why? Was he trying to protect her from false hope? Or did he mean to discourage her from trying to remember?

And was it her place to point out that Maggie just might be right? Not every choir sang Handel's masterpiece at Christmas. In fact, except for last year, the church choir never had. They generally preferred songs with which the congregation could sing along. Last year, though, the song had been a special request from Reverend Howard, and they had obliged.

More subdued, Maggie looked through the open doors into the sanctuary. "I suppose we should find a seat."

"There's room for you in my pew. Just follow me." Corinna led the way down the center aisle to the pew one-third from the front and took her seat next to Fern Howard. No sooner had Maggie sat down than she left again to speak to friends across the aisle. Ross, holding both their coats, sat on the end, staring straight ahead, his cheeks flushed.

"If her memory comes back, there's nothing you can do to stop it," Corinna said quietly.

He didn't glance at her, but a muscle in his jaw tightened. "I know."

"Are you afraid of what she'll remember?"

"Things were not good between us then."

"She knows that."

Abruptly he turned toward her, his gaze unforgiving. "She knows it in her head. She doesn't remember it in her heart."

A fanciful distinction for a man recognized by the world as ruthless. He didn't *feel* ruthless, though, when she clasped his hand. He felt very solid and human and, if the grip of his fingers around hers was anything to judge by, afraid. "And you think it will make a difference if her heart remembers. You think it will change the way she feels."

Slowly, miserably, he nodded.

"I would love to tell you that you're wrong," she said softly, "but I don't know that. I can tell you, Ross, that there's no problem in this world that love cannot overcome. There's no sin that can't be forgiven. But you've got to have faith."

He looked at her a long time, obviously wanting to believe but unable to.

Before she could say anything else, the lights flickered and all those visiting with friends, Maggie included, returned to their seats. After the opening prayer, Melissa, lovely in a red velvet dress that brushed her ankles, introduced each segment of the program. Agatha went onstage with the children, then joined the choir for their numbers. Corinna had been blessed in many ways, but the singing talent in the family had all gone to Agatha. Her solo was the highlight of the first half of the pageant.

Before anyone was ready, the last song had been sung, the final prayer offered, the candles extinguished, and the lights brought up. Corinna blinked, then glanced at her neighbors. Maggie was leaning against Ross, and their hands were tightly clasped. For the first time, she noticed, they were both wearing rings on their left hands—his a simple gold band, hers an impressive diamond. She looked contented. He looked . . . tormented.

Bowing her head, Corinna silently offered a quick and fervent prayer for them.

T HE CHRISTMAS TREE IN THE LIVING room was still beautiful, Maggie decided Monday morning, but it was badly in need of a few presents underneath. With Christmas only a few days away, there was no time to waste.

"Did we open the presents last year?" she asked Ross over breakfast.

He didn't pause in the peeling of an orange. "No."

"Where are they?"

"In the basement. Do you want them brought up?"

"Were they the same old things?" If they were duty gifts—no thought required, unwanted, unneeded—then, no, she didn't want them. They could stay in the basement forever for all she cared.

"If by that you mean that Lynda picked out most of my gifts for you, yes."

She made a face that he looked up just in time to see. It brought a hint of regret into his own expression.

"I'm sorry about that. It was an easy habit to fall into."

She brushed off his apology with a shrug. "We need to go shopping."

"All right. What do you want?"

She'd already asked for her emerald earrings. Beyond those, she couldn't think of anything that he could wrap and slide under the tree. Everything else on her wish list was difficult to tie up in bows—a baby, a long, happy marriage, promises and assurances and commitment. "Surprise me."

He laughed. "Oh, darlin', I can do that. They may not be *pleasant* surprises, but I can definitely surprise you."

"The night we decorated the tree, you said you would think about what you wanted. Well?"

He divided the orange in half, setting one piece on her plate, the other on his own. "A promise."

"And where can I buy this promise?"

"You can't. It has to come from your heart."

"All right. I have lots of that kind of promise. Which one in particular do you want?"

"The one that says we'll never let things get so bad again. We won't forget what's important again. We'll find compromises we can both live with. We'll make it good and make it last."

Compromises. There were no compromises for the biggest obstacle facing them now. She was going to have a family, and he would have to accept it. Period.

She pressed a kiss to his hand and smelled the sweet tang of orange. "You're so easy. I guess I'll have to come up with some ideas on my own."

"What about the promise?"

Her smile was as frivolous as his expression was serious. "I'm not telling. You'll have to wait until Christmas Eve to see."

Once the orange was gone, she said, "Let's walk downtown, go shopping for surprises, then meet at Harry's when we're done."

"Let's drive downtown so we don't have to carry the surprises home in our arms."

"Deal."

It was a beautiful cold morning with a cloudless sky of rich pale blue. "I'm starting over there," she said with a gesture across the street toward the combination gift and book shop. "I'll see you at Harry's."

She started to walk away, but he caught her hand, drew her close, and kissed her. It was simple, sweet, not the least bit inappropriate for a downtown sidewalk, and it made her heart ache. It was amazing that only a month before, she'd wanted him out of her life. Now, once again, he *was* her life—and life was *good*.

The gift shop was warm and smelled of the pot-pourri displayed in paper envelopes near the door. The clerk paused in the act of restocking the cards to greet her, then Maggie began wandering down the aisles. The displays of Christmas ornaments caught her attention, one in particular. It was a wreath of holly dotted with red berries, with a gold ribbon bow forming the loop for hanging. Seated in the center on the bottom curve of the wreath was an angel, its feet dangling, and hanging from the bottom was a tiny brass plaque bearing the year and a miniature bell. Maggie lifted the wreath from the display tree, making the bell jingle.

"Every time a bell rings, an angel gets his—or her—wings." From the opposite side of the counter, Noelle, the clerk from Melissa's shop, was watching her with a friendly smile. "It's a darling wreath, isn't it?"

"Yes." And it would be a perfect gift for all the angels in her life—too inexpensive to incur an obligation but enough to let them know they mattered. She gathered one each for the sisters, Melissa and Holly, Shelley and Emilie, holding them carefully in one hand.

"Here you go," Noelle said. "This is always helpful."

With a smile, Maggie accepted the basket. "I love Christmas ornaments. I have a ton, but I need one more."

"Since you like the wee angel so much, how about this one? It's even got a message on the back." Noelle offered a wreath from her side of the tree, identical to the others in every way except there were two angels, side by side and holding hands. On the back, in graceful script, was inscribed three simple words with incredible impact. THIS TIME FOREVER.

For a long time Maggie stared at the words. The promise Ross had asked for. It was perfect.

She added it to her basket, then looked up to thank Noelle. The woman was gone, walking out the door as the bell overhead rang. As she passed by on the sidewalk out front, she flashed a smile and a wave.

Maggie continued with her shopping. When she went to pay, the clerk chatted idly about the holidays and the weather, then broke off as she picked up the dual-angel wreath.

"Isn't that interesting? I unpacked every one of these myself, but I don't remember seeing any with two angels. And there's no tag on it either. How odd. Let me go check." Taking the ornament with her, she went to the display, then came back with a shrug. "It's the only one. I'll charge the same price as the others, if you don't object."

"I want it, whatever the price."

By the time Maggie settled in a booth at Harry's, the morning was over and she was all shopped out. The angel ornament was Ross's real gift, but she'd made several other purchases—a chenille muffler to help keep him warm, a nubby sweater that matched his eyes, a bottle of the cologne she liked best on him. She wished she could have thought of better ideas, but the man who had everything wasn't exactly easy to buy for.

She'd chatted with Maeve and finished her first cup

of coffee by the time Ross joined her. "Did you find everything you wanted?" she asked.

He shrugged. "I found some things I liked."

"What stores did you go to?"

"I'm not telling. You'll have to wait until Christmas Eve and see."

The words made her smile. It had been a long time since she'd looked forward to Christmas Eve—a long time since she'd known that her gifts from him weren't more of a surprise to him than they were to her.

"Hi there, handsome." Maeve turned over the inverted cup in front of Ross and filled it with coffee. "Maggie tells me you two have been Christmas shopping. Are you ready for the big day?"

"Almost."

"I *love* Christmas. It's the best time of the whole year. I always get misty-eyed over the season." With a grin, she pretended to wipe away a tear, sniffled, then asked, "What can I get you?"

Maggie ordered the lunch special—a steaming bowl of chili served with jalapeño corn bread—and Ross doubled it. When Maeve left, he reached for Maggie's hand. "Were you serious about inviting Tom to spend Christmas here?"

"Sure."

"He won't make you uncomfortable?"

"Of course he will—a little—but I can live with it. Do you want to ask him to stay with us?"

"I don't think he would. I don't even think he'll come, but he might surprise me. I've got to call him this afternoon. I'll ask him then."

"If he won't stay with us, I can call Holly and see if

she's got a room available." Remembering the interest her friend had displayed on Thanksgiving made her smile. "I think she would consider having him there her very own Christmas present."

"He's involved with someone," Ross warned.

"No, he's not. He's in a sexual relationship. His emotions never get involved."

"Whatever relationships he has, Holly's not his type."

"You don't know that."

"Every woman he's been with since I've known him has been exactly the same—"

"Beautiful, elegant, not too bright, bodies to die for, greed to match. And he's never fallen for any of them. He's never wanted anything more than sex from any of them. I think he chooses them because he knows they're *not* his type. They pose no threat. When they eventually leave, as they all do, he knows it won't be more than a minor inconvenience in his life."

By the time she finished, Ross was grinning. She put on a fake pout and demanded, "What?"

"You learned something from all those sessions with Dr. Olivetti, didn't you?" he teased.

"Oh, honey, I learned those things just being a woman. You men are our most intriguing topic of conversation."

He turned serious again. "If he comes, he'll treat you appropriately."

"I know. I'm not worried about that." She lifted his hand to her mouth and pressed a kiss to his palm. To anyone watching it looked perfectly innocent—but anyone watching couldn't see her tongue against his skin or feel his heart rate kick into high gear where her fingertips rested over his wrist.

"Forget inviting him to stay with us," he said, his voice husky. "We'll send him straight to Holly's."

"A gracious host would at least make the offer," she chided.

"But I'm not a gracious host. I'm a man in desperate need of his wife's attention, and I don't need company down the hall."

"We won't have company tonight or tomorrow or Wednesday," she gently teased. "That should take care of any desperation."

His gaze met hers and his fingers tightened around hers. "Three nights isn't enough."

"How many would be?"

He shook his head. "I can't count that high, Maggie. Forever. I'll need you forever."

ROSS SECURED THE LAST PIECE OF TAPE to the package in the center of his desk, then glanced around. The few gifts he'd gotten Maggie that were suitable for wrapping were wrapped—not as expertly as her own packages under the tree, but he'd managed well enough. One of the remaining gifts was tucked in the corner of his office with nothing more than a bow attached, and he'd just gotten off the phone from making arrangements to pick up the other in the morning.

He wasn't thoroughly pleased with several of the purchases—wasn't sure whether he'd made the right decision or simply the selfish one. Whatever his motivation, though, Maggie would be happy, and that was what counted.

It was Christmas Eve, and the sky was dark. Carols came softly from the stereo in the living room, and outside, Maggie was bundled up against the cold as she lit the farolitos. Tom was in town, a few miles away at the McBride Inn, and planning to join them later that evening for the midnight service in the square. Ross wouldn't be surprised to find Holly accompanying him.

He carried the gifts into the living room and placed them under the tree. It wasn't an impressive stack of the sort they'd become accustomed to in recent years, but it was more than enough because these were all gifts that meant something. Besides, this Christmas he'd already been given the best gift of all—Maggie.

For as long as she didn't remember.

For a moment panic gripped him so tightly that he forgot to breathe. Slowly he forced air into his lungs. According to Miss Corinna, there was no sin that couldn't be forgiven. God help him, he hoped Maggie believed that too. If she didn't, one of these days his life was going to crumble and he would have no one to blame but himself.

But until that day came, he would have a life worth living, and he intended to make the most of it.

He got his coat and went outside to slip up behind her and nuzzle her cold cheek. She gave him a smile so sweet that it made his muscles tighten, so full of love that it made his heart ache. Blind love. Totally-unaware-of-the-truth love. It would kill him to lose her again.

No problem that love couldn't overcome, no sin that couldn't be forgiven. He reminded himself of that before making an effort to push the fears back into the darkest corner of his mind.

"What time is Tom coming over?"

"Around eight. That'll give us time to eat, then walk to the square." Though they called it a midnight service, it actually began two hours earlier and ended at twelve. It was hard to imagine that Tom—the shark, as Maggie was fond of describing him—was willing to attend such a service. He had, in fact, received the invitation with a moment of blank silence before awkwardly agreeing.

But a year ago, wouldn't Ross's own attendance have been met with equal surprise? That night he'd meant to be in his office working when the church bells tolled the midnight conclusion to the worship service.

Instead, he'd been waiting to find out whether his wife would live or die.

This year he would be telling her how much he loved her—and praying that he would never lose her.

He followed her along the sidewalk as she lit the farolitos. When she finished, they stood on the sidewalk out front and gazed at the results. Maggie sighed contentedly. "Isn't it amazing how things change? Last Christmas Eve I lit the farolitos by myself while I waited for the service in the square, and I wanted everything to be perfect for the first Christmas in my new house, but I knew it wasn't going to be. I mean, you and me in the same room for an entire evening. Civility was definitely out of the question."

Far colder than the weather justified, Ross stared at her. He felt sick inside—so sick that his hands went numb. "You—did you remember that, or are you guessing?"

"I—I remembered . . . I think." Her expression turned more serious. "You don't want me to remember, do you?"

"I—it's not—" Breaking off, he clenched his jaw and said nothing.

"Why not? Do you think if I remember what we argued about, I'll leave you again?"

All he could manage was a hoarse whisper. "You did before."

"Before was different. I was going to leave you anyway, even if we hadn't argued. *You* were going to leave *me*." She slapped his arm, but it was merely a gesture, lacking force. "I *love* you, Ross. I want to be married to you. I want to live the rest of my life with you. And I want you to feel the same."

"I do!"

"Except where I'm looking ahead to forever, you're expecting me to walk out any moment now. Do you know how insulting that is? Do you know how that makes me feel to know that you don't trust me?"

"I trust you, Maggie, but I know what happened last year. You don't."

She folded her arms across her chest. "So tell me."

Tell her. It was through his own stupid carelessness last year that she'd learned his secret in the first place, and she'd almost died for it. If he told her now—bluntly, without mercy—*he* would be the one whose survival was at stake. He'd made her walk away from him once. He couldn't do it again. "I can't."

"Then forget it. I have."

"But someday it's going to come back, and—"

"And we'll deal with it." She hugged him tightly. "Have a little faith in us, Ross. We're strong. We can survive anything."

He slid his hands into her hair and held her for a hard, desperate kiss. "I love you," he whispered. "No matter what, I'll always love you."

"And I'll always love you," she whispered back. *"Always."* She started toward the house. Halfway there, she turned back. "Are you coming?"

"In a minute."

She came back for one more sweet kiss, touched his face gently, then went inside. He stood there in the cold, staring at the closed door.

She was going to remember. He felt it in some sick, hurtful place deep inside. She was going to remember, and all her talk about trust and faith and always would mean nothing. Love would turn to hate, as it had before, affection to scorn, and there was nothing in the world he could do to stop it. He couldn't tell her the truth and hasten the inevitable, and he couldn't walk away before it happened. All he could do was wait and love her and hope that that would count for something in the end.

He didn't think it would.

Feeling anxious and edgy, he started walking. He had no destination in mind but wanted only to burn off a little energy, to ease a little panic. When he came to the square in the center of town, he automatically turned into it.

In a few more hours it would be filled with people—virtually everyone in town attended the service—but at the moment it was deserted. The paths leading to the gazebo were dusted with snow, and drifts were piled around the shrubs. He walked through ankle-deep snow to the nearest bench, brushed it clean, then sat down.

Helplessness was a new feeling for him, and he didn't like it one bit. He was a powerful man accustomed to getting what he wanted when he wanted it. Even when Maggie's condition was at its most critical, every one of his demands had been filled almost instantly. A pilot willing to fly through a snowstorm to get her to the trauma center in Buffalo—no problem. Calling out the top doctors in the country on Christmas Day—piece of cake. The absolute best care money could buy—a done deal.

But he couldn't demand or buy his way out of this. There wasn't enough power or money in the world to find a happy resolution to this problem. She was going to remember, and she was never going to forgive him.

"You look a little lonesome sitting here. Mind if I join you?"

The question came from a slender woman with long, brown hair and familiar eyes. Noelle, nursery clerk, hospital volunteer, and first-class meddler. He wanted to tell her yes, he did mind. He wanted to be alone with his misery. Instead, he glanced at the opposite end of the bench, then away. "I didn't hear you come up."

"It's the snow. It muffles footsteps." She dusted the bench, then sat down. "Merry Christmas."

His only response was a grunt.

"Are you and Maggie coming to the midnight service?"

"Yes." He would be better off putting some distance between them, but it was too late for that. Hadn't he promised himself just that evening that he was going to make the best of however much time they had?

"How is she?"

He glanced distractedly at Noelle. "She's fine."

"How are you? And don't say fine, because anyone with eyes in her head can see that's not so." She turned on the bench so she was facing him. "She's begun remembering, hasn't she?"

"A couple of thin—how'd you know that?"

"You're worried that she'll remember what led to her leaving a year ago, aren't you?"

He answered even though he didn't want to. "What I did was unforgivable."

"Human beings have a tremendous capacity for forgiveness. As flawed as they are, they need it." Her smile appeared, then disappeared. "Nothing's unforgivable, Ross, especially for someone who truly loves you. Like Maggie."

"What I did was," he insisted, but she made a dismissive gesture.

"Two weekends. Three encounters. Bad judgment, immoral, certainly wrong, but not worthy of sacrificing the rest of your lives together—all the happiness, all the love, all the babies. And that's what you're doing, Ross.

You're risking your future. You're just waiting for it to blow up in your face."

"What—how did you—" Suspicion tightened his muscles. "Who are you?"

"Just someone trying to be a friend."

"How did you know—"

She laid her hand on his arm. "Your affair was wrong, Ross. It was a terrible mistake, and you've all paid the price. Last year your marriage wasn't strong enough to survive. Is it strong enough now?"

The answer was too painful to give aloud. Instead, he simply, bleakly shook his head.

"Are you sure?"

"I lied to her. I betrayed her. How could she forgive that?"

"What if the situation were reversed? If it was Maggie who'd had the affair, who'd lied to and betrayed you. Could you forgive her?"

"There would be nothing to forgive because she would never do it."

"That's what she thinks about you."

He knew she was right. Maggie had even said so one day over burnt burgers in the kitchen. *I always knew that there would never be another woman.* Which would be harder for her to hear? That there *had* been another woman? Or that she'd misjudged him so badly?

"What if the unthinkable happened? What if Maggie felt lonely and empty and hungry for just a little affection in her life—affection that you'd refused her? What if she found that affection with another man and, later, you found out? Could you forgive her?"

He would hate it like hell—would *hate* that another man had touched her, had kissed her, had found that incredible satisfaction with her. But could he forgive it?

If it was a choice between forgiving or living without her, no doubt. He'd lived without her before. He would gladly forgive a dozen affairs before doing it again.

Noelle smiled gently. "You could. You would. But, of course, you're a kinder, more compassionate, more loving, and generous person than she is."

"Not in this lifetime," he said scornfully. "Maggie is the best, sweetest, most honorable person I know."

"Then my guess is that she can forgive too. She's a bright woman. Once she gets past the hurt of discovery, she'll know what she has to do. She'll do the right thing."

He stared at the gazebo, shining with white lights in the dark night, weighing the confidence in Noelle's voice, hearing the certainty in Maggie's.

I love you, Ross. I want to be married to you. I want to live the rest of my life with you.

Have a little faith in us. We're strong. We can survive anything.

I'll always love you. Always.

Having faith. Believing in her and her love. Giving her credit for knowing her feelings as well as he knew his own. Could he do it?

Did he have any choice?

Noelle stood up. "You'd better go home. I imagine Maggie's wondering where you've gone."

He stood up, too, and took a few steps before turning back. "How did you know . . . ?"

With a smile, she shook her finger warningly. "A little faith, Mr. McKinney."

When she offered her hand, he accepted it, clasping it between both of his. "Thank you. I needed—"

"I know. Go on now. And have a merry Christmas."

He'd taken only a few more steps, when she spoke again. "I wasn't kidding about the rest of your lives—the happiness, the love, the babies. Bringing a longed-for babe into a loving home is never selfish, Ross. Maggie will be a wonderful mother, and in spite of your fears, in spite of your father, you'll be a wonderful father. Your sons and daughters, along with Maggie, will be the brightest blessings in your life."

Ross stared at her. For one odd moment when she'd spoken—*the brightest blessings*—it seemed as if the night had lightened around him. Maybe it had been the burden around his heart that had lightened, because when she said he would be a good father, he'd felt the impact of truth. She believed what she'd said, and for some reason her believing allowed him to believe it too. "How—"

She smiled sweetly, that bright, million-watt smile. "Faith," she said with a firm nod. Raising one mittened hand, she wiggled her fingers in a wave. "Go home, Ross. Your wife is waiting."

He nodded. Home was exactly where he wanted to be.

He cut across the snow to the nearest square of shoveled sidewalk, then looked back. Noelle had wasted no time leaving the park. She was already out of sight. And, oddly, from where he stood, he couldn't see any signs of her leaving. The snow in the direction she must have gone was smooth, unmarked. A trick of the lights, he was sure, but he didn't go back to confirm it. Instead, he pushed his hands into his pockets for warmth, then headed with long, purposeful strides down the street.

It was Christmas Eve, and Maggie was waiting.

Chapter Fifteen

MAGGIE STOOD FROZEN ON THE corner, unable to see for the tears that filled her eyes, unable to breathe for the sorrow that filled her heart. It was no wonder her mind had buried last Christmas's memories, no surprise that they'd sent her barreling up the mountain to certain disaster.

Anything could jog her memory, the doctors had told her—a sight, a sound, a smell—and they'd been right. The sight of Ross standing there, holding that woman's hand, hadn't just jogged her memory. It had broken open a flood of memories. Last Christmas Eve, Ross and Jessica in intimate conversation, her hand clasped familiarly in his until Maggie walked in on them. The gift addressed to Jessica, the one that had made Ross blanch, the one that had contained a small fortune in diamonds and sapphires that matched her dark eyes perfectly. The horrible guilt on Jessica's face, the utter blankness of Ross's expression, the sudden realization that had struck both Maggie and Jessica's husband, Kevin, at the same time.

Oh, God, she couldn't stand this! Not again, oh, please, not again!

Whirling around, she started toward the house, walking first, then picking up speed until she was running. Her feet slipped on the snow, but she caught herself and stumbled on. Her chest grew tight, her breathing labored, but still she ran—down the street, up the steps, into the house. She slammed the door behind her, leaned against it, and the first low moan escaped.

He'd had an affair! All these years she'd been so smug and secure in her certainty that he wasn't that type, that he had more respect for their marriage than that, that whatever else was wrong, he was too good and decent and trustworthy to betray her in that way, and all these years she'd been wrong! Not only had he done it, but with her best friend. *Her best friend!*

Damn his soul.

The pain was killing—the grief, the betrayal. She wanted to sink to the floor, to curl up and keen. She wanted to hit something—wanted to hit *him* and make him suffer. She wanted to scream and rage and sob until she had no voice, no tears, no feeling, and then she wanted to die.

He was on his way home—would be there in a few minutes, acting as if nothing had happened, as if he hadn't committed the single most unforgivable sin in a marriage. She couldn't face him, not yet, not while her heart was still breaking, while every part of her was agonizingly raw. She pushed away from the door and went down the hall. Last year she'd taken the time to pack her bags. Tonight all she needed was her keys, still clutched in her fist.

She let herself out the side door, took as deep a breath as the tightness in her chest would allow. She hadn't driven a car in a year, but she had no choice. It was the only escape available to her, and she needed escape before the emotions broke free of her rigid control and shattered her into a million pieces of pure sorrow.

"Maggie?"

Ross's voice came from the driveway. She couldn't look at him—at this man whom she loved so dearly, who had so thoroughly betrayed her.

"What are you doing? Where are you going?"

The serrated edges of the keys bit through her thin leather glove, giving her an actual physical pain to focus on. She squeezed harder as she slowly turned toward him. He looked unbearably handsome. Worried. Innocent.

Innocent. The man who'd indulged in an affair with her very best friend in the entire world. He wasn't innocent of anything.

Speaking was an effort that required easing some small bit of the control that kept her intact. She half feared that when she opened her mouth, nothing would come out but screams, and once started, they wouldn't stop until they'd consumed her. But there was no scream, no sob, not even a tiny hiccup. There were only two words—two cold, hard, damning words. "I remember."

He stopped a half dozen feet away and blanched. Just like last Christmas Eve. She'd been handing out the gifts, when she'd come to the elegantly wrapped box bearing the small gold foil seal of Ross's favorite jeweler. Jessica's name on the tag had surprised her. She never would have dreamed Kevin could afford even the least costly piece in the place.

She'd delivered the box to her friend with a flourish. "Looks like you've been a *very* good girl," she'd teased, but Jessica hadn't smiled. She'd looked mortified and tried to move the gift to one side, but neither Maggie nor Kevin had let her. Open it, they'd both encouraged, and, unable to avoid it, she'd done so.

Looking guilty as hell, she'd pulled the bracelet from the box and looked first at Maggie, then at Kevin. She'd avoided looking at Ross, but Maggie had looked and seen his own guilt. The weight of the stones had pulled the bracelet from Jessica's numb fingers, landing on the floor with a clatter, and some part of Maggie had died.

Just as some part of her was dying now.

Suddenly Ross exhaled the breath he'd been holding, and his shoulders rounded. "I'm sorry, Maggie," he murmured.

"*Sorry*. Are you sorry you had the affair? Sorry you betrayed us? Sorry you damn near destroyed me? Or merely sorry you got caught?"

"Maggie—"

"Was she the only one?"

"Yes."

"And I'm supposed to believe that? I'm supposed to take the word of a cheat and a liar?" Her words made him wince, and she felt the stab deep in her own soul, but she didn't regret them. She *wanted* to wound him. "My God, she was my best friend! I loved her! And you—you did *this!*"

"I'm sorry. Maggie, I'm so sorry." He came a step closer. "I don't know what else to say."

"Well, think of something, because that's not enough!" She was trembling now, on the verge of losing control. Anger. She needed anger. Anger was strength. "*I'm* sorry, Ross. I'm sorry I asked you to come here. I'm sorry I didn't divorce you the day I left the center. I'm sorry as hell that I ever knew you!"

That hit its target too, but he denied it. "That's not true. You love me. I love you."

"You have a hell of a way of showing it—sleeping with my best friend. Was that why you chose her? For maximum betrayal? Was it fun? Did you enjoy it? Did you laugh together about how incredibly stupid I was to trust you both?"

He closed his eyes for a moment, then looked at her again with such misery. "It was the biggest mistake in my life, but I can't undo it, Maggie. I'd give everything if I could. All I can do is tell you I love you and ask your forgiveness."

"Some things can't be forgiven," she whispered brokenly. "I think this is one."

Turning abruptly, she slid into the car and reached for the door. He stopped it with his hand. "Maggie, wait. You haven't driven in so long. I'll go. I'll leave. You stay here."

"I can't. I have to get away from here."

"I can't let you go." He reached for her arm, but she shrank away from his touch. Her action stunned him, made him still. She took advantage of the moment to jerk the door free of his grip. As soon as it closed, she locked it, then started the engine and threw it into reverse, backing into the street without looking.

She didn't know where she was going—just away, so far away that the pain couldn't follow, so far that she might find a blessed numbness that would allow her to survive. Before she'd gone twenty feet, the tears started—little ones at first that she dashed away with the back of her hand. Then they came faster, harder, scalding against her cold skin, making her whole body shake.

Wherever she was going, she knew it wouldn't help, knew there was no place far enough away to escape this heartache. They were strong, she'd told Ross, but that was a joke. He hadn't been strong enough to honor their vows, and this time . . .

This time *she* wasn't strong enough to survive.

M INUTE AFTER MINUTE PASSED, AND Ross remained in the same spot—unable to move, to think, to do anything but feel. He felt sore in body, heart, and soul. He never should have come to Bethlehem, never should have risked falling in love with her again—putting her through this again. She hated him, and with good reason. For whatever it was worth, he hated himself.

Finally, when the cold had succeeded in numbing

everything but the fear and the ache, he went inside the house and to the phone in the kitchen. The Walkers' phone number was in the address book there. He dialed it and heard the sounds of a family Christmas when Mitch answered. The reminder that he was more alone and lost this Christmas than ever before added another level to his pain.

"Hello?" Mitch repeated. "Is anyone there?"

Ross drew a breath. "Mitch, it's Ross McKinney."

"Merry Christmas. What can I do for you?"

"I—" A year ago he wouldn't have dreamed of making this call—would have been too proud, too protective of his damned reputation. Maybe if he *had* called then, there would have been no reason for some stranger living halfway up the mountain to make a later call for the sheriff and an ambulance.

"Ross? What's up?"

Another breath, this one deep enough to be painful. "Maggie and I have had a—a disagreement, and she's gone. She hasn't driven since the accident and she's upset, and—and I was wondering if—if you could have your people keep an eye out for her."

Mitch's response was quieter, more serious. "Sure. Give me a description of the car."

Ross provided him with that and the license number.

"I'll call the dispatcher now. She's also dispatching for the county tonight, so the sheriff's department will get it too. As soon as we hear something, I'll let you know."

"Thanks." Ross hung up, then wandered down the hall to the front of the house. Everything seemed so normal. The lights were on. The air was still scented with the aromas of the pies Maggie had baked this evening. The carols were still playing in the living room. The presents waited under the tree.

So normal. Except that Maggie was gone.

When the CD segued into the first strains of "Ave Maria," he punched the stop button with enough force to slide the stereo against the wall. He felt so damned helpless. So damned sorry.

And *sorry* meant nothing to Maggie.

His love meant nothing to her.

He meant nothing.

When the doorbell rang, it startled him. He didn't for an instant hope it was Maggie. He'd lost all hope when she'd looked at him in the driveway and said, "I remember." Lifting his gaze to the nearest window, he saw Tom's Porsche parked at the curb and remembered that they'd invited him for dinner before the service.

He opened the door as the bell chimed again. Tom followed him into the living room, took a look around, then, without even a greeting, asked, "What's wrong?"

"Who says anything's wrong?"

"You do. That expression. Where's Maggie?"

"Gone."

"Gone where?" Tom glanced around again as if he might spot her in some hidden corner. "You mean *gone*? What happened?"

"She remembered." Ross crouched in front of the tree and the gifts he'd placed there just a short time ago. It was frightening how desperately things had changed since then.

"Remembered what?"

He touched the smallest package, the one that held

the emerald earrings Tom had overnighted from the office. When he'd given them to her originally, she'd been thrilled, and when they'd made love later that night, she'd worn them and nothing else. He'd entertained some fanciful notion of doing so again sometime, but it wasn't going to happen.

Rising, he went to stand in front of the fireplace. After scrutinizing everything on the mantel there, he turned to face his lawyer—his friend. "That I had an affair. With Jessica Hinton."

For the first time in all the years Ross had known him, Tom reacted without thinking. "For God's sake, Ross, *why*?"

"I was lonely. She was available." He shrugged. "She was willing."

"A lot of women were willing, and they weren't your wife's best friend."

"It just happened. It was stupid and meaningless and we both hated and regretted it, but it happened and I can't change it."

Tom muttered something under his breath that sounded strongly of an insult. "Where would Maggie go?"

"I don't know."

"Have you called her friends?"

"One—the police chief. He's got his officers looking for her."

"She wouldn't go to Buffalo, would she?"

"I don't know."

Tom hesitated over what was apparently an unwelcome question, then asked it anyway. "She wouldn't hurt herself, would she?"

"No." Then the sharpness was replaced by a sudden resurgence of fear. "Not deliberately." Not that intent mattered. It hadn't been deliberate last Christmas, but she'd almost died anyway.

"Give me her friends' names. I'll call them."

Ross took him into the kitchen and pointed out the names in the address book. Then, from the island, he listened while Tom dialed each number, then repeated the same words. *My name is Tom Flynn. I work for Maggie McKinney's husband, and I'm trying to locate her. Have you see her this evening?* Each time he got the same negative answer.

When he hung up from the last call, Tom turned to him. "She's probably just driving around somewhere. I'll see if I can find her. If she comes back, call me on the cell phone."

Feeling sick inside, Ross nodded. He didn't accompany Tom to the door. He didn't say anything, didn't beg him to please bring her home safe. Tom was probably right. She was just driving around, trying to get her emotions under control. She would come home. She *had* to, because she loved this town, this house, and these people.

Even if she no longer loved *him.*

A SENSE OF DÉJÀ VU SWEPT OVER MAGGIE as she realized that she was following the same route she'd taken when she fled a year ago—the highway that led away from Bethlehem and Ross. That night the lanes had been coated with ice and snow, and driving had been treacherous. Tonight the road was clear, the sky was filled with brilliant stars, and the only treachery lay behind her.

Both nights she'd wanted nothing more than to get away from him . . . and nothing more than to run back to him. But how could she go back? How could she, when the mere thought of him with Jessica left her drowning under fresh waves of pain?

But how could she leave him when her heart, her future—her very life—lay with him?

Oh, God, she wished she were dead.

You don't mean that, Maggie.

The words were as clear, as real, as if they'd been spoken aloud, and they were full of conviction. She wished she shared that conviction. All she was sure of just then was that she couldn't bear this pain. She couldn't live with Ross or without him—couldn't forgive him and couldn't forget him.

Up ahead, the road widened, and a narrow lane forked off to the right. She remembered the place from her drive here with Ross, not from last year. That night she'd been too panicked to make note of where her accident had begun. She'd been afraid that she was going to die and convinced that Ross would be glad.

He wouldn't have been. She knew that now.

Suddenly her headlights illuminated a figure on the side of the road—a woman wearing a heavy parka over a skirt that reached to her ankles. Her hair was tucked under a knit hat, and a scarf was wrapped around her neck, obscuring much of her face. Even so, Maggie recognized her. She moved her foot to the brake pedal and eased onto the shoulder, bringing the car to a stop right in front of the woman.

Noelle opened the passenger door and bent to look inside. "Hi. It's a little cold out here. Can I come in?"

"Of course. What are you doing here? Did you have an accident?"

Noelle settled in the seat, rubbed her mittened hands together, then sighed. "The heat feels wonderful."

"What were you doing standing at the side of the road?"

"Waiting for you—and hoping that you wouldn't come along."

"Waiting for—" Maggie broke off. Clearly the woman had been out in the cold too long. "Where's your car?"

"I don't have one."

"Then how did you get here?"

"I think the more important question is how *you* got here." Noelle tugged off her mittens, searched through her pockets, then came up with a plastic-wrapped pack of tissues. "You look like you could use one."

Aware that she must look the very picture of *distraught,* Maggie took a tissue, dabbed at her eyes, and blew her nose. Then she settled her gaze on the other woman. "Why are you out here?"

"I told you. I was waiting for you."

"That's not possible. No one knew I was coming this way. I didn't even know."

Noelle shrugged. "I'm here, aren't I? Though I wish you weren't. I wish you were home unwrapping Christmas gifts with the husband you love more than anything in the world."

Maggie tried to combat the new tears that threatened with a scowl. "What do you know about that?"

"I know you love him and he loves you. I know that he hurt you deeply and that he regrets it more than words can possibly express."

Maggie was surprised, startled—and angry. "You *know* what he did?"

Noelle nodded.

"How? Did *you* have an affair with him too?"

"Oh, heavens, no. No, Jessica was the only one, Maggie. The only one ever."

Ross had said the same thing back at the house, but she had doubted him. Why did it sound more believable coming from this woman she hardly knew?

And *how* did this woman know?

She folded her arms over her chest and stubbornly stared ahead. "I'm not going to forgive him." From the corner of her eye she saw Noelle mimic the position.

"Oh, I wouldn't either. The man made a mistake. Now he's got to pay for it for the rest of his life."

"A *mistake*? A mistake is when you add a check in your register instead of subtracting it. It's when you buy regular coffee when you really wanted decaf. He was *unfaithful* to me! He dishonored our marriage! And he used my best friend to do it!"

Mildly, Noelle repeated, "Your best friend. You've been saying that a lot this evening. But, you know, Maggie, it occurs to me that a woman who would have an affair with your husband isn't really very much of a friend at all."

She wanted to argue the point, but how could she? Instead, she applied it in the opposite direction. "And a husband who would have an affair with *anyone* isn't much of a husband. He's certainly not worth keeping, and he sure as hell isn't deserving of forgiveness."

"What was he unfaithful to, Maggie? What marriage did he dishonor? There was nothing between you two but a piece of paper that you had both decided to do away with. It was all over but the formalities. Yes, the affair was wrong, but for all practical purposes, you'd already given up your claim on him. It was just a matter of time—very little time—before he would have been free to pursue a relationship with any other woman."

"Then he should have waited. There are no 'buts.' The affair was wrong. Period." Maggie made an impatient gesture. "I don't know why I'm having this discussion with you. I don't even know you. Why are you so interested?"

"Because I was here last year when this all started."

"Here—in Bethlehem?"

"Here." Noelle gestured to the area around them. "With you."

"I don't . . ." The denial trailed off as Maggie recalled that night. All the tears, the hurt, the anger—just like tonight. The fear when the truck began skidding out of control. The searing pain as it rolled down the mountainside. The sweet fragrance of the frigid night air as it filtered through the broken windows to surround her broken body. The realization that she was going to—

"Yes, you thought you were dying." Noelle's voice was as gentle as her touch on Maggie's arm. "I was with you in the truck. I stayed with you until help came, until I was certain you would be all right."

Maggie looked off to the ravine on her left. Though darkness hid it now, as then, she remembered it—the steep walls, the boulders, the trees. Getting down there required effort. It wasn't a walk in the park. "You live nearby?"

"No."

"You were driving past?"

"I don't have a car, remember?"

"Did you come with the paramedics?"

"No."

"Then . . . I don't understand."

"I was sent there to help you—to stay with you until you no longer needed me."

Maggie stared off into the darkness, traveling back a year in time. When the truck came to a stop, she'd slumped in the driver's seat, the crumpled metal holding her limp body upright. The headlights had shone at odd angles, and the windshield wipers had continued to sweep back and forth. The pain, so intense in the seconds of the crash, had eased to a distant throb as her life slipped away, and the voice had been distant too—

The voice. She'd been alone in the truck, but someone had spoken to her, comforted her. *Hold on, Maggie. Help is on the way. You're going to be all right. Everything's going to be all right.* Soft words in a softer voice offering hope that she had desperately clung to.

She twisted to look at Noelle, who shrugged. "I told you the truth. Help did come, and you are all right."

Maggie felt light-headed, the way she did when one

of the dizzy spells was about to hit. Maybe that explained all this—it was simply some bizarre hallucination coming from her damaged brain. But the woman looked real. Her hand on Maggie's arm had certainly felt real. She even smelled real—of cinnamon and pine and fresh, cold air.

"What are you saying?" Maggie demanded. "That you're some kind of guardian angel? *My* guardian angel?"

Noelle merely smiled, a sweet, simple gesture that somehow eased a small bit of the ache around Maggie's heart. Fighting against it—wanting the anger that accompanied the pain—she scowled. "I don't believe in angels."

"I bet you don't believe in miracles either, even though you got one of your very own last year."

"So I lived. It was a *medical* miracle, nothing else."

Noelle didn't look at all convinced—or offended—by her scornful words. "Last Christmas you received the miracle of life. This Christmas you received a miracle as precious—the gift of love. Maggie, how can you even consider turning your back on it?"

The ache in Maggie's chest intensified, and she had to close her eyes to stop the tears that burned. "He lied to me," she whispered. "He betrayed me. How could I even consider believing now that he loves me?"

"You're right. He did lie to you. He did betray you. But he didn't do it to hurt you. He was hurting himself, Maggie. He was lonely and confused. His marriage was ending. The girl who had loved him with all the intensity of her young heart had become a woman who couldn't bear his touch. You resented everything that took him away from you, and yet, when he was with you, you resented *him*. Do you remember that you didn't even share a bedroom?"

Maggie stared out ahead, but it wasn't the night-dark mountain she was seeing. Instead, her vision focused on a scene from long ago—another argument, another round of insults, hurtful words, scathing attacks. She was going to bed, she'd announced, and she didn't want to be disturbed, so Ross could use a guest room that night. And he did—that night, and every night that followed. The anger had gone away, the insults had been forgotten, but he had continued to sleep down the hall. He'd been waiting for her to invite him back into their room. She'd known it, and yet pride had kept her silent. And so she'd slept in her lonely bed, and he'd slept in his.

Until Jessica joined him.

A thin, bitter smile touched her lips. She'd thought Jessica was her best friend, but it turned out she'd never really known the woman at all. She had never known Jessica was the type to be unfaithful to her husband. She'd never dreamed she was the type to betray her closest friend.

She'd never, ever in her wildest dreams imagined that Jessica was Ross's type.

"She's not his type," Noelle chided. "But she was all the things you weren't. Warm. Friendly. Receptive. Willing to touch him. Eager to be touched by him. She was available, Maggie. *You* hadn't been available to him in a very long time."

The truth in those words made Maggie's voice defensive. "You're saying this is my fault."

"No, not at all. It was Ross's and Jessica's decision to have an affair. Only Ross and Jessica could have said no. They made the wrong choices, and they've had to live with the consequences." Noelle sighed, then drew a deep breath. "What I'm saying, Maggie, is that Ross was in a difficult place then. He was unhappy and hungry for affection. You know what that's like."

She did. Many were the times she'd been tempted to take drastic action to ease her loneliness—but she'd never gone through with it. And she'd never been tempted by anyone but Ross.

"I understand what you're saying," she said stiffly. "I understand loneliness and bad choices and mistakes. God knows, I've made plenty of my own. In my head I understand all of that, but in my heart—"

"In your heart you know that he's hurt you more than anyone else ever could. But you also know that he loves you more than anyone else ever will. You know how deeply he regrets it, how terribly he's suffered for it. And you know he would do anything in his power to keep you safe and healthy and happy."

"Anything except be faithful." Maggie said the words to remind herself, but she knew in some small, inviolable place that they weren't true. He was a different man. She was a different woman. They'd learned the hard way the things to treasure in life.

"You have two choices, Maggie. You can forgive him and spend the rest of your life with him, happy and in love. Or you can withhold forgiveness and live the rest of your life feeling much like you do right now. You should know from your mother's experience that pride is a poor companion. And you should know from your own experience that love is worth almost any sacrifice, including pride."

Maggie leaned forward, resting her head on the steering wheel, hiding her face. "I don't know how to forgive him," she whispered. "It hurts too much."

"Do you love him?"

"Yes, but—"

"There are no buts. Either you love him or you don't. Period. Do you?"

"Yes." She whispered the word soundlessly the first time, then repeated it with more conviction. "Yes. I do."

"Then go home. Tell him. Work this out with him."

Maggie felt a tender touch on her hair, a mother-soothing-child stroke. "You lost him once over this," Noelle said softly, "and you almost lost yourself. Don't let it happen again, Maggie. Go to Ross. Go home."

Go home. It was good advice. That was where she wanted to be—where she wanted to stay. Home. With Ross. Forever.

The knock on the driver's window startled Maggie, making her jerk upright. A sheriff's deputy stood next to the car, bent low so he could see through the glass. In the rearview mirror she saw his patrol car, the red and blue lights flashing. As her heart rate slowed to normal, she lowered the window and shivered at the sudden cold.

"Mrs. McKinney, are you all right?" the young man asked.

"Yes, I'm fine." And with surprise she realized it wasn't a total lie. She wasn't *fine,* but she felt better.

She *knew* she was going to survive this—she and Ross together. Intact. In love. Happy.

"Your husband's awfully worried about you, ma'am. Can I give you a ride, or are you okay to drive back into town?"

"I'm okay, really. I—I just needed some time." She managed a smile. "I'm going home now."

"I'll follow you. Just to make sure you get there all right."

She nodded and watched him walk back to his car before shifting her gaze to the sky. The stars were unusually brilliant tonight. Considering the night, it was fitting.

She rolled up the window, then glanced toward Noelle.

The seat was empty. She was alone in the car.

She looked ahead and off to the sides, then twisted around to look behind her. There was no sign of the other woman—and no way she could have gotten out of the car without Maggie hearing her.

So where was she? Real people didn't simply disappear.

But such a feat would be child's play to an angel.

Slowly she smiled. Maybe it was the night or those incredible stars up above. Maybe it was nothing more than her battered heart needing to believe. But this beautiful Christmas Eve, outside a town called Bethlehem, an angel seemed a perfectly reasonable explanation.

With one last glance around, she backed the car onto the side road, then headed back into the valley.

Back home to Ross.

• • •

H E SAT ON THE STAIRS IN THE SILENT
house, his arms resting on his knees, his head
bent. He didn't know how much time had passed. All
he knew was that his worst fears had come to pass and
there was nothing—*nothing*—he could do but sit and
wait, wearily twisting the worn band on his finger.

When the front door opened, he didn't look up.
Tom must have become better acquainted with Bethlehem tonight than he'd ever wanted to. No doubt he
was giving up the search. It was pointless anyway. No
one, not even Tom, could make Maggie come back.
No one could make right all the things he'd put
wrong.

The door closed, and footsteps moved across the
floor, coming slowly into his line of sight. Booted feet,
small feet. He jerked his gaze upward, and the ring
slipped from his index finger, fell to the floor, and
rolled to a stop between the boots. Maggie bent,
picked it up, examined it closely, then closed her fingers around it.

He had to try several times to make his voice work,
and even then the words were hoarse and thick. "Forget something?"

"Yes, as a matter of fact, I did." She disappeared into
the living room, then returned with a small package.
Kneeling a few steps below him, she held it out, and
slowly, without touching her, he took it. "Open it."

It was small, flat, wrapped in gold foil paper and
decorated with a gold mesh bow she'd tied herself. He
opened the package to find a Christmas ornament—a

wreath with two angels side by side, kissing. He touched it lightly, then glanced at Maggie. Her face was puffy, her eyes red, but her mouth curved in the beginning of a smile, and her expression was expectant.

"Turn it over."

He did. Written on the back was a brief message: *This time forever.* "Your promise," he whispered.

"You asked me for a promise and I made it. Now I'm going to keep it."

"But you didn't know—"

"I knew the important things. I knew that I loved you. I knew that you loved me. That's what matters."

His hand reached for her of its own accord. Deliberately he pulled it back. "What I did matters."

"Yes . . . but it can be dealt with. What's important is what you do now, what you do in the future." She became sweetly serious. "We were different people a year ago, Ross, in a different place. We can't let what we did then ruin the future we can have now. What we *can* do is ensure that it never happens again. We won't forget what's important. We'll make it good and make it last." She gestured toward the wreath. "My promise."

Abruptly her gaze shifted to the ornament. She took it from him and held it up to see better. "Hey, that's not the one I bought. On mine, the angels were holding hands."

"I like them kissing better," he said, sliding an arm around her waist, drawing her closer. "Maybe the clerk accidentally switched it with another."

"But she didn't have any others with two angels. She checked."

"Maybe she was mistaken. Maybe you were mistaken."

As he lifted her onto his lap, she gave him a wry look. "Believe me, I know the difference between this"—she clasped his hand—"and this." Wrapping one arm around his neck, she brought her mouth to his in a kiss that was instantly hot and needy and full of promise and love. When she finally ended it, he was breathless.

"Maybe . . ." His mind was blank, the words forgotten.

She rested her head on his shoulder and studied the ornament for a minute, then slowly smiled. "Noelle found this for me. She's an angel, you know. Maybe that explains it."

He thought of the young woman in the park who'd known his secrets, eased his fears, and disappeared without so much as one footprint in the snow—and he smiled too. "Definitely an angel."

She wriggled to retrieve the gold band from her jeans pocket, gave it to him, then extended her left hand. Ignoring her hand, he studied the ring for a moment. Sixteen years old, it had been through a lot. There were nicks and scratches, and, after being relegated to the jewelry box in favor of the diamond monstrosity, it had lost its luster. But the imperfections added character and the shine had been restored with a little TLC. It was as fitting a symbol of their marriage as any.

Solemnly he slid it onto her finger, then pressed a kiss to it. She gazed at it, then at him, with a look of supreme satisfaction. "And she brought us our own Christmas miracle."

A COLD CHRISTMAS EVE, SNOW ON THE ground, breathtaking stars in the sky, friends gathered round, and Ross at her side. Maggie couldn't imagine a more perfect moment if she tried, and so she didn't. She simply savored.

The high school choir was leading the crowd in one last carol, "O Little Town of Bethlehem." She didn't sing along. Neither did Ross, who held her so close that she imagined she could feel the steady beat of his heart through their coats. Surprisingly, beside them, Tom did sing along, and quite satisfactorily. Next to him, Holly was singing too—in between stealing glances.

As the last notes faded into the night, a hush fell over the crowd, broken after a moment by the pastor who offered the closing prayer. She had much to be grateful for, and she whispered a prayer to that effect. Then church bells from nearby rang in Christmas Day, and everyone turned to their friends and neighbors to offer greetings and wishes.

The Winchester sisters were the last to seek them out. "I would say that I hope Santa brings you your heart's desire," Miss Corinna said with a twinkling smile, "but it's obvious you've already got it. I'm happy for you both."

"Come and see us tomorrow. Bring your guest," Miss Agatha instructed.

"We will."

Miss Corinna hugged Maggie, then Ross. As she leaned close to him, Maggie heard her murmur, "Faith is a marvelous thing, isn't it?"

Indeed it was.

They made their way slowly to the sidewalk, where Ross left her with Tom for a moment while he spoke to a woman waiting to cross the street. He appeared to be asking a question, to which the woman nodded vigorously. When he rejoined them, Maggie asked, "What was that about?"

"You'll have to wait and see."

At home Tom wished them a Merry Christmas and good night on the sidewalk. He even gave Maggie a touch, just his fingers brushing her shoulder, before he left.

"I think he's warming up to me," she said with a laugh. "That's the first time he's ever touched me in eleven years."

"Come inside. *I* want to touch you."

"Sounds like fun." She let him pull her to the door and inside. Instead of heading upstairs, though, he guided her into the living room and to the tree, where he urged her to sit on the floor. "What are we doing?"

"Opening gifts."

She watched, amused, as he gathered the packages, then joined her on the floor. As he opened the sweater she'd picked out, she removed the paper from a long, narrow box. Jewelry—probably a necklace, she thought with the experience of years opening these boxes and just a hint of disappointment. However, when she lifted the lid, it was no magnificent necklace in the box. There was a charm made of metal and engraved with the year beneath a heart pierced by an arrow and the sentiment RM + MM.

"It's for the tree," he said. "When we plant it outside."

She swallowed hard over the lump in her throat and reached for the next package. Inside were the emerald earrings she'd always loved so dearly. When she reached for the third gift, he stopped her.

"I wasn't sure about this and the next one. When I bought them, I thought I was offering a reluctant compromise. I thought it was selfish agreeing to something I didn't think I wanted just so I could have you, but . . ." He swallowed. "I really do want this, and I'll be good at it, and you'll never be sorry. I swear."

Slowly he released the package, and she laid it in her lap, then peeled the paper away. Inside was a small paperback with a bright-eyed baby on the cover and ten thousand names inside. Tears welled in her eyes, then burst free when he brought the next gift in from across the hall. She knelt in front of the cradle, rubbing her hand over the delicately shaped curves, and all too easily imagined it providing a haven for the best-loved baby who ever lived.

Looking up at her anxious husband, she wiped away the tears. "Oh, Ross . . ." Before she could find the words, though, the doorbell rang and he disappeared to answer it. After a moment's quiet conversation, he returned—or, rather, was dragged back by the biggest, blackest, friendliest-looking creature she'd ever seen. As the dog bounded into her lap for an exploratory sniff and lick, she gave in to laughter.

"Remember your dreams? A man you loved, a

pretty little house, three kids, and a dog? Meet the dog." Ross sat down beside her, capturing some part of the animal's attention. "His name is Buddy, which is Old English for herald or messenger. You can look it up if you want," he said, gesturing toward the baby name book. "He was half starved and terrified of people when the vet found him, but he seems to have gotten over both. She says he's very gentle and great with kids."

Buddy settled in, half over her lap, half over Ross's, and gave a loud, contented sigh. Without disturbing him, Maggie twisted to wrap her arms around Ross's neck. "Thank you so very much—for the dog. The book. The cradle. The earrings. The tree tag. For loving me. For having faith in me." Her own words—words that he had listened to, taken to heart and acted on—echoed through her mind. *I would . . . marry a man whom I loved. We would have a pretty little house, three kids, and a dog, and we would live this incredibly normal, incredibly satisfying life.* They brought from her the same contented sigh Buddy had just given.

"Thank you, Ross, for making my dreams come true."

About the Author

Known for her intensely emotional stories, Marilyn Pappano is the author of nearly forty books with more than four million copies in print. She has made regular appearances on bestseller lists and has received recognition for her work with numerous awards. Though her husband's Navy career took them across the United States, they now live in Oklahoma, high on a hill that overlooks her hometown. They have one son.

The angel Noelle casts her spell on Bethlehem once more in Marilyn Pappano's new heartwarming novel, available in fall 1999 from Bantam Books.

When Dr. J. D. Grayson is approached by Noelle, posing as a social worker, about providing a foster home to the four Brown kids, he has a number of reasons to say no. He's single. He lives in a cramped apartment. He works odd hours. And the biggest reason: Becoming a foster parent requires a background check, and there are secrets J. D. doesn't want uncovered. But Noelle is nothing if not persuasive, and before J. D. knows it, he's got four children to care for.

No sooner have the kids settled in than a real social worker, Kelsey Malone, shows up. She doesn't know who gave custody of the kids to J. D.; certainly no one in her office did. When she conducts a background check, J. D.'s nightmare comes true. And it'll take all of Noelle's special magic to pave the way to happily-ever-after.